FAMILY
STORMS

Virginia Andrews® Books

The Dollanganger Family Series
Flowers in the Attic
Petals on the Wind
If There Be Thorns
Seeds of Yesterday
Garden of Shadows

The Casteel Family Series
Heaven
Dark Angel
Fallen Hearts
Gates of Paradise
Web of Dreams

The Cutler Family Series
Dawn
Secrets of the Morning
Twilight's Child
Midnight Whispers
Darkest Hour

The Landry Family Series
Ruby
Pearl in the Mist
All That Glitters
Hidden Jewel
Tarnished Gold

The Logan Family Series
Melody
Heart Song
Unfinished Symphony
Music of the Night
Olivia

The Orphans Miniseries
Butterfly
Crystal
Brooke
Raven
Runaways (full-length novel)

The Wildflowers Miniseries
Misty
Star
Jade
Cat
Into the Garden (full-length novel)

The Hudson Family Series
Rain
Lightning Strikes
Eye of the Storm
The End of the Rainbow

The Shooting Stars Series
Cinnamon
Ice
Rose
Honey
Falling Stars

The De Beers Family Series
Willow
Wicked Forest
Twisted Roots
Into the Woods
Hidden Leaves

The Broken Wings Series
Broken Wings
Midnight Flight

The Gemini Series
Celeste
Black Cat
Child of Darkness

The Shadows Series
April Shadows
Girl in the Shadows

The Early Spring Series
Broken Flower
Scattered Leaves

The Secrets Series
Secrets in the Attic
Secrets in the Shadows

The Delia Series
Delia's Crossing
Delia's Heart
Delia's Gift

Daughter of Darkness

My Sweet Audrina
(does not belong to a series)

FAMILY
STORMS

Virginia
ANDREWS

**SIMON &
SCHUSTER**

London · New York · Sydney · Toronto · New Delhi

A CBS COMPANY

First published in the US by Gallery, 2011
A division of Simon & Schuster, Inc.
First published in Great Britain by Simon & Schuster UK Ltd, 2012
A CBS COMPANY

1 3 5 7 9 10 8 6 4 2

Simon & Schuster UK Ltd
1st Floor
222 Gray's Inn Road
London WC1X 8HB

www.simonandschuster.co.uk

Simon & Schuster Australia, Sydney
Simon & Schuster India, New Delhi

A CIP catalogue record for this book is available from the British Library

Trade paperback ISBN: 978-0-85720-785-2
Hardback ISBN: 978-0-85720-784-5

Printed and bound by CPI Group (UK) Ltd, Croydon, CR0 4YY

FAMILY
STORMS

❧ *Prologue* ❧

"We gotta move," Mama said.

I had just closed my eyes and curled up as tightly as a caterpillar in the heavy woolen blanket. Over the past few months, I had grown immune to the variety of unpleasant odors woven into it. Most nights, I think I held my breath as much as I breathed anyway. I was always anticipating something terrible would wake me, so I never slept much deeper than the very edge of unconsciousness. My ears were still open, my eyelids fluttering, and the dreams that came tiptoed in on cat's paws.

It had begun to rain harder, and the wind blowing in from the ocean made it impossible to stay dry under the cardboard roof that Mama had constructed from some choice cartons she had plucked out of a Dumpster behind the supermarket. In the beginning, I would tremble with embarrassment while she sorted through the garbage. Now, I stood by quietly watching and waiting, as uninterested as someone who had lost all memory. I had learned how to shut out the world and not hear other people talking or see them gaping at us as they walked by. It was almost as if it were all happening to someone else anyway, someone who had borrowed my nearly fourteen-year-old body to suffer in and endure.

"Where will we go, Mama?" I asked.

"Home," she muttered.

"Home? Where's home?"

She didn't answer. Sometimes I thought she hoarded her words the way a squirrel hoarded acorns because she was afraid the day would soon come when she would have nothing left to say. Lately, she was saying less and less even to me. If I pressed her to talk, she would take on the look of terror that someone in the desert would have if she were asked to share her last cup of water. Consequently, I wouldn't talk very much to anyone, either. We both said only what was necessary. Anyone who watched us for a while would surely think we were actors in a silent movie.

I blocked my face from the drizzle and sat up. Mama was already stuffing her bedding into her suitcase, forcing it in as if it were screaming and fighting not to be locked away. She closed it and paused. The rain fell harder, but she stood there with her face fully exposed to it as if we were in bright sunlight, coating ourselves with suntan oil on the Santa Monica Beach the way we did years ago when Daddy was still with us. I knew she was looking at the ocean, expecting some boat to be rushing in to rescue us. A number of times over the past few days, she had told me she expected that to happen as we wandered up and down the beach searching for a good location to set up her Chinese calligraphy. Most people who bought any wanted their name in Chinese calligraphy and took Mama's word for it that she was doing just that. She could have been spelling out *toilet* for all they knew.

While she painted with expert strokes, I sat at her side and wove multicolored lanyard key chains that I sold for two dollars each. I usually began the day with a few dozen I had managed to do during the night. Between the two of us, we made enough to eat two, sometimes three, meals and occasionally have enough to buy some new article of clothing or old shoes from the thrift store. We had been doing this for nearly a year now, ever since we were evicted from our apartment and then from the hotel. Daddy had deserted us nearly two years before that.

Occasionally, someone would ask me why I wasn't in school. I would say I was on vacation or we were between locations and I'd be starting a new school soon. Most knew I was lying but didn't care, and when policemen looked our way, it seemed they either looked through us or didn't care, either. Sometimes I thought maybe we had become invisible and they could see right through us. Maybe it was painful to look at us. It was already past very painful to be us.

In the beginning, when Daddy first left, Mama had managed to keep us afloat, working first as a restaurant hostess and then as a waitress, but her depression led her to more and more drinking, and she had trouble holding on to any employment. Occasionally, she would sell one or two of her works of calligraphy to one of the arts-and-crafts stores. One of the better-known bars, the Gravediggers, had one prominently on a wall to the right of the bar. Mama told me it spelled *heaven.*

"The Gravediggers will take you to heaven," she joked.

Although I had never met her, my maternal grandmother was the one who taught Mama calligraphy. They had lived in Portland, Oregon. My grandparents had Mama late in life, and my grandfather, who was a fisherman, died in a fishing accident during a bad storm. Just like us, Mama and her mother were left to fend for themselves. Both of my maternal grandparents died before I was born, so I had never seen my grandfather in person, either. All I had were the few old photographs of her parents that Mama had brought with her. She told me they were taken when she was only ten, but her parents looked as if they could easily be her grandparents.

Mama said the struggle, which was what she called their lives after her father died, was responsible for aging and killing her mother. Her father hadn't made a lot of money and had had very little life insurance.

Despite our struggle, Mama would say that my daddy's desertion of us was no great loss. I knew she was just speaking out of anger. At least we ate and had a roof over our heads when he was with us. We never really expected to have much more. Daddy had barely graduated from high school and then enlisted in the army, where he learned some mechanical skills, and got a job as an appliance repairman when he was discharged. That was what he was doing when he met my mother at a bar in Venice Beach, California.

Mama had left Portland with a girlfriend right after

high school because her English teacher and drama-club coach lavished so much praise on her acting skills that she thought becoming a movie star was inevitable. She was in every one of her school drama productions since the eighth grade.

Of course, after endless rejection and only very minor acting opportunities, she blamed her teacher for ruining her life. "He got me full of myself until I couldn't see anything else, Sasha," she would say. According to her, he was right up there, just below Daddy, as the cause of all our troubles. "Beware of compliments," she told me. "Half the time people you know tell them to you so you'll like them more, not yourself."

She and her girlfriend were waitresses in the bar where she met Daddy. Her girlfriend was already going hot and heavy with someone she had met there, and according to my mother, "The writing was on the wall. I knew I'd be on my own very soon, and with what I was making, that was nearly impossible. The real possibility of my having to go home to Mama Pearl was looming. That's why I fell in love so quickly with a spineless, unambitious clod like your father."

She admitted, or rather used as an additional excuse, the fact that Daddy was very handsome, with his crystal-like cobalt-blue eyes, firm lips, and wavy light brown hair. I had his eyes but Mama's hair, which Mama said made me even more beautiful than she was.

"When I first met him," she said, "he looked like he could be a movie star himself. He had a sexy smile, the kind that could unlock anyone's chastity belt."

"What's a chastity belt?"

"Never mind that," she said. "He was built like a Greek god in those days, too, but I mistook his silence for strength. It took me a while to realize that most of the time, he was silent because he simply didn't know what to say. He never read anything, parroted whatever sound bite he had heard on television, and rarely went to a movie. At the time we first met, he had never been to the theater. Now that I think about it, Sasha, I must have been out of my mind."

She would eventually tell me that he had gotten her pregnant with me, and when he proposed, she thought maybe she should settle down and become a wife and a mother. She tried to make it sound as if I wasn't just a mistake. She said she was surely not going to be the famous movie star she had hoped to be, and she was just not tall enough to work as a model.

"Becoming a mother seemed to be the right thing for me to do. Besides, I needed you. I needed someone else. Your father wasn't much company."

There was no question, however, that she had once been very beautiful. Her half-Asian look was quite exotic, and she once had silky, long black hair down to her wing bones. Both men and women turned their heads to look at her when she sauntered down the street. I was proud to be walking beside her then. She walked like an angel, practically floating, her soft smile imprinting itself on the eyes of men who surely saw her often in their dreams. I wanted to be in that aura that rippled around her so I'd grow up to be just as special.

"If I would have had the sense to hang out where more well-to-do young men hung out, I'm sure I would have hooked a real catch instead of a mediocre clod. Almost as soon as we married, your father began cheating on me. He was never much help taking care of you. He hated having to stay home, so he would pretend he had to meet someone for a little while, maybe to get a better-paying job, and then not return until the wee hours and sometimes not until morning, bathed in the scent of another woman."

"Why didn't you go back to Portland?" I asked. "You said Mama Pearl's sister still lived there. Wouldn't she have helped you?"

"She had her own troubles and was fifteen years older than my mother. She was an old lady, and my mother's family wasn't happy she had married my father. His family wasn't happy he had married my mother. Everyone expects their children to make them happy," she added with a maddening laugh that always ended with her starting to cry, making me feel bad that I had asked anything.

By then, I was almost eleven. Daddy had just recently deserted us, but I was tired of hearing my mother complain about my father. It wasn't that I wanted to defend him. Even when I was only seven, I realized my father was not like the fathers of other girls at school. For one thing, he never came to a single parents' night and never seemed at all interested in my schoolwork. Sometimes I thought he wasn't interested in me, period. Once, when he and my mother were having an argument, which was most of the time, I heard him say, "Children are punishment for sins committed earlier."

"That makes sense when it comes to your parents," she told him. He never talked about his parents or his sister, and none of his family ever called or showed interest in him—or any of us, for that matter.

Mama and Daddy's fights usually ended with Daddy pounding a table or a wall and sometimes breaking something and then running out of the house with curses trailing behind him like ugly car exhaust.

I'll never forget the day we were evicted from our apartment. I was twelve, nearly thirteen, and home from school because I had a bad cough. We had no medical insurance, so Mama would always try to cure me with some over-the-counter medicines. More often than not, she would just tell me to take a nap or sit in the sun. She was in and out so much in those days that she hardly noticed when I was sick, and she was not taking very good care of herself, either. I knew she was with different men frequently and drinking too much. I hated it when she came home late at night and began babbling and crying. She would stumble and bang into things. I would bury my face in my pillow and refuse to help her.

Eventually, her good looks began to fade like a week-old rose. Her hair lost its rich, soft look until it no longer flowed. The ends were always splitting, and she wasn't keeping it clean. She finally decided to cut it herself. When she was done, it looked as if someone had hacked it with a bread knife, but even if she hadn't done it while she was high on some cheap gin, she wouldn't have done a good job.

It wasn't only her hair and her complexion that grew worse. Her figure seemed to stretch and bulge like the walls of a water-filled balloon. She couldn't get into her jeans and had to wear baggy skirts. Because we didn't have a car and she couldn't afford taxis, she walked so much in old shoes that her feet were always aching or blotched with ugly blisters. She took to wearing oversized sneakers.

I remember once looking out the window and seeing a woman walking up the street, her eyes glassy, her gait uneven, and thinking, *How sad. Look at that bag lady.* When she drew close enough for me to realize it was my mother, I was stunned.

But I was frightened more than anything. The little there was of my own world was falling apart. I had long since stopped having friends over to visit, and no one was inviting me. My attention span in school was bad. I dozed off too much and took little or no pride in my work. My grades were tanking. My teachers said I had attention deficit disorder, which only made me feel more different from the others. Teachers were constantly asking me to bring my mother to school. We had no phone by then, so they didn't call, and letters were useless. She considered everything a bill and read nothing.

Now that I think back, I realize my mother was really the one who was stunned. She must have woken one morning and realized just how badly off we were and how helpless she was. Instead of the realization driving her to be more vigorous in search of solutions, it caused her to retreat to the gin and whiskey. It almost didn't matter what it was as long as it was alcoholic and could jumble up her thoughts and fears to the point where nothing seemed to bother her.

However, to this day, I don't think of her as having been an alcoholic. I believe she really could have stopped if she had wanted to stop. She didn't have the courage to stop. It was ironically easier to look into the mirror and see someone she didn't recognize. Otherwise, she would have committed suicide.

I suppose if we could have afforded psychoanalysis back then, she would have been diagnosed as a borderline schizophrenic. Something that had begun too subtly for me to realize right away had been happening in her head. At times, I thought she was talking to someone else. At first, I thought that occurred only when she was drunk, but I quickly realized it was happening even when she was stone sober. I think the person she was talking to was herself before I was born, and even before she had met Daddy. From what I heard and could understand, she was warning her younger self not to leave home, that if she did, this could be how she would be.

Of course, it made no sense to me, and if I asked her what she was doing or whom she was talking to, she would look at me angrily, as if I were intruding on a very private conversation.

"None of your business," she might say, or "It's not for your ears."

Whose ears is it for? I wanted to ask. *There's no one there.*

But I kept quiet. I was actually too frightened to push much further, anyway. Who knew what that might cause to happen, and enough had already happened.

She wasn't home when the police came to the apartment the day we were evicted. The landlord had followed all of the necessary legal steps, but Mama had ignored it all. I was home sick. I opened the door and looked up at two burly sheriff's deputies. One took off his hat and combed through his hair with his fingers as if he were searching for a lost thought. He looked sorrier than the other for what he was about to do.

"Your mother here?" he asked.

"No," I said.

"Where is she?" the other deputy asked.

"I don't know," I said, and coughed so hard and long that they both stepped back, fearing infection.

"Jesus," the first deputy muttered.

"Do you know when she'll be back, at least?" the second deputy asked me.

I shook my head.

"We'll wait in the car."

They turned and went to their vehicle parked right outside our first-floor apartment. At the time, I didn't know why they were there. I thought maybe they had found my father and needed to tell my mother.

After I closed the door, I went to the front window and waited, watching the street. Finally, I could see her coming. She didn't look drunk. She was walking fast, swinging her arms, with her purse wrapped around the front of her body like some shield. She had told me she did that to avoid having it grabbed. "Not that I ever have much in it," she'd added.

The deputies saw her heading our way and got out of their vehicle to approach her. She stood listening to them and then just nodded without comment and continued to the front door. When she entered, she saw me standing there and shook her head.

"You can thank your father someday for this," she said. "Pack only what you really need. We can't carry too much. I'm not spending money on a taxi."

"Why are we leaving?"

"We can't live here anymore. The landlord got the police on us."

"Where are we going?"

"To a hotel nearby," she said.

It sounded good, but when we arrived, I saw how small it was. The lobby was barely bigger than our living room had been, and we had one room with two double beds and a bathroom.

"What about a kitchen?" I asked.

"We'll eat out when we want hot food. This will have to do for now," she told me.

Her best hope was that "for now" was forever, only I didn't know that. I didn't know how serious the dying going on in her head was. Because we slept in the same room, I woke up often to hear her nighttime chats with her invisible second self. Most of the time, it was done in whispers, but I often caught a word or two. None of it ever made much sense to me. *Maybe she's just dreaming aloud,* I thought, and went back to sleep.

She was doing it now as we trekked up the beach. The raindrops had become more like pellets. I kept my head down and lifted my eyes just enough to see her soaked old sneakers pasted with sand and mud plodding forward awkwardly.

"Where are we going?" I cried. I was tired and would have gladly just slept in the rain.

She didn't answer, but from the way she was moving her arms and hands, I knew she was talking to her imaginary self. I could see the top of a bottle of gin in her shabby coat pocket. There was no one else on the beach but us, so there was no one to appeal to for any help. I was feeling worse than ever. The only way I realized I was crying was by the shudder in my shoulders. My tears were mixed in with the rain.

Mama suddenly turned and started toward the sidewalk. I hurried to catch up. She carried her suitcase limply. It looked as if it was dragging. Even though I was exhausted myself, I wanted to help her, to take it from her, but she wouldn't let go of the handle.

"I'll carry it!" I cried.

"No, no. This is all I have. Let go," she said.

The way she looked at me sent a sharp pain through my heart. *She doesn't recognize me,* I thought. *My own mother doesn't know who I am. She thinks I'm some stranger trying to steal her things.*

"Mama, it's me, Sasha. Let go, and I'll help you."

"No!" she screamed, and tore it out of my grip.

We stared at each other for a moment in the rain. Maybe she realized her momentary amnesia and it frightened her as much as it had frightened me. Whatever, she turned and surged forward.

I sped to keep up with her. We were at a traffic light on Pacific Coast Highway, and it turned green for us. She stepped into the road, and I caught up with her to walk side-by-side. We were nearly to the other side when I heard car tires squealing and looked to my right.

The vehicle struck Mama first and literally lifted her over my head before it struck me hard in the right thigh. I saw Mama slap down on the pavement just before I fell and slid in her direction.

That was how my life began.

1

The Accident

The pain was hot.

Although I was lying faceup in the road and the rain was sweeping over me in a downpour, I no longer felt the slightest chill. It was as if electric heaters had been placed all around me. I heard myself groan, but it seemed to come from someone else. My first thought was that I was dead and this was the way a soul left its body. Any moment, I expected to be looking down at myself lying there on the road, shocked, my eyes two balls of blue glass, my mouth opened in a silent scream. Souls don't cry, souls don't laugh, but they can be surprised when they realize they are no longer part of their bodies.

Cars began stopping, some nearly rear-ending the ones that had stopped already. Looking through what was to me a curtain of gauze, I could see some men directing traffic, shouting at drivers, waving off the curious. I started to move, but the pain shot so fast and sharply up the back of my leg, up my back, and into my neck that I immediately

stopped and closed my eyes. I was vaguely aware of someone beside me, holding my hand. There was a man's voice
and then a woman's. I realized the woman was trying to get
me to talk. I heard more shouting. I tried to open my eyes,
but they wouldn't open. The noise began to drift off, and
then it came surfing back on the wave of sirens.

"Mama," I thought I finally managed to say. I wasn't sure
I had spoken. I drifted away again and then opened my eyes
when I felt my body being lifted. When they began to slide
me into the ambulance, I had a funny thought. I envisioned
a freshly made pizza being slid into the oven. Slices of pizza
were our lunch more often than not and sometimes all we
had for dinner.

I looked back and saw another ambulance. *They're getting Mama*, I thought, and that gave me some comfort. The
paramedic beside me was saying soothing things and putting a blood-pressure cuff on me. There was so much conflicting noise, mumbling voices, cars, people still shouting,
that I could make little sense of anything else the paramedic
was saying. Finally, the doors were closed, and I heard the
siren again as we began moving.

"Hot," I said, and lost consciousness.

I awoke in the hallway of the hospital emergency room.
My clothing had been removed, and I was in a hospital
gown. I saw what I knew to be an IV bottle and stand beside me. The tube was attached to my right arm. There was
a blanket on me, but there was no doctor, nor was there
a nurse tending to me. People were rushing around. No
one spoke to me. Another pair of paramedics wheeled in
another gurney, and I thought, *Maybe that's Mama*, but it

turned out to be an elderly man with oxygen leads in his nostrils. His eyes were wide, as wide as those of someone who saw his own impending death. They pushed him past me without even looking at me, but it frightened me.

"Mama!" I cried. I waited, but either no one heard me or no one had time to answer. There was little I could do but lie there and wait. My arms, shoulders, legs, and neck were throbbing so much I felt I had turned into a drum. My ears were filled with the beat of my heart and the chugging of my blood through my veins.

When I saw a nurse hurrying up the corridor, I called to her as loudly as I could. She paused, but before I could tell her anything or ask her anything, she said, "Someone will be with you soon. Be patient."

Don't you mean "be a patient"? I was the one who felt drunk now, not Mama.

I closed my eyes and tried to remember exactly what had happened. It had all happened so quickly. Mama was rushing through the rain as if she had an appointment. I ran behind her and kept calling to her. I was only a few inches away when I heard the sound of tires squealing. Right now, I could visualize the front of an automobile but little more.

Where was Mama now? Why had I been left in a hallway? Who had put me here? Who was looking after me? When I tried to lift my head, the whole corridor spun, and I was nauseated immediately. I kept my eyes closed and waited until the dizziness subsided, and then I opened my eyes slowly and took a deep breath. There was nothing I could do but wait.

Finally, I felt myself moving and looked down toward

my feet to see a different nurse pushing the gurney. She looked younger than the first nurse and had a shock of brown hair drifting out from under her cap and down over her right eye. As she pushed my gurney, she blew the loose strands away from her eye.

"What's happening to me?" I asked.

"You're going to X-ray," she said. "Just relax."

"Where's my mother?"

"You're going to X-ray."

Didn't she understand my question?

"My mother," I said.

"Relax," she told me. "We're having a bad night here. We're doing our best to get to everyone as quickly as we possibly can. I've got to get you processed before I see about anyone or anything else."

Processed? What did that mean? With all that ached on me, it was hard to keep talking, keep asking questions, and she didn't seem to want to talk much, either.

I felt myself being navigated through the corridor to an elevator. When I was in it, I hoped she would tell me more now that we were away from all the bedlam, but there was another nurse in the elevator, and they started to have a conversation over me as if I weren't even there. I heard them complaining about some doctor who hadn't shown up and another nurse who was always late.

"Like any of us want to be here on time?" my nurse said.

When the elevator door opened, the other nurse helped wheel me out and then went off in another direction. Outside radiology, there were two other gurneys lined up, one with a young man with a bloodstained face and a heavily bandaged arm and the other with an elderly African American woman. A younger African American woman stood beside her, holding her hand.

"Just try to relax," my nurse said again, and put a clipboard at my feet. "Someone will be out to get you soon."

"What about my mother?" I asked.

She walked off without replying. I began to wonder if anyone could hear me. Maybe I thought I was talking but I wasn't. The younger African American woman looked at me and smiled. The X-ray room door opened, and another patient was wheeled out in a wheelchair. He was an elderly man in a shirt and tie, wearing a blue cap with white letters that spelled "U.S.S. Enterprise." He looked perfectly healthy, even bored. A male nurse pulled the gurney with the young man into the radiology suite.

"Not much longer now," the younger woman told the older one.

"You hope," the older woman said. "You'll be on social security, too, by the time we get outta here."

The younger woman laughed. Then she looked at me again. "What happened to you, honey?"

"We were hit by a car," I said. "My mother and me, but I don't know where my mother is."

"Downstairs waiting, for sure," she said. "Took us five hours to get this far."

I was relieved to see she heard me. "I don't know how long I've been here."

"Long," the older lady said. "You drip through this place like maple syrup."

The younger woman turned to me and smiled as she

shook her head to tell me I shouldn't pay attention. "You'll be all right," she added, and turned to look firmly at the closed door as if she could will it to open.

I closed my eyes again. When I opened them, I realized I must have fallen asleep, because the two women were gone and there were two other gurneys lined up behind me. Finally, the doors opened again, the African American lady was wheeled out, and I was wheeled in. The young man bringing me to the X-ray machine was the nicest and warmest of anyone I had met so far. He assured me that he would do everything to make this easy and comfortable.

"Do you know where my mother is?" I asked him. Since he was being so nice, I thought he would give me an answer.

"Sorry," he said. "I'm just the X-ray technician. I'm sure someone will be getting your mother to visit you afterward."

"She was hit by the car, too," I said. "Was she here already?"

He paused, thought for a moment, and shook his head. "She's probably with the doctor somewhere else right now," he replied. "Let's get you going."

After my X-rays were taken, another nurse arrived to wheel me out and back into the elevator.

"Where am I going?" I asked.

"To wait for the doctor," she replied. "He'll look at your X-rays first. We have an examination room open for you, and I want to get you into it before someone else gets in there."

"What about my mother? She was in the accident, too."

"I don't know anything about her," she said. "I just came on duty."

She got me into the elevator and then out and into an examination room. I don't know how long I was in there before the doctor arrived, but I know I was in and out of sleep, and I was very thirsty. I called for someone to please get me some water, but everyone seemed too busy to hear me.

When my doctor finally arrived, I was surprised at how young he looked. He had curly light brown hair and a round face with thin lips and a small nose, so small it looked as if half of it had still not emerged. In fact, it looked as if his facial features were sinking into his skull. His hazel eyes were that deeply set. His skin was as soft and clear as a little boy's skin. Maybe he hadn't begun to shave yet, I thought, which I knew was silly.

"Okay, now," he said, as if we had been having a conversation that had been interrupted. "I'm Dr. Decker, one of the ER doctors here. I've called for Dr. Milan to look at you. He's an orthopedic specialist. The reason," he said, "is that you have a serious fracture of the femur."

"I don't know what that is," I said.

"It means your thigh bone."

He held up the X-ray for me to see and pointed to my right leg bone.

"This is your thigh bone. There are four distinct parts to it, and your injury is at the head. See?" he asked as if he were teaching a class. "Look where the edge of my finger is."

I nodded, even though I had no idea what he was pointing to.

"The reason it's serious for someone your age is that it can and most likely will affect the growth plate, the soft area of the bone located at the epiphysis near the head of the femur. As a result of all this, your right leg might end up a bit shorter than your left. So we want a specialist to handle the cast, okay? It might be a while."

"My head hurts, too, and so does my arm and my neck and shoulders."

"You've been banged up quite a bit. Luckily, nothing else is broken, but you do have a slight concussion. That's why you're nauseous and dizzy. In fact, I'm amazed you don't have a broken arm."

He lifted my right arm, and I saw the black-and-blue marks. They were ugly and frightening. I couldn't help but start to cry.

"Easy," he said. "I'll have the nurse give you something for the nausea. I don't want to give you anything else until Dr. Milan can get here. Okay?"

"What about my mother?"

"Your mother? What about her?"

"She was hit by the car first."

He nodded. "I'll check on it," he said. He patted my hand and left.

I expected the nurse to come in soon, but a long time went by before anyone came, and she wasn't a nurse. She wasn't wearing a uniform. She was an older lady with short gray hair that looked plastered around her head. She wore a pair of glasses with lenses so thick they looked more like the protective glasses mechanics wear. She approached me and lifted her clipboard.

"I'm Mrs. Muller. I work in admittance. You told the paramedic your name is Sasha Porter, is that correct?"

I couldn't remember telling anyone anything about my-self. Maybe I had been talking in my sleep.

"My name is Sasha Fawne Porter, yes. Fawne is spelled with an *e* at the end. That was the way my grandmother spelled her Chinese name."

"You said you were thirteen years old?"

"I'll be fourteen in two months."

She lowered her head and looked at me over her glasses as if I had said something outrageous. "What is your present address? Where do you live?" she followed quickly, as though I needed a translation.

Maybe I shouldn't have let her know my grandmother was Chinese. She remained poised with her pen and didn't look at me until she realized I wasn't answering her question.

"Don't you know where you live? What's your address?"

"We don't have an address."

"What do you mean, you don't have an address? I asked you where you were living." She had a thought. "Was it on a boat?"

"No. We live on the street, sleep on the beach," I said.

She stared at me and pressed her thicker lower lip over her upper one. It made the brown spot at the bottom of her chin look more like a teardrop. "How long has this been going on?" she asked, as if it was my fault.

"I don't know the exact number of days. A year, I guess."

"Where do you go to school?"

"I don't right now," I said.

She smirked and shook her head. "Where's your father?"

"I don't know. We don't know exactly. We think he went to Hawaii."

"Hawaii? So your mother and father are divorced?"

"No. He just left."

"Just left?" She nodded, as if she knew him, and tapped the clipboard with her pen. "Okay. What about other relatives here?"

"We don't have any here. My mother has an aunt and cousins in Portland, Oregon. My father's relatives are in Ohio, but we don't talk to any. I don't even know their names. His parents died a long time ago. He has a sister, but she stopped talking to him a long time ago, or he stopped talking to her." I nodded. Maybe these details were important. "Yes, Mama said he stopped talking to her."

"So you have no one to take responsibility for you?"

"Just my mother," I said.

"A lot of good that's going to do us," she muttered. She checked something on her clipboard and turned to leave.

"Where is my mother?" I called.

She paused and turned back to me. "Didn't anyone tell you?"

"No."

"Your mother is dead. She died instantly and was taken directly to the morgue."

2

Alone

The nurse who finally came to give me the medicine Dr. Decker had promised started to check my pulse and take my blood pressure and then gave me a tablespoon of some syrup for my nausea, which she said was all she could do for me right then. She saw that I had been crying. I started to cry again, and she told me I should try to be a big girl.

"That lady said my mother died," I said through my tears.

"Yes. Very sad, but you have to be a big girl now. It will make everything go that much easier for you."

A big girl? How does a big girl react to the news of her mother's death? I wanted to ask. *Doesn't she cry?*

The nurse looked up when Dr. Decker came in quickly. "What's happening?" she asked him, sounding a little annoyed.

"Milan isn't coming. Once he heard she's uninsured, he suddenly had another emergency."

"And?"

"I'll set the leg," he told her. "We've got to move her along. There's quite a backup out there."

"Tell me about it," the nurse said. "We should have a traffic cop."

"Okay, let's get to her." He finally looked at me. "We're going to get you on the way to getting better," he said.

He tried to explain everything he was doing every step of the way, but I had long since lost interest in myself and was only vaguely aware of the activity around and on me.

"This kid's practically in shock," the nurse said. "Besides the injuries, she just found out her mother died."

"The faster I get this done, the faster she'll get out of it," he said, obviously not wanting to stand around and have a conversation.

Get out of what, I wondered, *sorrow or pain?* I moaned, but because of my slight concussion, Dr. Decker said he didn't want to give me anything too strong for pain. He said he would prescribe some Tylenol, and he was sure it would help a little.

"Just hang in there," he said, and flashed a smile as if it were on a spring in his face.

After my leg was set, they moved me to a ward. It was nearly morning now. Through the window across from my bed, I could see the sunlight creeping up on the horizon as if it were afraid night would slap it back. Everyone else in the ward, six others who looked like mostly elderly women, seemed to be still asleep. To me, the one nurse in charge, Mrs. Stanton, appeared to be as old and as sickly as the other patients. Her face was so pale and her eyes so watery I thought one of them might have gotten up and put on a nurse's uniform. She settled me in and told me to try to get some sleep.

"Do you need anything?" she asked.

What a question, I thought. *Yes, I need something. I need my mother not to be dead. I need a home. I need to be in school and have food and clothes. I need to remember how to laugh.* I saw from the look on her face that if I had said anything like that, she might have been the one to laugh, so I didn't say anything. I hadn't said anything to anyone since that woman had told me my mother was dead and in the morgue. All I had done was moan and cry. Mrs. Stanton went off to check on another patient, and I closed my eyes.

I slept on and off. The clatter of dishes and trays woke me when breakfast was served. I looked at it but turned away and didn't eat or drink anything. The nurse who had replaced Mrs. Stanton shook me to tell me I should try to eat. "And you have to drink something. I don't want you to get dehydrated," she said, as if I worked for her. She stood there waiting to see me reach for the glass of juice and then handed it to me. I drank some, and she repeated that I should try to eat. "If you don't nourish your body, it won't heal," she warned. She said it as if it wouldn't be her fault or any doctor's. Whatever had happened and would now happen was my fault. It sounded as if she meant it was my fault that I had been born.

A different doctor stopped in to visit the patients in the ward. I heard the nurse complaining about me. He read the chart clipped to the bottom of the bed and then examined my bruises, checked my eyes, and listened to my heart and lungs through his stethoscope. His name tag read "Dr.

Morton." He looked older than Dr. Decker, but something told me he wasn't. Later, I heard he was interning.

"You've had quite a shock to your body," he told me. He looked at my chart and added, "Sasha. You want to eat and drink so you get stronger, okay?"

He was talking to me in a tone of voice he might use with someone only about five years old. I didn't reply, and he turned to the nurse and said, "We might need the psychologist to stop by for this one."

"Is my mother really dead?" I asked when I saw that he was going to move off.

He looked at the nurse.

"Her mother was hit by the same car," the nurse told him. "She expired at the scene."

"Oh. Well, what about . . ." He nodded at me.

"There are no other relatives listed. I'm sure Social Services has been contacted. Homeless," she whispered, but not low enough for me to miss.

"Right. You hang in there, Sasha. We're going to look after you."

He smiled at me, patted my hand, and moved on to the next patient. The nurse trailed along like an obedient puppy as he went from bed to bed.

Look after me? How were they going to do that? I wondered. How was anyone? Despite how terrible our lives had become, I wished Mama and I were back on the boardwalk selling her calligraphy and I was selling my lanyards. I wished we were back in the struggle. At least we were together then, and I had someone. Besides, she might have gotten better. Maybe she would have stopped drinking and found a place to work again, and I would have been able to return to school, any school. I used to feel tears come into my eyes when I would see other girls my age in their school uniforms, laughing and talking as they walked to school. The furthest thing from their minds was wondering about where they would sleep and what they would eat. If only I could somehow turn back time and change everything.

I closed my eyes and dreamed about it. Mama was pretty again, and I had new clothes and friends. We had at least as good an apartment as we had had with Daddy. Because Mama worked, I would start dinner for us before she came home. She would be so proud of me, and we'd laugh and tell each other about all the things that happened to both of us during the day. I'd have very good grades to show her, and then I would go off and do my homework. She would still do calligraphy, but now only for her own enjoyment. Because she was happier when she was doing it, she would do more elaborate pictures, and before long, she would be selling them to art galleries, not arts-and-crafts stores or bars. We'd have more money than ever, and Mama would start talking about buying a car.

"We'll go on trips every weekend, see beautiful things, and stop at nice restaurants along the way," she would say. "I told you. We can get along without him, and we can keep the struggle from doing us any more harm, because we're together, partners, mother and daughter, more like sisters, good friends."

She would hug me and hold me, and I would inhale the sweet scent of her perfume and hair, which was long and soft again. Men would be very interested in her, of course, but this time, she would be far more careful and go out only with responsible ones. Someday someone like that would propose to her, and our lives would improve tenfold. We'd live in a house, not an apartment, and Mama would not have to work anymore. This wonderful, well-to-do man would love me and be a real father to me. He'd come to parents' nights and do homework with me and want to show me things and take me places, just as any other girl's father would want to do with his daughter.

It occurred to me that most other girls would think my dreams were too simple, too ordinary. They would be dreaming of being popular singers or movie and television stars. They'd want big houses and expensive cars, even boats. They'd dream of jewelry and fashionable dresses and shoes, love affairs, and romantic adventures.

"Even your dreams are poor, pathetic," they might say, and not want to be my friends.

I'd have to be very careful about telling anyone about my fantasies. I'd have to pretend I wanted exactly the same things they did. In fact, I'd have to keep many things secret, especially our struggle. What I would certainly have to do is come up with a story. In my dream, when I explained this to Mama, she nodded, understanding my problem, and said, "It's best you tell them that your father was killed in a car accident. That way, they'll feel sorry for you and not mock you."

Exactly, I thought. Daddy was dead to me, anyway. It was almost not a lie.

I dreamed so hard I began to believe it was real. For a while, I was happy, and I felt no pain or discomfort, and then someone in another bed screamed with her own pain, and I was ripped out of my fantasy and dropped right back into this gray ward, with other patients who I found out were also uninsured homeless or deserted people. One lady told another we were all in the "human Dumpster."

How long would they leave me in there? I wondered. Would I have to be there until my leg healed? And then where would they send me? What was being done with Mama? Would I ever see her, or would she simply be taken away and buried somewhere without anyone present? She used to say she would end up in Potter's Field, a burying place for strangers, for people with no means.

"Where is Potter's Field?" I had asked her.

"There's one everywhere." She had looked at me, considering whether to tell me any more. I was thirteen by then and not attending school. Whenever she was sober enough, she always expressed regret about my not being in school and often tried to teach me things.

"It comes from the Bible," she'd continued. "My father was a Bible thumper. He would read aloud from it almost every night he was home. You know who Judas was, right?"

"Yes, he sold out Jesus for thirty pieces of silver."

"Good. Well, he regretted it afterward and went back to the high priests who had paid him. He threw the money on the floor. Afterward, he hung himself. The priests decided the money was tainted with blood and used it to create Potter's Field, where strangers and the poor were to be buried. They called it Potter's Field because it was located in a place where they mined clay for pots. As your father would stupidly say, that information and a dollar fifty will get you on the bus."

"But that's all it costs."

"Duh. That was your father's opinion of knowledge," she had told me.

It was almost impossible now to remember Mama from those early days, when she would have more sober hours than not. Before she began drinking for the day, her eyes were still clear; she was still standing straight and had a look of determination in her face. But that got to be less and less the rule and more the exception.

Sometimes I thought maybe an alien had gotten into her. The alien didn't have any of the self-pride and self-respect Mama used to have. Maybe Mama wasn't dead. Maybe just the alien in her had died on the highway, and she would wake up and come back to me. I was looking at the door of the ward just the way Mama used to look out at the ocean for that boat that would save us, hoping that she would suddenly just appear, smiling.

"It's going to be all right now," she would say. "We'll be fine, Sasha. I'm back."

I blinked when a tall woman dressed in a fashionable designer turquoise pantsuit with gold epaulets stepped into the doorway and caused my dream Mama to pop like a bubble.

This woman had thick light brown hair styled at shoulder length and carried a purse that matched her outfit. The nail polish on her long nails even matched her outfit. She gazed into the ward, looking carefully at each patient until her eyes came around to me. Once she saw me, she seemed to freeze, her eyes locked on me, her soft, puffy lips just slightly open. Whom was she trying to look like, Angelina Jolie?

I couldn't take my eyes off her. She had the look of a movie star, her makeup perfect, her complexion rich and peachy. But she looked somehow more important than a movie star. The regal way she held herself gave her an aura of authority, control, and power. The diamond ring on her left hand was so large that it seized on the ray of light spilling in from the nearest window and then seemed to brighten and become even more dazzling. She wore what looked like diamond teardrop earrings, too, and a necklace of small pearls.

A long moment passed before she stepped into the ward, and when she did, she stepped in as though she were trying to be careful, as careful as someone navigating a floor of mud. Maybe she thought the patients in the ward were contagious. She did look as if she was holding her breath. I waited when she paused at my bed.

"Are you Sasha Fawne Porter?" she asked.

She couldn't be someone from Social Services, I thought. Could she? Who else would be looking for me? Who else would know my full name?

"Yes," I said.

She nodded, opened her purse, and took out a very thin handkerchief to dab away something on her right eye. I saw nothing. Maybe she was wiping away imaginary germs. Why would there be a tear?

She focused on the area under the blanket where my cast was located.

"Are you in a lot of pain?" she asked, nodding at my legs.

"Only if I move too much," I said.

"I'm so sorry."

I looked at her and wondered why she was so sorry. "Are you with Social Services?" I asked, and she widened her eyes.

"Hardly," she said. She hesitated, and then she said, "I'm Jordan March. Mrs. Donald March."

The way she told me her name—announced it, I should say—caused me to scan my brain, searching for something in my memory that would tell me who she was. Had I seen her on a magazine cover? Was she really a movie star or on television, someone who visited patients in hospitals as an act of charity? Why would she think I would know who she was?

"It's your right leg that was broken?" she asked.

I pulled back the blanket to show her the cast. "My femur," I said, remembering Dr. Decker's description. "At the head."

"Yes, I know."

How did she know? Was she a special nurse? Or maybe she was a doctor. But she didn't call herself Dr. March. Would a doctor talk like that?

"You don't have any other broken bones, right?"

"No." If she were a doctor, she would have known that, I thought.

"But you're badly banged up," she concluded, her gaze fixed on my black-and-blue arms.

"I have a slight concussion, too. And my neck hurts, so

it's hard to raise my head." I don't know why I wanted to tell her everything. Maybe it was because there was no one else really asking me.

"Oh, dear, you poor, poor child."

Poor is right, I thought.

I watched her look around the ward. Some of the others were looking our way and listening. She didn't smile at anyone. She pulled herself back a little and blew a small breath through her nearly closed lips.

"Well, this won't do," she said. It seemed to be something she was saying more to herself than to me. "It won't do at all." She turned and walked out quickly.

"That your mother?" the woman nearest to me asked.

"No way," I said. "My mother is prettier." *Was prettier,* I thought, and then argued with myself. This woman was beautiful, there was no denying that, but Mama had that exotic look, and she was natural. She wasn't just beautiful; she was different. In Los Angeles, women like the one who had just been to see me were not unusual. Mama used to say, "It's the only place where women don't care that beauty is only skin-deep. Few want to go any deeper."

Mrs. March didn't return for nearly half an hour, and when she did, the ward nurse and a male nurse's aide accompanied her. The aide pushed a gurney right up to my bed. Mrs. March stood back to watch.

"We're moving you," the nurse said.

"To where?"

"A room. A private room," she added, the corners of her lips dipping.

She and the aide guided me carefully onto the gurney.

"Does she have any possessions?" Mrs. March asked the nurse when they turned to roll me out.

"Possessions? No, nothing," the nurse said. "What would she have?"

Mrs. March smirked. "A watch, maybe? Any jewelry? These people carry everything they own on them."

"She had nothing I know of, and there's nothing listed anywhere."

"I hope not," Mrs. March said. "Anyone who would steal from this child should be shot."

I looked back at the other patients in the ward. A few watched with curiosity and amazement.

"Just relax," the nurse said, and I lowered my head and waited as I was rolled along.

We went to an elevator. Mrs. March followed us all the way and stood quietly in a corner of the elevator as it rose to a much higher floor. She kept her head high and looked forward, not looking at me at all now. She said nothing to the nurse or the aide.

The door opened on a quiet corridor with walls that looked freshly painted and a floor that glittered in the sunlight pouring through one of the windows. I saw the nurses' station, with at least a half dozen of them busy with their duties. The nurse on the far side sat watching monitors. I could see that she was doing some needlepoint. There was none of the frenzy here that I had seen in the emergency room.

I was rolled down to a doorway and then into the room, which was nicer than any bedroom I had ever had. There was a light maple armoire on the left, a closet on the right, small tables beside the bed, and a television on a metal shelf across from the bed. The room had two large windows that looked toward the Hollywood Hills. The bed was wider than the one down in the ward, and the blanket and pillows looked brand-new. The nurse and the aide gently transferred me. The aide started out with the gurney, and the nurse turned to Mrs. March.

"I'll get her paperwork to the desk," she said.

"Thank you," Mrs. March said.

The nurse left, and Mrs. March stepped up beside the bed and looked at me. "Now, this is better, isn't it?"

"Yes," I said.

"I have a private-duty nurse arriving within the hour. Her name is Jackie Knee." She leaned toward me to whisper. "She's younger than most of the nurses here, more tuned in to girls your age. She actually worked at a plastic surgeon's clinic in Brentwood but now freelances on private-duty assignments. I think she makes more money."

She straightened up and just stared at me for a few moments.

"I've arranged for a well-known orthopedist, Dr. Milan, to examine you."

"Dr. Milan?"

"You know who he is?" she asked with a slight smile.

"He was supposed to fix my leg last night but didn't come because I have no medical insurance, so Dr. Decker did it."

"Really? Is that what happened? Well, he's coming today," she said firmly. "You can be sure of that."

"Who's paying for all this?" I asked.

"I am. Well, I should say my husband and I are."

"Why?" I asked, expecting her to tell me they were in charge of some charity.

She looked as if she wasn't going to answer. She turned away, looked out the window a moment, and then turned back to me.

"It was my daughter, Kiera, who hit you and your mother," she said.

3

Kiera's Mistake

I didn't know what to say when Mrs. March told me her daughter had hit Mama and me, so I just watched her as she began to pace back and forth, moving her hands as if she were speaking. I think she was trying to find the right words. Were there right words?

She turned, pressing her lips together. Then she took a deep breath and continued. "She was high on one of her recreational drugs. X they call it." She paused and turned to me. "Do you know what that is?"

I nodded.

"But you don't use that stuff, do you?"

"No," I said, but what difference would that possibly make to her?

"Good. Kiera has been more than a handful for us. She has everything any girl her age could possibly want. My husband, Donald, is one of the most successful builders in Southern California. Half the malls you see are malls he built, and he's busier than ever. He gives everything he can to our daughter. Kiera has her own car. She's already been to Europe twice. She has a wardrobe that's even bigger than my own, not to mention expensive jewelry and watches that would choke an Arabian prince."

She shook her head. "You would think any girl would be grateful for the life Kiera has, but this is not the first time Kiera's been in big trouble. Each time, my husband has bailed her out, pulled strings, saved her. The result is that she never learns a lesson. I told him. I warned him something bigger like this would happen, but he didn't listen, and now he's already busy saving her again. I told him this time he should let her pay the piper, but he won't have it. He's hired a top attorney, but this is not the first time. You can't even begin to imagine the money we've had to spend on attorneys because of her."

She spoke quickly and excitedly, and her face turned crimson. Then she took a deep breath, looked out the window, and relaxed her shoulders. "Of course, I understand why he's like this," she said. "And it's hard to blame him."

She sat in the chair near the bed. For a few moments, she just sat there with her head lowered. Her words and actions had captured my full attention. I was holding my breath in anticipation of the next outburst, but she began in a low, soft tone.

"We lost our younger daughter, Alena, to acute leukemia three years ago. We took her to the best doctors and the best hospitals in the country, but we couldn't save her. You can have all the money in the world, Sasha, and still not be happy. Anyway, Donald doesn't want to lose Kiera, too. I don't, either, but I think that his always finding ways to excuse her misbehavior will lead to us losing her. It's like a slow disease, just getting worse and worse. You're probably too young to understand all of this," she added, and sighed. "Forgive me for throwing it all at you like this, especially at this time when you're soaked in your own horrible trouble."

I didn't say anything.

She looked at me again, her eyes narrowing. "Maybe you're *not* too young to understand what I'm saying. Children who live harder lives grow up faster. I'm sure you've seen more than your share of the dark side, and now look at what's happened to you. I'm sorry. I really am, and I'm going to do whatever I can to make things better."

"My mother's dead," I said. "They told me she died instantly."

Her whole face seemed to tremble. She understood that I meant there was no way to make my mother better, there was no nice room for her or expert doctors to fix her injuries. No one could promise her anything anymore, so Mrs. March couldn't make things much better for me. Mrs. March looked as if she would cry and did turn away to dab her eyes with her handkerchief.

I certainly didn't feel sorry for her. I didn't care how unhappy she was or what terrible things had happened to her. Maybe that was mean, but I didn't feel like feeling sorry for anyone else except Mama and myself at the moment. Did she expect me to say it wasn't her daughter's fault? Had she come here and done all this for me so I would forgive her daughter and help her feel better?

"It's terrible. I know," she said, still looking away. "That poor woman. On top of struggling just to exist." She sighed and turned back to me. "How did the two of you end up living on the street? I see so many people pushing carts and sleeping in tents or just under something. Some of them look so young. I can't help but look at them and wonder how in the world they ended up the way they are, especially in this great country. Are there many children out there like you all over?"

"I don't know. We've been only here. We never left after we were turned out on the street. Mama said it would be the same for us no matter where we went, and at least it wasn't cold here so much."

She blew through her lips and shook her head as she looked at me. "You should be in school, going to parties, not worrying about where your next meal is coming from or where you will sleep. What did you two do, just beg?"

"No, my mother wouldn't beg. She sold her calligraphy, and I sold lanyard key chains on the beach. I made them myself."

"Calligraphy?"

"It's Chinese writing."

"Oh, yes." She smiled.

We heard a knock on the door. A tall man in a black suit and blue tie stood there. He had thick gray hair and ebony eyes, a gray and black well-trimmed goatee, and a Hollywood tan. I thought he might be her husband. He looked just as wealthy.

"I received your message while I was still at the orthopedic convention at Shutters, Jordan. I came as soon as I could get away."

"Thank you, Michael. This," she said, turning back to me, "is the young girl I want you to treat, Sasha Porter."

He nodded and showed Mrs. March a clipboard in his right hand. "I picked up her file on the way."

"This is Dr. Milan, Sasha. Please, let him examine you."

He stepped into my room and, without saying hello or even smiling at me, took the blanket off my right leg and looked at the cast. He shook his head.

"What?" Mrs. March asked.

"It's not set high enough. I see this sort of sloppy work all the time. I'll have to redo this. I'm sorry," he told me.

"Did you see the X-rays, Michael?"

"Yes."

"How bad is the break?"

"It's pretty serious, in a bad place, Jordan. I'll do the best I can, but nine times out of ten, for someone her age, there is a residual effect when it's that high up."

"Do what you can, Michael. I mean it," she said firmly. "Think of her as you would my daughter," she told him.

I was surprised that she could speak to a doctor so sternly, but he didn't seem upset. He nodded.

"I have a private-duty nurse coming." She looked at her watch. "She should be here any minute. I'm sure she can assist you."

"I'll change my clothes and come back," he said. He hurried out.

I was quite impressed with how easily Mrs. March could order people to do things. I imagined she could get anything she wanted done.

"Do you know where my mother is?" I asked her.

"I'm sure she's in the hospital morgue, dear. I'm sorry."

"Will I see her again?"

"It's not pleasant to see someone who has passed away, especially a young person." She took a deep breath and nodded. "But a daughter should say good-bye to her mother. I'll look into it for you."

"She used to be very, very pretty," I said.

"Well, you're a very pretty young girl, so I know that's true. Now, don't you worry. Dr. Milan will get you up and about faster than any other doctor around here can."

I turned away to look out the window. It was another sunny California day. How could the world be so beautiful after my mother had died? I didn't mean to, but I started to cry.

"Oh, God," Mrs. March said. She stood and looked at me.

Just then, the nurse she had hired came into the room. Mrs. March didn't wait for her to introduce herself or anything. She practically lunged at her.

"Dr. Milan is going to reset that leg right now," she told her. "The cast wasn't done correctly. You make our little patient as comfortable as possible. She's been through the most horrible experience, especially for someone her age."

The nurse nodded. She was younger than any I had seen so far, younger but heavier, too. Mama would have said she had a body like a turnip. When she smiled at me, though, I saw she was warmer and friendlier than any other nurses I had met. Somewhere under those heavy cheeks slept a pretty face. That was something else Mama might have said.

"This is Jackie," Mrs. March said.

"Hi, Sasha," she said, coming over to me to take my hand.

She knew my name without looking at the clipboard. That was good, I thought. Whether she was doing it for Mrs. March's benefit or mine, I didn't know, but she started to rearrange my pillow and raise the back of the bed.

"You should be at this angle right now," she told me. Then she looked at my chart. "She has a mild concussion," Jackie read aloud, and then looked at Mrs. March.

"I know," she said.

"Are you nauseous, Sasha?"

"I was. I'm not so much now."

"I'll have a neurologist in to see her today," Mrs. March said. Jackie nodded. Mrs. March looked at her watch. "You'll be here until eight?"

"Yes, Mrs. March."

"I'm arranging for another nurse."

"She might not need round-the-clock, Mrs. March."

"I'm arranging for another nurse," she repeated, and looked at Jackie Knee as if she would have her shot if she said another word about it. She just nodded and looked at me, smiling again.

"Don't worry. We'll have a good time together," she told me.

In a surgical blue shirt and pants, Dr. Milan returned with another male aide pushing a gurney.

"I need to take her to another room," he told Mrs. March.

"Of course," she said. "I'll be back later," she told me. "You do your best to cooperate with Dr. Milan, okay, Sasha?"

I nodded. What else would I do? I wasn't about to get up and run out, although I wanted to more than anything.

"I'll look into your seeing your mother," she promised before she left.

Later, while Dr. Milan redid my cast, Jackie tried to distract me by telling me about the time she had broken her ankle.

"My little brother left one of his toy cars right outside my bedroom door. I was about your age, too. I think I flew ten feet. I was rushing out to meet some friends. Of course, everyone signed my cast and wrote silly things on it."

I didn't think Dr. Milan was paying any attention to Jackie's babbling, but he said, "She'll be able to write a novel on this cast."

Afterward, I was taken back to my private room and discovered that Mrs. March had sent flowers to dress it up. There were five different arrangements. Jackie raved about them. I knew she was trying her best to make everything seem better than it was. She made sure I ate most of my lunch. Soon after that, another doctor arrived, the neurologist. He was older and nicer than Dr. Milan. His name was Dr. Sander, and when he looked at me and talked to me, I felt he really saw me. Dr. Milan could have been working on a big doll.

"Well," Dr. Sander said after looking at my eyes, "no concussion is pleasant or should be ignored, but you'll be fine in a week or so. I'll stop in to check on you again soon. For now, you just take it easy. Your nurse has what you need if you get nauseous again." He turned to Jackie. "You know how to reach me if you need to," he said. Unlike Dr. Milan, he said good-bye before he left.

Everything was catching up with me. I tried to stay awake, but not long after Dr. Sander left, I fell asleep and didn't wake up until it was time for dinner. Jackie was getting it all set up for me. I saw a pile of magazines and books and a few boxes beside them on the table to my right.

"What's all that?" I asked.

"Oh, you're up. Good. Mrs. March sent up some magazines and books she thinks you'll like. There's a DVD player in the box with a dozen movies for someone your age. She knows it's no fun just lying around here waiting to get better. Let me fix your bed so you can have your dinner, and then you can look at everything, okay?"

She moved the tray over after she raised my bed for me.

"This looks good," she said, lifting the cover over the plate. "But if you don't like the food, Mrs. March left instructions for me to send out for something you do like. You have no dietary restrictions."

"It's all right," I said, trying to sound casual.

Dietary restrictions? We had dietary restrictions, such as some days only two meals. When Mama and I were on the street, meals like this would be like Christmas dinners. She'd be really angry if I didn't eat it.

Jackie had her dinner served, too, and pulled her chair up to my bed table. She smiled. "When I was your age, I'd hurry my meal just to get to the dessert. My mother always had something great. This chocolate cake looks delicious."

"Did you know Mrs. March before she asked you to be here?" I asked.

"Yes. She had work done by the plastic surgeon I used to work for. She liked the care I gave her. We had a special place for the patients to recuperate, and I was her private nurse four times for surgeries."

"Four times?"

She laughed. "I'm not supposed to talk out of school, but yes, she had a full face-lift, work on her rear end, breast implants, and a bit of a tummy tuck, not to mention her lips."

"All at once?"

"No," she said, laughing again. "But all of it over four years, I think. I don't want to tell you how much it all cost."

"You know why she's doing all this for me?" I asked.

"I know she does a great deal of work for different charities. I think that's very nice of her. There are lots of very rich people who don't do anything for anyone else." She smiled and started to eat again.

"I'm not a charity case," I said.

"Oh?"

For a moment, I wondered if I should say anything. Maybe it would make Mrs. March angry and she would stop doing nice things for me, but then I thought about Mama lying in a morgue and lost any hesitation.

"Her daughter killed my mother and did this to me," I said. "She said she was high on Ecstasy."

She stopped eating. And for a few moments, she looked as if she should be the one in the hospital bed, not me.

4

People with Influence

I knew Jackie was thinking how much more horrible this was because I was a homeless child without anyone to care for me, and therefore I had to appreciate what Mrs. March was willing to give me and do for me. Another child who had a family would probably tell her to go to hell with her daughter.

"Well," she said after a few moments to gather her thoughts, "you just take whatever she gives you. You deserve it and more. Maybe her husband is afraid some alert attorney will come see you and get you to sue the Marches. A lot of money could be held in trust for you to have when you're eighteen. I bet that would bring your father back."

"Would it?"

"I imagine so. Of course, he might be returning just to get his hands on the money. How long has he been away?"

"Three years," I said.

"Three years? Has he called you often?"

"Never."

"Not even written or sent you things?"

"We don't even know where he really is."

"Well, don't you worry about it. Your first job is to get better."

"Maybe he'll come back when he hears what happened."

"He might not find out about it. I always read the news-paper from beginning to end, and I didn't see anything about this accident. I'm not surprised that the Marches were able to keep it out of the news, though," she added. "They are what you call 'people with influence.'"

She didn't have to convince me of that. Look at what Mrs. March had gotten done for me in so short a time.

After I finished eating, I began to look through the magazines and books. Most of it was what I would read when I could get my hands on it. I hadn't seen any of the movies she bought for me, and I had never had a DVD ma-chine you could hold in your lap. Jackie checked my blood pressure and temperature and then sat and read some of my magazines, too.

We spent the next two days like this. Mrs. March didn't return during those days, but I knew she called often to speak with Jackie. The nurse who came when Jackie left was older and less talkative, at least with me. She spent most of the night talking with other nurses. I guessed Jackie was right. I really didn't need the second nurse, because I slept through most of the night. I did look forward to seeing Jackie first thing in the morning.

Either because she really enjoyed talking about her fam-ily and her life or because she was just trying to keep me from thinking about things, Jackie told me all about her brothers and sisters, her parents, how she became a nurse, and her one disappointing love affair. She rattled on about her taste in music and things she loved to eat. It seemed there wasn't anything she didn't like. I enjoyed listening to her talk about her family. I imagined myself a part of it.

What was a family, anyway? Could just a mother and a daughter be considered a family, or did you have to have a father, too, not to mention at least one brother or sister? A house or an apartment didn't seem like much without a family living in it. When Jackie described her house, especially when all of her brothers and sisters had lived in it, I felt as though the house was alive, a warm place that embraced them and kept them happy and safe. How far that was from the cold apartment we had lived in and that small hotel room. How could I call either one a home?

Soon, though, instead of enjoying hearing Jackie describe her family and home life, I became sadder. Look at all I had been missing and would miss forever now. What sort of a woman could I become? I'd be like someone without any past. How could I ever do what Jackie was doing, describe my parents, where I lived? I'd be like so many of those homeless people I saw at the beach, panhandling or trying to sell something to survive. Their faces were caverns of despair, their eyes empty, a smile as hard to find as a decent meal or a place to stay the night. The sound of other people laughing was painful to them and to me. If one day we weren't there, no one would care; no one would look for us. Sometimes I wished the tide would come farther in and wash us all away. I was sure many people who saw us and shook their heads wished the same thing.

As I looked around my nice hospital room, I wondered where I would go from there. One day, the doctors would tell me I was recuperated enough to be discharged, but discharged to where? An orphanage? Some foster home? When I thought about that, I almost wished Daddy would come rushing back to get me, even if it was just to get himself some money. At least I'd be with someone who was supposed to care about me.

Late on the third morning, Mrs. March appeared and told Jackie she had arranged for me to be brought down to the morgue.

Jackie's face lost color, and she turned sharply toward me. "Are you sure?"

"I know it's very, very unpleasant," Mrs. March said, "but she wants to say good-bye. Am I right, Sasha? We don't have to do this if you've changed your mind, and Jackie's right to be concerned for you. It's ugly."

"I don't care. I want to see her," I said. Mama could never be ugly to me, I thought.

"Then you will."

She stepped out and returned with an aide and a wheelchair. I was helped into it, and the four of us went to the elevator. No one spoke all the way down to the morgue. My heart was pounding, and my eyes were filling with tears so quickly I had trouble seeing as we went down the corridor and through a pair of doors. A man in a white lab coat was waiting for us just inside and had me wheeled sharply to the right to avoid seeing anything else.

We entered a cold room. I saw no bodies, just what looked like a giant file cabinet.

"You stay with her, Jackie," Mrs. March said. "We'll hang back here."

I looked at her and the aide. He didn't seem unhappy about that, and she looked as if she was trembling. It got me trembling. Jackie wheeled me deeper in and up to a cabinet. The man in the lab coat looked at me, and then he pulled on the handle and slid Mama out. She was under a sheet. He lifted it, and something inside me shattered like a windowpane.

It didn't look anything like Mama, and for a moment, I hoped it wasn't her. Maybe she was still alive somewhere in the hospital. Maybe there had been a terrible mix-up. I looked at Jackie, and she shook her head. It was no good to pretend, to lie to myself. I knew it was Mama.

Tears were trickling down my cheeks. "Mama," I whispered. "I love you. I'll always love you."

I reached out to touch her face and then recoiled when I felt how hard and cold it was. Suddenly, I was very nauseous and began to dry-heave. Jackie whisked me around and away. The aide stepped forward.

"Let's get her back upstairs," Mrs. March said. "Quickly."

I kept my eyes closed and my head back until I was upstairs and in my bed. Then I slowly looked up at the ceiling.

Jackie rubbed my arm softly. "Don't think of her down there," she said. "That was no longer your mother. Think of her as being in a better place now, where she is always warm and happy and safe, okay?"

"Okay," I said in a voice so small I thought I had become three years old again. I closed my eyes and fell asleep.

Days passed. Mrs. March sent me more presents, more magazines and movies and boxes of candy. I could tell from the way other nurses looked when they gazed in at me that I was quite a curiosity. I had no visitors other than the doctors and my private nurses. I was sure that by now there were all sorts of stories about me. Despite Jackie and the gifts, I felt more and more as if I were in prison or in some cave in a human zoo.

Jackie tried to help me feel better about it. She got me into a wheelchair whenever she could and pushed me down to a small patio to get some air and sunshine. Except for a few visitors, only other hospital employees used the patio. Some ate their lunches out there. Jackie knew some people and introduced me. While I read or listened to music on the new iPod Mrs. March had sent, Jackie would move off and tell those people all about me. By the way they looked at me afterward, I could see that she had given them all the grisly details. I knew she didn't mean any harm, but soon, because of their looks of pity, I wasn't so eager to go down there anymore.

One afternoon, Mrs. March returned. I was sitting up in my bed and reading with my earphones on. They were plugged into the iPod, so I didn't see her or hear her, but out of the corner of my eye, I saw Jackie get up quickly and put her magazine down. I turned and saw Jordan March standing there. She looked as if she had just come from a fancy affair, and later she did say she had attended a charity luncheon. She wore a white wide-brim hat with a pink ribbon and a sleeveless V-neck dress, embellished with a pink scarf.

I took off my earphones.

"You can take a break now, Jackie," Mrs. March said.

Jackie nodded, smiled at me, and walked out. Mrs. March stepped up to my bed and smiled.

"I hear good things from your doctors," she began. "Your bruises are healing, the concussion has receded, and you do look a lot stronger. How are you feeling?"

"The cast itches," I said. "It's hard to get used to it."

"Yes, I imagine so. Dr. Milan says it's too early to know how the break will affect the growth of your leg, but it's important to remain hopeful. He's one of the best doctors in all of Southern California for this problem. Of course, when the cast is removed, you'll need therapy, and I'm arranging for all of that."

"Where will I have to go?"

"We'll see," she said, looking away for a few seconds. When she looked at me again, her face was full of sadness, the way it had been when we had first met and she told me about losing her younger daughter. I could see her eyes filling with tears. She took a breath. "I want you to know I've taken good care of your mother," she said.

Taken good care of my mother? She said it as if she meant that Mama hadn't died. Maybe that really wasn't Mama I had seen in the morgue. Maybe I wasn't lying to myself. I held my breath. I think she saw that I was misunderstanding her.

"What I mean is, I bought a plot in Greenlawn Cemetery for her. I wanted my husband to make my daughter come to the burial, but he wouldn't do that, so I went myself and made it as dignified as I could. I'll make sure you are taken to the grave as soon as you are able to go. I didn't have any stone put up yet. I thought you might want to have something besides her name and dates of birth and death. You might want something like 'Loving Mother,' whatever. You don't have to think about that right now."

At least Mama wasn't where she had feared she'd be, in that Potter's Field, I thought.

"I had one of our attorneys research your mother's family, and then I had any we could locate called, but no one wanted to attend the funeral. Your father was harder to find. He was in Honolulu for a while, and then he . . . well, he went off with someone to Australia. He hasn't responded to any calls or inquiries, I'm afraid. We have it from reliable sources that he has another daughter with this woman. I'm sorry to have to tell you all this, but I thought you should know. Any man who would desert a daughter like you isn't worth spending any time on, anyway," she added angrily.

"How old is his new daughter?"

"Not quite two."

Did he love her, I wondered, or did he think of her the same way he thought of me, as a burden, a punishment for his past sins, as he had told Mama children were?

"He just left you two one day? He didn't tell you he was leaving?" Mrs. March asked.

I tried to recall the exact details. That day, Mama had made a meat loaf because she said if he didn't show for dinner, we could keep it for lunch the next day. When he didn't return home hours after we had eaten, she had gone into their bedroom and come out with a look of shock and anger on her face. I was doing my homework in the living room.

"That bastard," she had said. I looked up and waited for her to explain. "He took all the spare cash I thought I had hidden from him under my panties in the top drawer of my dresser. So I thought I had better check my mother's jewelry, the ring and necklace and that cameo my mother gave me. It was worth a few thousand, at least. Guess what? That's gone, too. He went and pawned it all, I'm sure."

I didn't know what to say. She wasn't sobbing, nor were her shoulders shaking, but tears were streaming down her cheeks.

"I went into the closet and saw that he's taken a lot of his clothes."

"Why?" I asked.

"Why? Why?" She sniffed, looked up at the ceiling and then at me. "He's gone, Sasha. That glob of flesh and bones who called himself my husband and your father is gone. I knew he was seeing this woman over in West L.A. My guess is, he's moved in with her. I'll find out, and I'll get the police on his back. You can be sure of that."

She returned to her bedroom and shut the door. I could barely breathe. Just remembering it took my breath away now. How could Jordan March expect me to relive it?

"No," I said. "He never told us he was leaving. My mother thought he had moved in with another woman, but when the police checked, both of them were gone. Later, she heard that someone thought he had gone to Hawaii. She tried to find him, but no one really helped us."

"How terrible for both of you. Your mother had stopped working, right?"

"Yes, but she went back to working at a restaurant the next week, and for a while, everything seemed okay. She was sad, though, and tired and . . ."

"Began to drink?"

I nodded.

"So she lost her job eventually?"

"Yes, but she got another and . . ."

"The same thing happened."

I nodded.

"So your bills began piling up. There are so many people, especially women who've been deserted, who are just like that out there. You lost the house, I imagine?"

"We didn't have a house. We had an apartment, and the police came one day and told us we had to leave right away."

"Evicted? Yes, of course, that would happen. Where did you go?"

"To a hotel, but Mama wasn't doing well. She didn't have a job anymore, so we couldn't pay the rent too long."

"And that's when you went out on the street?"

I nodded.

"You said she sold calligraphy she created?"

"And I sold lanyards."

"Yes, which you made. That's sweet, but how terribly difficult it had to be. Where did you sleep, exactly?"

"Sometimes just under the tree, sometimes in a big box Mama made. For a while, we slept in an old deserted car, but then someone came along and took it away."

"You stopped going to school?"

"It was too far and hard for me to go. I didn't have my old clothes."

"Of course, and anyway, where would you do your schoolwork?" she said, nodding. "Didn't your mother try to get some help?"

How was I to explain what Mama had been like without making her sound terrible? I just shook my head.

"Your mother . . ." She hesitated and thought for a moment. I could see she was deciding whether or not to tell me something.

"What?"

"Your mother had quite a bit of alcohol in her at the time of the accident," she said. "I'm not saying that made it her fault or anything," she quickly added. "She was like that often, though? I mean, every day?"

I didn't say yes, but I didn't have to.

"I'm sure it made it all that much harder for you." She grew angry again. "That father of yours should be stood up and shot."

"Mama didn't want to drink whiskey," I said. "It made her feel better."

"Well, yes, I suppose . . ."

"She didn't have to think about us. She tried to change herself into another person so that she wouldn't have to think about all that had happened to her."

She stared at me. "That's very astute. You're a very bright young girl. I can see that, Sasha. It would be a waste to let you fall through the cracks. I'm sure you wanted to be in school."

"Uh-huh."

"I'm not usually someone who believes in fate. When Alena died, I knew there were some people who thought it was just something meant to be and that was why nothing we tried to do could stop it. It's like everything is designed, and we just follow the path we're given. Something like that. Donald believes that. I'd like to think that maybe some good could come out of Kiera being the one to have caused your accident, the injuries, and your mother's death."

I recoiled. *Good?*

"It brought me to you and you to me," she said. "I had a great loss when Alena died, and so did you when you lost your mother. We can help each other. Actually, you'll be helping me and Donald by giving us more to do with our lives, our family lives."

"How?" I asked.

She smiled. "I'd like you to think about something. I'd like you to come live with us, Sasha. First, we'll be your foster parents, and then, if you're happy, we will adopt you."

All I could do was stare at her. She wanted me to live with her? But I'd be living with her daughter Kiera, too?

"You'll only end up a ward of the state otherwise and be shipped off to some orphanage or multichild foster home," she quickly added. "You don't want that. Even your mother, in the condition she was in, that you were both in, avoided putting you there, and now that I have gotten to know you, it would make me very sad, too."

My continued silence unnerved her.

"Do you understand what I'm saying?" she asked.

I nodded, and she stood up.

"Okay. You just think about it. I'll be back tomorrow, and we'll talk again about it."

Jackie came to the door and hesitated, waiting to see if it was all right for her to return.

"You can come in," Mrs. March told her. "She's doing quite well, according to Dr. Milan."

"Yes, she is," Jackie said, smiling at me.

"We might only need you a few more days."

"Of course," Jackie said. She smiled at me. "In this case, I'll be glad to lose my job. She's been a delightful patient."

Mrs. March smiled and looked at me. "Yes, she's quite a wonderful young girl," she said. "Continue to take good care of her," she added, and left the room.

Jackie waited until she was sure she was gone and turned to me. "Well? What is she planning to buy you? What is she going to do for you now?"

"Have me take the place of her dead daughter," I said.

5
A New Life

Y ou mean she wants you to come live with her?"

"Yes. And if I like it, she and her husband would adopt me."

Jackie sat, a look of amazement flowing over her face. "I have never seen her house, but when I was working for the plastic surgeon, there was always a lot of gossiping about some of the patients. Some were famous movie stars, but I remember hearing that the Marches' house was bigger than any Hollywood movie star's or producer's and quite beautiful. In fact," she said, getting more excited, "I remember someone said it cost about one hundred million dollars. It's up in Pacific Palisades. Do you know where that is?"

"I think so."

"Wow. Well, what are you going to do? Did you say yes?"

"I didn't say anything," I said. "She wants me to think about it."

"Don't you give it a second thought," Jackie advised angrily. "Don't you be bashful now. You take everything that woman is willing to give you. No matter what. You deserve more than they're willing to give you, in fact. Take it gladly."

I didn't say that I would, but somehow, because Jackie had heard that I might live in the Marches' house and even be adopted by them, she looked at me differently. I could feel the gap between us suddenly widen, and I didn't like it.

Then, as if Jordan March had been listening in on our conversation, she sent more gifts. This time, it was clothes and shoes. Jackie unwrapped everything for me.

"This is all very expensive stuff. She wants to be sure you're dressed properly when you leave here and enter her world," she commented. Her voice didn't have the same tone of joy and wonder. I sensed the bitterness and wondered if I should be feeling it as well. "I bet this all costs more than I make in a week," Jackie added. "If this is any indication of what it's going to be like, you'll be fine."

"None of that replaces my mother," I said.

Instead of being upset, she smiled. "That's right. You keep that in mind. Take whatever you can get, but as I said, never let her and her husband forget that they can never give you enough. Sasha, don't ever feel like some charity case. Promise me that."

"I won't," I said, but I wasn't sure that I could keep such a promise. I wasn't even sure that I was going to say yes. I tried to imagine what Mama would have said before the struggle. Back then, she had so much self-pride. She wouldn't accept a nickel if she thought someone was giving it to her because he or she felt sorry for her. That's why she had worked so hard on her calligraphy.

"One of the worst things in the world," Mama had told

me, "is being obligated to someone, especially someone who won't let you forget why. So the best thing you can do for yourself is always earn what you get or deserve it, Sasha. That's what it really means to be free."

Mrs. March, however, had made it sound as if I was doing her more of a favor than she was doing for me. She was the one who was obligated. I wondered if her husband felt the same way. Would I be treated like some kind of princess? Should I ever be satisfied and happy when I was with them?

I knew Jackie gossiped a little with the other nurses about me and Mrs. March, because when they stopped by, they, too, looked at me differently. I imagined I was no longer just someone's charity case. Was this how it would always be from now on? People would no longer look at me with disgust, disapproval, or disinterest? Should I be feeling good about it? Mama was dead and buried. Everything, all of the gifts, the clothes, the promise of a new life, was designed to make me forget what had happened. *I won't*, I vowed. *I never will.*

With the cast on my leg, I always had a hard time falling and staying asleep, but this particular night was the worst. I dreamed that Mama was in the room with me, sitting beside my bed and looking at me. She wasn't my mother before the struggle, either. She was just the way she was on the day of the accident.

She was staring at me and twisting her hands around each other. "I'm sorry," she said. "I'm sorry I did this to you."

"You didn't do it, Mama."

"I did. I did. I can't sleep in my grave, Sasha. You're alone in the street."

"No, I'm not. I won't be, Mama."

"You are. I did this. You are," she insisted, and then she began to shrink in the chair. I reached out to stop it, but I couldn't get to her. She kept dwindling.

"Mama!" I screamed, and woke up.

I apparently woke up my night nurse, too. She came quickly to the bed. "What's wrong? Are you in pain? What?"

I looked up at her. Her face seemed as white as her uniform in the dim light, and she didn't look sympathetic. She looked upset.

"No," I said. "Nothing." I lay back, closing my eyes.

"You'd think the ceiling had caved in," I heard her say.

"It has," I muttered. "For me."

The next morning, I saw how nervous Jackie was. She didn't say any more about Mrs. March's offer to take me into her home, but it was clearly on her mind. The more she flitted about, trying to make me more comfortable, keeping the sun out of my eyes and the room cool enough, making sure I ate well, the more nervous I became, too.

Finally, just before lunch, Jordan March arrived. She was dressed in a bright blue pantsuit and had her hair pulled back so that her opal teardrop earrings in a gold setting were quite prominent. As usual, it looked as if a professional had done her makeup and she was ready to step onto the cover of some fashion magazine.

"How's our patient doing today?" she asked Jackie.

"Fine, Mrs. March."

"Take a break," she told her.

Jackie nodded and left without glancing at me, keeping her head down.

"Well, now, Sasha, have you thought about our little discussion yesterday?"

"Yes," I said.

"How do you feel about it? Do you want to come live with Donald and me? I'll have the therapist come to our house, and when you're able to get around, we'll get you into school again. In the meantime, I'll also arrange for a tutor to come to the house and get you caught up. We don't want you entering class behind the others, do we?"

I shook my head.

"Of course, if you're terribly unhappy, we'll look for other arrangements for you. What do you say? Will you come?"

She was sitting where I had dreamed Mama sat. It was almost as if Mama's spirit was there, too.

"Yes," I said.

"Oh, that's wonderful, Sasha. It really is." She leaped to her feet. "I have lots to do, lots to arrange. You'll be out of here the day after tomorrow. Dr. Milan will discharge you, and then he'll follow up on your treatment. Now, tell me some important things. What are your favorite colors? I took a guess with some of the clothes I sent up. Do you like the baby pink, the metallic blues, and this green? I love this green," she said, holding up a blouse I had not yet put on.

"Yes. Everything is beautiful," I said. What else would I say? I hadn't had anything new for more than a year. Everything Mama and I had managed to buy during the struggle when we were on the street was used, from some thrift store. Colors were faded and dull, and the clothes were often long out of style and never quite fit.

"I'm glad. Those were Alena's favorite colors, too. Actually, she liked anything that was bright and happy. She was a bright and happy girl, never depressed. You'll be like that someday, too, Sasha, I just know you will. I can see that it's not in your nature to be unhappy. You did such a good job of helping your mother, and I'm sure you weren't crying and complaining all the time. You've got that same energy in you. We'll go shopping to get you more, of course. For the time being, you'll have plenty, however. You're just about the same age Alena was and about her size. That's how I figured out what to buy you, you know. I bet you were wondering how I knew."

"No," I said. "I thought you could just look at me and see."

"That's right, I could. Well, there's a ton more to do, a ton. I'm going right over to Donald's offices to tell him about your decision. I'll try to stop by later, but don't worry if I don't. You can be sure that you're all that's on my mind."

She moved toward me as if she were going to give me a kiss, but the look on my face slowed her down, and she paused and then smiled quickly, grabbed her purse, and left. For a moment, it was as if all the air had gone out of the room with her. I felt the blood rush to my face. Of course, I knew Mama was gone, but it still felt as if I were deserting her, leaving her to be alone on the street. My father had deserted her and now me. I couldn't help it. I started to cry softly.

"What happened?" Jackie demanded as she stepped into the room. "Did she say she changed her mind, or her husband said no, or what?"

I shook my head. "No. I'm going," I said.

"So why are you crying?"

"I'm not going home," I said.

She froze and then nodded and moved to hug me.

"That's where my mother said she was taking us when we left the beach that night—home."

"You'll find a place to call home someday, Sasha. You'll make your own home when you're old enough. You'll marry someone wonderful and have your own children. You'll see."

I thanked her. Her words did give me hope. She was there the day I was discharged, and she followed Jordan March and me to the waiting limousine. I didn't know I'd be leaving in a limousine. I had never ridden in one. At first, I thought she had rented it, but I quickly learned that it belonged to the Marches. The driver was very tall, easily six foot four or five. He was slim but with such perfect military posture Mama would have called him a flagpole. He had a thick, well-trimmed black mustache, a nose that looked as if it had been pinched by the doctor who had delivered him, and coal-black eyes. Mrs. March called him Grover, which I would learn was his first name. His full name was Grover Morrison. He had been the Marches' limousine driver for nearly four years. I didn't know it yet, but the Marches owned five other vehicles, and Kiera had an additional one, the one she had been driving the night of the accident.

"You take care," Jackie told me after I had been

transferred from the wheelchair into the limousine. She stood in the open doorway.

"I will," I said. "Thank you, Jackie."

She nodded and backed away as Grover closed the door. He opened the door on the other side for Mrs. March.

"Well, now," Mrs. March said. "Are you comfortable?"

"Yes."

"I could put a pillow under your leg."

"It's all right," I said.

"Don't worry," she said, patting my hand. "Everything's going to be fine."

I wasn't worried as much as I was afraid. Before Daddy had deserted us, I had slept over at a friend's house. That was really the only time I had ever been overnight at the home of strangers, and now I was going to live with some.

"You'll have to wear that cast for months yet, Sasha," she said, nodding at it, "but Dr. Milan's arranged for you to be up and about on a crutch soon. In the meantime, we have the wheelchair for you. I've already told Mrs. Caro that one of her duties now will be to wheel you out onto the patio in the afternoon. I want you to get some color and fresh air and not be shut up in a room like you were in the hospital."

"Who's Mrs. Caro?"

"Mrs. Caro is one of my housekeepers and also our cook. We have four housekeepers. The one in charge is Mrs. Duval. She's been with us the longest and was actually Kiera and Alena's nanny as well. Her husband, Alberto, is what Donald calls our house manager. He is in charge of the grounds people, house maintenance, that sort of thing."

"Four housekeepers? How many people work at the house?" I asked as we started away from the hospital.

"Fourteen full-time," she said. "There's a lot to do. You'll see."

Neither of us had mentioned her yet, but I didn't see how I could go much farther without bringing her up. "What about Kiera?"

"What about her?"

"Does she know about me?"

"She knows about you."

"But does she know I'm coming to live in her house?"

"It's not her house," Mrs. March said quickly and sharply. Then she smiled and added, "Don't worry about it."

"But she knows?" I asked.

"Not yet," Mrs. March said. "Right now, I'm not concerned about what she thinks or how she feels about anything."

Her answer shocked me. How could such a thing be kept secret from her daughter? What sort of a family was this, anyway?

Maybe Mama and I, even during the struggle, had been more of a family after all.

It wouldn't be long before I knew.

6

Castle

*N*othing I had seen in magazines, on television, or in a movie had prepared me for what I was about to see. I had thought castles were only in Europe and only kings and queens lived like this. We turned off a main road, went down a side road, and began to climb a hill. As we climbed, I realized there were no houses along the way.

Mrs. March sensed my curiosity. "All this land is ours," she said, "on both sides. That's why there are no other houses on the road."

Eventually, we reached what I could only describe as a hidden entrance to the road on which the Marches' house was located. There were no signs, mailboxes, or anything, just tall, full pine trees on both sides, so that when anyone drove in, he or she couldn't see the March house just yet.

"This isn't a public road," she said. "My husband built it, and we maintain it."

They own their own road? How can anyone own his own road? I wondered.

We came to a tall, solid, light orange wall at least ten or twelve feet high. Now, just over the wall, I could see the top of the house and what looked like a tower. Just looking at the wall ahead of us wouldn't tell anyone it opened, but when Grover pressed a button by the sun visor above him, the wall began to part. It revealed a beautiful cobblestone driveway that curved upward toward what I could only call a storybook house.

"Is it a castle?" I asked breathlessly.

Mrs. March laughed. "Donald thinks so. He was determined to build something different, so he built what's called a Richardsonian Romanesque house. It has the round-topped arches over the windows and entryway and masonry walls with a pattern of ruby and white. And yes," she said, laughing again, "that tower makes it look like a castle, but Donald will tell you a man's home is supposed to be his castle."

As we approached and we could see beyond the high bushes and trees, the house seemed to unfold to my right and to my left.

"It's so big."

"It might be the biggest house in Southern California, for all I know. I forget, but I think Donald said it's ninety thousand square feet. There are three floors if we count the rooms in the tower. We've been here nearly twenty years, but I'm still furnishing it. I suppose it will never be finished, but that's what makes it fun to go shopping here and in Europe. There's furniture from all over the world. Persian and Turkish rugs, French chandeliers, cabinets from England, settees and chairs from Spain, tapestries from both France and Spain. You can understand why we need so many employees."

She pointed to her left as we drew closer. "Over there, you'll find the swimming pool and the tennis courts. You can't tell, but part of the house is our multicar garage. The garage entrances are all around the side, so it makes the house look much bigger. Of course, there is an apartment over the garage. That's where Mrs. Duval and her husband, Alberto, live. There's another maid's apartment for Mrs. Caro at the rear of the house. Everyone else comes to work from his or her own home. We have another entrance for servants and deliveries at the west end of the property.

"There are security cameras everywhere. Donald loves his toys. He has a movie theater in the house, with the most up-to-date equipment. There's a full gym and a small indoor swimming pool, which will come in handy for your therapy, I bet. The house has an intercom system, of course. Just think of all the fun you'll have discovering new things in it when you're up and about."

As we drew closer, I looked out at the beautiful gardens and fountains, the statues and benches, the rolling lawns and trees. No wonder so many people had to work there, I thought. There was so much to take care of. How could anyone be so rich?

As soon as we pulled up to the front, a short, stout, dark-brown-haired woman came rushing out. She wore a dark blue one-piece dress with a skirt that flapped about her ankles as she hurried down the stairs. Her hair was clipped into a tight bun. Right behind her was a tall, gray-haired man with a dark brown mustache sprinkled with gray hairs. He wore a plaid shirt and jeans.

"That's Mrs. Duval and her husband, Alberto," Mrs. March told me.

Grover got out quickly and opened Mrs. March's door. He went around to get my wheelchair and my things, some of which he handed to Mrs. Duval. He and Alberto unfolded the wheelchair and brought it to my door.

"Careful with her," Mrs. March told them.

Grover looked for a graceful way to get me out and then simply decided to put his right arm under me and embrace me with his left. He lifted me out easily and gently lowered me to the wheelchair that Alberto held.

"This is Sasha," Mrs. March said.

"*Hola,* Sasha," Mrs. Duval said. "Hello and welcome."

"*Sí,* welcome," Alberto said.

He and Grover lifted me and the chair and carried me up the stone steps to the entrance. Mrs. Duval and Mrs. March followed us. At the grand door, they waited for her instructions.

"Take her in and to the elevator," Mrs. March told them. "We're bringing her right up to her suite."

Elevator? Suite? Had I heard right? This did sound more like a hotel than a house.

They hurried to do so.

The entryway had a floor of golden marble, and there were small statues of ivory-white angels in niches on both sides of the darker marble walls. Above us was a large chandelier shaped like an opened hand, and ahead of us was a curved stairway with steps that matched the marble in the entrance. The banister was made of marble, too. Every-where I looked, I saw paintings and tapestries on the walls and pedestals with small statues.

Alberto wheeled me to the right, but before we went too far, a smaller, younger-looking lady with a pillbox chef's cap came hurrying down the long hallway. She didn't look much taller than five foot one or two, and her apron's hem was down to her ankles, making it look as if it was meant for a much taller person.

"This is Mrs. Caro," Mrs. March announced before she reached us. "Mrs. Caro, meet Sasha."

"Hello, dear," Mrs. Caro said in an accent I recognized as Irish only because Daddy had an Irish friend he had brought around from time to time. "My, what a pretty little girl," she told Mrs. March. "I'm fixing a nice lunch for you, dear."

"We'll let you know when she's settled in, Mrs. Caro. For today and perhaps tomorrow, we'll let her rest. Then we'll see about taking her out."

"Oh, of course, Mrs. March. I'll prepare some fresh lemonade," she said, and then asked, "You like lemonade?"

"Yes, thank you."

She smiled as if she rarely heard those words.

Mrs. March urged Alberto to continue, and he brought me to an elevator.

"We hardly use this," Mrs. March said when I was wheeled in. There wasn't room for Mrs. Duval, who had already gone up the stairway. "Donald thought it would be wise to have one, either to help us when we were too old or in the event of his wanting to sell, to have another attraction, an added advantage. If you ask me, it was just another toy for him, but now it does come in handy."

The elevator was slow. I saw that it could go up to the tower, too. When the door opened, Mrs. Duval was waiting for us. "I'll take her from here," she told her husband. Without comment, he turned and went to the stairway. Mrs. Duval wheeled me down another long corridor. More paintings and tapestries were spaced along its walls on both sides, with pedestals holding statues and busts here and there as well. We went almost to the end before she turned me into a room on the left. I nearly gasped.

Even in movies and magazines, I had never seen a bedroom this large. The walls were done in a baby pink, and the bed, which looked even larger than a king-size bed, had a cream frame with pink spirals, four posts, and a canopy. What surprised me, however, was the headboard. Embossed on it were two giraffes.

Before I could ask, *Why giraffes?* Mrs. March explained. "Giraffes were Alena's favorite animals. From the age of two or three, she was fascinated by them."

So, this was Alena's room, then. For someone who just weeks ago was sleeping in a carton on the beach, coming to such a house would have been overwhelming in and of itself. Even simply setting foot in it would have drowned me in amazement. The sight of it as we had approached it, the grounds, the landscaping, had taken my breath away and actually had numbed me. But now, realizing that I was stepping into the shoes and sleeping in the bed of Mrs. March's dead little girl did more than amaze and numb me. It actually frightened me. It was beautiful, the most beautiful room I had ever seen, but for a moment, it gave me the feeling that I was invading and violating another girl's sacred shrine. Prominent on one of the dressers was a picture of someone who was surely Alena. I avoided looking at it.

"Mrs. Duval and I have already gone through all of Alena's things and sorted out what we think would fit you properly," Mrs. March said as they brought me to the bed. "You don't have to put this on right now, but here's one of my favorite nightgowns." She lifted it off the bed where it had been neatly placed. She laughed. "As you can see . . . more giraffes. I'm afraid you're going to find them everywhere. She even had a toothbrush shaped like the neck of a giraffe with a giraffe's head. Donald went a little overboard with that stuff."

"Do you want her in bed right away?" Mrs. Duval asked Mrs. March. I looked up at her.

"I don't know. Are you tired, Sasha? You can explore the suite, if you like, or get into bed and rest. I imagine it's all been exhausting for you, considering you've been laid up so long and gone through so much. What would you like to do?"

Mrs. Duval pulled back the blanket in anticipation.

"I'll stay in the wheelchair a while longer," I said.

"Good. That way, you can have your lunch right over here," Mrs. March said, moving to her right to show me a separate sitting area. "This will become your private classroom, too, as soon as I have your tutor arranged. I was thinking we'd get that started as soon as we can, as long as you're up to it. You can work in here, don't you think?"

I wheeled myself toward it. There was a small table, a

desk with a computer, another television besides the one built into the wall directly across from the bed, and a very large dollhouse, large enough for a little girl to go into if she liked. Everywhere I looked, there were pictures of giraffes in different locales or just one or two close up. There was a beautiful painting of one as well.

The windows were low enough for me to look out, even sitting in the wheelchair. I wheeled to the one on the left and gazed down at the swimming pool, which looked huge, and the two tennis courts. Someone was cleaning the pool.

"That's an Olympic-size pool," Mrs. March said, standing over my shoulder. "Before she became very sick, Alena could do ten laps without stopping. I'm sure once you're fully recuperated, it will be great for your physical therapy. In no time at all, you'll be able to work up to ten laps, too, I'm sure. It's always heated, by the way."

There was a cabana with tables under a roof, a barbecue area, and what looked like a large hot tub, too. Around the pool were light yellow wood tables with yellow umbrellas. It looked more like the pool area in a hotel, not a home, but now that I was in it, I realized this house was bigger than many hotels. It would need everything to be larger and in bigger amounts than any normal house would. The hotel room Mama and I had slept in was probably no bigger than the wardrobe closet in this suite.

"Well, what do you think so far, Sasha?" Mrs. March asked. "Do you think you could be happy here?"

I looked up at her. Of course, there was a part of me that wanted to say, *Absolutely, this is like a dream,* but there was a part of me that still harbored anger and sadness. I was also reminded of the things Jackie had said to me. They could never do enough to compensate for what they had taken from me. Even all of this didn't come anywhere close.

"I don't know," I said, which obviously shocked Mrs. Duval and disappointed Mrs. March.

"It's understandable," she said, mostly for Mrs. Duval's sake, I thought. "You've been through so much so quickly. You need to catch your breath and get used to new things. I'd feel the same way," she added. "Well, don't hesitate to ask Mrs. Duval or Mrs. Caro or anyone, for that matter, for anything you want or need."

From the look on Mrs. Duval's face, I could see that she was thinking, *Need? What could she possibly want or need that she doesn't have already?*

I didn't know if I could blame her just yet for being insensitive. I had no idea how much she knew about me, about exactly what had happened or why I was there.

Another thought that was tying a knot in my brain was, where was Kiera? Where was her room? When would she and I meet? What would she say? What would I say? Did any of the people who worked there know what she had done?

"Okay, then, you look about, Sasha. Mrs. Duval will be bringing up your lunch soon. I have a few errands to run. All you have to do is pick up any of the phones in the suite if you need anything. Just picking one up rings Mrs. Duval's pager. That's another one of Donald's technical toys. I know sometimes Alena drove Mrs. Duval bonkers," she added.

"Only when she was sick," Mrs. Duval said sharply.

"Yes. She was a very thoughtful little girl, wasn't she?"

"The best. I can't imagine any little girl better," Mrs. Duval said, her eyes fixed on me.

"Well, let's not dilly-dally, as Mrs. Caro says. See you soon, Sasha." Mrs. March touched my shoulder and then turned and headed out.

Mrs. Duval hesitated. "Do you need to use the toilet?"

"No, not yet," I said.

"I'll go see about your lunch, then," she told me, and followed Mrs. March out. She closed the door behind her and left me in a silence so deep it made me feel as if I were asleep and dreaming.

It was truly like a medieval castle, with its walled-in grounds and security, its employees, some of whom I could see now cutting grass and trimming bushes. I was certain there was everything and anything that anyone like me could possibly want, if anyone like me could forget about love, especially a mother's love.

But to answer Mrs. March's question fully, no, I couldn't imagine ever calling this home. I was sure anyone else would think it strange, but as I sat there in my wheelchair and looked at all that was now at my disposal, I couldn't help wondering how and when I could escape.

7

Alena's Room

rs. Duval brought up my lunch on the same sort of cart I had seen at the hospital. I was stunned by how much food was on the tray. I thought maybe Mrs. March was going to eat with me, but she didn't follow Mrs. Duval into the suite, and I didn't hear her coming.

"Is this all for me?" I asked.

"Mrs. Caro made you one of her delicious chicken quesadillas, but in case you might not like it, she made a ham and cheese sandwich, and under here," she said, lifting a silver cover, "is a cheeseburger. There's a small salad for you and this piece of her homemade chocolate cake. This is the homemade lemonade she does. Do you think you want some ice cream, too?"

I sat with my mouth open. I would eat any one of the choices, but what would I do with the others? Maybe she'd take them back.

"I'll eat the chicken quesadilla," I said. I couldn't remember when I had eaten one last. "I don't need ice cream."

"Maybe you don't need it, but you can have it," Mrs. Duval said. "I'll bring some up later."

She turned to leave.

"But what about the rest? I can't eat everything."

"Just eat what you want and leave the rest," she said, shrugging. "That's what everyone does here."

After she left, I sat staring at the tray of food. There had been times when we were on the street when this much food would feed both Mama and me for a whole day. The thought of it being wasted and thrown out actually turned my stomach. Despite what I had said, I tried to eat more than I should have. I ate until I thought I would throw it all up and then stopped. Not long after, Mrs. Duval returned with a bowl of chocolate and vanilla ice cream.

"No," I said. "Please take it back. I can't eat any more."

She looked at me with indifference, put it on the tray, and rolled the food wagon out of the room. I closed my eyes and sat there trying to digest the food. Eating all of that food was stupid of me, I thought, but I couldn't change into a wasteful rich person overnight, could I? I dozed off in my chair and didn't wake until I heard voices outside. Fortunately, I no longer felt bloated and nauseous.

The voices grew louder, so I wheeled myself back to the window in the sitting room and looked out to see three teenage boys and four teenage girls getting ready to go into the pool. I had no idea what she looked like, but I knew one of them had to be Kiera March.

I concentrated on the four girls. One seemed too dark-haired and short to be Jordan March's daughter, but of course, I didn't know what Donald March looked like yet.

I thought all four of the girls were pretty, but one did stand out more, because she looked slim and tall like a model and had Jordan March's light brown hair, which she had similarly styled. All of the girls wore two-piece bathing suits. One of the three boys was at least as tall as the tallest girl, but the other two were short and stocky. They all jumped in ahead of the girls and started to race across the pool. The girls cheered, but the shorter boys were far outclassed by the taller, more graceful boy and fell behind quickly.

Moments later, all four girls were in the pool, too. Only one actually did any swimming. The other three bobbed and talked. I saw Mrs. Duval and Alberto arrive at the pool. Alberto carried what looked like a case of Cokes and began putting the bottles into a refrigerator in the roof-covered patio area. Mrs. Duval placed a tray of something on one of the poolside tables. No one seemed to pay any attention to them, but as soon as they left, the boys were out and at whatever was on the food tray.

Soon I heard some music start, and then the girls were out of the pool and dancing. One of the shorter boys went over to his bag and produced what looked like a bottle of some kind of whiskey. The tallest boy went to the refrigerator and filled glasses with Coke. He brought them to a table, and the shorter boy began adding from his bottle, and soon all seven of them were drinking, dancing, and occasionally embracing and kissing. No one seemed to be especially with anyone else. All of the girls kissed all of the boys.

I sat there mesmerized by the activity below me and wondered if anyone else in the house was watching from a window. None of the teenagers below seemed to worry or care. They began pushing one another into the pool, and then, to my shock, the boys, while they were in the pool, took off their bathing suits, swung them over their heads, and began swimming toward the girls, who screamed and rushed to the side of the pool. This went on until all of the girls were out and laughing.

The boys actually got out naked and put their bathing suits on in front of the girls, who, instead of being embarrassed, laughed. They all drank more, nibbled on the food, danced, and continued to tease and flirt. Finally, something drew their attention off to their right, and they quieted down. The boys went into the cabanas to change, and the girls followed. No one attempted to clean up anything. Tables were left with empty glasses and traces of what looked like half-eaten burgers, potato chips, and hot dogs. I leaned forward and struggled to see them walking off, but they were all soon out of sight.

I hadn't been in junior high school long enough and, of course, had never been in high school, but I had read about and seen enough of teenage romance to be curious about a group of girls and boys who didn't seem to favor anyone. None of them seemed to be boyfriend-and-girlfriend. Was this what was meant by an orgy? Nothing graphically sexual had occurred aside from the boys' nudity, but there was something different and strange about them. I couldn't help but be curious. Had the teenage world changed in ways I hadn't realized while Mama and I were living in the streets?

I heard a knock on the door and turned to see another maid, an African American woman quite a bit younger than Mrs. Caro or Mrs. Duval.

"You're Sasha, right?" she asked.

"Yes."

"I'm Rosie. Mrs. Duval sent me up to see if you needed any help going to the bathroom. I'm leaving for the day, so I gotta help you now."

"I don't need any help," I said. "I can do everything for myself."

"Okay." She started to turn and stopped. "Mind if I ask what happened to you? You got a disease or something?"

"I was hit by a car," I said.

"Oh, too bad," she said, and hurried off before I could add anything.

I was surprised she didn't know about me. If anyone else but the Marches knew what was going on, I thought, he or she certainly didn't gossip. Now that Rosie had mentioned the bathroom, I realized I did have to go. Because of the cast, it was hard to shift from my wheelchair to the toilet. I nearly fell twice but somehow managed to get it done and get back into the chair. At least I wouldn't have to depend on anyone for that, I thought happily, and went to watch television.

I tried to distract myself with a movie, but I kept my eyes and ears tuned to the door, anticipating Mrs. March and either her husband or Kiera. Hours later, Mrs. March did return, but she was alone. She burst in with an armful of packages.

"How are you doing, Sasha?" she asked, but before I could answer, she added, "I just had to buy these things for you."

She put everything on the table.

"Come, look. I was told that this is the newest iPod. Of

course, I didn't know what songs you'd like on it, but I had them download everything that's popular now."

"But you already bought me one of these when I was in the hospital."

"Yes, but the salesman told me this one is the latest version, and you can do so many more things with it. I'll leave it up to you to read about it. You teenagers are so much more adept at figuring out all this technology. Donald says we were brought up with pages to read, and you guys are being brought up with megabytes or some such thing. Anyway, that's that."

She handed it to me. One of those would have probably paid for food for Mama and me for a month or so, I thought.

Mrs. March held up the first wrapped box. "I stopped at what used to be my favorite clothing store for Alena's things, and they just got in these darling outfits for the fall and winter."

She began to unwrap the box, and before I could really see what was in it, she had unwrapped the next and the next, pulling everything out quickly. There were skirt-and-blouse outfits with matching caps, jeans with sequins, and two leather jackets, one light pink and the other light green. They felt butter-soft.

"What do you think?" she asked when she was finished unwrapping and showing it all.

"It's all beautiful," I said. I wanted to sound grateful, but she was flooding me with so much I didn't have a chance to appreciate any of it.

"I thought so, too. Now, more news. I had the guidance

counselor at the school Kiera attends contact the tutor he had recommended for us. Her name is Mrs. Kepler. She retired two years ago but is bored to death. Her husband does nothing but play golf. She'll be perfect, I'm sure. I've arranged for her to stop in tomorrow to meet you. Is that all right? We want you to be up to speed when the new school year begins."

"Where do I go to school?"

"You'll go to the private school Kiera attends, of course. It's just outside Pacific Palisades. Grover will take you and pick you up every day when that starts. I'm going to speak with Dr. Milan in a little while," she continued, barely taking a breath. "Do you have any complaints, pain, headaches, anything I need to report to him?"

"No."

"That's wonderful. It's so important not to linger in the hospital around all those other sick and injured people. It keeps it on your mind. There's plenty to distract you from that here."

She stood smiling down at me so long it made me feel a little uncomfortable. I deliberately turned away to look at the new iPod.

"Well," she said, "let's get your new clothes put away."

She gathered it all in her arms. I wheeled behind her to the walk-in closet. I had not yet looked into it, but now, when I did, I laughed to myself. I had imagined the hotel room that Mama and I had lived in not being much larger than a walk-in closet in this house. I was greatly underestimating. The closet was at least twice as large as that hotel room. It had a mirror and a vanity table in it and rows of clothing that probably rivaled the stock in most stores. How could any girl have been able to wear so much?

She paused as she hung up my new skirts and blouses and suddenly grew teary-eyed. She lifted one skirt, and I saw that it was hanging there with its label still attached. For a moment, it was as if she had forgotten I was there. Then she turned to me, still holding the skirt. After a deep breath, she nodded and said, "I'm being stupid again, I know."

"What do you mean?"

"When Alena was very sick, I went on a buying spree as I just did for you. Most of this," she said, pointing down the row of clothes, "she never had the chance to wear. I guess buying her new clothes, new shoes, anything, was my way of trying to deny what was happening to her. Here I am doing the same thing to you. I'm sorry. There is so much here that's still brand-new that will fit you. But I can't help it when I see something darling. When Alena was gone and I'd go into stores and see things she could wear and that would make her happy, I'd be tempted to buy them. In fact, I did buy some of this after she was gone. I know that sounds crazy to you, but . . . it helped me get by."

"I understand," I said. I really thought I did.

She looked at me and smiled. "I know you do. You're an exceptional young girl and will be an exceptional woman someday. I am determined to make you happy, healthy, and safe again," she said with such firm determination in her eyes that I couldn't help but believe her.

She hung up the rest, and we left the closet.

"Will I meet your husband tonight?" I asked.

"No. He's at a conference in Texas, something about

new home-building materials. I'm not sure when he returns. I don't pay much attention to his work. It will just be you and me for dinner."

"But what about . . ."

"Kiera is at a friend's tonight," she said, almost before the words were out of my mouth. "I wasn't going to let her go, but I thought it would be nicer if you and I had your first night here alone. Okay?"

I nodded. Did she know that Kiera and her friends had spent the afternoon at the pool? Should I mention it? I felt funny about spying on them. What if she asked me what I had seen?

"Did you take a nap, at least?"

"I dozed off for a while. I don't feel tired."

"That's amazing. I know the excitement of going somewhere new can wear you out, but I forget how much energy you young girls have. I'll come up later and help you decide what you'd like to wear to dinner." She moved toward the door.

Why was it important what I would wear to dinner if it was going to be just the two of us?

"Enjoy your new iPod," she said, and left.

I simply sat there staring after her. My head was spinning. I looked at the closet, the sitting room, the magnificent bed, the television on the wall, everything I could have ever dreamed of having up until now was there. We hadn't had very much before my father deserted us, but it still had been sad to leave it. How much more difficult had it been for a little girl to lie here and know she was dying and would leave everything, especially parents who adored her?

I embraced myself as if I could feel the cold sorrow closing in around me, even in the wonderful suite full of color and warm things. Then I looked at the bed. Could I sleep in that bed, and when I did, would I hear Alena March's voice, maybe her sobs and cries? Would I dream her dreams?

I could feel what Jordan March was hoping for when she brought me there, and it intrigued me and yet at the same time made me feel sick and afraid. She wanted to look at me, blink her eyes, and see her daughter returned.

I wasn't all that different from her.

I'd want to look at her, blink my eyes, and see my mother returned.

Either we'd both be happy or, in the end, both of us would end up blind.

8

Dinner

I fell asleep again in my chair. I had wheeled myself to the window in the sitting room and sat gazing at the pool, the tennis courts, and the beautiful grounds. I opened the window slightly and could hear the drone of the lawn mowers. Because the house was so high up on the hill, I could see the ocean just behind the tops of the trees. At this time of the day, it looked like blue ice but gradually reddened with the sinking sun.

When I was eight, my father brought home a doll he had found on a job site. It was in a basement next to a washing machine he was repairing, and he just put it into his tool kit. Although it was old, faded, and dusty, I cherished it, because it was one of the only times I could remember that he thought of me while he was working and brought me something. Mama bawled him out for giving me something so dirty-looking and seized it to put into our washing machine. I never saw another doll like it.

The doll was a sailor girl. Daddy didn't know what it

really was, but Mama did. She admitted it was something of a collector's item, because it was a doll depicting a member of the WAVES. She said she had a great-aunt on her father's side who had been a member of the Women Appointed for Voluntary Emergency Service, which was a U.S. Navy organization during World War II.

Once it was washed, the blue uniform had faded even more, but I thought it was the most beautiful doll in the world, and when I understood more about the WAVES, I began to fantasize about myself on boats and ships. Even during the struggle, when Mama and I were on the beach selling her calligraphy and my lanyards, I would look out at the sailboats and the bigger ships, and I would recall my fantasies.

Sailing off toward the horizon always seemed to be an escape from sadness and hardship. Nothing was as promising as the distant horizon. I envisioned myself standing at the bow and looking ahead toward a new life full of brightness and happiness. Mama was always on the boat with me, standing beside me or right behind me, with just as big a smile on her face, just as much hope in her eyes. We would never look back at the dark clouds.

I thought about my doll now as I looked out at the Pacific Ocean. I had played with it so much and kept it with me so much that the uniform thinned and the doll began to come apart. Mama tried sewing it a few times, but the threads would break. When I was older, I put it aside. Somewhere along the way, with our packing quickly, dragging our belongings along, it got lost. I told myself the doll had gone back to sea, back to that boat, to seek a better place than the places I could take her.

Now, I imagined her out there, sailing toward the horizon. I could vaguely make out a boat and watched it until I could see it no longer. *At least she's safe,* I thought. I smiled to myself and relived some of my childhood moments talking to my doll.

Mrs. March's return to help me decide what to wear for dinner broke the spell and ripped me out of the happier moments in my past and pulled me back to cold reality. It was as though I had lost my doll again.

"Let's look for something comfortable for you," she began, and headed back to that enormous closet. I wheeled myself to the doorway and watched her rake through the garments, pausing at some, shaking her head at others. What was she looking for? How could this be so important? I almost came right out and asked, but she plucked a blouse and a skirt off the rack as if she had found something she had tried and failed to locate many times. I saw the look of delight spread over her face.

"Yes," she said, talking more to herself than to me, "this was it."

When she turned and held it up to show me, I nearly fell out of my wheelchair. It was a sailor girl's outfit. I felt a hot flow move up from my chest and into my neck and face. The words crackled when I spoke. "Why that?"

"Alena was so excited when Donald bought our boat that I went right out and bought this outfit for her. When she tried it on, she didn't want to take it off. Donald and Kiera were away that evening, so it was just Alena and me for dinner. Even though we were alone, it was a very special night. I remember how talkative she was, how happy, and this was shortly after she had been diagnosed. Just like you, she refused to be depressed."

Just like me? What had I done to lead her to believe I wasn't depressed and unhappy? Did she think that just because I was overwhelmed with the house and the gifts, all of my sadness was dead and buried? Could she possibly believe that I had already forgotten what had happened to my mother?

I think she saw the look on my face and understood. Her smile flew off, and she grew serious as she approached me with the outfit.

"Oh, I know how unhappy and terrible you must feel," she began. "I don't want you to think for one moment that I don't know or don't care. I want you to remember and love your mother forever. I promised I would have whatever you wanted written on her tombstone, remember? As soon as you think of it, you tell me, and we'll have it done, and then you and I will go there to see it. But in the meantime, you've got to survive and grow and be healthy again. Don't blame me for trying to help you do that. I know you must hate me always talking about my Alena, but . . ."

"No, I don't hate you for that," I said quickly. I glanced at the framed photograph of her. "She was a very pretty girl, and I'm sure she was very nice."

"Thank you, dear. If you don't want to wear this," she added, holding up the skirt and blouse, "you don't have to. You can pick out something else."

"No, it's all right," I said. I almost told her about my doll but somehow felt that there were things so private that they still belonged only with Mama and me. Despite what Jackie called her charity, Mrs. March had not earned that trust. She was not my mother; she was not even a friend yet. She was simply someone who felt sorry for me and felt guilty because of what her daughter had done. It was I who was being the charitable one. I was letting her live with the guilt. That's what Jackie had told me, and it made sense to me now more than ever.

I reached for the outfit.

"Can I help you get dressed?" she asked.

I nodded, and she began by helping me take off the blouse I wore. She moaned at the sight of the fading black-and-blue marks and mumbled, "Poor child. What a horror you've gone through." She looked as if she was going to burst into tears, so I made sure to tell her that none of it hurt as much as it had.

After I was dressed in the sailor outfit, she wheeled me in front of the vanity table. I was amazed at how well it fit.

"Let's do something with your hair," she said, and began brushing it. "You do have beautiful hair, and thick, too. I bet your mother's hair was beautiful."

"Yes. She used to wear it down to her wing bones."

"I wish I could have long hair, but Donald says it makes me look older, and if there is one thing Donald hates, it's my looking older."

"What about him?"

"Men can always look older and call it distinguished, didn't you know?" she asked, smiling.

She opened a drawer in the vanity table and chose some hair clips. When I saw how she had shaped my hair,

I looked at the framed photo of Alena and realized it was very similar.

"There now," she said, stepping back. "Don't you look very pretty?"

"I hope someday I'll be half as pretty as my mother was," I said.

She kept her smile, but it lost its excitement and warmth. She nodded and turned me away from the vanity table. "I do hope you like Irish stew. Mrs. Caro makes the best."

"I don't remember ever having it," I said as she pushed me to the doorway.

"Well, you eat just what you want. She's made a special dessert for us, a surprise, too. Here we go," she said, and turned me down the corridor toward the elevator.

I had seen only a small part of the house when I arrived. When the elevator door opened, she pushed me to the left and around a corner. The hallway seemed endless, but along the way, she pointed out the game room, the formal dining room, the den and library, the entertainment center, and then a hallway that branched off to the right. She said that was where the indoor pool was located.

Right off the kitchen was what she called their informal dining room. No room in this house was small to me, but she called it one of their smaller rooms. It had a beautiful dark hardwood table with twelve cushioned hardwood chairs. The walls were paneled in a lighter wood, and a large window looked toward the rear of the property.

"Is that a lake?" I asked, looking out.

"Donald's lake, yes. It's man-made. He says he's going to

stock it with fish. What fun is that, right? It would be like shooting fish in a barrel, but once Donald sees something someone else has, he wants it, too. There are two rowboats. That's fun, at least."

She pulled a chair away next to the chair at the end of the table and fit me into that place. Two dinner settings, glasses, and silverware were already there. Almost as soon as Mrs. March took her seat, Mrs. Duval came through the door that led from the kitchen. She carried a bowl of rolls and a jug of water.

"Good evening, Mrs. Duval," Mrs. March said, sounding very formal all of a sudden.

"Good evening, Mrs. March."

"Doesn't our little girl look pretty tonight?"

Mrs. Duval paused after she poured Mrs. March's glass of water and looked at me as if I had just arrived. I caught the slight tic in her eyes, the little moment of surprise. She glanced at Mrs. March and then forced a smile and said, "*Sí, muy bonita.*"

Mrs. March looked satisfied. She leaned toward me as Mrs. Duval returned to the kitchen. "That means 'very pretty' in Spanish," she whispered. "Do you know any Spanish?"

"Not really," I said. "I mean, I know some words."

"Alena spoke fluent Spanish, because Mrs. Duval had been her nanny since birth. I'm sure you'll learn quite a bit just being around her. It's the best way to learn a language, better than in a classroom. That's what Donald says."

"I know some Chinese words because of my mother," I told her.

She didn't look that excited about it. "That's nice. Educating yourself as much as possible is important. I bet you are a good reader, too, right?"

Mrs. Duval brought in our salads and set them down without looking at me or speaking.

"I haven't read that much for a while," I said

"Of course. I understand. But you're going to see that Alena had a wonderful library in her sitting room. Unless you've already explored those shelves."

"No, I haven't yet."

"Getting Kiera to read anything is like trying to feed her cod-liver oil. She has barely passing grades. Donald's at his wit's end with that, and it isn't because we haven't paid for tutors. She never liked any, but I'm sure you're going to like Mrs. Kepler. Doesn't this salad look good? You like figs in your salad? We all like that. Alena loved it."

"I never had it before," I said, but I nodded. It did taste good.

That pleased her, and she became even more talkative, telling me about her own youth, her high school years, and her years at a private college she called "more of a charm school than a real educational institution. But I wasn't meant to have any sort of career," she added. "I was born to be who I am." She laughed. "That's what Donald says."

Everything was what Donald said, I thought. I couldn't help but wonder what he was really like and what he would think of me.

"Is he coming home tomorrow?" I asked.

"No. He'll be away the rest of the week, but that's all

right. We'll have plenty of company, with your tutor coming tomorrow, your doctor checkup, lots to do. No worries," she said. I was waiting for her to add, "as Donald would say," but she didn't.

The Irish stew was delicious. I had eaten so much for lunch that I couldn't eat as much of it as I would have liked, especially with Mrs. March continually warning me to leave room for our special dessert. After the dishes were cleared off the table, I sat in anticipation. Moments later, Mrs. Duval returned, carrying a tray with something on fire. Mrs. Caro was right behind her, smiling. It remained in a flame until Mrs. Duval lowered it to the table.

"It looks beautiful," Mrs. March said.

"What is it?" I asked.

"Banana flambé," she said.

Mrs. Duval served us each a dish, and Mrs. Caro added scoops of vanilla ice cream. I couldn't remember anything so delicious.

"Wait until Kiera finds out we had this. She'll be sorry she wasn't here," Mrs. March said, and then clapped her mouth shut and lowered her eyes.

"It's wonderful," I said. It brightened her face.

"I'm so glad you enjoyed your first dinner here, dear. I hope there will be many, many more, and all happy and delicious."

After dinner, she gave me a more detailed tour of the rooms we had passed on our way to dinner. There was so much to see. I simply couldn't take it all in, and I was very tired by then. This did seem to be one of those days that Mama called longer than twenty-four hours. Mrs. March realized I was getting very tired and brought me quickly to the elevator. In fact, she fell into a kind of frenzy as she rushed to get me up and into bed.

"I know I shouldn't get you this tired," she said as we went up in the elevator. "I just forget. I'm sorry."

"It's all right. I'm fine," I told her, but she had the look on her face that people have when they realize they've done something terrible.

She hurried me down the corridor to my bedroom. "I'll help you get ready for bed," she said. "I know you're exhausted."

"It's all right," I insisted, but she was at me, getting me out of the sailor outfit. Then, after I had on the nightgown she had laid out earlier, she pushed me to the bathroom.

"There's a brand-new electric toothbrush here for you, and different kinds of toothpaste. Alena hated the peppermint-flavored ones. She said they burned her tongue. This one is sort of plain. She liked it the best," she told me. "You should have had a sponge bath. I'll send Mrs. Duval in first thing to help you have one in the morning."

"I can bathe myself," I said sharply.

"It's no disgrace to have help when you need it."

"I don't need it," I insisted.

"Okay. She'll be available if you do. Remember, if you need anything, you simply pick up the phone, okay?"

"Yes."

She stood watching me brush my teeth for a few moments. "Let me help you get into bed, at least," she said when I finished.

I didn't say no. I thought I might need her to do that.

Despite someone's having come in to turn down the sheets while we were at dinner, the bed was a little high, and I was afraid of putting any pressure on my right leg. Mrs. March put her arms around me and guided me into the bed. Then she fixed the blanket and the pillow.

"Would you mind very much if I gave you a kiss good night?" she asked.

"I'd rather you not," I said, even more sharply than I intended.

Her face seemed to melt into a look of deep sadness. She forced a smile and wished me a good night's sleep.

How mean, I thought I heard my mother say.

"Mrs. March," I called. She turned abruptly at the door. "I'm sorry. You can kiss me good night."

She smiled and returned to kiss me on the cheek. "You're a brave little girl," she said. "Braver than I would be at your age. You must have grown very strong during your desperate time."

This is still my desperate time, I thought, but said nothing.

She turned and walked out slowly, shutting off the light and closing the door softly. There were so many lights on outside that the glow kept the room from being totally dark. I was glad of that, not that I was afraid of darkness. Mama and I had slept in too many dark and dingy places over the past year for me to have that sort of fear. Most of the time, the darkness had been more like a friend, keeping us from being seen by people who might prey upon us and take what little we had. Darkness became our cocoon.

But it wasn't like that now. There were probably not many safer places in the world to be than in this house, surrounded by its walls, lit brightly and protected by security cameras. Darkness made little difference. No, what frightened me the most was the utter loneliness I sensed, not only in Mrs. March's face and voice but also in the faces of her employees. When they looked at her, they, who had far less and were her servants, seemed to be pitying her.

I had come there to escape from loneliness, to escape from becoming no one in some orphanage or foster home. I wanted to hold on to my name and cherish my memories of Mama, but Alena March still haunted this house, this room. The thing was, she didn't haunt it because she wanted to haunt it.

She haunted it because her mother would not let her go.

Maybe she would never let me go, either. Maybe I should be more afraid of that than of anything else.

9

Mrs. Kepler

Mrs. Duval was there first thing in the morning to wake me and ask me if I wanted her to help with my bathing. I was prepared to refuse any help, but I saw something different in her face. Yesterday she seemed not only quite indifferent to me but even a bit resentful. Perhaps she had been thinking, *Who is this poor nobody who has stolen her way into Alena's world?* Perhaps she thought I wanted to take Alena's place and was taking advantage of Mrs. March. Maybe, like that maid Rosie, she didn't know the whole story. Maybe now she had learned about it all. There was warmth in her eyes, a welcome in her smile.

"Yes," I said. "Thank you."

Dr. Milan had made sure that I left the hospital with plastic bags to put over the cast. Mrs. Duval took one out of the case and fastened it so that the cast would not get wet. She then helped me into the bathroom, and together we managed to get the rest of me washed and dried. She brought me one of my new outfits to wear and then called down and had Rosie bring up my breakfast, which she set out on the table in the sitting area. Even with Jackie in the hospital, I hadn't gotten that sort of treatment.

While I was having breakfast, Mrs. March came in to tell me that my tutor, Mrs. Kepler, would be arriving in about an hour.

"After I introduce her to you, I'll leave and let you two work, unless you want me to stay."

"I'll be all right, I think," I told her.

I couldn't imagine why she would want to stay, unless she wanted to see how smart or how stupid I was. If I didn't do well, perhaps she would change her mind and send me away. I hadn't been much of a student during the last year when I was in school. Mama took some interest in my work, but she was always overwhelmed with something herself, even when Daddy was still with us, or maybe because he was. The fighting took its toll on her, and I recalled many mornings when she was too tired or depressed to get out of bed before I left for school. Often, I made my own lunch to take. I never blamed her. I always blamed Daddy.

Despite my attempt to be indifferent about my tutoring, I couldn't help but be nervous. Even when we were living in the streets, I didn't like being thought of as stupid. No matter what the circumstances, most people who looked at the homeless thought their failures were their own fault. How could anyone not manage a roof over her head for herself and her child? How could she not find enough food and clothing?

Mrs. March expressed her pity and her sympathy for Mama and me, but what did she really think about Mama?

Certainly, if her daughter had not been involved, she wouldn't have been there at the hospital to help me and wouldn't have seen to Mama's funeral arrangements. Perhaps she sent checks to charities or attended affairs as she told me, but did she really see the people the money was meant to help? More important for me right then was the question *Does she really see me?*

When Mrs. Kepler first appeared, I thought she was going to be as stern and as unsympathetic as the people who had walked past Mama and me on the street and either shook their heads in disgust or looked away quickly. Mrs. March had told her I had been out of school for some time, but she didn't say that her daughter had caused the accident. I could tell when we spoke afterward and I heard the way Mrs. Kepler made Mrs. March sound charitable.

"This is Sasha," Mrs. March said. "We want to get her up to speed so she can enter school on par with the other students who will be in her class. Sasha, Mrs. Kepler."

"Hello," I said.

Mrs. Kepler nodded, fixing her hazel eyes on me as intently as a doctor. She was a full-figured woman with dark-brown hair that showed gray roots. Nevertheless, she looked as if she had just come from a beauty salon. Her hair was nicely styled about her ears, with trimmed bangs. She stood about two inches shorter than Mrs. March but held herself stiffly erect. The weakness in her face was her far too thin lips, which looked in danger of disappearing entirely if she stretched them.

"What do you think of our little sitting area, Mrs. Kepler? It's quiet up here."

She studied the room for a moment as if it really mattered. It occurred to me that in her mind, she was being tested as much as I was and knew it. She was trying too hard to be a perfect schoolteacher.

"Yes, this will be fine," she said.

"I could have a blackboard brought up."

"No, that's not going to be necessary. There's just the two of us."

"I did try to make sure there were enough pens and pencils, paper, and such. Of course, the computer is there if you need it."

"I don't teach on a computer. Everything I need for now is right here," she said, patting her black leather briefcase. She walked into the sitting area to place it on the table. Then she looked around again and nodded. "Would it be all right if I opened these drapes to get more light?"

"Oh, of course. Let me help you," Mrs. March said, rushing to open the drapes.

"Why don't you come to the table, Sasha?" Mrs. Kepler said. She turned to Mrs. March. "I'll test her to see what levels she's at in math, science, reading, and history, and from there we'll know just how much we have to do to bring her up to speed."

"Yes, good idea. Would you like tea, coffee, a soft drink?"

"Not right now, thank you."

"Okay. Well, then, I'll have Mrs. Duval check back in an hour or so?"

"That would be fine," Mrs. Kepler said.

I noticed that after she said something, she pressed her

lower lip tightly against her upper one, crinkling her chin. It was a small gesture, but one I thought she had used on her students in her classroom, because it made whatever she said sound like words chipped in cement. Arguing or challenging her was out of the question.

"All right. Good luck, Sasha," Mrs. March said, and left.

Mrs. Kepler opened her briefcase and began to take out some papers. "Come closer," she told me, and I wheeled myself right up to the table. "Are you comfortable?"

"Yes."

"All right. You were in what grade before you left school?"

"Seventh."

"So you've basically missed the entire eighth-grade year?"

"I guess so."

"Either you did or you didn't. Did you attend any school after you left the seventh grade?"

"No."

"Then you missed a whole year, which would have been your eighth-grade year. I like to start with reading skills," she said. "Everything we do requires a good foundation in reading."

"I still read a lot even though I wasn't in school."

She looked at me long enough for me to feel she was finally seeing me. "What did you read?"

"Books other people on the street gave me from time to time. Sometimes we went into the library to get out of the rain, and I read there."

"What people gave you books?"

"Street people," I said, and she widened her eyes.

"I can just imagine what sort of things to read that was," she said.

"No, you can't," I replied sharply. She raised her eyebrows. "Unless you've been there," I added. "Not everyone was a bum. There were college graduates and people who had good jobs once. Someone gave me a copy of *Huckleberry Finn,* and someone else gave me a copy of *A Tale of Two Cities.*"

"Really?"

"Yes, really. I have no reason to lie about it. Not all street people are thieves and liars. Many try to keep themselves clean and have clean clothes, too."

I felt the heat in my face. I had never spoken to any of my teachers like that, but in my mind, any criticism of the street people was criticism of Mama, and I wouldn't permit it.

For a moment, I thought she was going to shove her paperwork back into her briefcase, shut it, and walk out, but she surprised me by finally smiling. "Well, you're not easily intimidated. Do you know what *intimidated* means?"

"Yes. Pushed around, made to give up or give in to someone or something," I recited.

"Okay, then. Maybe I'll be happily surprised. Let's get started."

She began explaining the tests she wanted me to take. We worked for hours. When Mrs. Duval stopped by to see if she wanted anything to drink, she had barely opened her mouth before Mrs. Kepler snapped, "Nothing, not now." She wouldn't tolerate the slightest interruption. I thought she would even make me work through lunch, but she agreed to stop so we could eat.

Mrs. Duval came up with the cart. Mrs. Caro had prepared chicken salad for us. I was afraid there would be a duplication of yesterday's mammoth lunch, but apparently the order had been put in earlier. We cleared the table, and Mrs. Duval served from the cart. It was when we began to eat our lunch that Mrs. Kepler stopped being the schoolteacher and spoke with warmth and concern. She wanted to know where I had lived and gone to school. I didn't know how much Mrs. March had told her about me and why I was there, but from the questions she asked and the way she spoke about Mrs. March, I was convinced that nothing had been said about Kiera.

"I'm sure this is all overwhelming for you," she said. Then she smiled and added, "It certainly is for me. I heard about this house, but until now, I had never set foot in it. I bet you feel a bit like Cinderella."

"Except there's no prince," I told her, and she laughed.

"No, I imagine not. There's not even a pumpkin."

Now we both laughed, and I finally relaxed. I hadn't thought I would, but I liked her. Even after lunch, she was different, warmer and more complimentary.

Mrs. March tiptoed into the room at about three o'clock. We were just finishing, and Mrs. Kepler was putting papers back into her briefcase.

"How is it going?" Mrs. March asked. Mrs. Kepler sat back and was silent for a long moment. I could see that Mrs. March was expecting bad news.

"I'm afraid I'm not going to earn very much money here, Mrs. March."

"Oh. Why not?"

"She's not as far behind as one would expect. Her reading skills are better than those of most of the students going into the ninth grade, I'm sure. She certainly has a very good vocabulary, and she picked up very quickly on the math, too. There are some weak areas with history and science, but most of that she's going to strengthen with her own reading."

"That's wonderful," Mrs. March said.

Mrs. Kepler rose. "I'll prepare the work assignments to help her catch up quickly. I'll start her off tomorrow and then stop by every other day for a few hours at most. I hope she'll get out a bit, get some fresh air and sun."

"Oh, yes. For sure. Mrs. Caro will be taking her out after lunch in the afternoons. You certainly can work on one of our patios, if you like."

"We'd like," Mrs. Kepler said, winking at me. "I'll be by tomorrow, then, same time. I'll bring the books."

"Wonderful," Mrs. March said. "Are you happy, Sasha?"

"Yes," I said, even though I thought she meant about everything and not only Mrs. Kepler's tutoring.

"I'll see you out," she told Mrs. Kepler.

"'Bye, then," Mrs. Kepler told me, and followed Mrs. March out of the suite. I heard Mrs. March's melodic laughter echo down the hallway.

Part of me didn't want her to feel better. Part of me wished she'd be suffering as much as I was, even though it wasn't literally she who had hit Mama and me. Just as Mama had once been responsible for everything I did, Mrs. March and her husband were responsible for everything Kiera did. Maybe her husband was more responsible, if I believed what she had told me, but still, it felt strange making anyone happy in that house. In that house, the cause of Mama's death resided.

From that house, Kiera March had emerged carefree and reckless, arrogant and self-centered. She had taken her drugs and, like some asteroid, come flying out of space to smash two people who had never done her any harm. Also like that asteroid, she was indifferent and unrepentant. *Look at how she was at the pool,* I thought. *She laughed and frolicked right beneath me.*

No, I hated the sound of laughter in that house. I even hated the sound of my own laughter. Eating well, trying to improve my education, wearing beautiful clothes, enjoying everything in that magnificent suite, suddenly felt more like a terrible betrayal. I almost wished I would never get better. I had to suffer in order to honor Mama's memory.

Try as hard as she will, I thought, *Mrs. March will not take the pain away from me.* When and if she did, it would be like me burying Mama again and again. These thoughts overwhelmed me. I sat there sobbing and made no effort to stop the tears from dripping off my cheeks. It reminded me of that night when the rain came pouring down over us, pelting us so hard that it was as if the heavens were expressing their anger.

Or maybe it was meant to be a warning, to make us stay on that beach and not dare try to cross that highway, not dare try to go home.

❧10❧

Family of the Blind

Probably because Mrs. Kepler had made an issue of it, Mrs. March sent Mrs. Caro up immediately to wheel me down and onto the patio. She found me crying and rushed to me.

"What's wrong, dearie? Are you in pain?"

"No," I said, wiping my face quickly. *Not the kind of pain you mean,* I thought.

"Oh, I know," she said. "Being brought like this to a strange house ain't easy, I'm sure."

I didn't say anything, but *strange* seemed to be the perfect adjective.

"Well, let's get you out in the sunshine and fresh air. It's no good being indoors so much, anyway. People heal better and faster when they get into fresh air."

She turned my chair toward the doorway.

"I grew up in Cork, Ireland, and I can tell you it wasn't always easy getting into the fresh air. When I tell my family back home that I live in a place where the sun shines at least three hundred days a year without rain, they're amazed."

She pushed me onto the elevator.

"You always live in Southern California?" she asked.

"Yes. My mother was from Portland, though."

"Don't say? Weather there can be like weather in England, I hear. You have any of your people still there?"

Her question didn't surprise me. I was sure everyone who was working there wondered why I wasn't with family.

"I don't know," I said.

"Yes, it's a shame how fast we all lose track of each other in this world. I have a sister I haven't seen in nearly twenty years now. She married a man who lives in South Africa. You know how far away that is?"

"Yes. It's at the tip of Africa."

"I bet you've been a good student. How did your schoolin' work go today?"

"Good," I said.

"You'll be up and around in no time, I'm sure. Right now, it looks like forever to you. I can't think of a better place to recuperate from anything," she added.

I looked up at her. Was it really possible that no one in the house except the Marches knew what Kiera had done and why I was there rather than with some relatives or in an orphanage? Mrs. Caro looked sincere. I wondered if Mrs. March believed that I would never say anything, or was she so confident that even if I did, no one would risk repeating it or discussing it? From the way she described her husband and how he always excused and buried whatever wrong things Kiera did, I imagined that he had given Mrs. March strict orders to keep it all from their servants.

It didn't take me long to understand that it was a house built on secrets and whispers. There was more living in the shadows than in the light, despite the bright chandeliers and lamps. A family that lived more in the shadows was a family of the blind.

The patio Mrs. Caro wheeled me to faced the pool and the tennis courts. There were two tables with chairs, a settee with a small table, and what looked like a pile of stones in a circle with benches around it. I asked Mrs. Caro what it was, and she said it was a fire pit to keep people warm when they sat out there on cooler nights. Right then, the sun was still high in the blue, nearly cloudless sky. It was about the same time of day as when I had seen those teenagers there. Would they return? What would happen when they saw me, if they did return?

"I'll set you in this shady spot," Mrs. Caro said. "Not too warm for you?"

"No. I'm fine."

"Will you be all right here by yourself for a while? I have to check on some things in the kitchen for tonight's dinner," Mrs. Caro asked. "It could be twenty minutes."

"Yes, I'll be fine," I said.

"I'll bring some fresh lemonade when I return," she said, and left.

I sat staring out at the beautiful grounds. There was so much to see. It was still hard to believe that one family owned all of this. Just a short while ago, the only space Mama and I had had to ourselves was bordered by the cardboard walls of some box. It almost felt as though I had been taken to another planet.

The Marches' estate wasn't just big; it was busy. Judging by the short time I had been there, it seemed there was never a time of day when someone wasn't working on something. Right then, two men were repairing a pole lamp on the driveway to my right, and two others were working around the cabana. One was touching it up with some paint, and the other was adjusting a door.

Wheeling myself out a little farther, I could look to my left and see part of the long driveway that curved around the side of the grand house to where Mrs. March had said the garages were. When I heard the sound of a vehicle, I leaned as far as I could to see if it was the limousine that had brought me. If so, it was probably Mrs. March returning. Instead, I saw what I knew to be a gold-colored Rolls-Royce. I had seen a few of them in Santa Monica, and Daddy used to vow that he was going to have one. Mama always mocked that and made him angry.

"You're lucky you can afford the old truck you drive," she had told him. "If you're going to have a dream, at least have the sense to dream about something relatively possible."

As the Rolls approached, I could make out a good-looking, light-haired man driving. He didn't look my way and followed the driveway around the house. Was that Mr. March? I was sure Mrs. March had said he would be gone longer. I watched and listened but heard and saw no one. When Mrs. Caro returned with my lemonade, I asked her if Mr. March had returned.

"Yes," she said.

"Is Mrs. March here?"

"She is. I told her you had been out here about twenty minutes, and she told me to take you up in a little while so you could rest, maybe take a nap before dinner. I'll have to get started in the kitchen soon myself."

I drank the lemonade and nodded. I couldn't make myself ask about Kiera, and Mrs. Caro said nothing about her. She offered to wheel me around to see the garden before we went up to my suite. Gardening had been and still was a passion for her. She bragged about the way flowers grew in Ireland, and she said, "My duties here make it difficult to get my hands into Mother Earth." The garden was so big. It looked like something in a park. Mrs. Caro knew the names of every flower, when they bloomed, when they should be planted, even how they should be nurtured.

"Here I am going off at the mouth when I have to get you upstairs," she said, realizing the time. She pushed me back into the house.

When we entered, I anticipated either seeing or hearing Mr. March, but there was no one around. We went directly to the elevator. I expected that I might meet him when we reached the bedroom floor, but again, the hallway was quiet and empty. I was a little tired and let Mrs. Caro help me into bed. She wasn't gone two minutes before I did fall asleep. I didn't wake up again until I heard the cart in the hallway. When Mrs. Duval entered, pushing it with my dinner tray, I sat up quickly. Why wasn't I going down to the dining room?

"Let me help you get up and to the table," she said.

"How come I'm not going downstairs for dinner?"

"Dinner's being served later," she said. "The Marches don't normally have dinner until eight-thirty, and Mrs. March said that would be too late for you." She saw the look on my face and added, "That's what she told me." She said it the way someone who didn't believe it might say it.

I got into my wheelchair, and she pushed me to the table, where she had set out the dishes.

"This is Mrs. Caro's special chicken dish, and she prepared a pudding for you, too. Just leave everything when you're done. Rosie will come to clean up," she said. "I've got to get down to prepare for the Marches' dinner."

Mrs. Caro's food was delicious, but I didn't have as big an appetite as I had expected. I listened for sounds of footsteps in the hallway but heard none. I had no idea where the Marches' bedrooms were but imagined they couldn't be too far away. This had been Alena's bedroom. I was sure Mrs. March would have wanted to be close. Finally, I did hear a door open and close and some footsteps, but they weren't heading in my direction. Moments later, there were more footsteps, but again, they didn't bring anyone my way.

After I finished eating what I could, I watched television but kept listening for someone coming. Finally, someone did, but it was only Rosie to clear away my dinner dishes.

"You left a lot," she remarked. "Mrs. Caro will be upset." To my surprise, she began to eat some of my leftovers. "This is much better than what we get," she told me. "Didn't you like this pudding?"

"I ate what I could."

"Can't let it go to waste," she told me, and finished it.

"There," she said. "Now Mrs. Caro won't be upset. Just don't tell anyone I finished your dinner."

She started to push the cart out and stopped.

"So, how did you get hit by a car?" she asked. "What, were you running where you shouldn't?"

"No. I didn't do anything wrong, and neither did my mother."

"Your mother? What happened to her?"

"She was killed," I said.

"Where's your daddy?"

"I don't know. He left us years ago."

She opened her mouth slowly and raised her head. "Oh. Well, now it makes sense," she said.

"What makes sense?"

"Mrs. March has been sponsoring little girl orphans, sending tons of money to these worldwide charities ever since her daughter died. She sits in her office and studies the pictures of those poor kids and compares them with the picture of her dead daughter. I've seen her doing it. She only sends money to those who look a little like her. You don't, but you're about her daughter's age and size, I guess."

She paused and looked at the doorway before turning back to me.

"Don't let her talk you into dyeing your hair."

"Dye my hair? Why would I do that?"

She shook her head. I watched her leave and then turned back to the television, but it was as if I could hear nothing, as if Rosie's words had put me into a daze. Hours passed. I prepared for bed and was just wheeling myself up to it when Mrs. March appeared.

"Oh, you're not asleep yet. Good. I'm so sorry I didn't get up here earlier, but Donald came home unexpectedly, and I had to spend all my time with him. He's always got a lot to tell me and new things for me to do."

I looked past her through the doorway but heard no one else. She saw where I was looking.

"Oh, Donald had some work to do in his office. He'll stop by some other time. Let me help you get into bed," she said, and moved quickly to my side. "Did you enjoy your dinner? Mrs. Caro said you ate almost everything."

"Yes."

"Good. Dr. Milan will be stopping by in the morning to check on you, so if there's anything to complain about, you make sure to tell him, okay?"

"Okay," I said.

She tucked me in, stood back, and smiled down at me. "Girls look so much smaller than they are when they're tucked into bed. No matter how old they are, they look like they could use a bedtime story. I used to read to Alena quite a bit. Would you like that?"

"Thank you, but I'm tired enough to fall asleep," I told her.

It didn't make her happy, but she kept her smile and then leaned down to kiss my cheek. "Sweet dreams," she said, then turned off the lights and closed my door as she left.

My second night there didn't feel any less strange than my first. I lay there with my eyes wide open and listened. There was a stronger breeze that night. I could hear it searching for nooks and crannies in the house, places, as

Mama might have said, to scratch its back. The darkness seemed quite different from the darkness I had known when we lived in our apartment, stayed at the hotel, and then slept at the beach. There were no street sounds or sounds of the ocean. Oddly enough, I missed all that. Street sounds gave me the comfort of knowing we were not alone, completely lost and forgotten, and the ocean was reassuring.

The silence enhanced my sense of loneliness. There was not only too much emptiness in this family; there was too much emptiness in this big house, too many places unused, untouched, unnecessary. Cemeteries weren't only for dead people; there were cemeteries for the living, as well, and despite all that was there, I felt encased in a tomb. I wasn't shut in because of any lock. I was shut in because there was simply nowhere else to go.

What good would Lazarus's resurrection have been if he had had no family to embrace him?

Thinking of Lazarus reminded me of Mama quoting from the Bible, reminding me that her father was a Bible thumper, but I was tired of crying for myself and for Mama. Sleep was the only balm to soothe the pain in my heart. I closed my eyes and waited as eagerly as someone waiting for a train that would take her home. It came mercifully quickly, and I was deep in it when the sound of my door opening and footsteps woke me abruptly. The lamp by my bed was snapped on. I wiped my sleepy eyes and blinked to focus on the beautiful tall girl who stared down at me.

"What are you, Chinese, Japanese?" she asked. When I didn't respond quickly enough, she added, "Don't you speak English?"

"I speak English. I'm part Chinese, yes," I said.

"What part?" She laughed. "I can't believe this," she said, looking around. "She put you in my sister's room. If she was going to do this, she should have at least put you in one of the guest bedrooms. There are enough of them, for crissakes." She stared at me a moment and then reached down to feel the sleeve of my nightgown. "What, are you wearing one of my sister's nightgowns, too? Jesus."

I pulled out of her grasp. "I didn't ask to be put in here and be given your sister's clothing."

"I bet you didn't. I bet you didn't ask for anything." She paused and shrugged. "Actually, I'm not saying you did. I'm sure it's all been my mother's idea. This is all just one of my mother's new ways to punish me. She thinks this really bothers me, her taking you into the house, giving you Alena's things, and letting you sleep in her bed. Who cares? Half the time, I don't know who the hell is in this house, anyway."

She paused again and stared at me. I stared back at her. I was disappointed. When I first had heard Mrs. March say her daughter had caused the accident because she was on Ecstasy and was a selfish girl who had been in trouble often, I had expected the face and body of some spoiled rich girl, overweight and even ugly, with distorted features.

Instead, this girl was the one I had picked out yesterday, the one with the model's figure and, now that I saw her close up, a model's attractive facial features, too. She had soft, not cold, azure eyes, beautifully shaped full lips, and high cheekbones. When Mama and I would watch television together, she would always remark about the good-looking actors and actresses and say it was much more difficult for them to portray bad guys.

"We want our bad guys to look bad, have scars or ugly faces. It's not the way it really is, Sasha, not out there," she would say, and she would nod at the window.

Out there was always a desert, a jungle, a rocky cliff to climb. We were always safer inside, even inside a dingy hotel room.

Looking up at Kiera March, I especially didn't feel a bit safer in that castle of a house with its walls and security. She was beautiful, but she was bad.

She smirked and shook her head. "I bet you're really enjoying yourself immersed in all this," she said, lifting her hands. "This suite's actually a little bigger than mine. Where were you sleeping before the accident, in a carton?"

"Yes," I said. "We were. On the beach."

She dissolved her smirk, widened her eyes, and lost her arrogance for a moment. But it soon came rushing back into her face. "Well, I don't care. It was your and your mother's fault. No one crosses that highway there. That's why there's no crosswalk."

"The light was green for us," I said.

"So what? It was still stupid. It was raining too hard to see anything. Anyone would have hit you two. I was just the unfortunate one to be there at the wrong time."

"Weren't you on some drugs?"

"Who says? My mother? No one proved that." She smiled. "My attorney is confident. He'll make things right."

"He can't make things right."

"Oh, yeah, why not, smart-ass?"

"He can't bring back my mother," I said.

Her lips trembled. "You know what? Go to hell." She turned and marched out of the bedroom, slamming the door behind her.

"I'm already there!" I shouted. "That's how come you're here!"

I waited, but she didn't return.

That silence I was beginning to hate was the only thing that returned.

❧ 11 ❧

Kiera

Mrs. March came into my room before anyone else arrived in the morning. I wasn't even out of bed. She was visibly upset.

"Was Kiera in here last night?" she asked.

"Yes."

"I thought so. I heard her complaining to her father. Did she say terrible things to you? What did she say?"

"She said you were punishing her by having me live here."

Mrs. March nodded. "She's right about that. Not that I want you to feel bad," she added quickly. "But I don't want her to forget and ignore what a terrible thing she has done. Don't worry. She won't bother you or do you any harm. I'm so sorry. She snuck in here without my permission. I'm going to tell her father to speak with her."

"Maybe I shouldn't be here," I said. "Maybe it's only causing more trouble."

"Oh, no, no, no. Don't you ever, ever, ever let that girl

make you feel bad or think such a thing. Of course you should be here. If you left, you'd only be making her feel good about what she did. You're doing both Donald and me a favor by being here. Sometimes I think that girl has no conscience whatsoever. I look at her and wonder how I gave birth to her. Alena was so different. No, don't you think about leaving. Dr. Milan will be here in a few hours. Let's just think about that for now, okay?"

"Okay."

"Good. Do you want any help getting up and dressed?"

"I can do it."

"I'll go see about your breakfast and talk to Donald about Kiera before he leaves the house. I'm so sorry." She hurried out.

I rose and went to the closet to choose something to wear. I wondered how anyone could decide with all of these choices. How important had this been to Alena? I didn't want to keep thinking about being in her room, using her things, but at the same time, I couldn't help but be curious about her. Was she spoiled, too? Did she get along with Kiera? How could anyone? What did she think when she realized how sick she was, or did they keep the seriousness of her illness a secret from her until she was near the end of her life? Secrets were very comfortable living here. It seemed only natural for the Marches to lie to one another.

And yet, I thought, surely she must have felt very sick and knew because of all the things she couldn't do any longer that she was in danger of dying. Even a doctor like Dr. Milan couldn't keep the truth from peeking out of his eyes.

I realized, however, that death is not something someone so young thinks about very often and probably not until he or she hears about a relative or a friend dying. I didn't, not even when life was so difficult for Mama and me. Somehow I always thought we'd get through it. Something would happen to change things and make us healthy and whole again. Even when I saw her get hit just before me on the highway, I still believed it would be all right. The ambulances were there. Someone was helping Mama.

And when that woman told me she was dead, that she had been killed instantly, it didn't set right in. I kept hoping and thinking that there was a mistake. Alena must have been the same way when she was getting sicker and sicker. She must have thought the doctor would make her better. One morning, she'd wake up and it would be all over, just the way a cold ends. The younger you were, the more of a surprise death had to be, I thought.

After sifting through some of the clothes, I chose a light-blue skirt and the blouse that went with it. Everything fit well, but the more comfortable I was in Alena's things, the more frightened it made me feel. I almost took the blouse and skirt off and put on what I had worn the day before, but before I could do that, Mrs. Duval brought me my breakfast.

"What time does everyone else eat breakfast?" I asked her.

"Mr. March is the first down always. He eats very early and leaves for work before Kiera even gets up and dressed most of the time, especially during the summer months. Sometimes, like today, he takes a little longer, and Mrs. March joins him. On weekends, it's usually different.

Everyone sleeps in. You look very nice this morning," she added. She smiled and left.

About an hour after I finished breakfast, Mrs. March returned with Dr. Milan. He examined me and said that one of the nurses at his office would stop by with a crutch for me to use.

"She'll show you how to use it so you can keep the pressure off that leg for a while."

"How long will I have to be in the cast?" I asked.

"We'll see. I'll get you over to my office for X-rays in three or four weeks. In the meantime," he said, looking around the suite, "you'll be fine. It doesn't look like you'll be lacking anything."

Nothing except love and a family, I thought. He and Mrs. March left together. I could hear them whispering in the hallway until they went down the stairs. Immediately afterward, Rosie came up to get my tray and dishes. She asked me how I was feeling and told me she thought Kiera was jealous.

"Jealous of what? Me?"

She laughed. "Well, she claims she's not feeling well and locked herself in her room. Mrs. Duval had to bring her breakfast, too, but it ain't the first time, and I'm sure it ain't the last."

After she left, I wheeled myself to the door and looked down the hallway. No one was there, so I continued a little until I heard music and laughter behind the door of the room next to mine. I imagined it was Kiera's and paused to see if I could hear anyone else. Perhaps one of her friends was already there. Whether she heard me or could see through some keyhole, I don't know, but suddenly, the door was thrust open and she was standing there in her bathrobe. She was holding a portable phone in her right hand. It happened so quickly that I flinched and wheeled myself back a few feet.

"What are you doing, spying on me?" she asked.

"No. I didn't even know this was your room."

"Right. You don't know anything. Just keep out of my face," she said, and slammed the door. I heard her tell whoever was on the phone that one of the annoying maids had come to check on something.

Still trembling, I wheeled myself back to my room and closed the door. Just knowing that Kiera was so close made me nervous. She had already shown that she could burst in on me anytime, even when I was sleeping. I doubted that Mrs. March could stop her.

Moments later, I heard someone else coming, and I was happy to see that it was Mrs. Kepler. She could see I was upset.

"Are you feeling all right? I know the doctor was just here."

"I'm fine," I said, but I didn't say anything more. What good would it do to tell her about Kiera March?

"Would you rather we work outside?"

"No."

"You're probably right. There are too many distractions out there. Let's get to it," she said.

She went through the history and science workbooks with me and set out the books she wanted me to read. Finally, she paused and said, "You do look worried, Sasha. I hope I didn't lead you to believe that you must finish all of this in a week."

"I'm okay," I said.

She still looked suspicious but continued with her explanations and instructions. I tried to pay attention as well as I had done the day before, but I couldn't help anticipating Kiera March again. Perhaps she would come in to interrupt us and mock me. I could see that Mrs. Kepler wasn't pleased with my responses.

Mrs. March stopped by to see if Mrs. Kepler was going to stay for lunch. She told her she thought we had done enough for the day. From the looks they were giving each other, I knew Mrs. Kepler wanted to speak with her privately. She said she would return about the same time tomorrow and then left with Mrs. March. I hoped she wasn't going to tell her that it was too soon to have me do the schoolwork. I was happy to have it, to have something that would take my mind off everything. In fact, by the time Mrs. Duval stopped in with my lunch, I had already done everything Mrs. Kepler had assigned for the day. I knew that would both surprise and please Mrs. March.

When she returned, because of what Mrs. Kepler had obviously told her, she wanted to know if she was rushing me too fast. "With your recuperation and all that's happened, maybe we should wait on your schooling and . . ."

"Oh, no. I like it," I said. "I've done everything she left for me to do."

"Really? Well, that's wonderful, Sasha. She'll be pleased. If you're not too tired, I thought I'd replace Mrs. Caro today and take you out. I'll wheel you along and show you more of the property. Would you like that?"

"Yes."

"Good. I'll be back in about a half hour."

Almost as soon as her footsteps died away down the hall, Kiera came into my bedroom. I had my back to the door and was looking through the science workbook. I caught her reflection in the window and held my breath. She was still in her robe, but her image appeared so silently that she looked more like a ghost. I turned around slowly.

"So, Mother is going to show you the grounds. How sweet," she said, coming into the sitting room.

How did she know that? Did Mrs. March tell her, or could she hear what went on in my bedroom? Was she always going to be spying on me? She looked at my workbooks and the books on the table, tossing them aside as if they were someone's garbage.

"And you're getting private tutoring, too. I'm sure you need it." She stopped and put her hands on her hips. "So, what, do you expect to live here forever?"

"I don't expect anything."

"Yeah, right." She continued to inspect everything in the suite and saw my new iPod. She picked it up. "What's this? My mother bought you this? This is better than mine," she said, and dropped it. "Oh, sorry. I hope it didn't break." She didn't make an effort to see or to pick it up.

She continued to stroll through the suite.

"It's been some time since I've been in here for any length of time, actually. Mother kept it locked up, you know. She had it cleaned regularly but wasn't keen on anyone else but the maid being in here. I see nothing has been changed for you."

She wandered past the bed to open the closet.

"I heard she's been buying you some new clothes, too." She turned to look at me more carefully. "But that's not new. That's one of Alena's outfits you're wearing. Aren't you ashamed to wear a dead girl's clothes? No," she said before I could respond, "you were probably finding clothes in garbage heaps to wear."

"I'm not doing anything your mother told me not to do."

"I'll bet. You know, my father's not happy that you're here. They had a big fight about it. She tell you that?"

"No."

"I wouldn't count on being here much longer."

"I told you. I didn't ask to come here."

"You won't ask to leave, either, but you will."

I turned away from her. She returned to the sitting room and looked out the window.

"You know, I saw you watching us the other day. I didn't tell the others, because I didn't want anyone to know you were here. They'd have all sorts of stupid questions. It's embarrassing."

"Embarrassing? I think what you did was more than embarrassing."

"Aren't you smart. Anyway, did you get a good look at everything going on at the pool, a good look at all of my friends?"

I didn't answer.

"You'd better not be telling my mother about anything you saw out there. It's none of your business."

"I don't tell on people," I said. "I don't care what you do, anyway."

"You don't tell on people? You told her I came into the bedroom last night, didn't you?"

"She knew you had come in, but don't worry. I won't tell her about what you and your friends did at the pool."

"Probably jealous. You liked what you saw, though, didn't you? Ricky and Boyd and Tony? But I guess you've seen naked boys plenty of times in the streets, huh?"

"No."

"You still a little virgin?"

"Now, that's none of your business," I fired back.

She laughed. "I forgot you're a street kid," she said. She said it as if she admired it.

"I'm not a street kid. We didn't want to be living on the street."

"We all have to do things we don't want to do," she replied. I waited to see what she meant, but she stopped talking, looked out the window, then turned and walked out of the bedroom quickly.

I felt like shouting something nasty after her but wheeled myself back to the table, picked up the iPod she had deliberately dropped, and looked at my workbook again. But it was harder than ever to concentrate on anything. *What am I doing here?* I wondered. Maybe I'd be better off in some orphanage after all. Maybe I'd be happy to have her father kick me out.

"Ready?" I heard Mrs. March ask. She returned wearing a different outfit and a wide-brim hat. "Don't laugh at my hat," she said, seeing where my gaze went. "It's beautiful out there, but I've got to be careful in the sun. When you're my age, it only makes you look older, makes wrinkles come faster."

She stepped behind my wheelchair and started to turn me toward the door.

"When I was a young girl like you and like Kiera, I never thought about it. Now, when I think about all those days I spent on the beach without any protection, I shudder. How stupid we were. I tell Kiera that all the time, but does she listen? No."

In the elevator, I wondered if she was going to ask me if Kiera had come into my bedroom again. She didn't, and I didn't tell her.

She smiled at me and nodded. "You're doing a lot better, I can tell, and Dr. Milan thinks so, too. Where you are when you recuperate can make a great deal of difference."

Mrs. Caro had said something similar. Was everything anyone said to me planned?

The elevator opened, and she pushed me out and toward the French doors that opened to the patio Mrs. Caro had taken me to the day before.

"I used to wheel Alena out here when she was bedridden. Even though the poor thing had a hard time sitting up, she looked forward to it. Those were my last beautiful days with her, and I know she lived longer because of it. Look at what a beautiful afternoon we have for you, Sasha. There's even a breeze coming in off the ocean today. Feel it? I'll take you for a ride to the ocean soon, too. We'll go to lunch. I used to take Alena to lunch before she became too ill to travel."

"Did you take Kiera, too?"

"Kiera never liked to go with us. Kiera may act tough, but she wasn't able to deal with her sister's illness and death. None of us really was, but we did what we had to do and for Alena's sake tried not to show our sorrow. It was better not to include Kiera."

"Didn't Alena want her to come along with you?"

"Oh, yes, but I found an excuse for Kiera not to be coming with us most of the time. Neither Alena nor I would have enjoyed ourselves. Now," she said, firmly changing the subject, "if we follow this path here, we can go around to the lake. I want you to see it close up. As I told you, Donald's very proud of our lake. He's always bringing someone in the construction industry here to see it, and it was featured in a prominent architecture magazine. When you are up and around, you can take one of the rowboats out. Did you ever row a boat?"

"No."

"Well, maybe I'll go with you the first time to be sure you're safe," she said. "After you start school, you'll probably make lots of friends and ask to bring them here. We'll ask that everyone wear a life vest, of course. The lake is seven feet deep and maybe deeper in some places."

Friends? I thought back to when I did have friends at school and when I would go to their homes or they would come to mine. It seemed so long ago that it was more like something I had dreamed. Would I have school friends again? All of them would surely be impressed if I brought them to the March house. The very idea of doing that set off all sorts of fantasies, but then I thought about Kiera and her threats and predictions. Maybe my days there were numbered. Maybe as soon as I was up on my feet again, I'd be sent away. Why even think about it?

We stopped at the dock, and I looked out at the lake. It was so still. Down on the left, the trees were reflected in the water, giving it a greenish tint. Toward the other side, I saw terns. They were visitors from the ocean. The two rowboats tied to the dock looked brand-new. Mrs. March stepped up beside me, folded her arms, and looked out as if she had never seen it until now.

"Isn't it beautiful?"

"Yes," I said. I hesitated but then asked, "Does Mr. March really want me here?"

She spun around and seemed about to say, *Of course.* Something she saw in my face made her pause. "Did Kiera say something terrible last night about her father?"

When you first meet someone, you can't help but wonder how much of the truth you should tell and how much you should hold back. It was something I had learned from the way Mama spoke to people, especially after Daddy had left us. Lying seemed to be an important way to protect yourself, and most people didn't seem to know or care that she was lying.

What should I do now? I wondered. *Get Kiera in more trouble?*

"I just wondered," I said.

"It's not for you to worry about," she replied quickly. "The reason I brought you here is to have your recuperation managed well so that you'll be up on your feet and get the opportunity to have a new, wonderful life. You let me worry about the rest of it, Sasha." She looked out at the water again for a moment before turning back to me. "I made a promise to your mother," she said.

"My mother? When?" Had my mother been alive for a while and no one had told me?

"At her burial, at the cemetery," she replied.

"Oh."

"I promised her that I would look after you, and I won't let anyone stop me from fulfilling the promise."

My daddy had made a lot of promises, I thought, and after we were thrown out on the street, Mama had made lots of promises, too. What was the real difference between a promise and a dream? Just like dreams, the day after, no one remembers them.

"Put your promises in writing," Mama would tell Daddy. "Not that it would mean much more," she would mumble to me.

A promise was a wish made of smoke, I thought. You could see it, but you couldn't grasp it, and you couldn't take it anywhere. You had to wait for the wind to see where it would go or if it would just disappear.

I had no doubt that Mrs. March wanted to fulfill her promise to Mama, but even she, sitting on top of that beautiful, rich world, was helpless when it came to putting her fingers around the promise of happiness when it was for herself and her family.

What could she really do for me?

❧ 12 ❧

Mr. March

Two nights later, I finally met Donald March. Mrs. Duval came up to my room to tell me that dinner would be served earlier than usual, and that Mrs. March had requested that I be brought down to the dining room.

"She said you should choose anything you would like to wear except a tank top. Do you need help with anything?"

"No," I told her.

"Then I'll be back for you in twenty minutes," Mrs. Duval said.

I couldn't help being very nervous, so nervous I could feel myself trembling. Kiera told me that her father would send me away, and although Mrs. March told me not to be concerned about it, that it was her problem, I still felt I'd be more uncomfortable in Donald March's presence than I would be sleeping in a cardboard carton. Maybe because we had had so little that anyone would want, neither Mama nor I had been terribly afraid out there. Everyone living in the street appeared just as unconcerned. Perhaps we all thought nothing more could happen to us. Now I was in what had to be one of the most expensive homes in the whole country, if not the whole world, and I knew deep in my heart of hearts that much more could happen to me there.

I had a difficult time deciding what to wear. When I started to choose something, I stopped to wonder if it was too fancy or not fancy enough. I had no doubt that Kiera would laugh at me, even ridicule me, in front of her father if I made the wrong choice. He might look at Mrs. March and smirk as if to say, *How could you bring someone so common and stupid to our home? I don't care what your reasons were.*

Because of my cast, I could only wear skirts or dresses, and I wasn't sure which dresses of Alena's were formal. Mrs. March had made such a thing of what I would wear when it was only the two of us. Why wasn't she helping me choose tonight? Wasn't this a more important dinner? Perhaps she wanted me to prove that I could make the right choice without her.

A full ten minutes had gone by, and I still hadn't decided. Mama would surely laugh at my panic attack, especially over something to wear, I thought, and finally reached out and took a plain-looking dark blue skirt and its matching short-sleeved V-neck blouse. I was surprised at how well the blouse fit me. Earlier, I had brushed and pinned back my hair with one of Alena's clips. I hesitated to take any more of her things. There was a beautiful gold watch, bracelets and earrings and rings, but I touched none of it.

Mrs. Duval looked pleased with my choices when she returned. "Ready?"

"Yes," I said, and she wheeled me out to the elevator.

"Mrs. Caro has made an Irish dish that Mr. March favors. It's called Dublin Lawyer. It's made with lobster. Have you eaten lobster?"

"Once," I said.

"Once? Well, you're in for a delightful surprise."

The elevator doors opened. My heart felt as if it was shrinking in my chest as Mrs. Duval wheeled me toward the formal dining room. When we entered, I saw that they were all there and seated. Kiera wore a yellow keyhole-bust cap-sleeved top and a black skirt. I had seen other teenage girls wearing something like it lately and had wanted one for myself. She looked as if she had been born in hers; it fit her that well. As we drew closer to the long, dark wood table, I saw that her skirt was barely below her knees. She wore the most beautiful turquoise necklace I had ever seen and looked as glamorous as any young movie or television star.

How plain I look in comparison, I thought, but then again, I never imagined ever competing with her, especially for her father's attention. I couldn't help but wonder if Alena had felt the same way. Two daughters not all that many years apart must have been vying for their father's favor constantly. Once Alena became seriously ill, that competition had surely ended with Mr. March doting on Alena. I remembered reading a story about two sisters in which one did become ill and the other, jealous of the attention she received, pretended to be ill herself.

Being an only child, I often wondered what it would be like to have a sister or a brother and to share my mother's love.

How could any mother have enough? It was clear to me that Mrs. March favored Alena, and Kiera perhaps still couldn't forgive her, even now, even with her sister dead and buried. Was that why she was afraid of my being there so much? I knew I wasn't any weight on her conscience, as Mrs. March had hoped I'd be. I wasn't sure she even had a conscience.

My gaze shifted to Mr. March, who sat at the head of the table with his elbows on the table, his hands clasped together, and I noticed his striking gold pinkie ring with a lapis, which I would find out later was his birthstone. He wore a dark blue velvet sports jacket and a black shirt opened at the collar. There was a gold chain around his neck with whatever was on it hidden under his shirt.

His light brown hair looked closer to blond. It was beautifully styled, with a slight wave in front. Against the color of his hair and his tanned face, his dark blue eyes were more prominent. They nearly matched his lapis ring. I could see that Kiera inherited most of her good looks from him, because the features of his face, his perfectly shaped nose and strong mouth, seemed as sculptured as hers were. He looked athletic, and later, when he stood, I'd see that he was a good four inches taller than Mrs. March.

He sat back when Mrs. March rose to take me from Mrs. Duval.

"Here she is," Mrs. March said. She put me to the right of Mr. March. Kiera sat across from him, and Mrs. March sat on his left. "Sasha, this is my husband, Donald."

"Hello," I said, or at least I thought I did. My voice seemed trapped inside my trembling body. I saw that Kiera had a look of disgust on her face.

Donald March sat back, still studying me. "How's your leg doing?" he asked as a greeting.

"It doesn't hurt anymore."

"Ugh," Kiera said. "Couldn't she put a shoe on that foot?"

Mrs. March pushed me closer to the table. My broken leg just slipped under it so she wouldn't have to look at my foot. She glared at Kiera and took her seat across from me.

"You're putting her in Alena's place, you know," Kiera said.

Mr. March raised his eyebrows as if he'd just realized that himself. The table could easily seat a dozen people. Why was Kiera sitting at the end? Shouldn't Mrs. March be sitting across from her husband?

"You could sit closer, Kiera."

"I'm fine where I am," she said. Then she smiled. "I can look at Daddy better."

I glanced at him. He obviously liked that and smiled back at her.

Mrs. Duval began to bring in our salads. Mr. March sat forward again and lifted his salad fork. Was that all he was going to say to me? I wondered as he began to eat.

"Sasha is off to a wonderful start with Mrs. Kepler, who says she has no doubt she'll have her up to speed before the end of the summer," Mrs. March said.

"Who's Mrs. Kepler again?" Mr. March asked.

"Her tutor, Donald, remember?"

"Oh, yes." He looked at me and nodded.

"I hate talking about the end of summer. I can't stand the idea of it ending," Kiera muttered. She pushed some of her salad off to the side. "Look at this! I keep telling her I don't like beets and artichokes. Why can't they remember?"

"Why can't you remember to hang up your clothes, especially those that we have dry-cleaned and pressed for you?" Mrs. March countered.

"I thought that was what servants are for," Kiera said.

"If you don't cherish the things we buy you, we shouldn't buy you so much."

"Whatever," Kiera said, shrugging. Then she smiled. "I'll buy my own things."

Mr. March seemed not to hear the exchange. He was too involved in his wine, bread, and salad. I began to eat my salad and thought it was wonderful. It had so many flavors and was crunchy, just the way I liked it. The hospital salad and the salads I had eaten at the March house before were not as good, I thought. Maybe special things were saved for dinners with Mr. March.

"We're going to have to do something with your fingernails," Mrs. March told me, smiling. "I'll take you to my manicurist."

I looked at my fingers. My nails were uneven, but the idea of trimming them and putting on nail polish was something I hadn't thought about for quite a while. Ages, it seemed. It was almost a foreign concept. Mama used to do them for me, but that was so long ago that it was like something I had seen in an old movie on television.

When Mr. March finished his salad, he sat back and turned to me again. "How long were you and your mother homeless?" he asked.

"Nearly a year."

"She lived in a carton, you know. Didn't you? You told me you did," Kiera added before I could admit to it or deny it.

"Yes, we did," I said.

"How did you bathe?" Kiera asked. "Or didn't you?"

"We bathed in the public restrooms. Mama always tried to keep us both clean."

"Yeah, right," Kiera muttered. "You need to take a bath as soon as you walk out of those places. I'd rather go in my pants."

"Kiera," Mrs. March snapped.

"Well, Kiera's not all wrong. It is quite difficult for people like that to take good care of their hygiene," Mr. March said. "It's lucky she didn't suffer from some disease."

"Who knows what she's brought into this house—or what Mother has brought into it, I should really say," Kiera said.

"I think, of all people, you should know what I brought into this house, Kiera, when I brought Sasha here," Mrs. March responded, her face reddening.

"No, Mother, I don't know. Do tell me."

"Please. Let's enjoy the dinner," Mr. March said sharply.

Rosie came in and began to clear away the salad dishes. Mrs. Duval followed with a tray holding the main dish, which she had called a Dublin Lawyer. She served it to Mr. March first and then to us.

"You're in for a special treat," Mrs. March told me.

"Just eating indoors is a special treat for her," Kiera said.

Mr. March poured himself some more white wine and then looked at Mrs. March.

"I'm fine," she said.

"Daddy, can I have some, please?" Kiera asked in a sweet, syrupy voice.

"I don't think . . ." Mrs. March began.

"White wine goes perfectly with this," he said. "It's harmless," he added, and looked to Mrs. Duval. She took the bottle and went around to pour a glass for Kiera.

"Thank you, Daddy."

He nodded. "This is as fantastic, as usual," he said after eating some Dublin Lawyer. "Give my compliments to Mrs. Caro, please, Mrs. Duval."

"I will, sir," she said. "Anyone need anything else?"

"My water glass is empty," Kiera said.

The bottled water was right in front of her. Mrs. Duval picked it up and put some in her glass. I waited to hear her say thank you, but she simply drank her water. Mrs. Duval looked at me and then went back to the kitchen. I started on my meal. It was delicious. I remembered the lobster Mama and I had had, but it was nothing like this.

"What did your mother do before things fell apart for you?" Mr. March asked me as he ate.

I looked at him. *Fell apart?* Did he mean before the accident or after Daddy left or before she met Daddy? I didn't know what to say.

"Before you were out on the street," he added, seeing my confusion.

"She was a waitress and she did her calligraphy."

"Really? Calligraphy?" He turned to Mrs. March. "You have something from our trip to China five years ago, don't you, Jordan?"

"It's in our bathroom," she replied.

"Right. So your mother did that sort of thing?"

"Yes. There's one hanging on the wall in the Grave-diggers bar," I said proudly.

Kiera laughed. "Gravediggers. What is it, a bar in a cemetery?"

"I've heard of it," Mr. March said, and Kiera lost her smile.

"Well, what kind of a place is that for whatever she called it?"

"She called it 'heaven,'" I said.

"The bar?" Mr. March asked me.

"No, the word she had drawn and painted, the calligraphy. She would tell me that people go to the Gravediggers to see heaven."

He stared a moment and then burst out laughing. "That's really clever," he said.

I looked at Kiera. She pressed her lips together and dug into her food as if she hated it and wanted to kill it first. Mrs. March laughed, too. "It is clever," she said. "Can you do calligraphy?"

"Yes," I told her. "I often did it with my mother, just as she had done with hers."

Mr. March's eyebrows rose.

"Well, we'll have to get you what you need so you can do some," Mrs. March said.

"I thought you said you sold lanyards on the beach," Kiera quipped.

"I did," I said. "My mother sold calligraphy."

What have you sold, I wanted to ask her, *besides unhappiness?*

But I didn't. I looked down at my food and continued to eat, thinking only of Mama and how pleased she would be to see me having such a wonderful dinner in so elegant a dining room with what was obviously expensive silverware and dishes.

She would have said, "You're in the pink, kiddo."

I was sure I heard it.

"What's so funny?" Kiera asked.

"What?"

"You're laughing. What are you laughing at?"

I shook my head. I hadn't realized I was smiling so widely.

"Well, there you are," Kiera said, nodding at me. "Smiling like an idiot. May I be excused, please? I have an important phone call to make."

"You haven't had dessert," Mrs. March said. "Mrs. Caro has made a very special cake in honor of Sasha."

"I don't need it. This was fattening enough," she said, pushing her plate away. There was at least half of her meal left. I had eaten every bit of mine. "Daddy?"

"Go ahead," he said. Mrs. March widened her eyes. "She'll only spoil our enjoyment pouting there, Jordan."

Mrs. March glanced at me. I could see that she wanted to respond but lowered her eyes instead.

"Thank you, Daddy," Kiera said. She rose and went over to give him a kiss. She looked at her mother and then brushed past me on her way out.

Both Mr. and Mrs. March were very quiet.

"You made a very nice choice of something to wear tonight, Sasha," Mrs. March told me.

Mr. March looked at me. I could see in the movement of his eyes and his mouth that he was just realizing that I was wearing one of Alena's outfits. I waited to see if he would say something, but he shifted his eyes down quickly and then turned to Mrs. March.

"I can't put off that trip to Hawaii any longer," he told her. "It's too big an opportunity for us to lose. Are you or are you not coming along?"

"I can't just now, Donald," she said, nodding at me.

"You have doctors, tutors, servants looking after her, Jordan."

"I just can't," she said.

Mrs. Duval came in with the cake. It was chocolate with raspberry and looked scrumptious. Mrs. Caro had drawn my name with the raspberries. Now I was glad Kiera had left. She would probably have thrown it up later.

"How beautiful," Mrs. March said.

After we had dessert, Mr. March said he had to make some calls and rose. He looked down at me and said, "It was nice meeting you."

He had been quiet the whole time we were eating dessert. Before he reached the door, Mrs. March said, "I'll be right back," and followed him.

I wheeled myself away from the table and turned toward the door, too. I thought I might wheel myself outside to the patio. I stopped before I reached the door, because I could hear them arguing in the hallway.

"Can't you be nicer to her, Donald?" Mrs. March said.

"I don't know why you're making us do this."

"We can't escape our responsibility, Donald."

"Who says we should? We can simply set up a trust for her and have her live with some foster family, can't we? You can involve yourself in all that, if you like."

"That's what she's doing here now, Donald. We're her foster family, but you're right. We should set up a trust for her as well."

"I don't know, Jordan. You saw how Kiera's reacting to all this. I don't know."

"I do. It's good that she isn't permitted to forget, to ignore and minimize what a terrible thing she has done, Donald."

"How can she forget with you harping on it so much?" he said sharply. I heard him walking away.

I knew I would be embarrassed to be caught listening and started to turn. Mrs. Duval was standing right behind me. She had heard everything, too.

"People say things they don't really mean," she told me.

Mama did, I thought, *but she was half out of her mind with cheap gin.*

What's his excuse?

13

Family

*W*hy stay here now? I asked myself. *For the big room, the clothes, the food, my tutoring, and my doctor,* another part of me replied. *Remember Jackie's advice. No matter what, take everything they want to give you. You deserve more than what they give you. Take it.*

I really didn't know what I should do. Except for Mrs. March's obvious sense of guilt over what Kiera had done and the servants speaking some kind words to me, I felt not only unwanted but in some ways even more invisible than I was when Mama and I lived in the streets. How lucky other young girls my age were to have loving parents and caring friends to whom they could go for advice and sympathy. I had only the memory of Mama when she was healthy and strong, now speaking to me from the grave.

"Oh, did you want to go up to your room?" Mrs. March asked when she returned to the dining room. She saw Mrs. Duval standing there, but Mrs. Duval went immediately to supervise the cleaning of the dining room. I saw that Mrs. March suspected that I had overheard the argument she had just had with her husband.

"I was going outside for a while first," I said.

"That's such a good idea. Let me take you." She got behind my wheelchair and started pushing me through the hallway, but this time she turned right. "We'll go to a different patio this time," she said. "This side of the house is better lit, and if we look east, we can see the lights of downtown Los Angeles."

She continued to talk, almost babbling, as we proceeded to another exit. The house did seem like a hotel to me. No wonder I couldn't think of it as someone's home. She pointed out some guest bedrooms and another, smaller living room.

"Donald had it designed just for the guests. He doesn't mind our having guests," she continued explaining, "but he likes us to have our private areas. Do you know who Citizen Kane was?"

"No," I said.

"It's a movie, actually, but in it, this man Kane builds an enormous mansion, which is actually modeled on the Hearst Castle. Have you ever seen that?"

"No."

"I keep forgetting how limited your life was," she muttered, more like someone chastising herself or someone else living inside her. "Well, anyway, Donald always got a kick out of a line in the movie suggesting that there were guests still there, guests Kane and his wife had forgotten. Can you imagine a house so big that you'd forget your own guests were still there? It could almost happen here, I suppose. At least, some of Donald's friends tease him about it."

I could see myself very easily being forgotten here.

She turned us through the smaller living room, which was surely bigger than the living rooms in almost all of the other houses in America, and then to the French doors that opened onto the other patio. She was right about the lighting. The grounds were illuminated like some major league ball field. There were more beautiful gardens, pruned bushes, and an area that seemed to be under construction. I asked about it.

"Donald's building a hedge maze," she said. "Like the one in Hampton Court in England." When I didn't say anything, she added, "Oh, but you probably don't know anything about that yet. You'll learn about such things in history when you return to school. There," she said, pushing me to the far left corner. "See downtown Los Angeles? Isn't it beautiful to be able to see it from here?"

"Were you always rich?" I asked.

"Rich?" She laughed. "Oh, well, yes, I suppose I was— or my family was, I should say. My father always says Donald interrupted my education. I was just graduating from Marlborough and on my way to attend Smith when I met Donald at a charity gala in Los Angeles. I had never met anyone like him. He was basically just starting out, but he was so sure of himself. You know how people often say there are no guarantees in life? Well, Donald behaved as if he had been given a guarantee of major success.

"But it wasn't only that. He was and is a very attractive man who believes your presentation is of paramount importance. My father believes the same thing. People usually, whether rightly or wrongly, judge you on first impressions, so it's essential to make the best first impression always. You'll never notice Donald looking sloppy or unkempt. He's never off duty, so to speak, whereas I'll let my hair down occasionally. Needless to say, my father loves Donald. In fact, he fell in love with him before I did."

She gave a trickle of a laugh. "I don't mean anything like gay love. He loved who Donald was and wanted to be. Can you imagine a father telling a girl just out of high school that this was the man for her? Oh, I know some people thought that was because my father believed I could never succeed at anything but being a wealthy man's wife." She laughed again. "Maybe that's true. So what?"

I don't know if she realized how much she had said so quickly or not, but she stopped talking and just stood there beside me looking out at the lights in the distance.

"What about your mother?" I asked, since she never had mentioned her.

"My mother was a rich man's wife," she replied, as though that answered everything. "Whatever my father said was gospel. She doted on my younger brother far more than me, anyway. He's a lawyer working for the Justice Department in Washington, a great success. They think he might become attorney general someday. I think every other sentence out of her mouth begins with his name, Gerald. Gerald Savoir Faire, his friends call him. You know what that means in French?"

"No."

"To know how to do . . . everything. Sophisticated," she

said, but she didn't say it with pleasure and pride. "I'm just kidding," she quickly added. "He's terrific. His real name is Gerald Wilson. We're supposedly descendants of President Woodrow Wilson, you know. That's almost royalty in America."

"What about Mr. March's parents?"

"That's a different story. Donald's father was married to someone before he married Donald's mother, and he has children with his first wife. He and Donald's mother had only Donald, and his mother died two years ago while on holiday with Donald's father and two of his three other children and their families."

She sighed deeply. "Aren't families complicated sometimes?" she asked, but she didn't look at me. She looked out, as if she were asking someone else.

We were both quiet, and then, after a few moments, she turned sharply and said, "Don't let Kiera's behavior at dinner and Donald's tolerance of her discourage you. You belong here now. I'm determined about that. Give it time. Everything takes time. Otherwise," she continued with a smile, "babies wouldn't need nine months."

What was she thinking and saying? That I was going to be reborn in nine months?

"I'm so happy we had this little chat. We have to do it more and more so we get to know each other better. Soon Donald will open up more, as well, and before you know it, we'll be like a family, a family for you. Okay? Don't be discouraged, okay?"

I saw that she wasn't going to stop until she got me to agree. I nodded, and she smiled.

"Good. What was it Scarlett O'Hara said? 'Tomorrow is another day'? Well, tomorrow is another day, and every tomorrow thereafter. Would you like to watch television in the entertainment center? We have a screen as big as some small movie-theater screens. When was the last time you went to a movie?"

I thought about it and realized that it had been soon after Daddy had left us. Mama had taken me to a movie to cheer up both of us. That was years ago, because we never spent money on a movie after that, and my school friends had stopped asking me to go to movies with them.

"Years ago," I replied.

"Years?" She got behind my wheelchair. "Years, and you live in the movie capital of the world? We'll do something about that, although once you see a movie here, you might not care about going to a theater."

As she wheeled me along, she described some of their theater parties. She said that her husband knew an important movie executive at one of the studios, and he brought them first-run films to watch. The elaborate parties she described and the things they had done were as foreign to me as rituals in Africa or the Far East.

When we turned into the entertainment center, she stopped my wheelchair abruptly. Kiera was there with one of the girls I had seen at the pool, but what they were watching on the screen was more surprising. A naked man and woman were embracing as they lay on a beach. Mrs. March adjusted the lights so the room was blazing.

"What the hell!" Kiera cried, and turned around. She and her girlfriend were snacking on popcorn. They sat on two large red leather seats with a wide arm between them on which they had the bowl of delicious-smelling popcorn.

"What are you watching? Why didn't you tell me Deidre was coming here tonight?"

"Daddy said we could," Kiera said. "And for your information, this picture is going to be nominated for an Academy Award. You're ruining it for us. Please turn off the lights."

"Hi, Mrs. March," Deidre said. She had auburn hair, smartly shaped, and was one of the prettiest girls I had seen.

"You can leave her here to watch if you want, Mother. I'm sure she's seen worse on the street."

Mrs. March seemed at a loss for words. She didn't move me or herself. The couple on the screen got up laughing and charged into the ocean, splashing each other.

"Deidre's mother would not like her watching this, I'm sure," she finally said.

"Are you kidding? She was jealous that she was getting to see it. Right, Deidre?"

"She was, Mrs. March."

Without further comment, Mrs. March turned me away and started out.

"Turn down the lights again, Mother!" Kiera screamed.

Mrs. March didn't. She continued to push me out and down the hallway.

"Thanks, Mother!" Kiera shouted after us.

"I'll take you up to your room. You can watch television in your own suite," Mrs. March said. I didn't look back at her, but from the way her voice trembled, I knew she was shaken.

As we went into the elevator, I realized that Kiera finally had told at least one of her friends about me, and surely once one found out, others would, as well. I wondered how she explained my presence in their home. Surely by now, her friends knew about the accident she had caused. One or two of them might have been with her in the car and probably high on drugs as well. They and their parents would have good reason not to let other people know what had happened.

After she had settled me in my suite, Mrs. March said that before going to bed herself, she would stop by again to be sure I was fine. She looked anxious to leave and hurried out, to speak with her husband I was sure. When she returned hours later, she didn't look much calmer. In fact, she looked as flushed as someone who had been in a nasty argument. I let her help me undress and get ready for bed, more out of sympathy for her than because of any need of my own. It seemed to help settle her down. After I was in bed, she tucked the blanket in around me, but she didn't leave. She pulled up a chair beside the bed and smiled.

"Did I tell you that when Alena was younger, she would often describe dreams she had? She loved telling stories, and to her, the dreams she had were often her best. Even Donald, as busy as he seemed, enjoyed having her go on and on. Only Kiera would complain that Alena didn't leave much time to talk or hear about anything else. Did I tell you about all that?"

"No," I said. What made her think she had told me? We didn't speak that much about Alena.

"Anyway, to help her get to sleep the next night, I would sit here just as I am sitting now, and we would think of ways the dream story could continue or how it might lead to another dream. Sometimes Donald would stop in and participate. Who'd ever think that something so terrible would happen to such a lovely little girl?"

She continued after a little pause of sadness, "It seems I keep apologizing to you for what goes on here. It will get better. I promise." She patted my hand and started to get up, but then stopped and looked at me. "You didn't have any storylike dreams last night, did you?"

"No," I said.

"Well, if you ever feel like talking about a dream you've had, don't hesitate to tell me, okay? Good. Sweet dreams, then." She leaned over to kiss me on the forehead. She put the chair back, smiled at me, and put out the lights on her way out, closing the door softly behind her. The house was quiet, but when I adjusted myself to get a little more comfortable, I heard the music start in Kiera's room. It was so loud that I was sure Mr. and Mrs. March had to hear it, as well, but it continued.

She's doing that deliberately, I thought. Why couldn't she use earphones? Perhaps her friend Deidre was still there and in the room with her. Maybe she was showing off, showing her how she could annoy me. I imagined her bragging about how she would drive me out of there soon. Finally, the music was turned down or turned off, and the silence returned.

It was still difficult for me to fall asleep. I anticipated Kiera bursting in on me again to make more threats, but she didn't. I also thought about what Mrs. March had said about Alena's dreams. I wondered if her dreams would somehow become mine if I remained there. Maybe dreams lingered like cobwebs. They were floating about looking to settle in another young girl's mind.

I half wished they would. My interest in knowing more about Alena seemed to grow stronger with every minute I was in the suite. Whether it was wishful thinking or not, I half expected that someday, she would reach out to me to tell me that she would help me.

"Don't worry," she would whisper, "I'm here."

I so needed a friend.

Even one who had died.

☙14☙
Unchained

Soon my days became more ordinary, or at least as ordinary as days living in such an enormous estate with servants could be. For the time being, Kiera seemed to lose interest in me and didn't come bursting into my room again. Often, she wasn't at dinner, and if she was, she acted as if I weren't even there. Perhaps she was convinced that my being sent away was only a matter of time and didn't require her interference or involvement. Mr. March was often gone on business or very involved in some project he was developing. I had seen little of him since our first dinner together. There was much to keep me busy, however.

Mrs. Kepler came to tutor me five days a week and always stayed the same amount of time. Dr. Milan came once more, and then I was taken to get the X-rays he wanted. He told Mrs. March and me that it was too soon to see if my right leg would continue to grow as normally as my left. I was instructed in how to use the crutch he promised, so the wheelchair was put away. The doctor wanted me to get more exercise and move about as much as possible, and I did feel myself getting stronger every day. As Mrs. Duval was fond of saying, there was light at the end of the tunnel.

Toward the end of the summer, Dr. Milan finally took off the cast, and I felt like a prisoner who had been un-chained. But I was walking with a limp. The doctor said I would for a while, if not forever. Still, I was so happy not to have something attached to my body that I almost didn't care. Suddenly, the world seemed bright again, and hope dared show its face on my horizon. How I wished Mama would have lived to see my recuperation.

On the way back from Dr. Milan's office, I told Mrs. March that I had finally decided what to have written on my mother's tombstone. From the way she reacted, I had the feeling she thought I had completely forgotten about it.

"Oh, you have? Why, that's very nice, Sasha. What have you decided?"

"Under her name and the dates of her birth and death, I want to write 'who showed her daughter a little bit of heaven.'"

I could see she didn't fully understand. How could I want to write something like that after being on the streets for nearly a year before her death?

"I don't know if it can be done," I added, "but I'd like to see her calligraphy of the word *heaven* right under that."

"Oh. Oh, yes," she said, now realizing why I wanted that. "That work she has on that bar's wall. How clever. Well, we'll just find someone who can get it done for us. Do you think that calligraphy is still on the bar wall?"

"I don't know. I saw it only once when she took me there to see it."

"Of course. How stupid of me to ask. How would you know, after all? I'll make some calls when we get home," she said. "But right now, I thought I'd have Grover drive us to your new school so you can see it. It won't be long before you'll be attending. Mrs. Kepler says you're ready for day one right now."

I sat back, nervous and excited. I used to love school. Before Mama and I ended up on the streets, it was a wonderful escape from the dreariness of the life we were living. Even when my girlfriends stopped including me in things, I still enjoyed being in my classes. The girls I used to consider my closest friends had still talked to me. They just didn't suggest anything that would bring us together after school, and then, when they learned that Mama and I had lost our apartment and were living in a hotel room, they had even stopped talking to me unless I spoke to them, and even then, they would answer quickly and look to get away. It was as if they thought what was happening to me and Mama was as infectious as some terrible disease. In the end, I almost didn't mind not attending school.

When we made a turn and Mrs. March said, "Here we are," I thought she was mistaken. All I saw were beautiful green lawns, trees, and bushes, but then the building just at the top of a small incline appeared. Right at the bottom was the sign, "Pacifica Junior-Senior High School."

"Turn in, please, Grover," she told him, and we started up the driveway. It wasn't like any school building I had seen, and it looked very new. Everything around it sparkled. Our building at my old school had graffiti smeared on some of the walls, and almost as quickly as it was removed, it reappeared. The windows never looked as clear and as clean as the ones in this building. The frames here looked freshly painted.

The building had two floors, and as we drew closer, I realized it was in an L shape. Off to the right, I could see the ball fields. One had goals for field hockey or soccer, and the other was a baseball field. There was a parking lot on the left with only a half-dozen cars in it.

"The school has a very nice cafeteria and tables outside if you want to eat your lunch outdoors," Mrs. March began. "At the rear to the left is the gymnasium, and right next to that is the theater."

"Theater?"

"Well, it's a really small theater, but it's equipped with the most up-to-date sound system. I should tell you now that Donald's . . . our company . . . built this school."

"He builds schools, too?"

"Just this one," she said, laughing. "It was almost done as a favor. A group of well-to-do people, including two state senators, decided to establish it about twelve years ago and practically begged Donald to take charge of construction. So, if you hear Kiera tell people that it's her school, that's what she means. Actually," she added after a moment's thought, "I think she believes it really is her school."

"How many students go to it?"

"I think it's just less than three hundred now. It's only for grades seven to twelve. There's a sort of sister elementary school that both Alena and Kiera attended. I'm sure you'll love it here. The classes aren't very big, so you'll get lots of personal attention."

Grover stopped, and I gazed out at it all.

"It looks better than any school I've ever seen," I said.

"The principal is a very nice woman named Dr. Steiner. She has a doctorate in education and has been the principal since the school was established. You're in Mr. Hoffman's homeroom class, and he's your math teacher, as well. I made sure you were in that homeroom. Your homeroom teacher is your personal adviser, too, and he's one of the best teachers in the school. So you can see, I'm getting everything set up perfectly for you. Doesn't it look wonderful?"

"Yes," I said.

"I thought you'd be impressed. Grover, you can take us home now," she said, and he started back down the driveway.

"Will Kiera go to school with me?" I asked.

"We'll see. That's something Donald has yet to decide. Seniors are permitted to drive to school. There's a parking lot for them." After a long moment, she added, "Her court hearing has yet to happen. Donald's lawyer has successfully delayed it, which is a legal tactic, but as I tell him, you can postpone and postpone, but inevitably you have to face the music. But let's not talk about any of that, Sasha. It only brings back terrible memories and pain for you."

I sat back and was quiet. Her saying not to talk about it didn't do any good. It was like unringing a bell. It couldn't be done. I had been wondering for months what was going to happen to Kiera. How could what had happened be completely swept under the table? Were rich people that powerful?

Perhaps to cheer me up further, Mrs. March delivered on her promise to get me whatever I needed to do calligraphy. She even bought me a beautifully illustrated book about it, and I saw some of the words Mama had copied. I had told her exactly what I needed, and it was all set up in the sitting room. I began to work almost immediately. I wanted to do a copy of Mama's "heaven."

"Don't make me sorry I got you all this," Mrs. March told me two days after I began work. I had done little of anything else. "You can't shut yourself away all day, you know."

She was right, of course. Now that I was free of my cast and did not have to depend on a crutch, Dr. Milan wanted me to take daily exercise. Mrs. March had a physical therapist come to the house to work with me every other day. "We've got to get your muscles strong again so you won't have any problem getting around in school," she said. The therapist, Sheila Toby, was very impressed with the Marches' indoor pool and, after some initial days of stretching exercises, decided we would do all of our work in the water.

One afternoon, Mr. March suddenly appeared to watch us. He was there for quite a while but said nothing. Later, when I was going up to my suite, he appeared in the hallway. I realized that this was the first time since I had come to his house that he and I were alone.

"You seem to be doing very well," he began. "I'm sure you feel stronger every day."

"Yes, I do."

I waited, expecting him to say, *Okay, since you're better and stronger, you don't have to live here anymore, and this idea of your going to Kiera's school is not really a good one*, but he didn't say that.

"I happened to glance in at the calligraphy you're doing," he continued, walking along with me toward my suite. "It's pretty impressive."

"Thank you."

"Tell me about it," he said.

"What do you want to know?"

"I'm not that familiar with it. Jordan bought something once, as I said, but I must admit, I didn't pay much attention to the explanation the salesman gave us at the gallery. I gather you told her exactly what you needed. What is needed?"

"I work with an ink brush, ink, a special type of paper, and an inkstone. Together, they are known as the Four Treasures of the Study."

"Really?" He smiled. "Go on. Tell me more."

We reached my doorway.

"The paper is weighed down with paperweights. Anything can be a paperweight, but my mother used to have wooden blocks that had pictorial designs on them, too. They had been her mother's."

"What happened to them?"

"I don't know. One day, they were gone and she used rocks we found on the beach instead. I think she might have sold them."

He nodded. "Go on in," he told me, and then he

followed me in and went to my desk. "So, what is this ink-stone?" he asked.

"You have to rub the ink stick on it with water to make the paint."

"Your mother did all this while you were homeless?"

"Yes. For her, it was more like . . . more like . . ."

"Therapy, relaxation?"

"No, I think something religious," I said, and his eyes widened and brightened.

"And for you?"

"The same," I said.

He smiled. He picked up the brush and studied it a moment.

"It has to be held a special way," I said.

"Show me."

I did.

"See, it's held vertically with the thumb and the middle finger. My mother told me you should be able to put an egg in your palm if you're holding it correctly."

He laughed and then tried it. I adjusted his fingers so that his ring finger and pinkie touched the bottom of the brush handle.

"This is hard," he said. "Must take a lot of practice."

"Yes. You start by practicing the Chinese character *yong* to master the eight basic strokes."

"And what does *yong* mean?"

"*Forever,*" I said.

"Now, what does the one you're working on represent?"

"It means *mother,*" I said.

"I know you must really miss her."

"Yes."

He nodded, keeping his eyes on my calligraphy. "Well," he said, "your art teacher should be happily surprised once he learns what you can do. He'll probably have you teach the class."

"Oh, I couldn't do that," I said.

"Sure you could. Let me see this when it's finished," he told me, and started to turn to leave. He stopped, and I looked at the doorway.

Kiera was standing there. From the look on her face, I knew she must have been there for a while and heard what we had been saying.

"What's up?" he asked her.

"Nothing," she said sharply, and hurried away.

He hesitated, and then he walked out.

Not long before our accident, after Mama and I had spent most of our day on Venice Beach's boardwalk selling her calligraphy and my lanyards, she had paused while we were getting our things together and just sat there staring at people.

"What's wrong, Mama?" I had asked. "Are you feeling sick again?"

"No, no," she had said. She'd smiled at me, and for a moment, I saw through her bloated face and tired eyes and saw the smile on her face years ago when she was beautiful and energetic. Nothing made me happier. I could go all the rest of the day without food and still feel content because I saw this smile.

"Then what, Mama?"

"I was just thinking how when they look at the calligraphy, they change."

"Who changes?"

"The people, the ones who pass by. It isn't until they're looking at the calligraphy that they suddenly see us as people. They look at both of us then, Sasha. Did you notice that?"

Now that she had said it, I realized it was true, and I nodded.

"Why is that, Mama?"

"The calligraphy, like anything beautiful, reminds us all about what we share as people. That's what your grandmother once told me," she had said. "But it wasn't until just now, today, that I realized what she meant."

She had smiled again and then continued gathering her things.

I looked down at my unfinished work and nodded, thinking about Mr. March, his softer tone of voice, his curiosity, and his smile.

"Now I understand, too, Mama," I whispered.

It was truly as if she had reached from beyond the grave to speak to me through my own calligraphy. It filled my heart with warmth and gave me the strength even to face the jealous face of Kiera March.

Someday, I thought—no, vowed—I wouldn't hate her as much as I pitied her.

But I knew that the journey to that place would be a long one and over a road full of many traps and dangers. I just didn't know how soon it would all really begin.

15

Judgment

A few days later, I learned that despite how powerful and influential Mr. March was and despite how good his attorney was, they couldn't put off Kiera's court hearing again. With only a week left before school began, she would have to go to court. No one discussed it in front of me, but I overheard enough to know the details, and by now, I understood that both Mrs. Caro and Mrs. Duval knew everything. In fact, Mrs. Duval apologized to me one day when I was sitting out on the patio that faced the pool, reading. Without my asking, she brought me a glass of Mrs. Caro's famous lemonade.

"Thank you very much, Mrs. Duval," I said, surprised. I started to drink, expecting her to leave, but she stood there looking out at the cabana. I could tell that she wanted to say something, and I waited.

"When you were first brought here," she began, "we all thought some organization had chosen you or singled you out for a special opportunity because of your accident and terrible loss and that Mrs. March had volunteered to take you in. She and Mr. March have done many wonderful charitable things. No one told us what or who caused the accident you and your mother suffered. We had some suspicions, but no one thought it was necessary for us to know the truth, so no one asked any questions."

I didn't say anything.

She shook her head. "If we had known the truth, we would have treated you better when you first arrived."

"You treated me just fine, Mrs. Duval. Everyone has."

"Not as fine as we would have if we had known how you lost your mother and who was responsible," she declared, and left.

I appreciated what she had told me, but I was worried that it would now cause even more friction between Kiera and me, especially now that her court hearing was scheduled. I felt the way Mama had always felt when she told me she was waiting for the second shoe to drop.

"What does that mean?" I had asked her.

"It means that when the second shoe drops, the whole ceiling comes down on you," she had told me. "The problem is, it doesn't happen right away, so you're always waiting for it, and that's nerve-wracking. That's the way my life has been with your miserable father. Every time the phone rings or someone comes to the door, I expect trouble."

Maybe that was why she had hated answering the phone and always made me look out the window to see who it was when someone came to the door before she would open it. I wished I had someone to do all that for me now, run interference. I had no doubt that the second shoe was about to drop.

Two days later, the Marches went to court. I practically locked myself away in my suite, reading, working on calligraphy, and watching television. The minutes went by like hours and the hours like days. Finally, a little before six o'clock, I heard footsteps in the hallway. I heard Kiera's door slam closed, and then I heard the recognizable *click-clack* of Mrs. March's stiletto heels on the tile floor as she headed in my direction.

"Well, that's over for now," Mrs. March said as she entered. I shut off the television. She came all the way into the sitting room and stood there looking at me. "The judge put her on probation, but only if she goes to serious therapy. If she doesn't go, she loses her driver's license indefinitely, so you know she'll go. What she'll get out of it is anyone's guess.

"I just don't want to think about it anymore," she continued. "Donald will handle the arrangements with the therapist. This is what we've come to in this country. A child will listen to a therapist but not her own parents. At least, that is what the judge believes. I can't say he's wrong."

I could see that she was waiting for me to say something, but I didn't know what I was supposed to say. *Good? That's all the punishment she gets? What?*

"I'm telling you all this so she doesn't tell you that the judge decided she was not at fault or something," Mrs. March continued. "She will probably tell her friends that, the ones who know the truth, but you should know different. I don't imagine any of this makes you feel any better, Sasha."

I realized that she thought I wanted to see Kiera get

a far more severe punishment. It certainly wouldn't have bothered me if she had, but on the other hand, it wouldn't have brought back my mother. At this point, I really didn't care. I didn't like her, and I didn't expect that any therapist would, either. He or she would have to have a magic wand to turn Kiera into a different person, turn her into someone who wasn't selfish and spoiled.

"Let's just concentrate on happy new things, okay, Sasha?" Mrs. March said. She smiled, looked around the sitting room as if she was worried that something had been changed, and then left.

Kiera said nothing to me about the judge's orders. In fact, she made more effort to avoid me, often finding excuses not to be at the table for dinner and then getting herself away from the house as much as possible so that we wouldn't even cross each other's path. I did learn that Mr. March had forbidden her to have any friends over to party. However, I wasn't sure whether he did that as a punishment or out of concern for me. Ever since Kiera had given me her logic for defending herself, a logic that essentially blamed me and Mama for being there in the rain, I imagined that she used the same argument with her father and maybe even with the judge. At least I was sure the judge hadn't accepted her excuse.

Perhaps Mr. March had ordered Kiera to avoid me so as to avoid any more conflict. After all, not only was I still there, but I had been enrolled in her school. She could no longer barge in to tell me her father was going to throw me out. I was sure that she was upset about that, as well as what happened the day after I completed my calligraphy of *mother.*

I brought it down to dinner the following evening, an evening when I was sure that Mr. March was going to be there. Kiera was there, too, this time. She looked as if she was going to burst out laughing when I arrived carrying the framed calligraphy, but Mr. March's exclamation of "Wow!" stopped her dead in her tracks. He rose and came to me to take it and hold it up.

"Isn't this something?" he asked Mrs. March.

She smiled. "Amazing."

"You know," he said, still holding my calligraphy and looking at it, "this gives me an idea for something. I'm doing this co-development deal with some South Koreans. We should do a logo in calligraphy." He smiled at me. "Maybe we'll hire you to do it, Sasha."

I didn't know what to say. He laughed and handed the calligraphy back to me.

"No," I said, handing it back. "I brought this as a gift for you and Mrs. March."

"Oh, how sweet," Mrs. March said.

"It'll look good in the entertainment center," Mr. March said. "Thank you."

He took it back with him to his seat and set it aside.

"How can you hang that up in the house? I don't know what it's even supposed to be," Kiera said. "No one will."

"We've got a number of works of art that few can figure out in this house that your mother bought," Mr. March said, laughing. "But at least we do know what this means," he said, lifting the calligraphy.

"What?" Kiera demanded.

"Sasha?" Mr. March said, looking at me.

"It means *mother,*" I said. *"Love."*

Kiera looked as if she had swallowed an apple whole for a moment and then began to stab at her salad. I took my seat and, during most of our dinner, answered questions that Mr. and Mrs. March asked about calligraphy. It was actually the happiest and most pleasant dinner I had had at the March house. Afterward, Mr. March asked me to follow him to the entertainment center to help choose the wall space for my art. Kiera went directly up to her room.

The day before school was to begin was the last day that Sheila Toby, my physical therapist, came to the house. By now, I was doing twenty laps in the indoor pool. Toward the end of the session, Mrs. March came in to watch, and when I got out of the pool, she handed me my towel and said, "That was terrific, Sasha. I bet you can do ten laps in our outdoor Olympic-size pool now, just like Alena could do before she got sick."

Before I could say anything, she turned to Sheila Toby to compliment her on the job she had done with me.

"It wasn't hard working with a young girl who is so cooperative and determined," Sheila said.

"Exactly. She starts the ninth grade tomorrow," Mrs. March said. "Come, let me give you your check," she told Sheila, and they left together.

I dried myself and dressed and then went outside to walk over to the lake. I was still limping, but I had no pain and did feel much stronger. I probably could swim those ten laps Mrs. March wanted me to swim one day, I thought, but I felt conflicted about it. Almost everything she had done for me and wished for me were things she had done and wished for Alena.

I imagined that was only normal for a mother who had lost her daughter and had someone else wearing her things and staying in her room. There was no way for her to look at me and not think of Alena, but that also told me that as long as I lived there, I wouldn't be Sasha. I wouldn't be my mother's daughter. No matter what Mr. and Mrs. March did for me, I thought, the moment I could leave and be on my own, I would.

Did that make me ungrateful? Did it make me as self-centered as Kiera? Whenever I thought that, I had to remind myself of what my private nurse in the hospital, Jackie Knee, had told me. I could never be ungrateful, because they could never do enough for me.

I sat on the dock and dangled my feet over the water. The breeze drew ripples in the surface of the lake. I saw water bugs navigating through some floating leaves and blades of grass. The rowboats tied to the dock bobbed and swayed gently, and on the far end of the lake, those terns I had seen sailed what seemed to be inches above the water before lifting toward the tops of the trees.

Tomorrow, I would return to school. I'd be back in a classroom but sitting among boys and girls who came from wealthy families. When they looked at me, would they immediately see how poor and lost I had been, despite my living now in the March house? Not my tutor, my physical therapist, my clothes and shoes, my manicured fingernails and styled hair—none of it could disguise the pain of the past and the loss I had suffered. If anything, I'd be more of a curiosity than any other new student would be. *How did this one get here?* they would surely wonder. *She doesn't belong here. She belongs out there.*

Despite what Mrs. Kepler said, would I look inadequate? Would my voice falter and crack when I was called upon to answer questions aloud? Would I do so badly on tests that I would quickly become the class dunce? And when they all talked about their possessions, their family travels, their rich parents, and brothers and sisters who might be in expensive colleges, fashions and styles, famous people they had met and seen, shows they had gone to and were going to go to, what would I do? What would I say?

My silence would reveal everything. No matter how well Mrs. March dressed me, despite my being brought to the school in a limousine every day and living in a bigger house than any of them, they would recoil and whisper, "She's an imposter. She doesn't belong here. She's not really one of us."

If I thought I had been lonely during my final days at my last school, what did I think I'd be at this one? Lonely would probably be a choice I would take rather than what I would find now. Wouldn't it have been better, wiser, for Mrs. March to enroll me in an ordinary public school? The other students wouldn't seem so superior. I'd be more comfortable. Why hadn't she thought of that?

And then there was Kiera, waiting and watching, hoping for me to fail. If I did something wrong or did poorly in class, she would pounce on her mother. I could almost hear her claiming, "This is embarrassing, Mother. She's dragging me down with her. You're making us the laughingstock of the school. Put her in a public school, at least."

I certainly wouldn't argue about it. I half hoped that was exactly what would happen. Of course, I expected that when any of the other students went to Kiera to ask about me, she would tell them that I was her mother's charity case, a girl from the streets, homeless, carrying some contagious disease. I could see her whispering in ears, especially the ears of the other girls in my class. She would sabotage me anyway. What chance did I have to succeed? Why even bother to try?

When I heard her say my name, I thought I was thinking about her so hard that I had imagined it, but she said it again, and I turned around to see her standing there. The sight of her startled me, and I got right to my feet.

"What do you want?" I asked her.

"What do I want? I want you to disappear," she said, and then smirked. "But that's not going to happen."

"So? What do you want?"

"Chill out," she said, and walked to the edge of the dock to look down at the rowboats. "I used to take my sister for rides," she said. "Especially when she first got sick."

Was she going to invite me to go for a ride? Maybe to drown me?

She turned to face me. "I've had two sessions with my therapist. Don't try to look surprised. I know Mother has told you everything."

"I'm not surprised that you're seeing a therapist, but I am surprised that you're telling me," I said.

"It wasn't my idea."

"Whose idea was it?" I asked, expecting her to say it was her mother's.

"My therapist's."

"The therapist's? Why?"

"It's part of my therapy, something I have to do."

"What is?"

"Talking to you. Not to get you to forgive me or any-thing like that," she added quickly.

"Why, then?"

"I told you. It's part of my therapy. I don't understand half of it myself, but if I don't do it . . ." She took a breath. "If I don't do it, he says the therapy won't work. Whatever that means. It could mean I would have to return to court, and then who knows?"

"What do you want from me?"

"Nothing. Just . . . I'll just talk to you," she said. She turned to walk away, then stopped and turned back. "Not that many people know about us, about what happened. I mean, what really happened. Just a couple of my very close girlfriends know. I'd like to keep it that way."

"What does that mean?"

"Don't you understand anything? I mean, keep your mouth shut in school. Just don't talk about it. No one has to know anything."

"They're going to want to know why I'm here, aren't they? They'll ask questions. They'll see that I come from a different world."

"They probably would. That's why I told Mother how hard this was going to be for me and that I wasn't going back to school unless she did something. Daddy agreed, and they made up a story about you."

"What story?"

"You're the daughter of one of my cousins who was killed in a car accident. My mother, who is a walking soap opera, wanted to take you in, and so you're here. That way, no one will know you were homeless and sleeping in a carton."

"Why didn't your mother ever tell me this?"

"She waits until the last moment for anything. She'll tell you about it tonight. We agree that it will make things easier for both of us." She started to turn and stopped again. "But I'm not driving you to school, and don't expect me to hang out with you there."

"I don't think there's anything I expected less," I said.

"Ha ha. Aren't you hilarious," she said, and walked off.

I smiled.

It was as if she had really been listening to my thoughts and had heard my fears.

Maybe I would do well at this school.

I sat on the dock again to watch the bugs and the birds and the ripples and the trees and all the clouds that floated softly across the blue sky like great white birds migrating to another horizon.

Just like me.

16

Another Horizon

Mr. March wasn't at dinner. He had a dinner meeting in San Francisco. Kiera obviously had not told her mother that she had revealed the story the Marches had created about me. When we were all seated, Mrs. March told Mrs. Duval to wait in the kitchen. She said she would let her know when to begin serving our dinner. Then she folded her hands on the table, looked down at them, and began.

"Both Mr. March and I have decided that it would be easier for both of you, but especially for you, Sasha," she said, raising her head to look at me, "if the other students in the school were not completely aware of your situation."

I looked at Kiera. She smiled and looked down.

"Situation?"

"What I mean to say is that it would be easier for you to assimilate if they all just assumed that you were part of our family. Which is something I am hoping you will actually become someday soon," she quickly added. "Anyway, for now, it would be better if you told your classmates that you were Kiera's cousin on Donald's side. That side is so mixed up no one would not believe it; not that many people know the details concerning his family."

"Don't forget the Chinese part, Mother," Kiera said.

"Please, Kiera, don't interrupt," Mrs. March said sharply. She turned back to me. "The story Kiera is referring to is simple. One of Donald's half brothers married a Chinese woman. You were born, and everything was fine until they were both killed in a car accident. That's when you came to live with us. Now, tell me, where have you visited outside California?"

"Nowhere," I said.

"Your story won't pass gas, Mother," Kiera sang.

"Kiera. You're not helping."

"All right, then," Mrs. March said. "Where have you been in California?"

"My father once took us to Santa Barbara, but I barely remember it."

"Wow, Santa Barbara," Kiera said.

Mrs. March glared at her. "That's fine. That's perfect. You'll just say that's where you had lived. If anyone wants more detail, you just tell him or her that it's too sad for you to talk about it. That should work."

"But what about my teachers, the principal?" I asked. "Don't they know the truth?"

"Dr. Steiner, the principal, knows, but no one else does or will. I can assure you of that."

"Unless she tells them," Kiera muttered, nodding at me.

"Why should she do that?" Mrs. March smiled at me.

"We just want you to succeed and be comfortable and happy at school, Sasha. Okay? You understand?"

"Yes," I said, and then suddenly thought, *I'm betraying Mama again, pretending she never existed.* "But I don't like lying," I added.

"Oh, please. Give us a break," Kiera said. "I can just imagine the things you told people when you were living on the street."

"That was different."

"Right. It's always different when you do it," she said. "I use the same excuse when I'm caught."

"I don't mean it to be an excuse. You just don't understand," I told her.

"That's the first thing you've said that makes any sense," she replied. "Who would understand?"

"Stop. Let's not talk about this anymore," Mrs. March said. "She understands, and that's that." She called for Mrs. Duval.

At first, I was happy when Kiera told me the idea about what other students and my teachers would be told about me, but now that I heard it from Mrs. March, I was more nervous about it. I was entering my new school life on a raft of lies. I'd have to be very careful about what I said to anyone about my past, where I had been, what I had been doing. One slip, and I would fall out of the raft and into the sea of turmoil that raged around someone like me.

Mrs. March was eager to change the subject. During the remainder of our dinner, she went on and on about how wonderful it was going to be for me at this new school.

"Are you getting her out of PE, Mother? I don't expect she can play any sport with that limp."

"She certainly can swim better than you can," Mrs. March said. "She'll do fine. Her teacher will be understanding."

"Miz Raymond? The only thing she understands is a vibrator."

"Kiera!" Mrs. March screamed.

"I don't think she has innocent ears, Mother. Look where she's been."

"I don't want that kind of talk at the dinner table. Your father is going to hear about this." She glared at her again and then turned to me and smiled. "Did you learn how to play an instrument when you were at your old school, Sasha?"

"Yeah, she played the lanyards, remember?"

"Kiera."

"No," I said. "We didn't have any instrumental music classes."

"Well you will here. You'll be in the senior high band. Alena played the clarinet."

"You're going to give her that, too?" Kiera asked.

"If she wants to play the clarinet, it would be foolish to let it just rot away, Kiera. No one stopped you from learning how to play an instrument."

"Yeah, right, the school band. There's nothing more appetizing than watching kids wipe their spit off mouthpieces."

"Don't listen to her. The band is highly regarded and goes on trips and is often asked to play at public events."

"Whoop-ti-doo," Kiera muttered. "You forgot to tell her she can wear the band uniform. There was nothing I hated more."

"I know you'll enjoy playing the clarinet, Sasha," Mrs. March insisted. "It will be wonderful hearing that sound in this house again. And with your artistic talent, you might consider joining the theater group and working on sets, too."

"She'd be better as an actress," Kiera said.

"Is that how you got your training?" I asked her. She actually reddened, especially after Mrs. March laughed.

"Alena could give it back to you just like that, too," Mrs. March told her.

Kiera pressed her lips together hard. Her face puffed up and looked as if it might explode. She pushed her plate away from her and stood up. "I have things to do," she announced, and walked out.

"If your father was here, you'd remember to ask to be excused, Kiera," Mrs. March shouted after her. Kiera did not respond. "He'll hear about this, too," she added. I heard Kiera pounding the steps on her way up the stairway.

Mrs. March shook her head, and we continued eating. It took her a while to calm down, and then she talked more about the school and how sad it was that Alena never got to graduate.

"When you arrive at the school tomorrow, go directly to the principal's office," she told me after we finished dinner. She walked with me to the stairway. "Grover will be waiting for you right outside after breakfast, and he'll be at the school precisely at the end of the school day. I'll be waiting to hear all about your day."

I nodded and turned to go up the stairway, but she reached out to stop me.

"Don't let Kiera's silly remarks disturb you, and don't be nervous, Sasha. You're going to do fine." She released my arm and smiled. "I always loved the first day of school. There's such excitement, such expectation. Go to sleep early," she added. "I'll be there to make sure you get up early enough." She looked up the stairway. "Half the year, I'm banging on Kiera's door to get her up."

I started up the stairway again.

"Oh," she said. "I'll have a wonderful surprise for you. I'll have it with me in the morning."

"What?"

"Well, it wouldn't be a surprise if I told you, now, would it?" she said. She smiled and walked away.

What would it be? More clothes? Shoes? Jewelry? Gadgets? Or a special lunch on the beach to celebrate my finishing my first week at school? I never thought I'd see the day when I would be so disinterested in all of that. How different I was from Kiera. She never saw a day when she wasn't interested in all of that.

Her door was closed as I passed her room, but she must have been listening for me, because the moment I entered mine, she was right behind me. I turned as she closed my door.

"What do you want?" I asked.

"Rules," she said.

"Rules? What rules?"

"Rules for you regarding me," she replied with her right hand on her hip. "I told you that Mother was going to tell you the way my parents were explaining you to everyone at the school, but that didn't include my rules."

I folded my arms and squinted at her. "I didn't think you followed any rules," I said and she laughed.

"You really are a scrappy street kid."

"Stop saying that."

"Okay, rule one. Never tell any of your little ninth-grade friends anything about me. I don't mean just about the accident. I mean anything you see here or hear here, especially. I'm never to be a topic of discussion between you and the other infants."

"That's easy. You're the most uninteresting person I've ever met. I won't be talking about you. There's nothing much to say."

"Rule two," she said, ignoring me. "Don't dare come over to me in the cafeteria or if I'm outside eating to ask for anything. My friends already know what I think of my so-called cousin coming to live with us. As far as I'm concerned, you don't exist. You're not there."

"That works for me," I said.

"Rule three. Do not come home blabbing about anything you see me do, especially if I have someone in my car with me after school. My father has forbidden it for now, but he'll change his mind about it soon.

"Rule four," she added quickly, to prevent any comment I might have about that. "Don't dare ever mention to anyone that I'm in therapy."

"I imagine most people who know you probably expect that you are," I said.

She glared at me and then smiled like someone who

had just discovered a big secret. "How do we know how old you really are?"

"What?"

"Maybe you're stunted or something, and you're really seventeen or eighteen."

"You mean because I seem to be as smart as you are? That's easy. You're not mentally seventeen."

"Keep it up, but remember this. Don't break any of my rules, or you'll be sorrier than you are."

She left, and I stood there for a few moments looking at the closed door. Alena couldn't have been happy to have her as an older sister, I thought. I went into my sitting room to watch television and get my mind off Kiera and the next day. I did go to bed early, but I didn't fall asleep for a long time. Would I be able to pull off the story Mr. and Mrs. March had created about me? That, plus wondering whether or not Mrs. Kepler was right about my readiness, was enough to keep me tossing and turning. Finally, I fell asleep, but I slept so deeply that if it weren't for Mrs. March shaking me in the morning, I wouldn't have gotten up in time. She looked more excited than I was.

"Although you're much older than Alena was when she first went to school, I feel as if it's the same sort of morning. She was such an independent little girl. She didn't want me to come along. 'I'll be just fine, Mother,' she told me. 'It isn't necessary for you to be there.' Can you imagine a five-year-old saying that? She never knew, but I was there watching her from a little distance to be sure she was all right.

"Well, don't worry," she continued, bringing my uniform

in from the closet. "I won't be following you. I'm absolutely positive you'll be fine. Come right down to breakfast as soon as you're dressed. Now, I've got to see if Kiera is up. Just because her father has permitted her to drive, she'll wait until the last minute for everything. I'll be waiting for you in the breakfast dining area," she said, and left.

I washed and dressed and fixed my hair quickly and then hurried down to breakfast.

"Was Kiera up?" I asked, taking my seat and seeing that she wasn't there.

For a moment, I thought Mrs. March hadn't heard me, she was that deep in thought. But she had.

"Surprise of surprises. She wasn't only up and ready, but she was on her way out. Seems she and a few of her friends decided to have breakfast on the way to school."

Mrs. Duval came in with orange juice, Mrs. Caro's home-baked rolls, and a tray of jams.

"Mrs. Caro's preparing your scrambled eggs just the way you like them," she told me. I had mentioned once that I liked them with cheese, and she often made them for me that way. "Mrs. Caro says a good breakfast is the best way to start at a new school," Mrs. Duval added.

"I agree. I'm sure Kiera and her friends won't have half as good a breakfast as you will," Mrs. March said.

I started to drink my juice. "Is Mr. March back?"

"No," she said. "He had to stay over an extra day."

I thought she was angry about it, but then she smiled. "That's okay," she said. "I'm busy today with charity committee meetings, a lunch at the golf club, and then some quick shopping at Saks in Beverly Hills before I rush home to hear about your first day. Here," she said, reaching down to take something out of her purse. It was a cell phone. "This is yours. My number is right here already," she explained, showing me. "You simply press one, and it calls me. So, if you need anything, don't hesitate."

"Thank you," I said, taking it.

"That's a very sophisticated cell phone. It takes pictures, but I'm sure you know all about those things."

"No. We never had one," I said, looking at it.

"Oh. Here's the booklet for it," she said, and gave it to me. "But for now, all you need to know is how to call me if you need me."

"This is the surprise you promised?"

"No. That's waiting in the limousine," she said.

Now I was really curious.

Mrs. Duval brought in my scrambled eggs and stood back to watch me gobble them up. My nervousness made me hungry. Afterward, when I went out to get into the limousine, I saw that Mrs. Duval and Mrs. Caro had joined Mrs. March to watch me go. Grover opened the door for me, and I looked back at them.

"Good luck, dearie," Mrs. Caro called.

"Yes, good luck," Mrs. Duval said.

Mrs. March stood, smiling but looking like someone who was smiling through tears.

I got into the limousine. All alone in the big automobile, I felt even smaller and more helpless than ever. Grover got in, looked back at me, winked, and then drove us away.

Then I turned and saw the gift on the seat. Slowly, I unwrapped it.

Mrs. March had bought me a leather book bag, which she had filled with pens and pencils, pads, paper clips, almost anything any student would need. On the outside of the bag, embossed in gold, she had my name, but because of the fictional biography, it read "Sasha March."

She had managed to justify changing my last name. Now I wondered if she would find a way to change my first name.

17
School

No one seemed to pay any particular attention to me when I stepped out of the limousine, even with a uniformed driver holding my door. Perhaps to the students at that school, it was nothing out of the ordinary to see one of them dropped off in a limousine. From the looks on their faces as they hurried into the building, shouted to each other, embraced, shook hands, and even kissed, I could see that most of the students knew one another. Except for the ones coming into seventh grade from elementary school, I wondered how many new students like me there were.

Since they didn't take much notice of my limousine, I wondered if they would take much notice of my limp. Even though it had been a while, I was still quite conscious of it. I walked as if the bottom of my right foot was stepping on hot coals.

When I entered, I saw the sign on the marble wall pointing to the principal's office. Everything looked immaculate, from the polished tile floors to the gleaming windows

and the glittering desktops I could see through open classroom doors. It wasn't a very big school lobby, so the chatter
reverberated all around me. A small blond boy, probably a
seventh-grader, bumped into me and then turned to flash
an excited smile, apologizing. Before I could respond, he
was gone. I walked slowly to the principal's office.

The front desk was already crowded with other students
who had questions and problems and two young women,
dressed almost as stylishly as Mrs. March, were answering
questions and passing out papers. I stepped up behind the
last student in line.

The lady on the right saw me and whispered something
to the other woman. Then she went around to the counter
gate and beckoned. I wasn't sure she was beckoning to me,
but she kept doing it until I pointed to myself and she nodded. All of the students waiting suddenly paused to look at
me as I went up to the gate.

"You're Sasha March, right?"

"Yes." I imagined she had been told that I was someone
with Asian features.

"I'm Mrs. Knox. Dr. Steiner wanted me to bring you to
her as soon as you arrived. Come through," she said, stepping back.

I followed her to the principal's office door. She smiled
at me and knocked.

"Yes," we heard.

She opened it enough to peer in and told Dr. Steiner I
was here.

"Send her right in, Louise," I heard her say. Mrs. Knox
stepped back and held the door open for me.

Dr. Steiner was a stout woman with a heavy bosom. She wore a dark brown skirt suit with a frilly-collared blouse. She had curly, gray-stained dark brown hair and looked about five foot two at the most. Except for lipstick, she wore no makeup, not even to cover what looked like tiny freckles or age spots on the crests of her cheeks. She was standing behind her desk when I entered and for a few moments simply stared at me the way someone would study a stranger to see if he or she was what was expected.

"Welcome to Pacifica High School, Sasha," she said, and nodded at the chair in front of her desk. "I'm Dr. Steiner."

I sat. I didn't realize it, but I was clutching my new book bag against my stomach as if I was afraid someone would steal it. It reminded me of the way Mama had worn her purse in front to avoid it being stolen when she walked through the streets. Dr. Steiner looked at the way I was holding my book bag, smiled, and sat. I relaxed my grip.

"I imagine you're a little frightened about entering a new school, but I want you to know you needn't be. I have a wonderful, bright, and caring staff working here. You'll discover we're like one big family," she said.

When she spoke, she sounded a little nasal, like someone with a bad cold. Her grayish blue eyes widened at the ends of her sentences. She had her left hand palm down on the desk, but she held her right hand up with her index finger out and pumped it up and down to emphasize what she was saying. When I didn't say anything, she continued.

"I've spoken with your tutor, Mrs. Kepler, and she is confident that you are ready for the ninth-grade work ahead of you. I have a high regard for her opinion, so I'm sure she's correct. This is your class schedule," she said, lifting a card no bigger than a pack of cigarettes. "Your classes and your teachers' names are on it. On the back is our motto." She turned it over and read, "Pacifica High School, where everyone strives to be all he or she can be."

She leaned forward.

"Despite your recent history, Sasha, there is no reason for you not to be all you can be. I want you to know that I personally will do all that I can to help you achieve that, and I feel confident that your teachers here will do so, as well. They're a dedicated bunch.

"Now, then," she continued, sitting back. "I promised Mrs. March that I would personally see if you had any problems and personally escort you to your homeroom. There is a very nice young lady classmate of yours, Lisa Dirk, who has volunteered to be your big sister for today. She has the same schedule you have and will show you around, okay?"

I could see that it was bothering her that I hadn't spoken.

"Is there anything you'd like to ask me before we go to your homeroom and meet Mr. Hoffman?"

"No," I said.

"No? Well, I'm sure there will be things as you get started, and if you can't get the answers from your teachers or other students, you come knocking on my door, okay?"

I nodded.

"I have been told you are artistic. I know that Mr. Longo, our art teacher for the senior high, will be excited about that."

"I don't know if I'm artistic."

"Sasha," she said, leaning toward me and smiling, revealing tiny teeth. "You will quickly discover that at this school, modesty is a disadvantage. Take pride in what you can do. Of course," she added, "many of our students take pride even though they can't do. I don't know all that much about you, of course, but I'm willing to bet that self-confidence doesn't come easy to you right now. I hope that will change." Her eyes narrowed. She sounded and looked as if it had better change. "Okay, then, come along," she said, rising. "Let's get you started on a wonderful school year. I'll take you right to your locker first and give you the combination."

She reached out for me as she came around her desk and surprised me by putting her arm around my shoulders. When she opened the door, I saw that the students who had been in the outer office were gone. Mrs. Knox and her associate both turned and looked at us with a surprised smile. Dr. Steiner still had her arm around me.

"Mrs. Knox. Mrs. Frazer, this is Sasha March, our newest student. Please make her feel at home. We're going to her locker and then to Mr. Hoffman's homeroom," she told them. "Man the fort."

They both nodded and looked at me as if I, not Kiera March, were the rich man's daughter. Was Dr. Steiner giving me this special treatment because of Mrs. March or because of what Mrs. March had told her about me? Whichever reason it was, I didn't feel good about it. I hoped this would be the first and last time I'd be singled out for any privileged treatment. It wasn't that long ago since I was last in school, and I remembered all too well how students would resent others whom their teachers favored.

When we stepped into the lobby, it was empty and very quiet. So was the hallway we entered. Where had everyone gone so quickly? Dr. Steiner saw the confused look on my face.

"The bell for beginning of homeroom has rung, but the bells don't ring in my office," she said. "I have enough outside noise as it is. Loitering in the hallways after the bell rings will get you into detention as quickly as anything else."

I couldn't help but wonder if Kiera had made it to school on time. After Dr. Steiner showed me my locker and gave me the combination, we continued down the long corridor. We walked to the last room on that wing of the building. When we entered, the dozen or so students all turned to look. Mr. Hoffman, a man Mama would have called as slim as a butter knife, stopped what he was reading and looked at us.

"Mr. Hoffman, here is your new student, Sasha March. Miss Dirk is to be her big sister today."

A chubby, dark-haired, light-skinned African American girl stood. She looked to Mr. Hoffman, who nodded, and then she came around the end of her row to us. She wasn't much taller than I was, and if it were not for her full, round, bloated face, she could be very pretty, I thought. She had unique-colored eyes that were like a very dark blue. Everyone else continued to watch us as if we were about to begin some traditional ritual of greeting.

"Hi. I'm Lisa," she said, extending her hand. I took it and nodded. "You're sitting right behind me," she added loudly, and the boy who was sitting there stood up and moved to the back of the row.

Dr. Steiner watched it all unfold and smiled with satisfaction.

"You're in good hands now, Sasha. Everyone be sure to make Sasha feel at home," she said, her voice, though still with that nasal quality, sounding very authoritative. She nodded again at Mr. Hoffman, handed me my class-schedule card, and left.

I followed Lisa to my seat.

"Welcome, Sasha. I was just explaining that this homeroom period will be extended so we can go through some of the rule changes at the school," Mr. Hoffman told me, and then said, "Number three."

The only rule change that made the students around me groan was the prohibition against cell phones being on during classes. Texting during class would result in suspension.

The redheaded boy across from me leaned over to whisper. "That's because Jean Trombly was caught cheating. Someone was texting her the answers on the test."

I just widened my eyes. And then I realized that the phone Mrs. March had give me was on. I quickly dug into my book bag, took it out, and shut it off. The phone made a musical sound as it went off, and everyone looked at me, most smiling and laughing. Mr. Hoffman didn't crack a smile. I shoved the phone back into my book bag quickly.

"Number four," he said sharply, and they all turned back to look at him. He went through five more rule changes before finishing.

When the bell to end homeroom finally rang, Lisa spun around quickly.

"Let me see your class schedule," she said. I handed it to her. "Oh, good, you're in instrumental music next. I was afraid you weren't."

"Instrumental music?" I hadn't looked at the card. She handed it back to show me.

"Room fourteen," she said. "It's a bit of a walk. What instrument do you play?"

"I don't," I said.

She tilted her head and pressed her lips deeper into their corners. "Weren't you playing an instrument in the school you attended before you came here?"

"No. We didn't have a school band."

"We have an orchestra. Not a band," she corrected, and I followed her out. "We have three full minutes between classes, so being late is considered serious. Two times late for classes will result in one day's detention. And you don't want to be in detention here. Mr. McWaine runs it, and he doesn't let students do anything for the whole hour. No reading, no homework, nothing but sitting up straight with your hands clasped. Not that I've ever been in detention," she added. "Have you?"

"No."

"You might get away with it because of your limp."

"I don't want to get away with anything because of my limp," I said sharply, but she didn't notice my annoyance, or if she did, she ignored it.

"That's the way to the cafeteria," she said, nodding to our left. "On Tuesdays and Wednesdays, they have pizza. It's thick and full of cheese, and you can ask for pepperoni to be put on it if you like. I love pepperoni. The juniors and seniors have their classes mostly down on this end," she continued. Then she leaned in to say, "Everyone's going to be asking me all sorts of questions about you. For starters, who was Chinese, your father or your mother?"

"My mother."

"Did you eat with chopsticks? I hate it. It takes too long to eat. My fingers are too fat and clumsy, anyway."

"We didn't eat with chopsticks at home," I said. "But always in an Asian restaurant. You shouldn't eat fast, anyway. It's not good for you."

"Oh, are you one of those health nuts?"

"No," I said. "I'm just nuts."

She looked at me and laughed. "You lived in Santa Barbara?"

I nodded.

"I've been there, of course. It's very nice. Do you miss it?"

"I miss a lot," I said sharply. I did, of course, only it had mostly to do with Mama.

She saw the tears in my eyes. "Oh, let's hurry. We've only got another thirty seconds." She began to walk faster. Keeping up with her made me limp more dramatically, and for some reason, I felt pain in my hip.

Just before we turned into the music room, she paused and said, "The music teacher's name is Denacio. Everyone loves him, but they still call him Mussolini. You know who that was?"

"Yes."

"Then you know not to fool around in here," she said, and we entered.

Nothing could have made me more curious. Why was I assigned to instrumental music? Didn't I have a choice?

Room fourteen was a bigger classroom, but the class was half the size of my homeroom. Mr. Denacio was tall and lean, with coal-black hair and a coal-black thick mustache. He had piercing ebony eyes as well. He had his jacket off and the sleeves of his white shirt rolled up to his elbows.

"Let's not waste time," he said when the bell rang. "I want to see how many of you really practiced over the summer, and don't think any of you can fool me about that."

The students around me went to their instruments. I stood there, feeling foolish.

"Okay," he said, nodding at me. "Sasha March?"

"Yes."

"I'm Mr. Denacio. I understand you're here to learn how to play the clarinet."

I stared dumbly. Before I could say anything, he reached back and picked up an instrument case.

"It's a pretty good piece," he said. "Just take your seat over there." He nodded at an empty desk on my right. "I'll get to you in a little while."

"I never played the clarinet," I said.

"No kidding. That's why you're here to learn, Miss March. Look around you. None of these geniuses knew anything much about the instruments they play now when they began here. This is why we call it an educational institution."

No one laughed, but everyone smiled. He handed me the instrument case, and I went over to my desk. Lisa was at the rear of the classroom, taking out a flute. I opened the case and saw the inscription on the inside cover.

Alena March.

Under that was her address, and at the very bottom was a tiny goldplated plaque that read, *We love you. Dad and Mom.*

I closed the case. Why hadn't Mrs. March told me she already had this for me? I had never said I wanted to play the clarinet. Would it be ungrateful of me to refuse?

I watched Mr. Denacio test every student. He complimented only two and told the others they had to make up for ignoring their instruments. Everyone was given something to do, and then he turned to me.

"Now, then," he began, "it just so happens I can use another clarinet in the senior orchestra. Hey, stop looking so worried. You're making me nervous." He finally smiled.

"I'm not nervous. I'm just surprised," I said.

"Surprised? Why?"

"I didn't know this was here waiting for me."

"Oh. Your aunt brought it in last week. She didn't tell you?"

I shook my head

"Well, I guess it is a surprise, then, but a nice surprise, right?"

I looked at the case and shrugged.

"Enthusiastic, I see. Okay, you're what I call a challenge, and why shouldn't I have one the first day of school? Why should anything come easier to me?"

He opened the case and began to show me how to put the clarinet together, set up the reed, and hold the mouthpiece correctly. He told me to hold it between my teeth, pretend to say "doo," and blow.

"That's it," he said. "Blowing long tones will get your abdominal muscles used to the pressure."

I did it again and again, and he smiled.

"That's a pretty good sound. Something tells me I have my new clarinet player," he said. He said it as if he had been waiting for me for a long time.

It gave me chills, because sometimes that was just the way Mrs. March made me feel.

I looked back at Lisa, who lowered her flute and smiled. Maybe it was my imagination, but it looked as if everyone was looking at me and smiling.

It was as if everyone from Dr. Steiner down had been waiting for me, as if they had all known that what would happen some rainy night on the Santa Monica highway would deliver me to this very place.

❦18❦

Fast Learner

"Y ou were a big hit with Mr. Denacio," Lisa said after the bell rang. I put the clarinet in the locker assigned to me. She put away her flute, and we were on our way to English class. "I could tell, because he always looks annoyed when he gets a student to start from scratch. He'd like everyone who enters his class to be concert-ready.

"So tell me the truth," she said almost in a whisper. "You really did play the clarinet at your previous school, right?"

"No. I didn't."

"Then why was an instrument left here for you?"

"It was meant to be a surprise."

She nodded as if she understood why I wasn't telling the truth. "Everybody tells little white lies here," she said.

"I don't."

She smiled coyly again and continued walking silently. I had little opportunity to speak with any of my other classmates until our lunch break. All the time I was with her in my classes and on the way to them, I could see that Lisa was using me to make herself look more important. When we entered the cafeteria, that was even clearer. Students who were eager to learn more about me looked up from their tables in expectation. She took her time deciding where and with whom we should sit and finally decided on a table with three other girls.

We set our books down first, and Lisa introduced me to Charlotte Harris, Jessica Taylor, and Sydney Woods. Charlotte and Jessica had light brown hair cut and styled almost identically. Sydney had auburn hair brushed shoulder-length. I didn't think any of them was particularly pretty, but after Lisa introduced them all to me and me to them, they acted and spoke as if they all had won teenage beauty contests.

Lisa began by telling them as much about me as she knew. I was a little more nervous, because all of them had been to Santa Barbara frequently, and I thought they would be asking me detailed questions about stores and places to go. I waited to hear what they liked about it and quickly agreed.

"Isn't there a place you liked more?" Sydney Woods asked me.

I pretended to think about it and then shook my head. "We didn't go out to eat that much, and my father hated the beach."

That was certainly true about Daddy, I thought. Mama practically had to drag him the few times he did come along, and all he did was complain about hot sand or the water being too cold.

"So, how did you get that limp? Born with it?" Jessica Taylor asked me.

"No, car accident," I said quickly.

While I was eating, I saw Lisa lean over to whisper in her ear. How long was it going to take for everyone in the school to hear the story the Marches had created for me?

"My parents know your aunt and uncle," Charlotte Harris said. "They say they are one of the richest families in Southern California. Is that true?"

"I don't know," I said. "I don't know the other rich families."

Everyone laughed, and when they saw that I didn't mean it to be funny, they looked at each other and laughed harder. Later, that was the information that flew around the school: "Sasha doesn't know the other rich families."

I told myself I didn't care, but who doesn't want to make new friends? Before the day ended, I saw Sydney Woods talking to some of the girls in PE and obviously imitating my limp as she recited my now-famous line: "I don't know the other rich families."

New girls are a threat, I thought—not that I saw myself as prettier or smarter or even simply nicer than the girls in my class. For a while, at least, I was a bit of a mystery to them and the boys. It was practically impossible for me to enter any room or even walk down the hallway to class without being watched and studied. I was even more self-conscious of my limping, and by the time the bell rang to indicate that the last class was over, I felt like a clam that had crawled completely into its shell.

Apparently, Lisa had decided that she would be better off not clinging so closely to me after that day.

"I guess you can get around yourself now, huh?" she asked as we headed toward the parking lot.

I had books in my new book bag and carried my clarinet in my other hand. Mr. Denacio had given me instructions on what to do. He said I had to practice every night for an hour at least and added that he would know if I hadn't.

"Yes, thank you for helping me today," I told Lisa.

She flashed a smile and then hurried to catch up with the other girls. They all laughed as they exited the school. Before I got to the door, Dr. Steiner called to me from the doorway of the principal's office.

"I hear you had a good first day," she said.

I thought, *Yes, I wasn't stoned to death.* I simply looked at her.

"That's what your teachers have been telling me. I didn't speak to Mr. Cohen yet, your history teacher, since you just finished the class, but all of the others think you'll do just fine, and Mr. Denacio is quite impressed. Did you enjoy the day? Was Lisa a good big sister?"

I tried to sound enthusiastic, but I could almost see her brain clicking.

"It's not easy for anyone to start somewhere new," she said, lowering her voice a bit, "but it has to be especially difficult for you, Sasha. I understand, and I'm confident you'll blend in well here. Concentrate on the schoolwork. Everything else will come in due time."

I thanked her and walked out. A few of the girls in my class had been watching us through the door. They rushed to catch up with Lisa and the others. Everyone turned to look my way. Did they think I had complained about them? They weren't laughing. They looked like a coven of witches mumbling curses in my direction. I watched them continue to their cars. Mothers waited in most of the cars, but I saw a few fathers. Grover stood by the limousine waiting for me, so I hurried toward him.

Before I reached him, Kiera caught up with me. Her girlfriend Deidre was with her, as well as one of the boys I had seen at the pool. Kiera deliberately bumped into me, and I turned.

"Oh, sorry, coz," she said. "So how did your day go? Feel like a little fool yet?" She walked off laughing. The boy smiled but turned to see my reaction. I lowered my head and continued to the limousine. Suddenly, it had become my cocoon, and I couldn't wait to be shut away inside.

Mrs. March was waiting for me when we drove up. She came toward us so fast that for a moment, I thought she was going to be the one to open my door and not Grover.

"I couldn't wait to hear how it went," she said when I got out. "I spoke with Dr. Steiner. I was so happy with the good reports about you. Did you like the school, your teachers? Isn't it wonderful?"

"Yes," I said. Anything else might have caused an earthquake. "But you didn't tell me you had brought this clarinet for me."

"Oh. Didn't I mention that? I thought I had. Apparently, Mr. Denacio thinks you could be a natural. I'm so happy for you. I bet you can't wait to go up to start your homework. Alena was like that. Kiera couldn't stand it. No matter what Kiera did or said, she couldn't get Alena to put off her work. She was such a responsible little girl, as I'm sure you are."

For a moment, I wanted to do something that would

change her mind about me, even though she was right. I did want to get right to my homework. I was so happy to have it. After all, it had been a year since I had been asked to do anything for school.

"Did you make any nice friends?" she asked as we entered the house.

"Not yet," I said.

"Oh, I'm sure you will. Mr. March will be calling soon. He was anxious to hear about you, too."

"Was he?"

"Why, of course, Sasha. That school was his precious other child. He takes personal interest in it."

"Oh," I said. I thought he wasn't so interested in me, per se. He wanted to be sure the school lived up to its reputation for excellence. Mrs. March didn't realize the difference, I thought, and I went up to my room, where I did go right at my assignments.

I was so involved in it all that I didn't realize how much time passed. Mrs. March came in to tell me that we would be having dinner soon, but that wasn't the main reason she had come.

"Did you see Kiera at all today?" she asked.

"Yes, at the end of the day."

"Thank goodness for that," she muttered. "I was afraid she had cut school the first day. Last year, she and some friends did that, as if it were some sort of great accomplishment. Her father was furious."

Not furious enough to take away her driving privileges, I thought.

"Do you have any idea where she might have gone after

school? Did she say anything to you? She doesn't answer her cell phone."

I shook my head.

She looked concerned but then shook it off to smile at me. "Well, let's concentrate on you for now. Come down to dinner in ten minutes, and tell me all about your homework. We're not holding up dinner for Kiera," she said, and left.

When I went down, Kiera was still not home, and Mr. March wasn't there, either. It was once again just Mrs. March and me. She asked more questions about school and my teachers, but before I could really answer, she would go on again about Alena and her first days. I thought she was babbling to keep from showing how nervous she was about Kiera still not being home. Finally, just before we were going to have dessert, we heard her come in. Instantly, Mrs. March rose, intending to greet her before she went upstairs, but Kiera surprised her by coming quickly to the dining room.

"Sorry I'm late!" she cried.

"Where have you been? Why didn't you answer your cell phone?" Mrs. March demanded.

"I didn't see you had called until I was on my way home and thought you'd be at dinner, Mother. I was being considerate. See? When I am considerate, you complain."

For a moment, she threw Mrs. March off, but then Mrs. March got right back on track. "Where have you been? Why didn't you come right home after school? Both your father and I told you to do so. You didn't take anyone in your car, did you?"

"Oh, no, and that was such an inconvenience. I had to go with Clarissa in her car so no one would ask me why I couldn't take anyone."

"To where?" Mrs. March practically screamed.

"To Paula Dungan's house. I told you we had all decided to form a homework club."

"What?" Mrs. March looked at me to see if I knew. I said nothing, and she turned back to Kiera. "You never told me such a thing. A homework club?"

"We're seniors, and this is a very important first half of the year, Mother. Most of us will be sending out college applications soon."

For another long moment, Mrs. March just stared at Kiera.

"I'm hungry," Kiera said, and she went to the kitchen doorway to tell Mrs. Duval she was ready to eat. Then she went to her seat and poured herself some water. Mrs. March had still not returned to the table. She stared at her. "What?" Kiera asked.

"You never told me about a homework club."

"I did so. I told you that it was going to be difficult for me, because I have to go to that stupid therapy every Tuesday and Thursday after school. If I don't do well this first half, it's because of that."

Mrs. March returned to the table silently.

Kiera smiled at me. "I bet you haven't even started your homework," she said.

"I'm almost done," I told her.

"She went right to it after school, just like Alena," Mrs. March said, quickly coming to my defense.

Kiera shrugged. "They probably made it easier for her."

"Of course not," Mrs. March said.

Kiera shrugged again. "The kids will be coming here every other Wednesday until I get out of this therapy junk. Then I can have them here two or three days a week." She turned back to me. "I heard you made quite an impression on some of the girls in your class."

"Oh?" Mrs. March said.

"Yes," Kiera said. "She's got them all limping."

She laughed at her own joke just as Mrs. Duval brought in her dinner. Mrs. March sat back, looking as if all of the air had gone out of her lungs. I began to eat my dessert. Kiera was an expert when it came to throwing her mother off, I thought. First, she frustrated her with her responses, and then she went on to talk about things that she knew would interest her mother: what the other girls were wearing, what she had learned about where their parents went for the summer, and who had bought what for their homes.

I began to feel invisible again and asked to be excused.

"I want to finish my homework and practice the clarinet fundamentals," I said. They were like magic words for Mrs. March. I, too, knew how to manipulate her when I wanted to do that, but it didn't make me feel any better to compare myself with Kiera. She looked at me with a mixture of anger and awe. She realized then that I was more than a street girl. I could play on her field. I was a much faster learner than she had expected, and for the first time, I thought she might be afraid of me. I could almost hear her concerns.

For the first time in a long time, since Alena's death, actually, there was real competition in the house for her parents' attention. Soon it might be for their love, as well, and that was more than she could stand.

Maybe, Mama, I thought, *this is how we get our revenge, our justice.*

Why else would I be there?

19

Nightmares

Because I really believed I had seen those things in Kiera's face that night, I began to settle more comfortably into school, as well as into the mansion. I made some acquaintances in my classes, but no one struck me as a possible best girlfriend. Maybe it was because of my limp. Maybe it was because of my looks. Or maybe it was because of the rumors that circulated about me, rumors Kiera probably had planted. Whatever the cause, I felt a gap between me and the other girls, a gap that seemed to be widening and not narrowing with every passing day.

As the first weeks and then months went by, I heard of parties some girls in my classes had, but no one ever invited me to any. I knew there were girls who got together on the weekends and went to movies or to hang out in malls, where they could flirt with boys, but no one had asked me to join them. Sometimes I felt that girls were friendly to me just in the hope that I would invite them to the March house. When they talked about it and I said nothing, they usually drifted away.

Mrs. March continually asked me about my days at school and how I was getting along with the other girls. I tried to sound as upbeat as I could, and she accepted it, either because she believed it or because she wanted to believe it. Reports about my initial work began to flow back to her and Mr. March. When he was home for dinner, he would compliment me about it, and Kiera would either sulk or try to ignore it. What really got to her, I thought, was how quickly I was picking up the skills to play the clarinet. Mr. March was even more impressed than Mrs. March and came to my suite a few times to listen to me practicing.

Kiera tried her best to make my accomplishments sound insignificant, especially after I played my first piece of music just before dinner one night in the living room. She didn't want to listen, but both Mr. and Mrs. March insisted. I tried not to look her way, because her sour expression was enough to make Mr. Denacio himself fumble the notes.

"I can't believe how quickly she learned how to read music," Mr. March said when I finished.

"Maybe she already knew," Kiera suggested. "From her old school."

"We had no orchestra, no band," I said. "The school had major cutbacks in financing, and art and music were dropped."

"We know that to be true," Mr. March said.

"Well, her mother might have taught her stuff," Kiera insisted.

"I don't think so," Mrs. March said, her eyes fixed on me

with such adoration I had to blush. "She had other things on her agenda." She turned to Kiera. "Like survival."

Frustrated, Kiera went into retreat. She didn't say anything more about me or my past. When our first report cards came out and I had all A's, she was practically a candidate for a straitjacket. She had nothing higher than a C and had two C-minuses. Mr. March looked disappointed, but it was Mrs. March who went after her at dinner that night.

"You told me you and your friends formed this homework club for after-school sessions because the first half of your senior year was so important, didn't you?"

"These teachers hate me," Kiera moaned. "They resent us because we're so rich."

Her father looked up. "Why, did someone say something to you that would indicate that?"

"They don't come right out and say it, Daddy. They're too smart for that, but I can see it in their faces."

"That's ridiculous," Mrs. March said. "Every girl and boy in that school comes from a wealthy family. How else could they attend with the tuition being as high as it is? No one would single you out for that, Kiera. It's a pathetic excuse for your failure to care about your work."

"Your mother's right, Kiera," her father said. "If a girl like Sasha can do so well, considering her background, you can, too. I want to see more of an effort from you."

Her face deflated. Her eyes filled with tears. She looked at me and bit down on her upper lip. "It's the therapy!" she cried. "It's driving me nuts. I can't think."

"You could go to prison if you don't follow through on that," her mother said.

Kiera looked to her father, but he didn't disagree.

"Well, you'll just have to put up with me until I'm finished with it, then," she said in the exact manner and tone of a spoiled girl. She went back to her pouting and pecked at her food.

I didn't gloat, but inside I felt good about myself for the first time in a long time. It inspired me to work even harder. I was beginning to enjoy the clarinet, as well, and some nights I practiced for close to two hours. I overheard Kiera complain to her father about the noise, but he told her just to put on her earphones like she did most of the time. That brought a smile to my lips.

Kiera wasn't yet at the point where she would talk to me during the school day, but I did often notice her watching me when I was with other students in the cafeteria. A few times, I ate outside with some of my classmates, and I thought she was going to come over to say something, but she didn't. I thought she was looking at me differently, too. I didn't see the disdain or disrespect as much. It was more as if she was curious about me, which only made me feel even better about myself.

Usually, if she did say anything to me after school, it was sarcastic or biting, but one day, she followed me out and said, "You're hanging around with nerds and losers. If you stop, the other girls might invite you to something." She didn't wait for me to reply. She kept walking to catch up with her friends.

Did I hear right? I wondered. From her tone, it sounded as if she was trying to give me good advice, looking out for my interests. What was she up to now? Had Mr. and Mrs.

March come down on her for not being friendlier to me? Had she been promised something if she was? I couldn't imagine ever trusting her or believing her, and yet there was a part of me that wanted to do just that.

All I should want to do is hate her, I thought. It was easier to hate her when she was so aggressive and arrogant and mean. I hated her for being rich and pretty and popular with her friends, too. However, somehow, no matter how I tried to fight it back, I was beginning to pity her. In her mind, she was losing her father and had already lost her mother. Maybe she was becoming more of an orphan like me.

With all that I was being given materially as well as emotionally now, it was sometimes hard to remember that I was an orphan. One afternoon, whether she had intended it or not, Mrs. March reminded me. As usual, Grover was there to take me home at the end of the school day, but when he opened the rear door for me, I saw Mrs. March sitting there smiling. I was so surprised that I didn't move.

"Get in, silly," she said.

I did, and Grover closed the door. Mrs. March had said nothing the night before or at breakfast to indicate that she would be with Grover. I first thought she was on her way back to the mansion and had timed it so she could detour with the limousine to the school, but that wasn't it.

"I'm taking you to see something," she said.

"Where?"

"You'll see very soon. How was your day?"

I showed her a math test I had taken. I had gotten a ninety-eight, and I had an A on my English essay. She looked at it all and widened her smile.

"Mr. March has gotten to where he's actually bragging about you. I heard him talking to Mrs. Duval yesterday. We're all very proud of your accomplishments in so short a time, Sasha."

"Thank you."

I saw that we were not going in the direction of the mansion.

"Where are we going?" I asked again.

"To see a promise fulfilled," she replied. "Is it true that you might actually be in the spring concert this year?"

"Mr. Denacio mentioned it, but he didn't say for sure," I replied.

She nodded but looked as if she knew something more. "It would be something for a first-year instrumental student to be included in the school's senior orchestra. I knew the clarinet would come naturally to you."

I had to admit that I didn't think I would enjoy playing it as much as I had.

"You deserve your moments of happiness," she told me. "That's what today is about."

She sat back, and we drove on. Soon it became obvious to me where we were heading, and the realization made me tremble in a way I hadn't for some time. Minutes later, we turned into the cemetery and drove as far as we could before Mrs. March and I had to get out and walk the rest of the way to Mama's grave. As we drew closer, I realized why she had brought me.

There on the tombstone was the inscription I had wanted. Under Mama's name and dates, it read, "who showed her daughter a little bit of heaven." And beneath that was the calligraphy for *heaven*. It looked just like Mama's work hanging in the Gravediggers.

Mrs. March stood back and smiled as I stepped up to the stone and touched the engraved words. The engraving certainly made the tombstone special, but as I stood looking at it, I simply couldn't imagine Mama lying below, shut up in the dark, cool earth. Most of the years we had been together, she had felt trapped, trapped by Daddy's betrayals and failure to provide for us as well as he should have, trapped after he had deserted us, and then trapped by our terrible fate. She had certainly trapped herself with her drinking, and now death had trapped her. How could I free her?

"Is it like you wanted it?" Mrs. March asked. Without turning, I nodded. "I'll wait for you in the car, Sasha," she said, and walked away.

I felt my legs weaken and sat on Mama's grave with my forehead just touching the cool headstone.

"Don't worry, Mama," I whispered. "I haven't forgotten you. I'll never forget you, no matter how much they give me or do for me, no matter where I go and what I become. You will always be with me."

I thought I was going to sit there and cry, but I didn't. Instead, I tightened up inside with a resolve that made me feel stronger, harder. I took some deep breaths, and then I kissed the tombstone, rose, and started back to the car.

When I got in, Mrs. March said, "I was hoping this would please you and not make you sad, Sasha."

"Yes, I'm pleased. Thank you, Mrs. March."

She stared at me a moment, looking a bit hurt. What did she expect me to call her, "Mother"?

"Let's go home, Grover," she said, and we drove out of the cemetery.

Neither of us spoke for quite a while. I stared out my window. Just before we were home, she told me that for the first time since I had arrived, she had to go away that coming weekend with Mr. March.

"It's a traditional thing we do this time every year. We meet some of Donald's old friends in San Francisco and go to Carmel. I'll leave very specific instructions with Mrs. Duval, who is quite capable of looking after things, and after you, while I'm gone, and I'll call often."

"I'll be okay," I said.

"Of course you will. Why shouldn't you?"

I thought she might add that Alena had always been okay while she was gone, but she said nothing more. The night before they left, both Mr. and Mrs. March warned Kiera not to take advantage of their absence. Even Mr. March sounded firm and threatening. Kiera kept her head down and didn't come back with any smart remarks. The last few days, she had come home right after school and shut herself in her room, and when she returned from her therapy sessions, she not only shut herself in her room but also refused to come down to dinner.

At first, I thought all of this was her way of playing her parents again. She was hoping to punish them for forcing her to fulfill her obligations to the court and continue the therapy she hated, but she said nothing about it to them when she was at dinner. To my surprise, in fact, she showed them her math and science tests, on which she had received high-B grades.

Mr. March looked very pleased. "This is very good, Kiera," he said. He turned to Mrs. March. "Some people just take a little longer to wake up to what's important."

"Yes," she said, but she didn't look as convinced about any change as he did. "Do keep it up, Kiera."

Because of some change in her schedule, Kiera had a therapy session on the Friday the Marches left for their extended weekend holiday. As usual lately, when Kiera returned, she went directly into her room and asked that her dinner be brought up. I ate alone. Both Mrs. Duval and Mrs. Caro kept appearing to talk and keep me company. They both seemed nervous for me.

"Don't worry," I told them. "I've eaten alone many times."

"I'm sure you have, dearie," Mrs. Caro said. She sighed deeply and returned to the kitchen.

Afterward, I watched some television and then practiced some music Mr. Denacio had given me. By nine-thirty, I was feeling tired enough to go to sleep and prepared for bed. After I put out the lights and slipped under my blanket, I listened to what I thought of as the grand house's sad silence, but suddenly I heard a different sound. I listened harder and then rose and pressed my ear to the wall between Kiera's suite and mine. I was sure of it now. She was crying. It wasn't someone on television. It was Kiera.

Full of curiosity, I put on my robe and stepped into the hallway and up to her door. I stood there for a moment, listening. Again and again, I heard the distinct sound of her sobbing. It was a sound that every part of me should enjoy,

I thought, but I didn't feel the satisfaction I would have expected or hoped to feel. I even tried to ignore her sobbing and turn to go back to my suite, but it was as if my feet were glued to the floor. I had no idea what I expected, but I knocked softly. Her sobbing continued, so I knocked a bit harder, and then it stopped.

"Who is it?" I heard her ask.

"Sasha," I said, anticipating some nasty remark to send me back to my own suite. Instead, she opened the door.

She was in her nightgown. Her hair looked as if she had been standing in an open convertible going seventy miles an hour. She wiped tears away from her cheeks and turned to go back to her bed, surprising me again by leaving her door open. I stepped in and closed it behind me.

"Why are you crying?" I asked. She lay on her back, staring up at the ceiling.

"It's the therapy," she replied.

"Oh," I said, waiting for her to complain, but she surprised me again.

"It's been giving me nightmares."

"Nightmares?"

I stepped closer to her bed. I saw that she had taken off her clothing quickly, tossing it every which way, a blouse on the floor, her skirt on a chair, socks and shoes at another place on the floor, her panties beside them. In fact, the room looked as if someone had entered it in a rage and attacked it. Books and magazines were on the floor by a table, and items on her vanity table were turned over, uncovered, and scattered.

"What sort of nightmares?" I asked.

Still looking up, she spoke like someone in a trance. "Nightmares about that night. I can't get your mother's face out of my mind. I told my therapist, and he said that was good."

She finally looked at me.

"Can you imagine that? He said it was good, good that I see her almost every night now, good that I dream about that night. I don't sleep. I feel like I'm coming apart inside, and he nods and says, 'You're making progress, Kiera. That's good.'

"Every time I go to see him now, I begin to shake. He has this calm, soft voice, but it doesn't make it any less painful. And it makes it painful to look at you," she added in a louder, strained voice, her lips trembling. She turned away to illustrate her point.

I certainly didn't want to feel sorry for her, but I couldn't get myself to say anything nasty, either. I was waiting, probably hoping for her to do or say something that would drown any sympathy I could possibly have for her, but she sobbed and then wiped her eyes and sat up.

"What I hate about him, my therapist, is how low he makes me feel without saying anything. It's like he's become a mirror."

"Mirror?"

"Yes, a mirror in which I see myself differently. I see what I've become to the people I love, how much I've hurt my parents."

She took a deep breath and looked at me silently for a long moment.

"I hated you the first day my mother brought you here.

I wanted to hate you forever, but my therapist pointed out that I was doing that to make myself feel better. If I could hate you, I could live with what I did much more easily, but hate doesn't ease the pain or stop the nightmares, and you've been . . . been far nicer to me than I would have ever been to you if the situation was reversed. In fact, I've tried hard to get you to hate me even more."

"That's true," I said.

She wiped away some more tears and smiled.

"When my mother put you in Alena's room and gave you Alena's things, I really hated you, but you've never taken advantage of it. I complained. Oh, I complained to both my mother and my father, but I saw it only brought more pain to them, so I stopped complaining. When I did that and when I talked about you with my therapist, I realized I was trying to hate you for being so much like Alena."

"Why would you hate me for that? Didn't you like your sister?"

"Of course I liked her. I loved her." She looked away and then turned back. "I wanted to be more like her, wanted to have my parents believe that and see that, but I couldn't, and then you came, and you could. My therapist made me realize all this."

"I'm not trying to be like anyone," I said.

"You don't have to try. You just are." She sighed, lifting and dropping her shoulders. "My mother doesn't know how close Alena and I really were. There were many, many nights when I went to her when she was sad and when she came to me. I hated that she got so sick. I hated everyone who was healthy. I even hated my parents for not giving her healthy genes, and I especially hated the world and God. Yes, I wasn't there as I should have been when she was dying. I couldn't face it. I wasn't strong enough.

"Maybe you can't believe this, but I was looking forward to being her older sister, to guiding her through the dangerous channels we all pass through as girls. I wanted to be there for her when she had her first boyfriend. I hated being left an only child. I hate it now. Everything I've done to displease my parents was done in anger.

"So," she concluded, "I have the nightmares."

"I'm sorry," I said. I really did feel sorry for her now. "But what can I do?"

"You can help me," she said quickly.

"Me? How could I help you?"

"You're just about Alena's age, what she would have been now. Maybe you'll let me be your older sister."

"Sister?"

"I'm not saying I won't still suffer. I can't ignore what I've done. Your limping about is clearly in my face every day, no matter what I do to forget, but as my therapist says, maybe it's better to confront what I've done and not try to ignore it."

"I'm not sure I know what to do," I said.

"You don't do anything, silly. I do it all. You're being kept like a prisoner here, and it's all my fault. You should enjoy being a teenager, too. I'll take you to places, to the malls, movies, parties."

"Parties?"

"I want all my friends to know you are part of my family now. I'll admit I have a selfish motive. I want to stop feeling terrible and having these nightmares, and I want people who think I'm so terrible to see me as a better person. If you're with me, they will. Well?" she asked when I said nothing.

Maybe I was very much like Alena. Maybe I was incapable of hate and being mean, and maybe my being with Kiera would change her. I tried to think of it as a selfish thing, too. I would enjoy living there more if we weren't at each other's throats.

"It's all right with me," I said.

She smiled and reached out for my hands. "Let's make a pact, then," she said. "Let's swear that we'll try to be like sisters."

"Okay," I said.

She squeezed my hands gently, and then she let them go and fell back to her pillow. "Do me a favor," she said.

"What?"

"Just return to your room and play the clarinet for a while. Will you?"

"Play my clarinet?"

"Yes."

"Okay."

"Thank you. It will put me to sleep, a good sleep," she said, and closed her eyes.

I stared at her a moment, and then I left, feeling as though I was the one who might begin to have nightmares.

20

New Friends

Oddly, that night, I thought I played the clarinet better than I ever had. It was as if Alena possessed me for a while and had me do it well enough to help her older sister get through her own darkness. Afterward, I went to sleep feeling contented, too. I felt safer knowing that Kiera needed me.

For the first time, she was up before me in the morning. She knocked on my door, which was already different behavior for her. Usually, she would just burst in as if I didn't have any right to privacy, especially in her dead sister's suite. I thought it was Mrs. Duval and that I had overslept and was missing breakfast, but I saw it was early.

"Yes?"

Kiera peeked in first. "Hi," she said, and entered. She was already dressed in a pink and blue tennis outfit and wore a blue wristband. I had never seen her look as fresh and as buoyant this early. She practically bounced over to my bed.

"Get up, get up!" she cried. "We're having an early, simple breakfast, and then I'm going to teach you the fundamentals of tennis so that eventually we can play doubles. I've had all sorts of professional lessons, as you can imagine, so I'm qualified to give instruction. I'm not terrific, but I'm pretty good, better than most of the girls in my circle of friends, for sure. And it won't take you long to be as good as, if not better than, them, too."

"I've never played tennis."

"That's the point, silly. That's why I want you up and out there with me this morning." She smiled coyly. "I have a few friends coming over to play later, swim, and have lunch. I got my parents' permission," she added quickly.

"Really?" I said, feeling a little excitement but not rushing to get up.

"I know what's troubling you. Stop worrying about your limping. You get around pretty quickly when you want to, and you'll see that in doubles, you don't have to move that fast, anyway."

"But I can't expect to be too good at it, good enough to play with you and your friends."

"So? None of us is going to be in any tournaments. It's just for fun. Stop arguing. If you're going to call yourself a March, you have to live up to the March reputation for self-confidence, if not downright arrogance. My father happens to be an excellent tennis player. My mother, however, is a professional sideliner."

"Sideliner? What's that?"

"Someone who sits on the sidelines, silly," she said. "She worries about breaking a fingernail even more than I do."

I couldn't help but laugh with her, even though it felt wrong to make fun of Mrs. March. Kiera was so light-hearted and happy, I didn't want to ruin her mood. I had gone to sleep wondering if everything she had said and claimed she wanted was just words that would drift away with all of the broken promises I had heard in my life, but this morning, that didn't seem to be happening.

I started to rise, and she went to the closet.

"Alena had a very cute tennis outfit that should fit you," she said, and began to look for it. While she did, I went to the bathroom and prepared to get dressed. She was waiting with the outfit when I came out, and she stood there watching me try it on.

"You have a pretty good figure for your age," she said. "With the right clothes and makeup, no one would say you were only fourteen. I didn't have boobs and a rear end like that until I was sixteen."

Her comments brought unexpected heat to my face. I caught my image in the closet wall mirror and saw that my cheeks were crimson. It wasn't that I never thought of myself as becoming a woman. I used to worry about it when Mama and I were living in the streets, in fact, because I had not gotten my first period. I expected that our poor diet would have an impact on my development, perhaps stunting me. When my first period came, I was excited and told Mama. She had looked at me and started to cry.

"I can't be happy for you," she had said. "Not now."

But I wanted to be happy for myself. *I'll be all right after all,* I thought. Mama had once had a beautiful figure, and when I looked at myself from time to time, I dared to think

I might get to look just like her, like she was before this had all happened to us.

Kiera laughed at the way I blushed. "You're embarrassed, aren't you?"

"No," I said, but not very convincingly.

"Don't you ever think of yourself as being sexy?"

"Not really."

"I bet you never really had a boyfriend, did you?"

"Not the way you mean," I admitted.

She sat on my bed and looked at me. "The way I mean? What other way is there?" She smiled. "One of the first things I wondered about you was what happened to you living on the street. I mean, what happened to you sexually."

"Nothing," I said quickly. "My mother and I were rarely, if ever, separated, day or night."

She shrugged. "It wouldn't have been so terrible if you had some experiences, but on the street, you could pick up some diseases, I'm sure."

"I was only thirteen when we went on the street."

"I lost my virginity at fourteen," she replied casually, and then leaped to her feet. "We'll talk about all this later. Let's get to breakfast. There's a lot to do before they get here."

I followed her down to breakfast. Everyone was surprised to see Kiera up so early, but it was the look on Mrs. Duval's face that nearly made me laugh. Not only was it because both Kiera and I were wearing tennis outfits, but also because there was a new tone of excitement and friendliness between us. Mrs. Duval's eyebrows rose, and she hurried back to the kitchen to say something to Mrs. Caro, who found little ways to observe us at breakfast, too.

Afterward, Kiera took me out to the tennis court, and with more patience and expertise than I ever imagined she would have, she began to teach me the fundamentals. We were out there for nearly two hours before we took a break to have something cold to drink. I didn't know if she was deliberately hitting the ball softly back to me the whole time or if that was as good as she was, but even with my limp, I found I could do decently for someone playing for the first time. She continually complimented me.

"I knew you could do this," she said. "In fact, you're doing a lot better than I did when I picked up a racket. My father was so frustrated, I thought he would give up on me. I guess he did. He hired professionals."

We sat at the pool cabana and sipped Mrs. Caro's famous homemade lemonade. Despite how well we were doing together, I remained on the lookout for some sign, some remark, something that would reveal that Kiera was just being nice to me to please her parents. Nothing like that occurred. In fact, she seemed even more interested in our being closer, and she was more willing to be honest with me than she had been the night before.

"I watched you all during these first months at school," she confessed. "I saw how badly your classmates were treating you, especially those snobby girls. In the beginning, as you know, I was hoping that would make you so unhappy that you'd want to leave no matter what my mother promised you." She laughed. "I was always complaining about you to my friends."

"How much did you tell them about me?"

"Not much. Only one of my friends knows the truth about what happened, and that's Deidre, who was in the car. The rest of my friends couldn't understand my attitude toward you. How could I hate my cousin so much? What was the big deal about her living in my house? A dozen more cousins could move in, and no one would notice in my house, they would say. I couldn't explain anything to them, so I didn't try. They're my friends, but they think I'm a bitch anyway. Half of them, if not all of them, are as well. You've heard of a coven of witches? Well, my girlfriends and I are a coven of bitches."

She laughed. Her being unconcerned about what other people, especially adults, thought of her intrigued me. Did she have that self-confidence only because her father was so rich? Not constantly worrying about the impression you were making or if people were looking at you with pity and disgust was very attractive to someone like me. No matter how Mama and I looked as if we were indifferent when we were on the streets, I know I was never anything but ashamed.

"What are you going to tell your friends about me and you now?"

"Simple. I had a change of heart. They know I'm capable of that always, and besides, I don't have to explain myself to them. They're lucky I let them be my friends."

She smiled and leaned toward me. "I can see that shocks you. You've got to develop an attitude, Sasha, especially with those snobs in your class. Tell yourself you're better than they are and you will be," she declared. She sat back. I supposed she thought she was acting like a big sister now, giving me worldly advice.

"Which of your friends are coming over?"

"Deidre, who you know was in the car with me that night, is coming over today. So is Margot. I'm the closest with Deidre. Her father's a business attorney and does lots of business with my father, so she and her family were always trusted. Margot is my next-best girlfriend, but I don't confide in her as much. And of course, none of the boys knows anything, so don't worry. Boyd Lewis and Ricky Burns are coming with Deidre and Margot. You've seen them here before," she said, and added, "completely."

She laughed, and I knew she was referring to their swimming nude.

"Is one of them your boyfriend?"

"Boyfriend? Not the way you're asking. We don't think of ourselves as with one or the other. In fact, last year, we all went to the prom as a group."

"You don't like one more than the others?"

"I like playing the field and so do they. Forget that *Romeo and Juliet* stuff, Sasha. It's only in the movies, and it gets boring. There's nothing as dull to me as going steady. Don't you know what we all are? We're friends with benefits. Ever hear of that?"

I shook my head, and she laughed.

"Friends with benefits have sex but don't have romantic relationships." Before I could ask anything else, she leaped to her feet and cried, "Here they come!"

A black Mercedes convertible with its top down was

rushing up the drive. We could hear the girls screaming and laughing as the tires squealed.

"Boyd is such an idiot," Kiera said, but she said it as if being an idiot was great. She shouted and waved, and they got out and started in our direction. They were all carrying small bags and tennis rackets. The girls were in tennis outfits as cute as Kiera's, and the boys, whom I recognized as the taller two of the three who had been there that afternoon, were in short white shorts, tank tops, and white caps. Despite what I thought would happen and even what she seemed to have anticipated, none of them appeared surprised to see me there.

"Everybody knows Sasha, right?" Kiera said.

"Right. Hi, Sasha," Boyd said. He was as blond as a blond could be, I thought. He wore his hair long, but it was neatly styled. Like most of the boys in the school, he had a light tan, but even his tan couldn't hide the freckles that randomly ran over his forehead and down his temples.

"She's a tennis player?" Ricky asked. He had dark brown hair and soft brown eyes. A little taller with wider shoulders than Boyd, Ricky looked more athletic, and I thought he was better-looking.

"What makes you think you are?" Boyd asked him before Kiera could respond. The girls laughed.

I had met Deidre before at the house when she had come to watch a movie with Kiera, and I had seen Margot with Kiera often at school. She was much shorter and overweight. From the way I saw her following Kiera around, she looked content to be in her shadow.

"Sasha is just learning," Kiera said. "Don't make a big thing of it," she added in a threatening tone.

"Who here isn't just learning?" Margot quipped. She smiled at the boys. "About everything." They all laughed, and she looked quickly to Kiera to be sure she had said something Kiera would appreciate.

"Whoever sits out takes Sasha on the other court and practices with her. Make sure she has the right form," Kiera said.

"She looks like her form's all right to me," Boyd said.

"Will you shut up and just do what I say? Didn't I tell you he was an idiot?" Kiera asked me as we headed for the tennis court. Everyone laughed. "Before we're finished, you can come in for me and get some experience."

"I can't be any good yet."

"Breaking news," Ricky said, turning back to me as we walked. "None of these girls is."

That started a playful argument and some challenges. Deidre was the one who sat out the first set, so she and I went to the second court. Before we did anything, she paused, looked at the others, and then leaned toward me.

"Hey," she said. She had her hair cut short, in almost a pageboy style. I hadn't noticed it before, but she had a dimple in her left cheek that flashed in and out when she spoke and smiled. "You're doing a very nice thing for Kiera. I think it's really big of you."

I had forgotten for the moment that she was the one who knew everything. From the way she spoke, I assumed that Kiera had told her about her therapy, too, and even what she would ask of me. I didn't know what to say, so I just nodded.

"Let's hit a few balls easy," she said. "Kiera showed you

how to hold the racket and swing so you don't develop tennis elbow?"

"Yes."

"That's the most important thing. I'll keep an eye on it for you."

She went to the other side, and we began. Just like Kiera, she hit the ball softly right to me, which made me look better than I was, I'm sure. Before she changed with Margot, she showed me how to hit backhand and practiced it with me. Margot was just as considerate and nice. I couldn't help wondering if they were really this way or if they were afraid of Kiera, who kept an eye on us even while she played.

As she had promised, Kiera asked me to step in for her. "Just for a few minutes," she told me.

I was reluctant, but both of the boys insisted, too, and when I did take Kiera's place, I didn't do so badly. At least, that was what they all told me.

The whole time, I felt strange about how I was reacting to being with Kiera and her friends. I would never say I wasn't having a good time—a very good time, in fact—but the more fun it seemed, the more guilty I felt. They all continued to be very nice to me, and once, when Boyd made a slightly sarcastic remark about my being inoculated to live in the same house as Kiera lived in, she pounced on him so hard he seemed to wither under her words. I felt sorry for him and told him it was all right. I knew he was just joking.

Afterward, our lunch was brought out for us just as it had been when I saw them at the pool that first day. Rosie brought a tray of hamburgers, salads, and chips. I waited to see if one of the boys or even one of the girls would pour some whiskey into our drinks, but this time no one did. We sat at the tables, and I listened to them gossip about other kids in their classes. Even though I had nothing to say, I felt that they were including me. Every once in a while, one of them would ask if I knew this one or that one. Of course, I knew no one. Margot's comment each time was, "You're lucky. Isn't she, Kiera?"

"We're all lucky," Kiera said, and gave me a look to indicate that we shared some deep secret. I saw that Margot was actually jealous.

Afterward, we all did go swimming. Kiera, Margot, Deidre, and I went into the house so Kiera and I could get our suits. The boys changed in the cabana. I was nervous about it, of course, expecting a replay of what I had witnessed before, but everyone seemed different, a lot more restrained. I couldn't help but wonder if it was only for my sake. The boys fooled around, teased, and splashed, but no one did any nude swimming and when the music came on, they danced and invited me to join them. I refused, but Boyd insisted, and then he and Ricky pulled me onto the dance floor, and both danced with me, one turning me toward him after the other had danced with me a few minutes. I was very self-conscious about my movements, but no one seemed to notice or care. I couldn't even recall when I had danced last, but I was sure it had been in our apartment, when Mama and I had still been living in an apartment.

Later, when we were all pretty much exhausted, we sprawled on chaise longues and sipped lemonade. The afternoon sun was falling below a row of trees to the west, and the cool air was refreshing. I had to admit to myself that I hadn't felt this content since I had arrived there. Everyone was so quiet that I thought they had fallen asleep.

Then Boyd spoke up. "Hey, what are our plans for tonight? I think we should go to this new, fabulous pizza joint on Venice Beach that Julian was talking about yesterday," he added before anyone could reply. "Afterward, we could do the boardwalk and gape at the freaks. What do you say?"

Kiera turned to me sharply. "I'm not in the mood for Venice Beach," she said, still looking at me. "Let's do Westwood."

"Boring," Boyd sang.

"We'll buy you a yo-yo," Kiera said, and the girls laughed. "Besides, I thought we all wanted to see the new Belly Boys movie."

"You'll see that?" Boyd asked, excited.

"What do you say, Sasha?" she asked me. "Want to see the Belly Boys movie?"

"I don't know anything about it," I said.

"Perfect reason to go," Kiera said. "We'll meet you guys at the Big Burger. I want some shoestring french fries."

She rose, which the others took as the signal that the day at the March mansion had ended. Ricky screamed that he didn't want to leave. Boyd pulled him to his feet, and then everyone walked together to the front of the mansion, where Boyd had parked. Before they got into Boyd's car, they all kissed Kiera, and then, to my surprise, they kissed me, too. We watched them drive off.

"I have completely crazy friends," Kiera said. "But I wouldn't have it any other way. What do you think?"

I nodded. Who was I to challenge her, anyway? I could barely remember the names of any classmates I had once considered friends. As Mama might have said, beggars can't be choosers.

And I was still feeling like a beggar.

I had no way of knowing, but it wouldn't be long before that feeling would change.

21

Night Out

Mrs. Duval looked nervous about my spending the day with Kiera. When Kiera told her we were going out for dinner and a movie, she wanted to know if Mrs. March was aware of it.

"I spoke to her this afternoon, and she didn't say anything about your taking Sasha anywhere," Mrs. Duval said.

Kiera groaned. "I'll call my mother and have her speak to you again, Mrs. Duval. Chill out."

To my surprise, Mrs. March did not call Mrs. Duval after Kiera spoke to her. She called me. "What's Kiera up to, Sasha?" she asked as soon as I went to the phone.

How could I even begin to explain what had occurred? I certainly felt funny doing it over the telephone in a quick conversation. Instead, I simply told her what we had been doing. "Kiera offered to show me how to play tennis, and then we had lunch by the pool with some of her friends and went swimming. Now everyone is going to dinner and a movie. Should I say no?"

She was quiet so long that I thought she might have lost the call on her cell phone. "What brought on this sudden generosity on her part?" she finally asked, but it sounded more like she was asking herself a question aloud.

"Her therapy," I said, looking for a shortcut.

"Is that what she said?"

"Yes."

I heard Mr. March in the background asking questions. She must have put her hand over her phone, because it all sounded muffled.

"All right, but I want you to be very careful, Sasha. I wish I was there to decide about all this, but I can't be."

"I'll be all right, Mrs. March," I said.

"Yes, you will, or someone is going to hear about it," she said. "I'll call you first thing in the morning."

Not long after I hung up, Kiera came to my suite. She had clothes in her arms. "My mother hasn't bought you anything worth wearing," she began, "and Alena's things are okay for just getting around, but there's nothing for going out. You'll look great in this. I've outgrown them but hardly wore them."

She held up the skirt, which didn't look as if it would cover much. Before I could say anything, she pretended she was running a fashion show.

"I have one of our newest creations, Madam. This is a red and black buffalo plaid miniskirt with what they call flirty inverted pleats and a black scalloped lace hem."

She put it up against me.

"You must surely agree, Madam, that this will be perfect for you with this black top," she said. "Please, try it on, or our designer, Monsieur Daddier, will have a stroke and a half." She snapped her fingers and called for champagne.

I laughed at her antics.

"That's not too much of an exaggeration. I've been to these fancy-schmancy boutiques and fashion shows with my mother. It's enough to make you puke. Go on, try it all on already."

I did. The skirt was the shortest I had ever worn, and the top was so tight it felt like another layer of skin.

"Beautiful. Only you can't wear a bra with that. It looks stupid. It's no big deal anymore, Sasha," she added when I showed surprise. "Don't worry about your nipples. I'll show you a little trick, no shows," she said. She stepped back and looked at me hard for a moment. "You know, I think I remember Mother buying Alena some boots that would go with this. Let me look."

She went into the closet and was out so quickly that I suspected she had known exactly where they were. They were a pair of high black boots with black fur at the top.

"Try them on. You look like the same shoe size."

I had secretly tried on some of Alena's shoes, and they had fit, so I knew these probably would. After I put the boots on, Kiera smiled.

"Wow, you're really hot. I might get jealous," she said.

Of me? How could someone who looked like her ever be jealous of me? I looked at myself in the full-length mirror. The girl who looked back at me looked so different that, for a moment, I imagined I was looking through a window at someone else and not at a mirror. Did I dare wear this?

"Now that I see you, I've got to rethink what I'm wearing," Kiera said. "C'mon."

I followed her to her suite. This was the first time I had seen her walk-in closet. It was a little bigger than Alena's, and despite the way Mrs. March had been buying Alena clothes, Kiera's looked fuller. It didn't look as well organized, but Kiera seemed to know exactly where what she wanted was located. She told me to sit on the chair at her vanity table while she tried on one outfit after another— skirts, tight jeans, and dresses. She asked my opinion about each outfit, but they all looked great to me.

Finally, she decided on a pair of designer jeans with sequins up the sides and across the waist. She matched it with a blouse that wasn't as tight as mine but left a naked midriff. Then she went to her jewelry and found a pair of earrings for me, as well as a gold necklace. After I had everything on, she looked at me and shook her head.

"Makeup," she declared, and sat me down at her vanity table. I had never used lip gloss or mascara or eye shadow. As she applied it, she told me why I needed it. She used some blush and then decided we couldn't go out without my having my nails polished.

"We don't have time to do a real manicure, but let's get some color on those fingers," she said. "Didn't you ever do any of this?"

"Once my mother did my nails, but she didn't like me wearing lipstick yet. She didn't wear much makeup herself. She had such a beautiful complexion. Once," I added.

She nodded and averted her eyes. "I never really got the chance to do much of this with Alena," she said, as if she had to match my loss with her own. Then she smiled. "But now I have you."

She did my nails. She said she would have liked to do more with me but declared that we had to get moving. We hurried out. I couldn't help feeling very excited, but when we reached the bottom of the stairway, Mrs. Duval was there and nearly dropped her jaw to the floor at the sight of me.

"Mrs. March said you have to be back by eleven," she told Kiera, her eyes still fixed on me.

"That's very unlikely," Kiera said. "I won't drive fast, and the movie doesn't end until ten forty-five. It will be closer to midnight."

"I'm just telling you what your mother told me."

"Well, I'll explain it to her when she returns," Kiera said. She didn't sound condescending or nasty. She made it seem like nothing anyone should have the slightest concern about.

Mrs. Duval turned to me. "You be careful, Sasha," she said.

"She's with me, Mrs. Duval."

"That's why I said it," Mrs. Duval replied, and walked away.

"That woman has come to hate me," Kiera said. "She can't wait for me to go off to college or something. She used to love me." She sounded as if it saddened her, but then she smiled and added, "Oh, well, you can't get everyone to love you, can you? Let's go."

When I got into Kiera's car, the excitement of wearing those clothes, changing my image with the makeup, and going to socialize with older kids took a backseat to my realization that I was in the automobile that had struck Mama and me. A feeling of dark dread washed over me. It was truly as though I were committing a sin. I was surprised that Kiera hadn't thought of what this meant. Maybe she had but was just better at burying it. She seemed to be in an entirely different place, a place where she could remember only what she wanted to remember.

"Oh, this is really exciting," she said. "I feel like I'm taking my younger sister out for her first big night on the town."

She drove very slowly and carefully through the gate and turned down the road. Because of my silence, she asked if I was all right.

"Yes," I said, but my voice sounded small, the voice of someone lost.

"Don't you be nervous about being with these guys," she told me, misreading my silence. "They may be a few years older, but they're not an inch better than us."

Us? Was she trying to make me feel better by including me, or did she really believe that? I knew little about psychotherapy, but now I wondered if it could really be this effective. She had been going to therapy for some time. Why would the court send her if the judge didn't believe it might change her, help her?

As if she could read my thoughts, she said, "I can't wait to tell Dr. Ralston about this. He'll surely be impressed, and maybe he'll see an end to my therapy. Therapists can keep you going for as long as they want and keep that cash register ringing along the way."

She looked at me. This time, I was sure she had read my mind.

"That's not why I'm doing this with you, Sasha. I don't really care if the therapy goes on for the rest of the year. My father can afford it, and it's no big deal. The fact is, Dr. Ralston is easy to talk to now. I don't resent him as much."

"Really?"

"Let's not talk about it anymore, especially in front of these lamebrains, okay?"

"Why do you like them if they're lamebrains?"

"Simple. Because they're fun," she said, and laughed. "It's all about fun. You'll see," she told me, and drove on.

When we got to Westwood, Kiera parked, and we walked two streets over to meet her friends. The four of them were there already and also ready to complain about how late Kiera was, but when they saw me, they were speechless for a moment.

"Who's this?" Ricky asked, smiling. "This is not your little square cousin, is it?"

"You look terrific, Sasha," Boyd said. They both looked impressed. I didn't know what to say.

Kiera spoke up for me. "I made a few small improvements with her clothes and makeup. It's no big deal. Don't salivate in the street, Boyd. It's unbecoming."

"Oh, I'm becoming," he said, and everyone laughed.

We went into the restaurant. Maybe it was my imagination, but I thought the people already seated watched us from the moment we entered.

"There are UCLA college boys here," Deidre whispered, "and they're looking at you."

"Me?"

"Get used to it," Margot said. "As long as you hang out with your cousin."

I glanced at the college boys who were looking our way and smiling. Was she right? They were looking at me? It wasn't so long ago I had thought no boys would be looking at me with any interest, and not only because of my limp. Despite all I had now and all I had been given, the magnificent mansion in which I lived, the beautiful private school I attended, I couldn't help believing that the stigma of Mama's and my street life lingered. Somehow they would see through the expensive clothes and see the stains. Maybe they would still smell the odors of the street on me, no matter how much perfume I used.

Right from the first day I had entered Pacifica Junior-Senior High School, I had feared that someone might recognize me. So many people had walked past Mama and me while we were selling on the sidewalks or the boardwalk. Why wasn't it possible that one of these students, if not more, might look at me and think, *Isn't that the same girl who sold lanyards on the boardwalk?* Maybe one of these UCLA college boys was thinking that right now.

"Don't look back at them," Kiera whispered. "They'll get annoying if they think any of us is showing interest."

I looked down quickly, and she slipped me the menu.

"The burgers are out of this world here," Boyd told me.

"Since you're not from this planet, it makes sense that you'd know," Deidre told him.

"I've sent you out of this world from time to time," he retorted.

"Shut up," she said.

Everyone laughed, but I didn't. Why were they always trying to hurt each other if they were such good friends?

"You're wrong, anyway, Boyd," Ricky said. "I'm the one who sent her out of this world. You barely got her off the ground."

"Big shots," Margot told me, pointing her thumb at them. "Or should I say single shots?"

"Ha, ha," Boyd said. "It takes only one shot to hit your target."

Fortunately, the waitress came over, and they stopped their game of insults. It took so long to get served and to eat that we had to rush to make the movie. I held them all back with my limping, but no one seemed to care if they made the movie in time or not. It was just something to do. In the theater, I ended up sitting between Kiera and Ricky. He smiled at me and let his hand drop over the seat arm so that it was against my thigh. During the movie, his fingers played with my miniskirt. I didn't know what to do, but when he lifted it a little to touch my thigh, I jumped, and Kiera turned.

"What's going on?"

"Nothing much," Ricky said. "That's the problem."

"The problem is, you don't have any patience," she told him.

"That's Ricky," Boyd said. He was on Kiera's other side and leaned over her to talk to me. "PE Man," he said, jerking his thumb toward Ricky.

"Shut your mouth," Ricky told him.

Boyd laughed and sat back.

Ricky didn't bother me for the remainder of the movie, which had some very funny scenes but was basically pretty stupid, I thought. I didn't say so, because the others, including Kiera, seemed to think it was great. Later, after we parted to go home, I asked Kiera what Boyd meant when he called Ricky PE Man.

"He was just teasing him," she said.

"I know, but I don't know what that means."

"It means premature ejaculation. You know what that is?"

"I think so," I said. I wasn't really sure.

"It's when a boy, a man, gets excited too fast and the girl gets nothing out of it."

"Oh."

"Anyway, I can tell you for a fact that it isn't true, so don't worry about it."

I looked at her. She knew for a fact?

She smiled. "Hey," she said. "Don't look so shocked. Relax. This is your first day of real class in the real school. Here, I'm the best teacher. And," she added as we reached her car, "it's tuition-free."

She laughed, but something told me it wasn't tuition-free.

Something told me there was a price to pay.

❧22❧

The Price

Mrs. Duval will be happy," Kiera said as we drove through the opened gate just before eleven-fifteen.

"How will she know what time we arrived?" I asked.

"You'll see."

Sure enough, when we parked and went into the house, Mrs. Duval was there to greet us. Kiera glanced at me and smiled.

"As you can see, Mrs. Duval, you didn't have to worry. Both of us are still in one piece," Kiera said.

Mrs. Duval said nothing. She watched us go up the stairs, Kiera giggling.

"Did you have a good time today?" she asked when we reached her suite.

"Yes, thank you."

"No, thank *you*, Sasha," she said, and then she surprised me even more by hugging me. "Sweet dreams," she said, and went into her bedroom.

I hurried to mine. It was still difficult to think of it as

mine. There was so much of Alena in it, not haunting it as much as continuing to possess it. I slept in what had been her bed with her choice of headboard. Most of the clothes I wore every day had been her clothes. Her pictures were still on the dressers, tables, and walls. I wished it was different, wished that her things were gone and it was really my bedroom suite, but I felt guilty wishing that. I now knew as well as anyone that those you loved died gradually after their funerals. The blood of their immortality consists of the memories you have of them. As they are gradually forgotten or thought of less and less, they drift farther away, closing the lid on that darkness. Mrs. March, as would any mother, refused to close the lid.

Perhaps by embracing me, if that was really what she was doing, Kiera was avoiding the pain of losing her sister. Would I be doing the same thing in relation to Mama if I accepted Mrs. March even as a surrogate mother? Could you really slip people in and out of your family the way you slipped your feet in and out of different shoes? It seemed so mean and horrible to me right now, but I knew that people did it all the time. Husbands and wives remarried and slipped new spouses into the spaces beside them on their beds, into the chairs across from them at their dinner tables, and into their arms when they danced.

Maybe loneliness was worse than grief after all. The guilty feeling that followed and grew as you began to accept someone else and bury your loved one deeper could be overcome. In the beginning, you did that by using anger. How dare the one you loved so much die? How dare he or she not fight off death, defy fate or destiny, or drive away some mysterious plan God supposedly had? There should have been some greater resistance so as not to leave you alone.

After that, you thought, if the person you loved was just as loving of you, he or she wouldn't want you to be lonely. When you found someone else, it was almost as if you were building a new relationship for your loved one who had passed away as much as for yourself. Why add grief to the soul already struggling in the afterlife?

Mama would want me to have someone fill the role of a mother—and a father, too. Mama would want me to have an older sister looking after me. Mama would want me to be happy and safe and healthy. After all, she drank whiskey and gin not only to escape who she had become but also to escape feeling guilty about not providing for me. I was like a can tied to the tail of a dog or a cat. No matter how fast she ran or what turn and twist she made, I was there, clanking behind her, reminding her of just how deep down she had fallen. Maybe that was why she refused my help carrying her suitcase and why she ran so blindly in the rain that night. Maybe she was only trying to escape.

Okay, I thought as I sat on the bed while I was still dressed in the clothing Kiera had chosen for me and still wore the makeup. *I'll put on Alena's clothes. I'll accept Mrs. March's affection. More important, I'll accept Kiera and let her be my big sister, at least for now, at least until I can stand as alone as anyone can stand. I'll try not to forget Mama, but I won't use her as a reason to reject any of this anymore.*

It was fun being with Kiera and her friends. It was exciting. I liked being a regular teenager, flirting, laughing, saying outrageous things. I wanted to have their dreams and possess that same invulnerability that made them reckless, carefree, and rebellious. Up to now, since Mama's death, I had been in some sort of cloudy, vague place. Because of the fiction that had been created about me, I no longer had my name. At least, with Mama, even on the street, I knew who I was. Whatever space we found in the parks, on the beach, even in that deserted automobile, became ours, whether it was for a short time or not. There was nothing I could call mine in my new place. It was funny to think about it, but I was living in one of the biggest homes in Southern California, and I was still homeless.

So, don't blame yourself for accepting Kiera's friendship, I told myself. *Don't go to sleep feeling guilty. If you need to justify it, justify it the way Jackie Knee, your nurse, proposed. Be selfish now. Take whatever you can get, even their affection. Embrace it. Turn something into yours.*

I gazed at myself one more time before taking off the clothes and washing off the makeup. As recently as just days ago, I would never have imagined myself looking and feeling like this. A new kind of energy had entered my body. I could see it in my eyes and could feel it everywhere, tingling right down to the small of my stomach. I loved the new feeling.

I looked back at the bed as if I expected to see my old self lying there, looking as lethargic and lost as ever but angry at me for leaving her behind.

Go away, I wanted to tell her. *Go your mousy way into the shadows, and drown yourself in self-pity. Dwell on your limp. Practice your "Yes, sir" and "No, sir," and remain a beggar hoping for some handout of love. Do that while I seize the tail of the wind.*

My old self disappeared like smoke. With a new bounce in my steps despite my limp, I prepared for bed, and when I went to sleep, I didn't think about Alena and my sleeping in her nightgown and in her bed with her favorites, the giraffes, above me. I thought about myself and about the way those UCLA college boys had been looking at me.

For the first time in a very long time, I couldn't wait for morning.

I was already dressed when Kiera came around. She was still in her robe and slippers. "Why did you get up so early?" she complained. "It's Sunday."

"I couldn't sleep anymore," I said. "I felt so awake and anxious to start the day." She saw and heard the change in me and smiled. "I'm hungry, too."

"Me, too. I know. We could have breakfast brought up to us. Let's have it in my suite. It's like room service in the best hotel, after all," she said, going to the phone.

I was sure that when she picked up the receiver, Mrs. Duval thought I was calling.

"This is Kiera," she said. Although Mrs. Duval would certainly recognize her voice, Kiera obviously liked to announce herself as if she were a princess. "Sasha and I will be taking breakfast in my suite this morning, Mrs. Duval. I'll have my usual Sunday breakfast, and Sasha will have . . ." She listened and then shook her head. "I don't know if she wants that." She put her hand over the mouthpiece. "Do you want your usual cheese and egg omelet?" She grimaced and shook her head. "Or what I have?"

"I'll have what you have," I said. I knew that on Sundays, she had a cup of fruit sorbet with a dab of whipped cream, coffee, and glazed doughnuts. Mrs. March always complained about the way Kiera ate.

"She'll have exactly the same as me, Mrs. Duval. Thank you very much." After she hung up the phone, she laughed. "She didn't sound pleased, but they're here to please us, and not vice versa. I'm going to go take a quick shower. Oh," she added at the door, "I sorta agreed we'd go to Disneyland today. Ricky's getting his father's SUV. It will hold us all. They'll be here in about an hour."

"Disneyland?"

"Yes. Have you ever been there?"

"No, but . . . when will we return?"

"I don't know. What's the difference?"

"Homework left to do," I said.

"We'll get to it when we can. If we can," she added with a smile. She paused and tilted her head a little as she looked at me. "What are you wearing? I think Alena wore that to someone's baptism. Don't worry. When you come into my suite, I'll have something better for you."

"Okay," I said, and she left.

I looked at the clothes I had put on. Mrs. March sort of suggested things for me to wear by organizing the front of the walk-in closet so I could go from outfit to outfit. I hadn't thought much of it, but I certainly didn't want to go to Disneyland dressed the way I would dress if I were going to a baptism.

I had always wanted to go to Disneyland, but for Mama and me, it was too expensive after Daddy deserted us, and when he was still there, he never wanted to take me or spend the money. I imagined it would be more fun going with Kiera and her friends, anyway. I knew it was at least an hour away. It would certainly take up the whole day.

I gazed at the clarinet. Besides the homework I still had, I was also supposed to spend a good hour on the new music Mr. Denacio had given me to practice on the weekend. He was so good at detecting when you didn't practice. Somehow, I thought, I'd get it all done.

Before I went to Kiera's suite to have breakfast, my phone rang. It was Mrs. March, and from the tone of her voice, I suspected that Mrs. Duval had called her as soon as she had hung up from Kiera's call.

"How are you this morning?" she asked.

"I'm fine, Mrs. March."

"Where did she take you last night?"

I told her about the restaurant and the movie and added that we had come right home after the movie. I also said that Kiera had driven carefully. Mrs. March was quiet a moment and then asked if any of Kiera's friends had tried to get me to smoke something or take something.

"No," I said. "Nothing like that happened. They were all very nice."

"Nice?" she said, as if I had said something good about Nazis. "Just be very, very careful with them and with Kiera," she reiterated. "Okay, we'll be flying into L.A. about five. I look forward to seeing you at dinner and hearing more about your day and night."

It was on the tip of my tongue to tell her we were going to Disneyland, but I hesitated, and she said good-bye. *Oh, well,* I thought. Surely Kiera knew we had to be back by dinner. She knew when her parents were returning. It would be all right.

She was still in her robe but drying her hair when I entered her suite.

"Ricky called," she said after she turned off the hair dryer. "He wanted to be sure you were coming along."

"Really?"

"He says there's something fresh about you."

"Fresh?"

"I explained that you were a virgin," she said, making it sound as if I had come from another country, maybe another planet.

"Oh. What did he say?"

"What do you think?" she asked. I waited. "He said too bad."

She laughed hard just as Mrs. Duval brought in our breakfast.

"Perfect. Thank you, Mrs. Duval," Kiera sang.

Mrs. Duval looked at me as she put the tray on the table. "Be sure to take your vitamin," she said. "Mrs. March was concerned."

"Oh, brother," Kiera muttered loudly. "You've already told my mother what we're eating for breakfast?"

Mrs. Duval turned to her. "You should be taking your vitamins, too, Kiera, especially the way you eat."

"I don't think I look so bad for it, Mrs. Duval."

"I'm not talking about the outside of you," she replied.

Kiera groaned.

Mrs. Duval shook her head, looked at me with a warning in her eyes, and left.

"I hope she didn't make the coffee as weak as she has been making it," Kiera said, coming to the table. "Oh, your clothes are laid out on my bed there. You can change after we enjoy our nutritionally worthless breakfast."

Now that I started to eat what she ate, I wondered why I had not asked for my special eggs. It was too much sugar, and just looking at it actually made me feel a little nauseated. She finished her sorbet almost before I had started.

She grimaced when she sipped her coffee. "It's more like tea. My mother tells her to make it like this for me."

"Your mother called me," I said as I nibbled at the doughnut.

"This morning?"

"Yes."

She stopped sipping her coffee and put her doughnut down. "Probably after Mrs. Duval let her know what you were having for breakfast. What does my mother expect you to be, her little spy now?"

"No," I said.

"What did you tell her about our day together?"

"Nothing bad. I told her we had a very nice time."

She thought a moment and then shrugged. "Whatever," she said, and went at her doughnut.

After we ate, I put on the outfit she had chosen. It was a pair of slightly destroyed denim shorts with raw cuffs and a tank top that read "Fresh Air Turns Me On." I was surprised at how tightly the shorts fit. There was something uncomfortable in the rear, and I reached in and discovered a tag.

"You never wore these?" I asked.

"Oh," she said. "I probably never noticed." She grabbed some scissors and cut it off. "They look perfect on you."

"I think they're too tight."

"That's perfect, silly. You don't want to look like some old lady."

The top hung loose, however—too loose, I thought. My bra was half out. "I'm swimming in this."

"I'll give you a shell to wear instead of your bra," she said. "It'll look great."

When she put on what she was going to wear, I thought she looked more conservative. Her jeans weren't tight, and she layered a shirt and a top but wore her bra.

"I'm not sure I look good," I said, gazing at myself in her full-length mirror.

"Trust me, you're dynamite. Now let's go find a reason to explode," she said. Her phone rang. "We'll be right down," she said, and hung up. "They're pulling in. Let's go."

We almost left the house without anyone knowing, but Mrs. Duval spotted us just as we reached the front door. "Where are you going?" she asked, hurrying toward us. "Your parents will definitely be home for dinner," she added.

"We're going to Disneyland with friends, Mrs. Duval. Didn't I mention it this morning?"

"No, you didn't."

"Didn't I? I'm sorry. We probably won't make it back in time for dinner. I'll call you if we can."

Before Mrs. Duval could respond, Kiera opened the door and shouted at Ricky and the others as they pulled up to the front of the mansion. She grabbed my hand to pull me out, and I looked back at Mrs. Duval. She gazed at me and shook her head as if I were about to step off the edge of a cliff.

It made me hesitate but only for a moment. The boys were howling as we stepped out.

"Who's that foxy girl with you, Kiera?" Ricky called.

The laughter and shouting replaced my worry with excitement. It hadn't been that long ago that I was desperate on a street. *Now look at yourself,* I thought.

You're a foxy girl.

23

Happiest Place on Earth

*K*iera decided that I should sit up front with Ricky
since this was my first trip to Disneyland. On the
way, everyone argued about the best rides and events. The
boys liked Pirates of the Caribbean the most, and the girls
favored Alice in Wonderland. I was surprised to hear that
most of them had been there a dozen times at least. Because I didn't want to look and sound like some wide-eyed,
dazzled child, I didn't want to say it, but I felt like Alice
in Wonderland when we arrived and started down Main
Street.

I was surprised at the attention I was receiving. Everyone wanted to show me something he or she liked. I
was rushed along from one ride to another. Whether or
not Kiera had coached the others about making me feel
wanted, I did feel like part of their group and as if I had
been for some time. Ricky was especially attentive and sat
with me on every ride, especially Autopia. Boyd and Margot were right behind us in their car, deliberately bumping

us every chance they had, but it was all great fun. I had never laughed and screamed so much.

After lunch, we went to Indiana Jones and then to Alice in Wonderland. Both Ricky and Boyd were ecstatic when I voted with them on best attraction and created a tie. The girls weren't upset. We joked about it and finished the day by going to the 3-D show of *Honey, I Shrunk the Kids.* I had not even looked at the time once and was shocked to see that it was nearly six-thirty. There was no question now that we would not be home for dinner. Kiera didn't seem at all nervous or upset about it. On the way home, we stopped at one of Deidre's favorite restaurants. By the time Ricky drove through the Marches' gate, it was nearly nine-fifteen.

No one worried about doing homework. In fact, nothing about school had been mentioned all day until Ricky said he'd see me the next day at school. Kiera and I got out and watched them drive off. I felt exhausted, but it was a happy sort of exhaustion that I would welcome again and again. I thanked Kiera. She had paid for everything for me, of course.

"Ricky seems to genuinely like you," she commented as we opened the door. "He's usually very critical of younger girls."

I basked in the compliment, but only for an instant, because Mrs. March came marching out of the living room with a look of anger I had not seen before.

"Earthquake coming," Kiera whispered.

"How dare you keep Sasha out all day and have her miss dinner?" she began. "Your father is too angry to come out of his office."

"She didn't miss dinner. We stopped on the way home."

"I don't mean that, and you know I don't mean that, Kiera. We worked out our travel schedule so we could have dinner together when we returned. And why didn't you answer your cell phone? Either of you?" she asked, looking at me.

"I didn't have mine with me," I said.

"Come to think of it, neither did I," Kiera said. "Everyone I wanted to talk to today was with us, anyway."

That brought blood into Mrs. March's face. For a moment, rage choked her throat, and she couldn't speak. Then she looked at me again. "What are you wearing? Where did you get those clothes?"

"They're mine," Kiera said.

"I never saw them before. Those shorts are inappropriate."

"Please, Mother, don't be a prude."

"And they're surely not warm enough."

"They were," Kiera said. "We weren't exactly on a hiking and camping outing. Can we go upstairs now? We both have homework."

"I'm very disappointed," Mrs. March said, stepping back. She was saying it mostly to me.

"You wouldn't have been if you had come along. Disneyland was great today. The lines weren't that long and . . ."

"Go to your room, Kiera. We'll discuss this tomorrow," Mrs. March said.

I lowered my head and followed Kiera to the stairway.

"My father's not as angry as she claims he is," she whispered as we went up. "Otherwise, he'd be out here, too."

I didn't say anything. The look of disappointment on Mrs. March's face was not only sobering, it was a little frightening. Maybe now all her of kindness and generosity would end. Perhaps she no longer saw me as being as good and as nice as her Alena. If anyone had told me months ago that I would fear being sent away, I would have practically laughed because it seemed such a ridiculous possibility. How could I ever get to care much about being with the girl who was driving the car that night or the family that protected her? All of the gifts, the money, the clothes, and the wonderful new school would not buy my forgiveness.

"Don't worry," Kiera said, seeing my silence and concern. "She won't be as angry tomorrow. That's the way she is."

"I'd better finish my homework," I said, and hurried to my bedroom.

When I entered it, I felt even worse. It was as if I had let down Alena as much as Mrs. March. *I thought you were going to be me for my mother,* her picture said to me. *I'd never have done that.*

Looking at myself in Kiera's clothes suddenly disgusted me. I took them off as quickly as I could and put on one of Alena's nightgowns before getting to my homework. It took me so long to finish that there was no time to practice the clarinet. I was so bleary-eyed by then anyway that I couldn't stay awake and, in fact, overslept.

Mrs. March came in to wake me. "You'll have to rush," she said, and then she just left without another word.

I got up quickly. I could hear her yelling in Kiera's bedroom, and a door slammed. I dressed as fast as I could and hurried down to breakfast. Mr. March apparently had left already. Mrs. March was at the table but had her head in her hands, her elbows on the table, and didn't look up when I entered.

"I want you to be sure to come directly home after school today," she said, still looking down at the table. "Do not permit Kiera to talk you into coming home with her and sending Grover back without you." She raised her head. "She wants you to go back and forth to school with her, but I refuse to permit it. In fact, I don't want you riding with her anywhere unless I specifically say. Understand, Sasha?"

"Yes."

"I don't know what went on here exactly while I was away, but I'm not pleased," she concluded.

"I'm sorry," I said.

Kiera sauntered in and poured herself a cup of coffee. "They're still making the coffee too weak," she told her mother after sipping some.

"I think you have more important things to think about than the strength of your coffee, Kiera."

"We just went to Disneyland, Mother. Don't make it into a federal case."

Mrs. March narrowed her eyes. "Rein yourself in, Kiera. You're heading for another major disaster," she warned.

Kiera smirked and nibbled on a pastry. Then she just threw it down, got up, and left. Mrs. March didn't say anything, even to me.

I finished, got my things, and hurried out to the limousine. After being with Kiera and her friends, hearing their laughter and seeing their joy, it was even more depressing to be alone in the big vehicle. If anything, it made me feel as if I had shrunken again and was back to being the mousy little girl with a limp.

After homeroom, I dreaded walking into Mr. Denacio's class. The moment I took out the clarinet, his eyes shifted with suspicion. I hadn't played for more than thirty seconds before he stopped me.

"You didn't practice at all, did you?"

"No," I said.

He didn't say anything. He nodded and went to the next student, but that sort of quiet reaction of his was worse. I felt his disappointment and his conclusion that I was finally like most of the others and would not be anyone special after all. It was like almost getting to the top of a mountain and then sliding all the way back down. I wanted to cry. I tried to be enthusiastic for the remainder of the period but couldn't get my energy level up and was happy when the bell rang.

I wasn't as alert in any of my morning classes as I usually was and actually went into a daydream during math. I missed the entire explanation of a problem, and when called upon, I didn't know where we were in the lesson. There, too, my teacher didn't reprimand me. He just looked at me as if I had let him down and went on to another student. By the time lunch period came around, I felt as if I had stepped in quicksand and was nearly in it above my head. I certainly had no appetite.

But before I could settle into my funk and cry to myself, Ricky grabbed my arm. "We're eating outside," he said.

I looked at him with surprise. It was one thing to do things with Kiera and her friends on the weekend, but for them to want me with them at school, too, was quite another. My classmates and the girls with whom I usually sat looked up with as much surprise as I had when I filled my tray and followed Ricky out to their table.

He made a place for me, and I sat beside him.

"Why so sad a face?" Margot asked immediately.

"Not that it's any of your business, but my mother gave us a hard time for missing dinner with her and my father last night," Kiera said quickly. "I suppose that's still bothering her."

"Hey, don't mope, Sasha. It was worth it," Boyd said. "It was the best time I've had there."

That started us all reviewing the day at Disneyland. Before I knew it, I felt upbeat and happy again, especially with the way they were including me in everything they said. When the bell rang, Ricky helped me with my tray, and we walked out of the cafeteria together. Out of the corner of my eye, I saw the way Charlotte Harris, Jessica Taylor, and Sydney Woods were watching us. When Ricky and I parted in the hallway, they approached me quickly before I entered class.

"How come Ricky Burns is so interested in you?" Charlotte asked.

"Did you go out with him?" Sydney followed before I could answer.

I looked at the three of them. When I first came to the school and met them, I was of no interest. They mocked my limping and never thought to invite me to anything once I didn't invite them to the March mansion. They rarely said a word or sent a smile my way.

"Who's Ricky Burns?" I asked, and went into the

classroom, leaving them stone-faced behind me. I laughed to myself.

When I sat and looked back, they were in deep conversation among themselves and Lisa Dirk, my first-day big sister who had had nothing much to do with me thereafter. They all looked my way, and I smiled at them.

I did much better in my afternoon classes. Before my last class, Kiera tapped me on the shoulder and asked if I wanted to go with her after school. "We're heading to the Century City Mall."

I hadn't told her that her mother had forbidden me to ride with her without her specific permission and didn't want to do it now and start her on some tirade.

"I can't," I said. "I have too much to do."

"You're missing a great time," she sang. "If you change your mind, let me know as soon as the bell rings, and I'll send Grover back home without you."

I couldn't deny that I wanted to go, but I was too frightened this time. I deliberately took longer to leave my last class. Even so, Kiera loitered near the doorway.

"Change your mind?" she asked.

"No, I can't, but thanks," I said.

"Too bad," she said. "Tomorrow I have to go to therapy."

"I know. I'll see you at home."

"Home? Right," she said, and left me quickly. I saw her meeting the others in the parking lot. Ricky looked my way, shrugged, and then followed everyone else.

Did he really like me much? I wondered. I was fourteen, a girl who had never had a boyfriend or even a boy just interested in her, and a senior at my new school was looking at me romantically after spending only two days with me and his friends. He was one of the best-looking boys at the school, too. I hated seeming so young and innocent. I tried to talk and act more like Kiera when I was with her and her friends, but running home that afternoon probably made me look like a child again. Tomorrow they would have no interest in me, I thought, and my classmates would not be so friendly, either.

I sank back into a deep funk and remained there all the way back to the March mansion. When I entered the house, I headed for the stairway, waiting to get into my homework so I could have time to practice the clarinet. I paused when I heard some loud voices and realized that it was Mr. and Mrs. March. When I heard my name mentioned, I turned toward the living room and listened.

"You're not making any sense, Jordan," Mr. March said. "You said you brought this girl here to save her from the streets and the orphanages or whatever. You wanted her to have a family, right?"

"Yes, but . . ."

"So why wouldn't having Kiera as an older sister make her more part of our family? And look what good this can do for Kiera. It's her way of achieving repentance, feeling remorse. Her therapy is going well, and now you want to stop her from being too close or influential with Sasha? It makes no sense to me. If you're that worried about Kiera being a bad influence, then maybe it would be better if we found another home for Sasha," he said.

Mrs. March was quiet. I held my breath. "It would be terrible to send her away now," she finally said.

"Well, then?"

"Okay, Donald, I'll try to keep an eye on both of them for now."

"If there's one thing we don't need, it's more tension in this house," he said.

They were both so quiet that I thought they'd be coming out and see that I was eavesdropping, so I turned away quickly and headed for the stairway. Once in my suite, I sat and pondered what I had heard. What was Mrs. March agreeing to let me do? I was as conflicted as she was at the moment.

On one hand, I wanted to be with Kiera and her friends, go out, go to their parties, go on their trips, everything, but on the other hand, I wanted to do well in school, too. Kiera and her friends didn't seem all that interested in school or concerned about their grades.

It would be like walking on a balance beam, I thought. Could I do it, do both?

If I fell this time, the fall might be too long and deep for me to make any sort of recovery, and then where would I be?

Probably following Mama's ghost on some backstreet and wondering how I had become so trapped in my recurring nightmare.

24
Rules

*M*r. March was at dinner that night. This time, Kiera made sure she was there, as well. She didn't come to my room when she returned from the mall. I thought she was still upset about my deciding not to go with her and the others after school, but when she came down to dinner moments after I had arrived and taken my seat at the table, she smiled at me and apologized for not coming to my suite to fetch me.

"I wanted to be sure you got some of that homework done," she said. Then she looked at her father and added, "They give students in the ninth grade more work than they give us seniors. I remember." She turned to her mother. "You remember, Mother. I was complaining about it when I was in ninth grade, and they told you it was the transition grade from junior high to high school."

Mrs. March nodded but said nothing. Her eyes betrayed her deep suspicion of Kiera's sudden sweet talk. No one said anything while Mrs. Duval and Rosie began serving.

Then Mr. March clasped his hands and began what was obviously his and Mrs. March's compromise. "I'm pleased to see you including Sasha in some of your activities with your friends, Kiera, but you have to remember that for now, along with being younger than you, Sasha is a different sort of responsibility for us. We are acting as her foster parents, and therefore it doesn't begin and end with us.

"Naturally," he continued, looking at me, "we don't want her to feel strange or different. We want her to feel she's part of our family. However, we have to supervise her activities more closely. We need to maintain more control, follow more rules. So, before you decide to go anywhere with her, you must get either your mother's or my permission. We want her curfew maintained. For now, we don't think it's appropriate for her to be out later than eleven."

"Even on weekends?" Kiera cried.

"Even on weekends," her father said.

She shook her head, glanced at me, and looked down.

"The second we hear of any misbehavior, and you know by now what I mean by misbehavior, around her or including her, everything changes for both of you, understand?"

Kiera said nothing. She did glance at her mother, with what I thought was a look of such disgust and rage that it would surely have turned my heart into stone if I were Mrs. March.

"Now," he said, sounding softer, "if you're going straight to school in the morning and if you return straight home after school on the days you're not attending therapy, Sasha may ride with you. It would free up Grover and the limousine for your mother's use and mine at times."

Kiera started to smile.

"But if I hear of any bad driving, speeding, or anything of the like, I will take away your driving privileges, and of course, we'll forbid Sasha to go anywhere with you."

"We have to come right home all the time? Sometimes we like to get a snack or something, Daddy."

"If there is any change, call your mother and get her permission first," he said, relenting.

Kiera looked satisfied but wasn't. She was an expert when it came to manipulating her father.

"May I just say, Daddy, that it's very difficult for us to go to a movie or a house party or anything, for that matter, and have to be back by eleven on weekends. Half the time, the movie doesn't let out until nearly eleven, just like it did the other night. It's not good to have that sort of pressure on someone. I'll end up driving too fast just to make the curfew. Either I do that or not include Sasha in things."

"Eleven is late enough for a girl in the ninth grade," Mrs. March said.

"Not in today's world," Kiera countered.

"Let's leave it between eleven and twelve," her father said. "Call it the pumpkin factor."

"Pumpkin factor?" Kiera asked.

"Cinderella," I said.

Mr. March smiled. "That's right, Sasha. Remember? At twelve, her carriage turned into a pumpkin."

"Which one of us is Cinderella?" Kiera asked impishly.

I thought she was also looking for some clear expression of affection from her father, but before he could respond, her mother did. "I hardly think it's you, Kiera," she said. "You already live in a castle."

"You're right, Mother," Kiera said. She turned to me. "Then maybe Sasha will get her prince after all."

Her father laughed, but her mother didn't. She heard something I heard, too. It sounded more like a threat than a promise of something nice. After that, the conversation changed to other topics, mostly between Mr. and Mrs. March. When we left to go up to our rooms, I wasn't sure who had won the argument I had overheard earlier, Mrs. March or Mr. March or Kiera. From the expression on Kiera's face, I was sure she believed she had.

"Don't worry," she told me, "we'll find ways to avoid coming right home on the days I can drive you."

"As long as I can get done what I have to get done," I said as a caution.

She didn't hear me or care to. Instead, she went into her room after she said, "Ricky really missed you after school today."

Her comment really distracted me. I had to concentrate harder to complete my homework and get to the clarinet. I was determined to impress Mr. Denacio in the morning, but a half hour into my practice, I had very bad cramps. I knew what it was; it was my time of the month, but it hadn't been this bad since I began to be regular again.

I don't know if it was because of our poor nutrition or simply the stress that came with living in the streets, but I had hardly begun to have periods before we were evicted from the apartment and then had to leave the hotel. In those early days, Mama was always there for me, but once we were on the street, I was on my own. I made sure I always had what I needed, but sometimes I would go weeks overdue, and once I went nearly two months. Since living with the Marches, I was clock-regular. I had merely forgotten that it was my time, but the severe cramps were more than a reminder; they were an alarm bell.

I prepared for my flow to begin and then curled up in bed, which was the way Kiera found me when she came to my room to tell me about something very secret. For a moment, she didn't realize what was happening to me. I had my eyes closed and my hands pressing on my tummy. She really didn't look at me. She entered and began to pace.

"I've been debating telling you about our secret club," she began. "There are the three of us, Deidre, Margot, and me, but we inducted Marcia Blumfield and Doris Norman recently, so now there are five of us, and . . ." She paused when she really looked at me. "What's your problem?"

"Monthlies," I said.

"Monthlies? What are monthlies? Is that what you call it?"

"My mother did. I have very bad cramps this time."

"Isn't that something? I was just going to ask you about your period. Are you regular?"

"I am now," I said, "or have been since I've been here."

"Well, that's good. Don't worry. I have something for cramps. I'll go get it."

"You do?"

"Of course I do. Do you think I want to be all twisted up like you are right now? Besides, we have to stick together through pain and pleasure." She started out, then paused and turned. "Which, by the way, is the motto of our secret club."

"What secret club?"

"The one I was considering telling you about. Now," she added, "I definitely will."

She sauntered out, leaving me as confused as ever, but if she could help stop my cramps, I wouldn't care what silly thing she had to say next. She returned quickly and handed me a glass of water and a pill.

"What is it?"

"Something my doctor prescribed. It works fast. You'll see."

I took it and swallowed it down with water. "Thanks."

"No problem. I have more if you need it in the morning, but they usually work overnight."

Even though the cramps didn't lessen, I lay back and breathed easier. "What were you talking about before? I really wasn't listening."

"I know. It's not important right now. I'll tell you about it later. Hey," she said, starting out again. "You don't have to rush to get up. You're going to school with me tomorrow. I know a shortcut Grover doesn't know. Night." She left quickly, as if she had to talk to someone or do something.

Kiera's pill worked wonders. I felt a lot better in the morning and let her know at breakfast.

Mrs. March rose a little later than usual and entered just as we were talking about it. "What pill?" she asked immediately.

"My monthlies pill," Kiera said, teasing me.

"What?"

"You know what happens to us monthly, Mother."

"I repeat. What pill?"

"The one Dr. Baer gave me for cramps."

"Oh," she said. She looked at me. "I didn't know you were having any problems, Sasha."

"It's not a federal case, Mother. She came to me, and I helped her," Kiera said.

I practically spun around in my seat. *Came to her?*

"I'm getting tired of hearing that stupid expression, Kiera. I'm sorry your father taught it to you. No, it's not a federal case, but Sasha should know to come to me with her problems," Mrs. March said. She didn't sound angry as much as hurt.

Kiera shrugged. "I just happened to be around at the right time. It's not . . . it's no big deal."

Mrs. March stared at her a moment and then turned slowly back to me. "How are you now, Sasha?"

"I feel better, Mrs. March. Thank you."

"You know you can come to me with any problem, no matter how big or how small."

"I know. Thank you."

"We might stay after school tomorrow," Kiera said. "Mr. Bowman is casting for the school play."

"You would go out for the school play?"

"I might," Kiera said. "It's my last chance to do something like that, and I know Sasha will be interested, if not in being an actor, maybe in helping with the sets."

"That would be nice."

Again, I looked at Kiera. We had never discussed anything like that, and besides, I didn't recall any casting for the school play being announced. Afterward, on our way to school, I brought that up.

"That's because he hasn't announced it yet," she said. "Don't worry. I'll just tell her I made a mistake. It's next week. I got the dates confused."

"You can't lie to your mother all the time, Kiera."

"Who's lying all the time?" She laughed. "Just when it's absolutely necessary, and tomorrow it's important that we don't go right home."

"Where are we going?"

"To a meeting."

"Meeting? What kind of meeting?"

"A meeting of the secret club I was trying to tell you about last night. It's at Deidre's house."

"What kind of club is this?"

"It's the VA."

"VA? Isn't that something to do with veterans?"

She laughed. "Absolutely. Everyone in the club is a veteran."

"Of what?"

"Sex, silly. VA stands for Virgins Anonymous," she said, laughing.

"I don't understand."

"You will," she said. "And it will be the most exciting club you've ever been in."

"I've never been in any."

"Perfect. You're a virgin when it comes to clubs, and tomorrow, we'll end that."

She sped up. I tried to ask more questions, but she said I should just be patient and promised I wouldn't be disappointed.

I wasn't disappointed at school. Once again, Ricky asked me to join him at lunch, which once again captured the attention of my classmates. I could almost feel the buzz about us growing with every word we spoke to each other and every step we took beside each other.

"I might be able to get my father's boat one of these weekends," Ricky told me on our way back to class. "It's at Marina Del Ray. If I can, we'll all go to Catalina Island. You ever been?"

"No," I said. I was sure I sounded like someone locked in a closet. No matter what place they all discussed or mentioned, I had not been there, and as far as I knew, all of them except Deidre thought I was Kiera's cousin. Either because Kiera would come down on them if they did or because they were just being kind, no one wondered aloud how I could not have done half of what they had done. I did hear Kiera whisper to Margot that my family was poorer relatives, but from what I could see of the Marches, ninety-eight or ninety-nine percent of the country was poorer than the Marches.

"Great. It's always fun to show someone places and things for the first time," Ricky said. It seemed, at least for now, that there was nothing I could do or say that would discourage his interest in me.

I was having a better day all around. Although Mr. Denacio wouldn't say anything nice about my playing that morning, I could see that he was cautiously optimistic about me again. I did better in all of my classes and got a ninety on a pop quiz in history. I could feel my confidence growing stronger all day and was quite convinced that I could walk that beam. I could do it all.

Grover was there waiting for me after school. I didn't see Kiera, but I knew she was off to her therapist. Grover rarely said anything to me, but this particular afternoon, he smiled and asked how my day had gone. I think he saw something new, healthier, and stronger in me and wasn't afraid that he might do or say something that would send a stampede of tears down my cheeks.

I even felt better about being in the limousine. I didn't feel shut up and alone. Maybe I was catching Kiera's arrogance, but I sat back and looked out the window at the other students emerging. I deliberately lowered my window so they could see me, too. Lisa Dirk stared at me a moment and then lifted her hand to wave. I flipped my hand like a queen I had once seen in a movie, and Grover drove us away.

Cinderella was in her carriage.

No pumpkins here, I thought.

❧25❧
Conspirators

*E*ven though Deidre and Margot know you a lot better now," Kiera began just before dinner, "they're still a little nervous, and the other two are very nervous, about my bringing you to a meeting of the VA club. It's a very private, secret club. You've practically got to take a blood oath that what you see and hear at Deidre's tomorrow after school will never leave your lips, even if you're not accepted. Can you promise to do that?"

I put down my math book. I had gone at my homework with a vengeance, partly because I was afraid that when she returned, she would take up all my time again, and I wouldn't have time to finish or practice the clarinet.

"Maybe I shouldn't go, then," I said.

"Oh, no. I've assured everyone that you're not the sort who betrays friends. In fact," she said, twirling a strand of her hair, "I told them you were very excited about it after I described it to you. I told them that in your heart, you were one of us and definitely no prude. However, for this first time, I wouldn't advise you to talk too much. Just listen, and look at me if anyone asks you anything you're not sure about or think you should answer."

"You didn't really describe it all to me, Kiera."

"We've got to leave something for a surprise," she protested. "Believe me, you're not going to be disappointed."

"What do they really know about me?"

"Just what we've told them. I added that your mother was controlling, and you were frustrated. That's why you never had a real boyfriend or even a friend with benefits. Except for Deidre, of course, they all bought everything I told them."

"Can't you at least tell me exactly what we do at this club?"

"We talk and advise and help each other."

"With sex?"

"You'll see. It's better if you see and hear it all yourself."

She stepped over to the dresser and looked at one of the pictures of Alena. There were about a dozen in the suite, but I noticed only one with both Alena and Kiera. Most of the others were of Alena with Mrs. March or both Mr. and Mrs. March. Either Kiera had been the one taking the pictures, or she simply hadn't been around when they took them.

She lifted the one on the dresser and studied it a moment before putting it down softly.

"How old was she in that picture?" I asked.

"Ten. This was a school photo taken when she was in the fifth grade."

"She would have been a very pretty woman."

"We have the exact same eyes and nose." She turned to me. "My therapist thinks it's healthy that I see you now as more like a younger sister. I told her how my mother was trying to come between us."

"Come between us?"

"She had a good explanation for it," Kiera went on, pacing now, like some teacher explaining a new idea. "She said my mother was jealous of our budding new relationship."

"She said that?"

She paused and looked at me with those narrowed eyes.

"She said my mother wants to dominate you, and the more she alienated you from me, the easier it would be for her to turn you into Alena. You don't want to be turned into someone else, do you? Or do you?"

"No, of course not," I said.

"Good." She stepped closer. "Just be alert. My mother will continue to warn you against me, if not call me the devil outright. That's why she was so angry when she saw you dressed in the clothes I gave you and wearing the makeup I put on you. That's why she wasn't for me taking you to school. She'd love to have you locked up in that limousine going and coming and then locked up in this room. She even has our servants working for her that way. They're all a bunch of spies, so be careful about what you say and do in front of any of them."

She smiled and relaxed her shoulders.

"But don't worry. My father sees through all that. He'll be on our side more and more."

I didn't say anything for a moment. She was making it sound as if there was a war going on in that great house, and now I was the prize, the spoils.

"Don't you love your mother?" I asked her.

She shrugged. "I love her the way a daughter is supposed to, I guess, but I've always gotten along better with my father, and after Alena was born, my mother didn't seem to care much about it, anyway. She doted on Alena. I could do nothing right, and Alena could do nothing wrong. It's back to that since you came," she said, but then she smiled again. "I don't mind. I'm fine. And so will you be, because I won't let her turn you into someone you're not. You've become . . . my cause célèbre. How's that? I learned something in French class," she added with a flair as if she were on a stage. "Oh, I heard Ricky's planning on getting his father's boat and taking you and the rest of us to Catalina one of these weekends."

"Yes, he said one of these weekends."

"His father makes him work every other weekend in one of their pharmacies."

"One? How many do they own?"

"About ten, I think. He expects Ricky will become a pharmacist, too, and take over someday. They have a beautiful boat. He hasn't invited many girls. I told you he likes you. I hope he can get it. His father lets him take it because he trusts him. My mother won't let my father give me use of the boat, even if I have someone like Ricky do the driving. Someday, though." She took a deep breath and smiled. "For the first time after a session of therapy, I've got an appetite. See you downstairs," she said, and left.

I rose and looked at the picture of Alena she had been looking at so intently. I didn't think they had the same eyes and nose, not at all. Alena's features were more doll-like, and her eyes looked warmer, friendlier. According to

Kiera, Alena was only in fifth grade when the picture was taken, but she had an innocence that did remind me of myself, vulnerable, eager to trust and believe in someone and in the future. It wouldn't be all that difficult for Mrs. March to turn me into this girl. I was closer to her than I was to Kiera.

I returned to my homework and even got in twenty minutes of clarinet before I went down to dinner. Everyone was there. Kiera gave me a knowing smile, winking slightly as if we were conspirators now, both working her parents, manipulating them.

During dinner, Kiera reminded Mrs. March that we were staying after school to audition for the school play. Before her mother could say or question anything, her father went on and on about his own dramatic experiences when he was in high school.

"I was in a play called *Harvey,* the one about the invisible big rabbit."

I wasn't familiar with it, and apparently, neither was Kiera. He went on to tell us practically the whole story.

"Oh, Daddy!" Kiera cried when he described the ending. "That sounds like so much fun."

"It was. It is. In fact, your school should do it. At least, you guys should read it or maybe get the movie."

Mrs. March moved her dish to the side and said, "We have had that movie in our theater, Donald, and Kiera was bored and left."

He looked stunned for a moment, thought, and then nodded. "Yeah, I do remember that. Right."

"I was younger then," Kiera said quickly. "Besides,

you never told me you were in the play when you were in high school, Daddy. I would have paid more attention and watched it to the end."

"He did tell you that, Kiera," Mrs. March said softly, "right before we began watching it."

"Well, I don't remember." She looked at me before firing back at her, "You're always finding something wrong with me."

"I'm just . . ."

"Just jumping on every opportunity you can to make me look bad in front of Sasha," Kiera added, and leaped to her feet. "I don't know why I'm still in therapy. I go there, make some progress, and then come home to have you ruin it," she moaned, and left the dining room.

The silence that followed was as deafening as that right after a bomb.

"Donald," Mrs. March finally said, "she can't . . ."

He put up his hand for silence. "Let's just finish our meal in peace," he said, and that was how we ate it, the three of us performing a show of simple gestures, passing dishes, salt and pepper and butter, as if we all were deaf.

When I went upstairs, I heard Kiera sobbing in her suite and knocked softly on her door.

"If that's you, Mother, go away."

"It's Sasha," I said.

She opened the door and then turned away quickly and returned to throw herself on her bed.

"You see? You see why my therapist is right? You were there!" she cried, and pounded the mattress. "No matter what I do or say, she's ready to destroy me." She turned to face me. "How can anyone be a better person in this house? Tell me that, will you? You were there. You saw it. You heard her."

She waited for my response. I didn't want to take sides, but I nodded.

"Well, we just have to stick together more," she said, sitting up. "Next time she's critical of me, something I do or say, you might come to my defense, say something."

"What could I say?"

"Say . . . 'Kiera's trying.' Just say that. My father will pick up on it. I can see he likes you. Maybe then my mother will get off both our backs."

I didn't think she was really on my back, but I didn't disagree.

Kiera smiled and reached for my hands. "Thanks for stopping by to see how I am, Sasha. That's very sweet of you. I don't deserve it, of course. I don't deserve even your being civil to me, but I plan on deserving it someday. Now, go practice the clarinet. I know it's important to you and you want to do well. Besides, I like hearing it through the wall."

I started toward the door.

"You can leave my door open a little," she said. "And yours, too. That way, I'll hear you better."

"Okay, but I'm not that good yet."

"You're better than me, not that that says much."

"Didn't you ever play an instrument?"

"The heart," she said.

"You mean the harp?"

"No. The heart," she said, and laughed.

For a moment, I thought she did look like Alena, innocent, young, and vulnerable.

Downstairs, you became deaf, a voice of warning inside me said. *Up here, you became blind.*

I practiced for more than an hour before getting ready for bed and reading ahead in my English textbook. I had forgotten that I had left my door open. Before she said anything, Mrs. March must have been standing in my doorway a while just looking in at me. I finally sensed someone and lowered my textbook.

She smiled. "Seeing you lying there like that, reading, reminded me so much of Alena. She was a voracious reader, unlike Kiera. She read all of those books you see on the shelves here, every single one. I know, because she would spend hours telling me the stories or talking about the characters. She always got so involved. She'd talk about her books with anyone who would listen."

She stepped in.

"It used to break my heart when she tried describing a story to Kiera, and Kiera would brush her off, tell her it was silly or a waste of time. I know Kiera can be a very exciting young woman, Sasha. She is beautiful, and boys trail after her like ants following honey, but she hasn't quite reached the level of maturity and responsibility she should, and I worry about her. Now I have to worry about you, as well. Please be careful," she said. "I know how easy it is to fall into traps when you're the age you are. Is there anything you want to tell me?"

"No. I'm fine, Mrs. March."

"I hope someday you'll be able to call me Mother. Not

that I want to replace your mother," she quickly added. "I just want us to be closer."

"That's still difficult for me to do right now, Mrs. March," I said.

I saw how hard she took my answer. For a moment, she looked like she might burst into tears, but then she managed a smile. "Of course. Everything has its proper time and place."

She gazed around, smiled again, and said good night, closing the door softly behind her. Less than a minute later, the door opened again. I thought she had forgotten something, but it was Kiera.

"You left my door open a bit, remember?"

"Yes."

"I heard everything she said. I don't read. I wouldn't listen to Alena. I'm not mature and responsible. See what I was saying? That was a lie. I always listened to Alena. She would sit on the floor next to me and tell me her stories while I sat there filing my nails or doing my hair. Why, she'd even come in while I was soaking in the tub and sit on the bathroom floor and recite them."

Now she was the one who looked as if she might burst into tears.

"I hope you never call her Mother," she said. Then she turned and rushed out, closing the door sharply behind her.

It sounded so ridiculous, even outright funny to say it, but I muttered to myself, "Maybe I was better off in the streets."

26

The VA Club

I was nervous from the moment I got into Kiera's car the next morning and never stopped being nervous all day. I did well enough in instrumental class to avoid any looks or words of dissatisfaction from Mr. Denacio, and I got an eighty-eight on a vocabulary test in English, but all through the day, I would have these moments when my heart would race and I would have a shortness of breath. I knew that this was because I was attending Kiera's secret VA club meeting and because of our lying to Mrs. March about a school play audition. If and when she found out, she would be very upset that I had gone along with it, but I felt that if I changed my mind, Kiera would return to the way she had been when I had first arrived.

I was good at keeping it all to myself. Ricky was the only one who sensed anything different about me. Kiera and her other friends were their usual buoyant selves, laughing, gossiping about other girls and boys in their classes and teachers as well. No one noticed that I was especially quiet.

It wasn't until the very end of lunch period that anyone said anything about the VA club. Deidre came up beside me as we were all leaving for class and said, "We're all looking forward to you coming today."

Before I could say anything, she walked away and left me with Ricky, who now looked even more suspicious.

"What was she whispering about? What are you she-devils up to today?" he asked.

The first thing that came to my mind was that if I said anything that even suggested we were meeting after school, he would mention it, and Kiera and the other girls would think I had already betrayed them.

"Nothing very important," I said. "Girlie stuff."

"Well, that's no fun," he replied, and walked the rest of the way wearing an impish grin. Kiera never mentioned any boys knowing about or going to the VA club. Was that one of the surprises that awaited me?

When the final bell rang to end classes, my heart felt like a yo-yo. Kiera was at my classroom door before I got to it myself. She must have run all the way from her wing of the building the second the bell rang. She had told me that sometimes she faked a desperate need to go to the bathroom just to get a head start on leaving.

"C'mon," she said. "We can't stay at Deidre's longer than we would have stayed for a play audition, remember."

I followed her out as quickly as I could. I hated it when she or someone else made me move so quickly that my limp became more pronounced. I knew there were students, even in my own classes, who ridiculed me. I didn't see any of the other girls in Kiera's group of friends when we reached the parking lot. When I asked about them, she told me they had already left. Deidre had actually feigned an excuse to leave before the last period.

"They always get excited when we agree on a possible new candidate for the club," she said as we got into her car. "There are lots of girls who would love to join, but we're very particular. Usually, we don't ever consider a new student to the school, but since I vouched for you and all of them except Deidre believe you're my cousin, they agreed. Excited?"

"I don't know. I still don't know or understand what the club does."

"Oh, you will before today's meeting ends." She stopped the car as we reached the driveway to the parking lot and turned to me, her face tightened into a look of seriousness and intensity I had not seen. "Nothing we can do together, nothing we say or promise each other, will ever bring us closer together than you being in the VA," she said. "I can assure you. We're closer than real sisters, and every girl in the club would rather tell her most secret thoughts and things to one of us than she would to her own real sister."

She drove out. I sat back, impressed. Never had I dreamed I'd be close friends with girls older than I was and in a new school, too. Now, according to Kiera, I would be even more special. I felt as if I had stepped onto a rocket ship, and it wasn't only because of Kiera's driving, either. Trips to Disneyland, parties, boat trips, all of it lay before me like some promised land filled with delight and pleasure. *Months from now,* I thought, *I won't even remember living on the streets.*

Deidre's house was in a gated community. The guard

checked off Kiera and opened the gate for us. All of the houses were big and beautiful, but none was even half the size of the March mansion. That didn't mean Deidre's family's home wasn't a big, beautiful house in Pacific Palisades, too. As we approached, Kiera told me more about her. First, she explained that none of them talked about each other much with anyone who wasn't a member of the VA club.

"We hold each other's trust sacred," she said. "Any of us gossiping about any one of us would be considered worse than being a serial killer, but I can tell you more about Deidre now. Deidre, as you know, is an only child. I became friendlier with her than I was with the other girls because I frankly felt like an only child, especially after Alena came along. I think you're beginning to understand why.

"As I told you, Deidre's father is an important business attorney with beautiful offices in Century City. Her mother works with her father. She's his personal secretary. I think she became that because most men hire beautiful women to become their personal secretaries and then have affairs with them.

"Look, everyone's here already," she said, nodding at the three cars parked in the driveway. We pulled in behind the one on the right and got out.

Deidre's house was a sprawling Spanish-style hacienda with a large courtyard. It didn't have views of the ocean because of the tree line on the west side, but it was high enough to capture the sprawling vistas and the lights of sections of Los Angeles on the east side. Deidre opened the arched front door before we reached it.

"Everyone has to take off her shoes today," she said.

"We just put in a new carpet in the living room, and my mother is anal about it."

Kiera kicked hers off, and I slipped out of mine. We put them next to the four other pairs there and followed Deidre over the tiled-floor entry, down a hallway, and into the living room, where the girls were sitting on settees. There were some soft drinks on the table and a bowl of popcorn with smaller bowls, but I was glad to see no whiskey. It looked as harmless as a gathering of teenage girls could look.

"Everyone knows who Sasha is," Deidre began. "Sasha, you know Marcia Blumfield and Doris Norman."

"Hi," Marcia said.

"Right," Doris said. She sipped her soda and shifted her gaze to Kiera.

"Sit anywhere you want," Deidre said. She flopped into the big armchair to the right of one of the settees. Kiera sat beside Margot, and they made a place for me. "If you want something besides soda, let me know," Deidre said. "Don't spill anything or drop anything on the floor, or I'll have my mother visit you late at night."

The girls laughed. I sat, and Kiera poured herself a Coke. She looked at me and offered some, but I shook my head.

"Who's first this time?" Margot asked. "I was first the day we inducted Doris."

"It might be instructive for Doris to lead off, then, don't you think?" Deidre said.

"You mean since the last meeting, no one's made lovey-dovey dangerously?" Marcia asked.

They all laughed again.

"Okay, I go first, then," Doris said. She looked at Kiera. "Unless I'm wrong."

"You're not wrong," Kiera said. "Go on."

"Well, you all know my father owns and operates a bowling alley in Manhattan Beach. On weekends, I often go in to waitress at the café. I've always had a crush on the bartender's son, Crawford."

"Crush. Give me a break," Margot said. I noticed how she looked at Kiera after practically everything she said to see if Kiera approved.

"Well, what would you call it?" Doris fired back.

"Hunger," she said, and everyone laughed, even Doris.

"Okay, hunger. No matter how I flirted with him whenever he was there, he didn't seem to notice or care. Last weekend," she said, smiling, "he did."

"Doesn't sound dangerous to me," Marcia said.

"I didn't get to it yet, genius."

I wanted to ask why it had to be dangerous but remembered Kiera's warning about asking questions. She must have sensed it, however, because she turned to me to explain.

"Sasha's probably wondering about this 'dangerous' thing, right, Sasha?"

I looked at the other girls. They were all focused on me. "Yes," I said.

"We came up with the idea to add some additional excitement," Kiera said.

"You mean you came up with it," Deidre told her.

Kiera smiled. "Whatever." She turned back to me. "You see, Sasha, some of the recent sexual episodes described here were quite mediocre."

"You say," Deidre told her. "I was quite satisfied the last time."

"It takes so little to satisfy Deidre," Kiera said, and everyone laughed again, including Deidre. "Anyway, a suggestion was made by *moi* to the effect of performing the ultimate sex act as close to in public or in the presence of a third party as possible, trying not to be discovered, of course. Therein lies the danger. Which brings us back to Doris. Go on, Doris," she said.

"Crawford hung around longer than usual this particular day. I could feel his eyes on me, and he was flashing that cute, sexy smile of his. To my surprise and delight, I might add, he waited until I was finished with my shift, and then he and I had something to eat and drink, mostly drink. He snuck me some of his vodka. His father asked him to get something for the bar in the storage room, and I went with him. When we got there, we began to kiss."

"Storage room?" Marcia moaned. "That's hardly dangerous."

"Will you wait!" Doris said, stamping her foot.

"She's right. Don't rush her. Don't ever rush it, girls," Kiera said. Everyone smiled. "Go on, Doris."

Doris sent some eye darts at Marcia and continued.

"He was trying to undo my skirt, and I said, 'No, not here.' I remembered our new VA pledge."

"Where did you go?" Margot asked, leaning toward her. All of the girls looked more interested now.

"I took him by the hand to an area right behind the pins. We made love to the sound of strikes and splits," she said proudly.

Marcia grimaced, shaking her head. "That's not much. I don't think it was possible for anyone to see you."

"You don't bowl at my father's bowling alley. Anyone looking past the pins might have seen us. That counts, doesn't it, Kiera?"

"It counts. It wasn't as dangerous as Margot's time with Perry Gordon just under her father's home-office window, however."

Doris looked disappointed. "Well, I thought it was clever," she said. "And it got Crawford very excited, just like you said it might. He couldn't believe I wanted to do it there."

"It was clever. That was very good, Doris. I don't mean to say it wasn't," Kiera told her, and her sour, disappointed expression flew off her face, to be replaced by a satisfied smile. She nodded at Marcia.

"From the look on her face, I don't think Sasha understands us or what we're talking about or what we believe," Margot said. Everyone turned to me.

"I thought I would let you guys talk a while to whet her appetite," Kiera said, and then turned to me. "You know what Alcoholics Anonymous is, right?"

For a moment, I lost my breath. She knew very well that I knew what Alcoholics Anonymous was. It was a place my mother should have been regularly, even before we were on the street. I glanced at Deidre and saw the way she was staring at me, poised to see my reaction. Every part of her face was perfectly still. She wasn't even blinking.

"Yes, I know what it is."

"Well, then, it's simple to understand," Kiera said.

"Alcoholics go there to swear off alcohol. We meet here to swear off virginity."

As if they anticipated my reacting with shock or negativity, they each pounced with a defense.

"Why should boys be the only ones to be ashamed of being virgins?" Margot asked.

"Why should they be the only ones to enjoy having sex whenever they can or want?" Marcia added.

"Why should boys be the only ones who can brag about how good a lover they are?" Doris asked.

"Why do we have to be the ones who always say no?" Deidre asked.

"Most boys, the ones who really are good lovers, don't want to be with virgins, anyway," Kiera said. "When they are, they always act as though they're doing the girl a big favor."

"What we do here is support each other, advise each other, and protect each other," Deidre told me. "Any girl out there on her own is vulnerable and afraid. You're very lucky Kiera has brought you here. You may not realize it now, but you will soon enough."

"She thinks she doesn't have to worry because she's only fourteen," Kiera said, as if she were reading my mind.

"I was only fourteen the first time," Margot said.

"I wasn't quite fourteen," Marcia said.

"I confess. I was almost fifteen," Doris said.

"The way you look, you're not long for virginity, anyway," Deidre said. "When Kiera dresses you and gets you made up, you look at least eighteen, nineteen. That's why all those college boys were looking at you that night in Westwood."

"You don't have a mother or a father," Marcia said, "but every girl here will tell you it's easier for her to come to one of us than to go to her mother with questions. What mother would accept the VA club? Even though she probably lost her virginity when she was about our age, she'd make you feel terrible even thinking about it."

"Exactly," Doris said.

"Well, what do you think?" Kiera asked me. "Want to be with us, part of us, the sex sisters?"

They all smiled.

"Or do you want to be on your own out there?" she added.

I looked at each of them. They were all anxious to hear my answer. "I thought that once you lost your virginity, you couldn't get it back."

"No, not physically back," Deidre said, "but you can become a mental virgin, which is just as stupid."

"I'm still not sure about what I have to do," I said.

Doris laughed the hardest.

"First, you take the oath, and then you get the tattoo," Deidre said.

"What tattoo?"

"Girls?"

They all stood up. Doris and Marcia undid their jeans and lowered them as they turned to show me a tattoo of VA done in a fancy script just above the crack in their rears. Deidre and Margot lifted their skirts to reveal the same one in the same place, and then Kiera rose, lowered her jeans, and showed me hers.

"We'll take you to get yours on Friday after school," she said. "I think Sasha should have hers done in calligraphy.

Her mother used to do calligraphy, and she's doing it in art class now. Anyone have any objections?"

No one spoke.

"Deidre, you schedule the tattoo, and tell him what we want him to do."

"First the oath," Deidre reminded her.

"Yes, the oath."

"And then?" I asked, my heart thumping.

"And then we help you break out of physical and mental virginity," Margot said.

"She began her period yesterday," Kiera told them.

"No rush," Doris said. "I trust her. She looks as innocent as I did."

"Hardly," Marcia said. "When you were born and your father asked what you were, a boy or a girl, the doctor said, 'Slut.'"

They all laughed. Doris threw a pillow at her. Marcia threatened to throw her drink at her.

"Watch the rug!" Deidre screamed.

"There's one major added benefit," Margot told me when things quieted down again. She looked to Kiera.

"She's right. When we say we'll help you break out, we'll make sure you break out with the right boy."

"No one knows the boys at school better than we do," Deidre said.

"The oath!" Doris cried.

"The oath," everyone else chanted.

Deidre reached under the chair and produced a diary. She brought it to me, and all of the girls stood up.

I looked at Kiera. "What is this?"

"This diary contains every member's description of her first sexual experience," Deidre said. "When you've had yours and you write it into the book, you can read the others. Place your right hand on the notebook."

Were they serious? Was this some sort of joke? There wasn't a smile on anyone's face, and no eyes betrayed any humor. No one was going to leap to cry "April fool" or anything. They couldn't have looked more serious in church.

I put my hand on the notebook.

"Repeat after me. I, Sasha Porter, do solemnly swear to share my most secret sexual thoughts with my sisters and with no one else."

I repeated it.

"I hereby renounce virginity, and I will never betray any sister's trust or speak of the VA club with anyone who is not a member."

After I repeated that, all of the girls placed their right hands over mine. They all closed their eyes as if in silent prayer. I closed mine.

Each one hugged me and returned to her seat.

"Now, then," Kiera said, smiling. "Let me tell you how I made love dangerously this week."

Like kindergarten students gathering around their teacher to hear a story, the girls leaned forward. Despite what Kiera was about to describe, I found myself lost in my own thoughts.

More a single question.

What had I just sworn to do and to be?

27

The Oath

I was really proud of you in there," Kiera said as we drove home. "A couple of the girls were worried you were too young. Of course, they don't know your history. Growing up in the streets, seeing the things you've seen, has made you more mature than they are, I'm sure."

"I didn't see much more than poor people struggling to eat, Kiera."

"You know what I mean."

I didn't, but I didn't disagree with her. If she wanted to believe those things about me, fine. Right now, it looked like something of an advantage to have her think that way about me.

"But you can't keep going to school dressed like a character in *Alice in Wonderland* or something," she continued. "I'm going to give you more of my things to wear. My mother has to realize you're not a ten-year-old, and boys won't take you seriously if you look like you just walked off *Sesame Street*."

"Ricky seems to like me," I said.

"He's one of us. Besides, he's only one boy. You don't want to become dependent upon one boy this early. That's the whole point of our club. Girls get into this frenzy to have a relationship. Heaven forbid they not be asked out on a date or not have a date to the prom or something. We're free of all that anxiety and pressure." She smiled. "And it drives the boys crazy because we act so indifferent. We're in more control of our own destinies. You see the point, right?"

"Yes," I said. I did see the point. What she was saying made me feel a little better about what I had just sworn to do and to be.

Luckily, Mrs. March wasn't home when we arrived. I didn't have to greet her with my face full of deception immediately. We went right up to our rooms, but Kiera wanted me to come into hers after I settled in so she could choose some clothes for me to wear to school. That was where Mrs. March found us. Kiera had at least five outfits laid out on her bed.

"What's all this?" she asked as soon as she entered Kiera's suite.

"Clothes I'm lending Sasha, Mother. She doesn't have anything really fashionable. Alena's things are just not right for her now," Kiera said.

"Fashionable? I hardly think the clothes you wear to school are what I would call fashionable, Kiera."

"They are to me and to my friends, Mother," she said with what I thought for Kiera was remarkable control. She even smiled at her. "You just forget what it was like to be a teenager. I'm sure your mother complained about the things you wore."

Mrs. March stepped closer to examine what was on the bed. "I don't remember you wearing these things."

"Why am I not surprised?" Kiera said, rolling her eyes. "Sasha likes them," she added.

I hadn't really expressed any opinion yet, but Mrs. March looked at me as though she had caught me in a betrayal and then relaxed her shoulders like someone accepting defeat.

"How did the audition go?" she asked.

"Neither of us was thrilled with it," Kiera said. "We're rethinking it."

"Why?"

"Mother, will you ease up a little? Sasha has enough pressure adjusting to a new school, making new friends, learning the clarinet, and everything else."

Again, Mrs. March turned to me for a reaction. I was silent. *I'm already deep in a lie,* I thought, and felt trapped.

"Very well," she said. "I'm meeting your father at Palmeri for dinner. Don't give Mrs. Duval or Mrs. Caro any grief." She left.

I knew Mrs. March was very upset with us, but Kiera looked as if she couldn't care any less about it. She continued pulling clothing off hangers and tossing what she liked onto the bed with cries of "This will look great on you! This is perfect!"

She stood back from the clothes. "You need some jewelry, too, and I have a watch you could have. Here," she said, taking the watch off her wrist and handing it to me.

"But it's your watch."

"I have more than twenty, silly."

"Twenty?"

"Those are real diamonds in it, by the way."

I put it on my wrist.

"Looks nice on you."

She dumped a box of earrings, bracelets, and necklaces onto the bed beside the clothing she had laid out and began putting the outfits together with the jewelry. She had so much I thought she could open her own jewelry store.

"Is any of this very expensive?" I asked.

"It's all very expensive. I don't buy junk, and I don't let my parents buy me junk, not that they would. You have nothing here that would make you ashamed to wear," she said.

"I don't mean that. I don't want to lose anything expensive. It makes me nervous."

She laughed. "First of all, Daddy has some kind of insurance policy on our jewelry, and second, I could replace anything anyway, even without insurance, so don't give it a second thought. I don't. There," she said, stepping back. "You have a different outfit for every day of the week with the right accompanying earrings, necklaces, bracelets, and rings. Start trying things on. Oh, wait a minute!" She examined my ears. "You don't have pierced ears. Didn't your mother ever want you to get your ears pierced?"

"No. She didn't think I was old enough."

"Damn. Most of these earrings are useless. We have to get your ears pierced. We'll do it this weekend."

I looked at the watch she had given me.

"Will you stop being such a worrywart about your homework? I'll leave you alone after dinner. Promise," she said, holding up her right hand.

I began trying her things on and was surprised at how well everything fit me. Everything looked and smelled new, too. She raved about it all. All of the tops were skin-tight, shirred, with plunging necklines. The skirts were short and also tighter than I would normally wear. There was a fuchsia halter-top dress that left little to the imagination. In fact, I thought what she was giving me was even sexier than the clothes she wore.

"Are you sure I can wear all of these things to school?"

"Of course you can. You're not dressing much differently from most of the other girls. Besides, if you have it, flaunt it," she said. "That's my motto, and it should be yours, too. You have a great figure."

I was still reluctant. "Your mother was very upset about it."

"Of course she is. She has you in Alena's room, playing Alena's clarinet, and wearing Alena's things. We know why, and we know how we both feel about that, right?"

"Yes," I said.

"Good. I'm starving," she declared before I could say anything else. "Let's go eat dinner. Keep that on. I love the expression on Mrs. Duval's face when she sees you in something I would wear." She seized my hand and pulled me along.

She was right about Mrs. Duval. Her eyes widened, and she shook her head softly, mumbling to herself as she went back and forth from the dining room to the kitchen.

At dinner, Kiera reminded me about getting the club's tattoo on Friday.

"That's when we'll get your ears pierced, too," she said.

"What will be our reason for not coming right home after school?" I asked. Mrs. March probably would approve of pierced ears, but I couldn't imagine her approving of tattoos.

"I'll tell my mother I had to stop at the mall to pick up some makeup. That's one thing she understands and approves of, cosmetics. Besides, it is the start of the weekend. We don't have to rush home to do homework—not that I ever do, anyway."

"Does she know you have a tattoo?"

"I don't bathe in front of my mother anymore, Sasha, and certainly not in front of my father. Besides, they both know that if I wanted to do something like that, I'd do it with or without their permission."

I was still quite nervous about doing it, but I felt I couldn't back out now without turning all of the girls against me. Kiera didn't talk about it any more. She went on and on about different boys and other girls at school whom the club members were considering, and she told me more about each of the girls themselves, especially whom I should listen to more and trust more. It was truly as if I had been taken into her confidence now, and there was nothing she wouldn't tell me. She lived up to her word after dinner, however, and didn't disturb my homework and practicing of the clarinet.

Grover picked me up after school the following day, as Kiera had a therapy session. During the day, I did notice that more boys were looking at me because of the clothes I was wearing. Both Ricky and Boyd made a point of telling me I looked hot, and all of the girls in the VA club complimented me. I saw the envy in the faces of the girls in my classes, too.

"You'll need us more than ever," Deidre whispered. "Boys will be coming at you like flies to honey. Make no promises or commitments until you speak with one of us."

I thought I had felt as if I were floating when I had just entered such a school, but now I really was lightheaded and happy. I dared to think that maybe I was beautiful; maybe I was just as pretty as or even prettier than Kiera.

Grover was surprised and amused by how many boys accompanied me out to the parking lot, each trying to get me to pay him some special attention.

"I guess you're adapting pretty well," he said before driving off. He rarely said anything, so I was pleased and actually felt myself blushing. I waved when I saw Kiera driving away, but she didn't notice.

Either because we were friendlier now and she was assuming more of a big sister's role or because she had reached some important realizations about herself, Kiera complained less and less about her therapy and behaved much more nicely and kindly toward her mother. I still saw the suspicion flashing in Mrs. March's face, but even she began to relax more. On Thursday night, after dinner was over and we were heading up to our rooms, Kiera claiming that she was trying hard to do better in her schoolwork, Mr. March asked me to follow him to his office.

"I'd like to speak with you a moment, Sasha."

Kiera paused, too.

"You can go up, Kiera. I just need to talk to Sasha right now," he said.

Kiera looked at me with fear and warning in her face, but she didn't linger. Mrs. March followed Mr. March and me to his office. He smiled at me as soon as we entered.

"There's nothing wrong, Sasha," he said. "You can wipe away your look of anxiety. On the contrary, there's something right."

He went to his desk and took a cigar out of a box. "Have a seat," he said, gesturing with his cigar toward the red bullet leather chairs. I sat, and he lit his cigar.

"You could wait until she leaves, Donald," Mrs. March said. "Not everyone loves the stench of cigar smoke."

"Oh. Sorry. Does this bother you, Sasha?"

"No, sir."

There had been a time not so long ago when the aroma of a lit cigar would have been more like perfume when compared with the odors surrounding me.

He leaned against the front of his desk.

"First," he began, "I want to thank you for giving Kiera a chance to redeem herself when it comes to you. You have every reason to hate every cell in her body. I know it looks like I'm totally aloof from all that goes on here, but I assure you, I'm not. Both Mrs. March and I have kept in close contact with Kiera's therapist, and we're very happy with her progress."

"We hope it's real," Mrs. March said.

"I think Dr. Ralston would be a better judge of that than we would, don't you, Jordan?"

"I'd hope so. I have a closet full of Kiera's broken promises to us both."

He shook his head slightly at her, puffed on his cigar, and turned back to me. "In any case, you've been very generous in permitting her to rework herself into decent behavior. I'm also impressed with the influence you've had on her. Now, even more important perhaps, I wanted to tell you how pleased I am to hear about your own progress and achievements. I must admit I was wary when Jordan, Mrs. March, wanted to have this arrangement, but I'm very happy to be proven wrong. Is there anything you need? Anything I can do for you?"

I looked at Mrs. March. She was finally smiling warmly.

"No, sir. I have more than I ever dreamed I would have," I said, and he laughed.

"You and me both, Sasha. You and me both. Okay. I just wanted to have this little talk. Don't hesitate to come to me if I can do anything more or if anything bothers you, okay? I know you have Mrs. March to rely on, but I want you to know you have me as well."

"Thank you."

He smiled and went around to his desk chair. I rose, glanced at Mrs. March, and then hurried out and up the stairs. Kiera was waiting for me at her doorway.

"What did he want?" she asked. "Was he trying to get you to tell him something? My mother must have put him up to it. Well?"

"No, nothing like that," I said. "He wanted to tell me how pleased he was with how things were going between us and how both of us were doing now," I said. "He told me not to hesitate if I needed or wanted anything."

"My father said that?"

"Yes. He was very nice, nicer to me than ever."

She studied me a moment to see if I was telling the truth and then smiled. "That's my father. He can be a real charmer when he wants to be. This is great. Mother might ease up on us. Okay. Get to your homework," she said, and went into her room.

On Friday as planned, all of the girls in the VA club met us after school and followed as Kiera drove me to a tattoo parlor in West L.A. The man doing the tattoos looked as if he was tattooed on every possible area of his body. There was a snake up his right arm beginning at his wrist and what looked like a chain up his left arm. He even had a tattoo on his throat.

All of the girls followed us into a small area in the rear, and the tattooing began. It wasn't pleasant, and twice I was on the verge of screaming that I wanted him to stop, but Kiera stood right beside him, and the girls were right behind her. Afterward, I looked at it in a full-length mirror by holding another mirror to catch the reflection. It looked bigger than theirs, and he had done what they had asked, a form of calligraphy.

They insisted on celebrating. Kiera called Mrs. March and told her we had gone to the mall so that I could get my ears pierced. She asked her to let us hang out and go for pizza with some friends. Minutes after she hung up, my phone rang, and Mrs. March asked me if we were doing what Kiera had said we were doing. Kiera knew, of course, that it was her mother calling me, and she watched and listened. I had no choice but to lie.

"Let's get to the mall," Kiera said. "We really do need to get your ears pierced, remember?"

Instead of going someplace for pizza afterward, however, we all went to Marcia's house. She had a younger brother, but her parents had left for a weekend in San Diego and had taken him along. Kiera had told me that Marcia's father owned car dealerships up and down the coast. A girl whose parents were only middle-class would have a hard time being friends with members of the VA club, I thought. She would always be intimidated by their clothes, their jewelry, and their cars. That feeling was reinforced when I saw Marcia's family's home, a sprawling two-story in a place called Brentwood Park. She had a live-in maid, too, but her maid had the night off.

We did order in pizza, and then, to my surprise, boys began to arrive. Ricky and Boyd came first, and then three other boys followed—Tony Sussman, Jack Martin, and Ruben Weiner. They were all seniors as well. In fact, I was the only one there who wasn't. As before, no one seemed particularly involved with anyone else. When they danced, everyone was dancing with everyone. I saw the vodka being added to the soda and juice, but when Marcia offered me some, Kiera interfered.

"Sasha doesn't drink," she said. She said it so sharply that Marcia looked as if she had been slapped.

"Well, excuse me. I didn't know we had a Mormon in the club."

"She's not a Mormon. I promised my mother I wouldn't let her get into any drinking after what happened to her parents, remember? They were killed by a drunk driver."

"Oh. Sorry," Marcia said, turning to me and looking as if she would burst into tears.

Kiera seemed to wink with her whole face. She leaned over to whisper, "She needs to drink to have fun. You and I don't."

Later, Ricky spent more time with me. We sat and talked and ate.

"I've got to work tomorrow," he said. "I have next weekend off, and I'm sure I'll get the boat."

"I've never been on a boat," I said.

"You will be next weekend." He looked at the others and then brought his lips to mine. It wasn't a quick peck, either. It was a soft, long kiss. I closed my eyes, and when I opened them, I expected that everyone would be looking at us, but no one was.

We kissed again and again before the party ended, but we didn't do much more. I wasn't disappointed, but I was anticipating it. When Kiera announced that we had to leave, Ricky followed us out. He kissed me again before I got into the car. I knew Kiera was watching.

"See you soon," he said, but he held on to my arm. Then he leaned in, bringing his lips to my ear. "I hear you were inducted into the VA club," he whispered. "I hope I'm the one."

He turned and walked back into the house before I could respond, not that I knew what to say. When I got into the car, Kiera asked me immediately what he had whispered. I told her. I was surprised that he knew about the club.

"He's okay. He has the Good Sexkeeping Seal of

Approval," she said nonchalantly, and started the car. As we drove out, she slowed down and turned to me, "But as for him initiating you, that's not his decision—or yours, for that matter."

"What do you mean?"

"We'll bring it up at the next meeting, and the members will vote on it. There are four other boys who are approved for initiations, right now only four boys."

"You mean everyone votes on which boy each girl is with for the first time?"

"Of course. That way, no one makes a serious mistake. When I said I was going to be your protective older sister, I meant it," she said. "It's the least I can do for you, and I appreciate your letting me do it. We're all sisters now. The members of the club think clearly and carefully about each girl's sexual experiences. Everyone there has far more experience than you have. Why shouldn't you benefit from their experiences? Believe me, my mother wouldn't be any sort of adviser when it comes to sex. Sometimes I think she and my father stopped doing it.

"Despite what some people tell you, sex for the first time is the most important time. Our four boys know how to make love to a virgin. There have been no complaints," she added, smiling.

We drove on.

It was on the tip of my tongue to ask, but I didn't. *Whatever happened to love?*

ᴖ28ᴖ

Decision

A strange thing happened at school during the days that followed. The more I hung out with the older students, whether at lunch or talking to them in the halls between classes and going with Kiera and the others to malls or restaurants, the more invisible I became to my classmates. Those who had once been impressed with my being so lovey-dovey with a senior boy were now indifferent to me. No one said hello or even nodded at me. They walked past me as though I weren't there.

I continued to do well in class and improve on the clarinet, but when Mr. Denacio announced that I would have a seat in the senior band and issued me a uniform, everyone else in the class took it as if it had been expected. It wasn't so much an achievement as simply another assumed step. *Big deal* was written across their faces. Ironically, Kiera and the club members were the only friends I had. No one my own age would give me the time of day.

One Wednesday, Kiera told me that we were having a

meeting of the VA club at Deidre's house after school on Friday, and I was the main topic. She asked me how my period had been since she had given me her pill. I had gone through it far better than any time I had had it before and told her so.

"My doctor says we should take the pill afterward, too," she said. "It will prevent you from having those severe cramps next time. These are for you. Take one every day now."

I thanked her and took one every morning as her doctor had prescribed. As Friday drew closer, I was even more nervous for the VA club meeting than I had been the first time. After all, it was to be all about my first sexual experience.

The other girls were already there when we arrived, sitting in the same places. They all looked very serious. I saw the pictures of four boys on the coffee table: Ricky, Boyd, Ruben Weiner, and Tony Sussman. Deidre brought a chair for me and put it in the center so I'd face all of the girls.

"We didn't ask you last time," Margot began, "but how much experience do you have? How far have you gone with a boy?"

I looked at Kiera, but she was just as serious and stone-faced as they were.

"All I've ever done with a boy I did at Marcia's party with Ricky," I said.

"Just kiss?" Marcia said, squinting and crinkling her nose as though kissing were more disgusting. "What, did you grow up in Disneyland?"

"There's no reason to pick on her," Kiera said. "You

weren't exactly Miss Sophisticated when we brought you into the club."

Marcia blushed and sat back.

"That still leaves Tony out. He moves too fast, assuming the girl has been on the verge," Deidre said. "Everyone agree?"

They all nodded, and she turned Tony's picture over.

"Can she go on a date? Will your mother permit it?" Doris asked.

"I doubt it," Kiera said. "My mother refuses to see her as anything but a ten-year-old, and she has this thing about added responsibility for her."

"She doesn't look ten now," Margot said. "I want to know where you got that fuchsia outfit you wore the other day."

I looked at Kiera. Hadn't she ever worn it?

"Like it will look as good on you," Doris muttered.

"Can we get on with the business at hand?" Kiera said sharply.

"Ruben uses his love machine," Deidre says. "It's an SUV. All the seats go down, and he throws an air mattress in it. It feels like a waterbed."

"You should know," Doris said, smiling.

"Like you don't?"

Doris laughed.

"In any case, he'd be better if it was going to be a straight-out date, don't you think?" Deidre asked. Everyone nodded, and she turned his picture over.

"It's between Boyd and Ricky, and we know how you feel about Ricky already," Marcia said.

"Ricky's usually the most gentle," Doris added.

"I prefer Boyd," Margot said.

"It's not your initiation. It's hers," Doris told her.

"Boyd is more professional about it. He spends more time on foreplay," Margot insisted.

"I think this should be a secret ballot," Kiera announced. "There's a little too much personal business going on here."

"Whatever," Margot said.

Deidre produced a sticky pad and handed each girl a sheet.

"I don't have a pen," Margot said.

"Use your lipstick," Doris told her.

"Then everyone will know it's my vote. That's not a secret ballot."

"I'm just kidding, stupid."

Deidre got up, walked out, and returned with pens for those who didn't have any.

"Just an *R* or a *B* is all that's necessary," Kiera said.

I watched as they spread out to vote. It wasn't until they all handed their folded papers to Kiera that the full realization of what they were deciding for me hit me. I had sworn their oath, and I had gotten the tattoo, but I wasn't confident that I could go through with the rest of it, especially if they had chosen Boyd. Kiera didn't announce the votes. She opened each slip and put it on the right. She put none on the left.

"It's settled," she said. "Unanimous. Ricky."

"When?" Margot asked immediately.

"As it happens, we're all going on Ricky's boat

tomorrow," Kiera said. "I didn't say anything until I knew for sure and knew this would be the vote for sure. I mean, Boyd will be there, too, but Ricky's the one."

"And you can make it dangerous, too," Margot said, "if it happens on the boat."

"No, that wouldn't count as dangerous," Kiera said. "It's only us. Besides, you wanted real privacy the first time, as I recall. I heard Tony almost had to use a sheet with a hole."

"That's not true!" she cried.

Everyone laughed.

"Let's have some music," Deidre declared, "and order some Chinese."

Everyone rose to congratulate me as if I had done or would do something historic. Maybe I was naive about sex, but I knew that what they expected me to do, what I would do, was not all that much of an accomplishment, except, of course, that it would make me solid with these girls. I'd be part of their family, and for an orphan, that was some accomplishment.

"I bet you're really excited," Kiera said after we left Deidre's house.

"This is all supposed to happen tomorrow on Ricky's boat?"

"Sure. It has two staterooms. Don't look so worried. You'll do fine."

She made it sound like a performance or a test. When we arrived home, however, we were both almost grounded. Mrs. March had learned the truth. The drama teacher had not held auditions for the play yet. She intercepted us just before we were about to go upstairs.

"In here," she commanded, standing in the living-room doorway.

Kiera and I looked at each other. On the way into the living room, she whispered, "Whatever it is, let me do all the talking."

Mrs. March was alone. She stood with her arms folded under her breasts and nodded toward one of the settees. We sat.

"What now, Mother?" Kiera asked.

"What now? Why did both of you lie to me about the auditions? There were no auditions that day. Well?"

"I was too embarrassed to tell you that I had made a mistake and misread the date on the bulletin-board announcement. We actually went to the auditorium and felt like idiots. At least, I did. It wasn't Sasha's fault, so don't blame her."

"But you continued the lie, giving me that story about changing your minds," Mrs. March said, looking from Kiera to me. I couldn't look directly at her.

"Yes."

"Why? Why wouldn't you just tell me the truth? You made a mistake?"

"I didn't think you'd believe me, and besides, we really did decide not to do it."

"Where did you go that day?"

"Nowhere. We just killed some time riding around and then came home. It's not a federal case, Mother. It's not like we did some terrible thing instead."

"I don't believe you, Kiera."

"Don't believe me. Ask Sasha."

She looked at me. "Is what she's saying true? You just rode around?"

"Yes," I said softly, almost too softly for her to hear.

"I'm very disappointed in both of you. Why don't I see you working on your calligraphy anymore, Sasha?"

"I've done a little, but with my homework and clarinet practice . . ."

"And the time you're wasting riding around," she completed for me. "This is very discouraging. Alena never lied to me, ever."

"Oh, please, Mother. She had her little white lies, too."

"Never," she insisted. "Your bad habits never rubbed off on her. She was too good, an angel. That's why God took her back."

Kiera looked away, and when she turned back, her eyes were filled with tears.

"You just love making me out to be the bad one all the time. You did it when she was alive, and you still do it now. You hate me!" She leaped to her feet and ran out of the living room.

"Kiera!"

I sat there, frozen.

Slowly, Mrs. March turned back to me. "I don't hate her," she said. "She's my daughter. Of course I love her. I wouldn't put up with all her antics if I didn't care for her and love her, but I'm not one of those mothers who are so blind they will not see. I know her faults. Pretending, ignoring, excusing will not help her to change and improve. And you won't do her any good by supporting her when she lies or disobeys."

She took a deep breath and sat on the settee opposite me. After a moment, she looked up at me. "Sasha, I think, as Donald does, that it's wonderful you've found a way to get along with Kiera and perhaps help each other, but you must be wary. She has too many years of successfully manipulating both her father and me. She's an expert at it. Will you be careful?"

"Yes, Mrs. March."

"I don't mind your being a normal teenager, but please, be careful. I take my responsibility for you very seriously. Remember, I made that pledge to your mother the day she was buried."

I nodded, now nearly in tears myself.

"Donald is so happy at how things are going or seem to be going. I won't say anything to him about this, but no more lying, okay?"

"Okay, Mrs. March."

"Oh, I hate that 'Mrs. March.' At least call me Jordan," she said. She smiled. "So, you got your ears pierced?"

"Yes."

"Kiera has plenty of earrings to lend you. That's for sure. Alena always wanted her ears pierced, but we never got around to it." She was quiet a moment and then smiled again. "Donald is planning to take us all on a little trip, perhaps to San Francisco. Won't that be nice?"

"Yes, Mrs. . . . Jordan."

"Good. Okay, I won't keep you."

I rose and started out. She held her smile and then turned away. I paused once after I walked out of the living room and looked back at her. She suddenly looked like the saddest person in the world, alone, bedecked in expensive jewelry and her designer outfit, her hair recently cut and styled. But instead of looking wonderful, she looked like someone trapped and chained by her wealth, lost and alone with nothing but her expensive possessions to keep her warm.

Kiera's door was open. She wasn't crying, but she was facedown on her bed. She heard me enter her suite and turned.

"Why didn't you run out with me?"

"You jumped up and ran so fast I didn't know what to do," I said. It was the truth.

"What did she say? Did she tell you how terrible I am again?"

"No. She said she loves you, but she was worried. She liked that I got my ears pierced."

"That figures. Oh, well," she said, shaking off her rage and smiling. "At least I got us out of that one, even if she tells my father."

"She said she wouldn't."

"Did she? Great. I was afraid she would get him to lay down some new restrictions and ruin tomorrow. Perfect. We'll tell them both about it at dinner. Be sure you look and sound very excited about it." She studied me a moment. "You are, aren't you? You're not going to back out now?"

"No," I said, although I could hear a chorus of voices inside me saying *yes*.

"I'm going to take a bubble bath. Come in to talk if you want," she said, and headed for her bathroom.

I went to my suite and just sat for a while looking out the

window. It was odd, I thought, but it wasn't until now that I realized I didn't even have a single picture of my mother. Everything we owned had disappeared in the road that night. Maybe it had all been tossed aside as junk. The sacks and the suitcases had been battered and stained. There had been some pictures in Mama's suitcase, but we had had nothing else of any real value. I couldn't recall anything that would have had our names. We had no address. If it had all been left on the side of the road, some other homeless person or persons might easily have come upon it and taken what they could use.

Of course, my thoughts went to the next day. *I like Ricky,* I thought. He was certainly very good-looking and so far very nice to me. It was exciting being with him. But to do what I was about to do, for the reasons I was about to do it, was troubling to me, and not because I was afraid. I wasn't old enough to have spent much time thinking about losing my virginity, but whenever I had thought about it, it was in terms of romance and love. Just doing it to get it over with diminished it, made it seem like such a common exercise. Was it just me? Why didn't these other girls feel and see that too?

Maybe they didn't really believe in love. From what I could see and what I heard them say, none of them had a particularly strong feeling for any one boy. If one of them had such a feeling, she surely kept it secret from the others. I had always dreamed of having a boyfriend who took me to school dances, movies, and restaurants. Maybe we would be too young to be really in love, but we would like each other so much that it would seem that way, and when we eventually broke up to go our separate ways, maybe for college, we would be broken-hearted, at least for a while. Years later, married to other people, we would meet and smile, almost laugh, at how intense we had once been. Yet in our heart of hearts, we would wonder what it would have been like if we had gone on together. The wondering would last only a second, but at least we would have had that.

None of the girls in the VA club would have anything remotely close to that. What would their memories of high school be like? How long could they continue to mock and belittle other girls who had had long and deep affections for boys in the past? Would they wake up one day years from now and realize what they had missed and lost and, most important, what they had given up when they treated their first sexual experience as just something they had to get over with?

I was tempted to go into Kiera's bathroom and sit beside her while she was in her bath and talk about all this, but I was afraid that the moment I brought it up, she would carry on with how I was not only betraying her but making her look bad to her friends. She might even find a way to blame it all on her mother, and things would return to the way they had been, a house full of thunder and lightning which would only bring us all to some new great tragedy. Whether Kiera would blame it on me or not, I would think I had caused it when all I had to do was make love with a boy I admittedly thought of as handsome and exciting.

How I wished I had a real mother to talk to now, even a mother who was in and out of sanity the way Mama was when we lived on the streets. I'd know when I could talk to her, when her mind was clear enough to hear me and care.

But I didn't even have that.

It was at times like this when I knew just how lost and alone I really was and that no amount of money, no house, no special school, nothing, would fill the great and deep hole in my heart.

❧29❧
Initiation

*K*iera was really very clever when it came to manipulating her father. I watched and listened to an expert
at dinner that night. The excitement and sweetness in her
voice was so well crafted, as were her smiles, her looks at
me, and her way of bringing me in at the right times to support what she said. She had a way of tilting her head just
slightly to the left while rolling her eyes to the right to look
cute and innocent. She tossed back her hair with a flick of
two fingers and pursed her lips as if she was sending her
father a kiss across the table.

I looked at Mr. March as Kiera described what our
outing on Ricky's boat was going to be. Mrs. March's face
was more like a mask, nothing moving, her eyelids barely
blinking as she listened. Although Kiera never came right
out and said it, she implied that Ricky's father was going to
keep close tabs on us. She reminded her parents that she
had been on Ricky's father's boat before and how well it had
gone. The weather was going to be perfect for boating, too.

Most of all, this would be the most exciting thing I had ever done. She made it sound as if all the others, Ricky, even his father, were going along with this outing for my benefit. How could her parents reject it?

"Well, it sounds like you two are in for a great time," Mr. March said. "I'd take you myself, but I'm having so many problems with this project in Oregon that I've got to work all weekend. I don't know why I took on doing anything with Rick Stanton," he said to Mrs. March. "His preparation is always so sloppy."

"I couldn't agree more," Mrs. March said curtly, "but not because of Rick Stanton. You're taking on too much, Donald. We need you to spend more time with us."

The way she said "we" made it clear, at least to me, that she meant herself. He nodded and promised that he was going to cut back. He said he had already rejected two major projects. Kiera glanced at me as he spoke, a look of victory and satisfaction in her face. There was no other discussion about our going on Ricky's boat. She was happy they had gone on to other topics. Secretly, I had been hoping that they wouldn't let us go and my crisis would be postponed for a while, but I should have realized that there was little or nothing Kiera didn't get the way she wanted.

"I've picked out some things for you to wear tomorrow," she told me after dinner. "Boyd's picking us up at nine."

The outfit she had chosen looked more like a tennis outfit to me. When I put it on, I thought the skirt was too short, but she insisted that it was perfect. She gave me another watch to wear, with a band that matched the colors of my outfit, and different earrings, too. This watch, like the other, had diamonds.

"Now, don't worry about becoming seasick or anything," she said. "That pill I gave you actually helps prevent that, too. Don't ask me how or why. It just does. Tomorrow's your day, and we won't permit anything to ruin it."

I felt as if I were on the high seas already when I went to bed. I tossed and turned, struggling to fall asleep. The conflicting arguments going on inside me were fierce. I was caught in an echo chamber. A strong part of me was screaming how wrong it all was. I was doing it for the wrong reasons, and I would regret it for the rest of my life. The other part of me kept reminding me of what I had now and what I would have afterward. For a girl who had had few, if any, friends most of her life and none during the entire past year, the idea of being part of a group like the VA club brimmed with great promise. I'd be included in everything. I'd have trusted friends in school and out of school. Boys would like me even more. And besides, I had already gone too far. I had the tattoo. I had lost any chance of having friends my own age. They all thought I was too snobby because I was hanging around with the seniors. If I didn't do this, I'd be all alone again.

Sometime just before morning, I fell asleep and slept so late that Kiera came rushing with panic into my suite.

"You're still in bed?" she cried. I groaned and turned over to look up at her. She was already dressed in her boating outfit. "It's after eight! Get up. Get dressed. Get ready. I'll be back in fifteen minutes. You know my mother will make a big deal of us having a decent breakfast. C'mon.

And don't forget to take your pill," she said, ripping the blanket off me.

I ground the sleep out of my eyes, sat up, and then, still half asleep, jumped into the shower to shock myself awake with cold water. I was just putting on my boat shoes when Kiera returned.

"Let's go," she said. "My mother is already wondering if you're sick or something. If you don't look good and full of energy, she'll find a reason to stop us. C'mon," she urged.

I hurried out after her.

Mrs. March was in the dining room waiting for us. "Are you all right?" she asked me immediately.

"Yes."

"She just stayed up too late doing her homework. You know how she is about her homework, even on weekends," Kiera said.

Mrs. March looked at me suspiciously but said nothing. I had to eat more than I wanted so she wouldn't think something was wrong with my appetite. At least, Kiera did most of the talking for us both, describing the day that lay ahead in Catalina and reminding her mother how much fun they'd had there when her father had taken them. She made the point of reminding her that Alena was alive then and loved the day.

"Never mind all that. You'd better make sure both you and Sasha are wearing your life jackets on that boat," her mother warned.

"Oh, of course. Ricky follows all the regulations to a T. What are you doing today, Mother?" she asked to throw her off.

"I'm meeting Deidre's mother for lunch at the Ivy," she

said. "It's a lunch meeting we've both been looking forward to for a while now." She made it sound as though they were meeting to discuss her and Deidre.

"That's nice," Kiera said without missing a beat.

"I want to hear from both of you periodically," Mrs. March said. "You both have cell phones, and this time they're not to be forgotten or turned off. Is that clear?"

"Of course, Mother. It's when we go on excursions like this that they come in most handy. We need to be excused now so we can both do last-minute things. Boyd will be here in ten minutes."

"Don't make any more mistakes, Kiera," Mrs. March warned. "There's no room for any more mistakes."

"That's all in the past, Mother. I'll let someone else make mistakes."

"Don't belittle what I say, Kiera."

"I never do, Mother. Sasha?"

I stood up and looked at Mrs. March. If she would or could ever see the hesitation in my face, she would see it now, I thought, and maybe she would forbid my going, but her mind was somewhere else. She nodded and looked down. Kiera tugged me, and we headed back up to our rooms. I was still brushing my teeth when she cried from my doorway that Boyd was there.

"Hurry up," she said, "before my mother finds some reason to stop us. Believe me," she continued as we went down the hallway, "she wishes she could."

"Why wouldn't she want us to have fun?"

"It's a long story, but it's because she had such a boring childhood. She's just jealous."

I shook my head as she descended in front of me. How could a daughter think her mother was jealous of her? Mothers wanted their daughters to have better lives than they had, didn't they? She certainly wanted a better life for me, even if it was just to ease her conscience. Besides, I couldn't believe Mrs. March had a boring childhood. Kiera just had a definition of "boring" that was different from most people's.

Deidre was waiting for us in the car with Boyd.

"The others are meeting us at the dock," she said. "Hurry up." When we drove off, she turned and leaned over to whisper, "Ready for VA day?"

Kiera pushed her to turn around. "Don't spook her," she said. "She's nervous enough."

"Nervous about what?" Boyd asked.

"Being on the same boat with you," Kiera said.

"Yeah, right. You have nothing to worry about as long as I'm there, Sasha," he said.

Ricky's boat was impressive. He had told me it was a seventy-five-foot Hatteras motor yacht. While everyone else waited, he took me on a tour to show me the galley, the salon, the master stateroom, and the guest stateroom. After that, he brought me up to the pilothouse, where I was to remain with him as he got us under way. Despite the conflicts going on inside me, I was very excited. When he started the boat and we were bouncing over the water, I couldn't help but squeal with delight. He let me steer for a while, too. Boyd started whining about not being permitted to do half the driving, as Ricky had promised, so he let him come up with Marcia, and he and I went down to join the others in the salon.

Kiera looked pretty cozy with Ruben Weiner, and

Deidre was practically on Tony Sussman's lap. Margot was sprawled on a sofa with Jack Martin. The way everyone was smiling at us gave me the jitters. Did all of the boys also know what was supposed to happen on the boat?

"Looks crowded in here," Ricky said. "Come on. We'll go to the front of the boat, and you can feel the wind and sea spray."

He took my hand and led me out. It was more exciting at the front of the boat. He pointed out Catalina and some of the other boats traveling to and fro. Because it was so bumpy, he held me around the waist, and we stood like that for a while. Afterward, we returned to the salon. I saw that Margot and Jack Martin were gone.

"Margot and Jack are in the guest stateroom," Kiera whispered. "You have the master, of course."

I glanced at Ricky.

"He already knows he's been chosen," she said.

Whether it was the prospect of really going forward with this or because this was my first time on a boat at sea, I don't know, but I felt the blood drain from my face and a wooziness come over me. I faltered for a moment as my legs turned into jelly beneath me.

Ricky saw it coming and had his arm around my waist again. "Whoa," he said, and scooped me up to carry me to the sofa.

"No," Kiera said, seizing his arm. "She needs to be in the bed."

He nodded and carried me to the master stateroom.

"I'll get Boyd to slow down. That will help," he said after he lowered me to the bed.

I closed my eyes. My stomach was doing flip-flops.

After he left, Kiera came in.

"Perfect," she said, as if I had planned it all out and was pretending. "We'll wait until the boat is docked."

"I'm not fooling," I said. "I feel sick."

"You'll get over it," she insisted. "Rest a little."

"But you said the pill would prevent this from happening."

"Everyone's different, Sasha. Don't be silly. I was hoping it would work for you, but I guess it doesn't. Next time, we'll get you to wear one of those patches to prevent seasickness. Relax. The best is yet to come."

"I don't want to," I said. "I don't feel good."

"What are you talking about? We go through all this effort to make it easy for you, and you want to back out now? Relax. You'll feel lots better after we dock, and that will be the best time for your initiation. Besides, you don't want to disappoint the girls after they voted to include you, and you especially don't want to disappoint Ricky," she added. "I'll be back in a few."

"I think I'm going to throw up."

She stood glaring at me for a moment and then sighed and shook her head. "Okay. If you have to throw up, go into the bathroom. I'll see if Ricky has anything onboard that will help," she said, and left.

I closed my eyes and kept my hands on my stomach while I fought back the urge to vomit. No one else was this seasick. I was embarrassed. The feeling didn't pass. I was about to get up when Ricky and Kiera returned. Kiera was holding a glass of something with a blue tint.

"We called Ricky's father, and he told us where this was in the galley," Kiera said. "You drink it all down as fast as you can."

She came to the bed. Ricky helped me sit up, and I took the glass. It didn't look like anything anyone would want to drink.

"Drink it fast," Kiera emphasized, "and you won't mind the taste."

I looked at Ricky. His face was so serious, his eyes intense. Was he that way because he thought that somehow this was his fault and he felt sorry for me?

"If she has a bad time, I'll never stop hearing about it from my mother," Kiera told him.

I looked at the glass again, took a deep breath, and gulped the contents. Kiera took the glass back immediately, and Ricky lowered me to the pillow again.

"Just rest. We're almost at the dock," he said.

Kiera was looking down at me in the strangest way. After a moment, they both left. I closed my eyes again and listened to the hum of the engines. I felt the boat slowing down, but I never felt it being docked. I fell asleep, I think, or maybe it would be better described as passing out.

The first thing I realized when I opened my eyes was that I was naked, and everyone was standing around the bed looking down at me, but their faces were going in and out of focus. Was I dreaming?

Then I saw the top of Ricky's head. He was moving between my legs and lifting them at the same time. Faces continued to go in and out and then diminished, as if I were looking at them through the wrong end of a telescope.

When I felt him pushing into me, I was sure I heard a soft chanting that sounded like "VA, VA, VA." I know I cried out. My whole body was shaking. *It's really happening,* I thought. *This isn't a dream.*

I don't know how long it lasted. Minutes seemed to float into each other. I wasn't even sure how many times Ricky was there. At one point, as if they were all suddenly bored, they filed out, and I was alone with him for a while. Then he left, too.

When I woke up again, I was dressed. I could feel the boat moving. I sat up. The stateroom spun and then settled. My stomach was still woozy but not as bad as it had been. I called for Kiera. I could hear them all laughing. There was music, too. I struggled to get to my feet and opened the door. Everyone but Ricky was in the salon. They were drinking vodka. I saw the bottle on the table. Deidre noticed me first and called out. They all stopped talking and laughing and looked at me.

"I hope you're feeling better, Sasha," Kiera said. "I can't bring you home seasick. My mother called, and I told her you were on the island. She tried your phone next and then called me back, and I told her you left it on the boat. Remember to say that," she added, and sipped her drink.

Everyone continued to stare at me.

"I want to talk to you," I said.

"So talk. We don't keep secrets from each other, remember?"

Everyone laughed.

I started to cry. "I want to talk to you," I insisted.

She groaned, finished her drink, and stood. "Will you

all excuse me? Babysitting duties call," she said, and came to the stateroom.

I closed the door.

"What?"

"What did you give me to drink?"

"I don't know. Something Ricky's father had on the boat."

"I don't know what happened to me. I think . . . was I raped?"

"Raped? You were initiated, Sasha. Don't think of it as being raped."

"But I think everyone was there."

She smiled. "No one was there but Ricky."

"I . . . it was like a rape."

"I told you. Don't think of it as a rape."

"What should I think of it as?"

She thought a moment and smiled. "Think of it the way you would think of a toothache. Now it's over," she said, and walked out.

30

Lies

I kept to myself for the remainder of the trip. No one tried to get me into any conversations, anyway. It made me feel like yesterday's news. Even Ricky was aloof and indifferent. He never asked me how I felt. When we docked in Marina Del Ray, Kiera called to me to hurry along. She was anticipating another call from her mother any minute.

"I'll call her first and let her know we're on the way home once we're started," she said. That seemed to be the only thing that mattered to her now.

As I stepped off the boat, I saw the way the others were looking at me. None of the girls said good-bye or "See you later." They all simply stared at me. When I looked back at them, they were huddled and whispering.

"Is everyone angry at me?" I asked Kiera after we got into a taxi she had waiting.

"Don't ask, don't tell," she replied, and laughed.

"What does that mean?"

"It means what happens in Vegas stays in Vegas, Sasha.

Don't go blabbing about our trip. I'll describe some of the things on Catalina that you missed," she added. "Just in case my mother gives you the third degree or something."

She then narrated her version of our story, even elaborating on what we all had for lunch.

"Did you really do all that?" I asked.

"Of course," she said. "Why would I lie to you?"

"It's not that. I can't believe I slept through it all."

"Don't mention being seasick. You can say you were a little woozy but you got over it," she instructed. Then she put her earphones in and turned on her iPod and sang along. I couldn't remember when she had looked and acted so happy.

After the taxi dropped us off, I turned to her and said, "So now I'm a full-fledged member of the VA club, huh?"

She paused at the front door and looked at me with the most curious expression on her face. "Pardon me?"

"The club," I said.

"I don't know what you're talking about, Sasha," she said, and opened the door.

I hurried in after her to pursue and understand, but before I could say anything else, both Mr. and Mrs. March came strolling out of the entertainment center, laughing. They paused when they saw us.

"Hey," Mr. March called. "How was your day, girls?"

"Miserable," Kiera said, and charged up the stairway.

I stood looking after her with just as shocked a face as they had. She didn't look back. She pounded her way up as if she were trying to stamp out bugs on the steps.

"What happened?" Mrs. March asked me as she

approached. "When I called, she said you were all at a restaurant and were having a great time."

I shook my head. What was I supposed to be saying? Had Kiera forgotten to prepare me?

"Did something bad happen on the boat?" Mr. March asked, stepping up beside Mrs. March. "No accidents, I hope."

"No," I said.

"Well, then, what is it?" he asked.

"I don't know," I said. "I'll go talk to her."

"What the hell . . ." He looked at Mrs. March, who just shook her head.

I moved quickly to get away from them, fearful that I would say the wrong thing. Kiera had her door closed, so I knocked. She didn't open it or respond.

"Kiera? What's going on? Your parents are confused, and so am I." I looked back to be sure they hadn't followed me up. "What am I supposed to say?"

She opened the door partway and looked out at me with a face so full of anger it took my breath away. I stepped back.

"Tell them whatever lies you want," she said. "I'm tired of covering up for you."

"What?"

She slammed the door. I stood there dumbfounded. When I looked toward the stairway, I saw that Mrs. March had come up and was standing there gaping at me. I hurried to my suite and went in quickly. My head was spinning. I was still woozy and a little confused from what had happened on the boat, but this added so much weight to it I felt as if my head had turned to stone. I sat on my bed, dazed, my heart thumping. I hadn't closed my door, so I heard Mrs. March knock on Kiera's door. Instead of the usual unfriendly "What do you want?" I heard the door being opened, muffled voices, what sounded like Kiera crying, and then the door being closed.

I sat absolutely still, trying to hear something more, but I heard nothing for the longest time. Then I thought I heard heavy footsteps in the hallway and got up to listen at my doorway. I heard Mr. March ask, "What's this all about?" Then he, too, went into Kiera's room, and the door closed again. I closed my door softly and retreated to my bathroom. From the moment I had stepped off the boat, I could think of nothing else but a hot shower. I felt so dirty inside and out. I decided to wash my hair as well. Afterward, I wrapped a bath towel around myself and went to my vanity table to blow-dry my hair and brush it out.

The shower had refreshed me, but I could feel the deep fatigue in every muscle in my body, even in my bones. My eyes wanted to close and did for a moment. When I opened them, I saw both Mr. and Mrs. March captured in the mirror. They were standing behind me, looking very upset. I spun around.

"Sasha," Mrs. March began. "Do you have a tattoo very low down on your back?"

For a moment, I couldn't speak. My throat tightened so hard I couldn't breathe. Why would Kiera have told them about that? There was no other way, no other reason, they would be asking about it.

"Yes," I finally said.

"I'd like to see it," Mr. March said, more to Mrs. March than to me. "Now," he emphasized so sternly that I winced.

"Please turn around again, Sasha, and undo the bath towel so we can see the tattoo," Mrs. March asked. She looked as if she was going to burst into tears any second. "Please," she added.

I fumbled with the towel so I could open it and cover the front of my body while lifting the towel enough to expose the tattoo.

Mr. March stepped closer and looked at it. "Where's Alena's digital camera?" he asked Mrs. March.

"Donald, please."

"Where is it?" he practically shouted at her.

She looked flustered for a moment but then went to a drawer in the desk and took out a camera. She brought it to him. He turned it on and took a picture of my tattoo.

"You ask about the rest," he said. "I'm going to my office to send this to have it checked."

He left the suite, and I wrapped the towel around myself again. I had no idea what I was supposed to do or say. Had someone informed Kiera's parents about the VA club? Were we all in trouble? Mrs. March, her body looking as if it was slipping off her bones, slinked over to a chair and sat.

"Kiera is upset," she began. "She says you stole her boyfriend today, Ricky Burns. She says you were intimate with him on the boat and didn't care that everyone knew it. She says you seduced Ricky."

It felt as if a sheet of ice was sliding from the back of my head down my back, over my stomach, and down my legs to my feet.

"That's not true," I said.

"She was so upset that she broke down and confessed

about other things. She told us she took you to buy those clothes because you wanted them, and she thought we'd want her to make you happy."

"What?"

"I knew they weren't her clothes. They looked new, and they fit you."

"That's not true, either. She's lying. I don't know why, but she is."

"She said it was your idea to lie about the play audition."

"No."

"Otherwise, why would you go along with it? She says you have a reputation as a big flirt in school, and all the boys were after you, and she was frankly embarrassed about it since we had described you as her cousin. She claims she tried to get you to calm down, but today was the end. You could have had any boy on the boat, but you chose Ricky just because he was her boyfriend. She says that you were plotting and conniving to get your revenge in subtle ways, this being one."

How could she say these things? I thought. I wasn't going to let her get away with it.

"No, no, Mrs. March, I didn't choose Ricky. They did."

"Who's 'they,' Sasha?"

"The other girls . . . the VA club," I said.

She stared for a moment, looked away, and then turned back to me. "Now, what is this supposed to be, the VA club?"

"Virgins Anonymous. That's what this tattoo is about. It's calligraphy of the *V* and the *A*. All of the girls have a tattoo there."

"What's Virgins Anonymous? I don't understand."

"All of the girls in the club have given up their virginity to be members, and everyone has sex regularly with any boy. Kiera brought me to be a member, and they approved of me. I swore a vow on a notebook that contains the description of each girl's first time. We meet regularly at Deidre's house, because her mother works with her father and she has the house free after school. No one was supposed to talk about it, but Kiera's lying to you about me. I didn't ask for new clothes, I didn't ask for the tattoo, and I didn't steal her boyfriend. What happened was that I got seasick very quickly on the boat, and Ricky put me in the master stateroom. I wasn't supposed to get seasick. Kiera said those pills she had given me would prevent it."

"What pills?"

"The pills to make my periods less severe. Here," I said, rising quickly and going to the drawer beside my bed. "I'll show you."

I opened the drawer and stared down in disbelief. The pills were gone. I looked carefully through the drawer.

"She must have taken them back," I said under my breath.

"Sasha, Mr. March is very, very upset."

"It's not true. None of what she's saying is true!"

"Get dressed," she said, rising. "We're all going to have a talk downstairs in Mr. March's office. I'm sick to my stomach."

I started to cry. She looked at me but not with the same compassion and sympathy I used to see in her face.

"Just get dressed. I'm calling Deidre's mother right now," she said, and left.

I couldn't stop sobbing, but I put on some clothes, making sure not to wear anything Kiera had given me. I wanted to confront her first, but she was already downstairs sitting in her father's office. She had her hands clasped on her lap and looked straight ahead, as though she was the one being accused of everything, as though she was the one so damaged and hurt.

Mr. March sat at his desk. Mrs. March was sitting across from Kiera.

"Just sit anywhere, Sasha," Mr. March said.

I looked at Kiera, but she wouldn't look at me. Nevertheless, I sat on the settee, too.

"Do you belong to or did you join a club?" Mr. March asked immediately.

Good, I thought. *They found out the truth. It serves her right.*

"Yes."

He held up a printout of the digital picture he had taken of my tattoo. "Is this the club's logo?"

"Yes, it is," I said.

"Hell Girl?" he asked.

"What?"

"That's what this calligraphy represents. I had it confirmed."

"No," I said, shaking my head. "It spells 'VA.' That's the club Kiera had me join, the VA club."

Kiera blew air through her lips. She smiled at her father. "Did you ever? VA club?"

"The girls took me to get the tattoo," I said quickly. "All of them."

"Do you know where this supposedly occurred?" Mr. March asked.

"Somewhere in L.A. I don't remember the address. If I saw it, I'd remember."

"First," Kiera began, "you know, Daddy, that someone under eighteen can't get a tattoo in California legally. Why would anyone risk his business to give her that ridiculous tattoo?"

"She's right. Sasha?"

"I don't know why he did it. Maybe they gave him more money," I said now, feeling real panic. "She has one. They all have one."

Kiera turned slowly. "Did you see it? Is that what you're telling my parents now?"

"Yes," I said, nodding at Mr. and Mrs. March. "I saw it on all of them in the same place."

Kiera stood up, undid her jeans, and lowered them. She turned to her father and mother and lowered her panties. Then she turned to me, and I gasped. It was gone.

"This is beginning to sound like *Psycho*," Kiera said as she pulled her jeans up. "I don't really care what my parents decide to do about you," she told me. "What you did with Ricky was mean. I'm not going to lie for you anymore, though. I can tell you that."

She turned to her parents.

"Haven't I tried to be a good older sister to her? I've lost friends because of her and some of the crude things she says. Now she goes and seduces Ricky after I talk him into taking us to Catalina on his father's boat. Don't just take my word for it. Ask my girlfriends. Go on and ask her if she's still a virgin or ever was when she first came here. Go on. You can have her examined if you don't believe me."

I couldn't keep the tears from streaming down my face. The looks on Mr. and Mrs. March's faces felt like knives in my heart. They both looked drained of any warmth and hope. I felt as if I were looking at them when they had first heard their younger daughter was terminally ill. I felt terminally ill. Kiera, always alert to an opportunity, had her finish perfected and perfectly timed.

"I told you, Mother. I warned you," Kiera said with a voice soft and sorrowful. "She's not Alena. She took advantage of you. She probably did know how to play the clarinet but pretended she didn't."

Mrs. March started to cry.

Kiera turned to me. "You're not my sister. You never could be," she said, and walked out of the office.

I took deep breaths to stop myself from crying. My chest ached. Mr. March rose and paced a bit behind his desk. Mrs. March stopped crying, wiped her face with her handkerchief, and, after a deep breath herself, turned to me.

"I spoke with Deidre. She confirmed Kiera's story about what happened on the boat," she began. "She doesn't know anything about any VA club, and her mother confirmed that she has no tattoo on her lower back."

"Deidre's lying for her," I muttered weakly.

"I called some of the other mothers, and they checked their daughters, too. No tattoos, Sasha."

"Theirs weren't permanent, then. They showed them to me to fool me," I said. "I'm not lying. I didn't seduce Ricky

Burns on his boat. They gave me something to drink that was supposed to help my seasickness, only it made me feel weird. They were all in the room. I was raped!" I cried.

Mr. March stopped pacing and looked at Mrs. March. "This is no good, Jordan. We're talking about a first-class scandal here."

"I know," she said in a voice of defeat.

He pointed at me. "You don't go making such an accusation, Sasha. Tom Burns is an influential businessman. His chain of pharmacies is one of the most successful in the state. He'd destroy us in such a fight. I don't want to hear that you've told this story to anyone at school. Is that understood? Is it?"

"Yes, but it's true."

"Don't dare speak it," he said, punching each word. He turned to Mrs. March. "I want you to move her out of Alena's room for now. Put her in one of the guest rooms away from Kiera. I don't know what's wrong with you, Sasha," he said, turning back to me. "Maybe your life on the streets made you sly and clever in your battle to survive. Maybe you saw an opportunity in Mrs. March. She's taken the loss of our daughter very hard. Maybe I need to send both you and Kiera to therapists. Whatever. But for now, I want no more talk about any of this. I'll look into seeing what the best alternatives for you are. For the time being, go to the school we have had you going to. Do your work, and stay out of trouble. Come directly home after your school activities, and do not go out and about on weekends. Am I clear?"

"Yes."

"You did impress me when you first came here. I have to believe that indicates you have good qualities. My advice is for you to nurture them and nothing else. You want to add anything, Jordan?"

"No," she said.

"Tell Mrs. Duval to move her things immediately, then."

She nodded and looked at me. "Go up and put together what you want to take to the guest room, Sasha. I'm sorry, but Mr. March is right. We want you away from Kiera."

"And out of Alena's room," he emphasized.

"Someday you'll know that I wasn't lying, and you'll be sorry," I said. "And I'll feel sorrier for you than I do for myself."

I walked out and up the stairs, but I felt like a sleepwalker. When I reached Kiera's room, she opened the door. She must have been waiting right there, listening for my footsteps. She stepped out and smiled at me.

"I feel I should tell you something," she began. "The second set of pills I gave you . . ."

"Where are they? What about them?"

"They were fertility pills. Ricky's father owns a drugstore chain, remember? He can get anything. Maybe you'll have twins."

The heat that came into my face made me feel that I would go up in flames.

"Why did you do all this to me?" I asked.

She smiled. "My parents started to love you more than they loved me. That was the way it was when Alena was alive, and I wasn't going to let it happen again. Aren't my friends loyal? They're so wonderful.

"Besides," she said, losing her smile of satisfaction to the hard, cold face I had first known, "I told you. It was your mother's fault. She shouldn't have crossed the highway there." She closed the door softly.

I felt like someone in a coffin who wasn't really dead watching the lid being shut.

31
Darkness

Although the guest room wasn't as large as Alena's suite and didn't have a sitting area where I could set up my schoolwork, it was luxurious, with a king-size bed and a thick-carpeted floor. It had a very nice bathroom, too, but the room was in a wing of the house that was darker and lonelier, not that I wanted to be anywhere near Kiera ever again. She claimed the same about me and wouldn't eat dinner if I was at the table at the same time. Her father accommodated her wishes and ordered Mrs. March to have me served my dinner an hour earlier than when they ate. Every night of the following week, I ate dinner alone in the kitchen nook. By now, all of the servants working for the Marches knew that something was seriously wrong, but no one asked me any questions about why I was being isolated, nor did anyone speak much more to me than was absolutely necessary, even though I could see sympathy in both Mrs. Duval's and Mrs. Caro's faces. I imagined they were all worried about losing their jobs.

Grover was driving me to school again but was back to his silent, formal ways.

I didn't know what to expect when I returned to school on Monday. At first, no one noticed anything really different until lunch hour, when I ended up sitting by myself. That was when the buzz began. The stories about me couldn't have been passed around quicker even in a general announcement over loudspeakers.

I had no idea exactly what the girls were saying about me yet, but Lisa Dirk couldn't wait to be a messenger. She came sauntering over and slid into the seat across from me.

"How come you're sitting all by yourself?" she asked. It was obvious that she knew the answer. My senior girlfriends didn't want me, and I didn't want them.

I didn't reply. I just ate with my gaze focused on nothing, least of all her.

"Is it true what we hear?" she asked. "About you and Ricky Burns?"

I put my sandwich down and leaned toward her. The expression on my face frightened her, and she pulled back.

"I don't know what you heard, and I really don't care."

"We heard that you threw yourself at him on his boat. You called him from a stateroom, and you were naked," she blurted.

"They're spreading lies about me," I said, even though I knew it would be useless and a waste of time to defend myself. It was like holding back a waterfall with your bare hands. They were a chorus of gossipers, and I was a lone, lost voice.

"I'd never guess you were like that," Lisa said, ignoring my denial. "To go after a senior boy so desperately is sad."

"Sad?"

I was holding back a flood of truth with a dam made of paper. It was charging down my tongue. I was moments away from telling it all. *I'm not Kiera's cousin. While she was high on some drug, Kiera ran my mother and me over and killed my mother. Her mother took me in, enrolled me in this school, and made up that story.*

For a moment, I thought I had actually shouted it all, broken through the dam, but I quickly realized that what kept the dam secure was my fear that telling the truth about myself would only alienate me even more from my classmates. Who would want to be friends with a homeless girl? No one in that school would want to be seen talking to me. That was for sure.

I couldn't skip all of that and defend myself by telling Lisa I had been raped, either. Mr. March had forbidden me to say it. I could only swallow it all back and ignore everyone, but that was hard to do. By the end of the day, I felt covered in cobwebs of lies and distortions. There wasn't an eye not looking my way or a tongue not wagging about me. I might just as well have been walking around naked. My limping was nothing when it came to drawing attention compared with the globs of mud thrown at me. In fact, they almost didn't notice my limp, because they were too busy elaborating on the lies about my sexual exploits and sly ways. They saw only this promiscuous new student who probably had a bad reputation at her old school. In their minds, that was why I was so mysterious when it came to my past.

I did the best I could in my favorite class, art, but when I tried to start a new calligraphy project, I could only think of the horrible tattoo on my back and sat there for the longest time staring at blank paper. Mr. Longo kept coming over and encouraging me, but by the time the bell rang, I had hardly begun anything. I was the same earlier in music. I played my clarinet mechanically and so poorly that Mr. Denacio threw one of his famous fits.

"If I don't see an improvement in you soon," he threatened, "I will have to reconsider appointing you to a position in the school band."

I didn't protest. I had no enthusiasm for anything and plodded my way through the corridors from class to class. Occasionally, I caught sight of Kiera looking at me from across a hallway. At one point, I thought she looked amazed at how well her plan had succeeded. She seemed in awe of herself.

Ricky never gave me a second glance. A few times, I was tempted to walk up to him to ask him how he could be so cruel, but he and Boyd were always laughing, and I was sure that if I did speak to either of them, they would make me feel foolish and even more embarrassed than I already was.

Except for band practice on Tuesday and Thursday, I returned home immediately after school and went up to the guest room. I didn't start right in on my homework as I used to do. I sat for quite a while just looking out the window, wondering what I could possibly do now and where I would eventually end up. I was terribly worried about becoming pregnant. I had no idea what I would do if my period didn't come. I wanted to visit Mama's grave, hoping that somehow she would talk to me and tell me what I should do, but I was afraid to ask Mrs. March for anything.

Mrs. March didn't say much to me all week. When we

confronted each other, she looked as sad and as lost as I did. I was numb by now, but she still appeared to be on the verge of new tears. She did tell me that Mr. March was still researching what was best for me under the new circumstances. I understood that this didn't include my staying with them even like this. Sometimes, when I thought about all that Kiera had managed and how they had accepted everything she and her friends said as being true, I became more angry than sad for myself. I recalled the advice from Jackie, the nurse, and was tempted to threaten them with a lawsuit. I'd find my father, and he'd come back to do it.

Oddly, though, no matter how poorly I was being treated now, I couldn't harden my heart against Mrs. March, and I actually felt sorrier for Mr. March. Kiera had him so tightly wrapped around her finger that he couldn't see. Eventually, he would suffer some great tragedy. I went from wishing for it to chastising myself for wishing such evil things on someone.

In the midst of my misery, my loneliness in the dark side of the March mansion where my own footsteps echoed, I would find myself recalling some happier, sunnier moments with Mama, even on the streets after we had sold more than we had expected. She would splurge, and we'd have ice cream sundaes or get foot-long submarine sandwiches and sit out on the beach as if we were back to being as we once were. She didn't buy any alcohol with the extra money, so she was more like my mother again. She would tell me stories about her own youthful days in Portland, her boyfriends in high school, the plays she had been in, and the parties afterward.

I had heard many of the stories before, but for me, they were like the fairy tales other parents read to their children. Kids never heard them enough. You could recite them and know exactly what was coming next, but there was something special about having your mother or father read them repeatedly to you. It made you feel safe, wrapped securely in their love and in the magic they could conjure with their voices. The hard, cold world was kept outside. Nothing bad could happen, and you could slip softly into a comfortable sleep, unafraid of the darkness it necessarily had to bring along with it. There was always the promise of tomorrow.

Now there was no promise of tomorrow, and the cold, hard world had found its way to come back at me. There was no escape, no safety, and the darkness that came with sleep now was terrifying, not because it brought old ghosts and nightmares but because it made me blind and afraid to take another step forward, to have another thought, to dare to make another wish.

On Friday, Kiera broke her vow of silence when it came to me and approached me in the cafeteria, but it wasn't to express any regret or remorse. She didn't sit at my table. She stood across from me, keeping her distance as if she were afraid I might attack her.

"I see you're still having trouble making new friends," she began, nodding at the empty chairs.

"I'm not looking for new friends yet, but when I do, I'll be more careful about choosing them," I replied.

"You don't have to be careful about it or worry about it. I doubt you'll be here that much longer, anyway."

"Wherever I go can't be worse," I said, and she laughed.

"Ricky's having a party tonight at his house. His parents are beginning a short Mexican Riviera vacation. We'd invite you just for entertainment, but everyone's afraid you might steal away another boyfriend."

I was silent. I felt my insides trembling, but I wasn't going to cry or even look sad and frightened. Instead, I said, "I feel sorry for you."

"You feel sorry for me? That's a laugh. When you end up in some foster home, sleeping in a two-by-four bedroom and going to some inferior public school, think of me. I'm going to think of you tonight. You can call it a celebration of sorts."

"You're good at what you do, Kiera, I won't deny it, but with all your money and your things, your cars and trips, you really don't have much more than I do. You're lonelier than I am, in fact."

"You're crazy," she said, but my firmness threw her. I could see her losing some of her confidence and arrogance.

"You had me believing that you really did have a good relationship with your sister, but I know now you couldn't possibly have had that. I imagine there were times when you wished bad things would happen to her, and when they did, you hated yourself. You know what?" I added, scooping up some fruit with my fork. "I think you still do."

For the first time, I saw blood rush into her cheeks and her eyes blaze. She was also speechless. There was so much anger in her eyes. I looked away, and she walked off, but I caught her looking at me every once in a while. There was no question in my mind that she was wishing she could do more harm to me. I had cut deeply past her hard steel surface and touched that place where all of her fears and regrets slept, waiting for something or someone to nudge them awake. Maybe now she would have bad dreams and fear the darkness, too, I thought.

Ironically, it didn't make me feel better to be able to hurt her, even after all she had done. I knew that for most people, that would be a weakness. How could I survive in a world where people were so cruel to one another if I didn't enjoy revenge?

I think the trouble was that I had grown too close to Alena. Dead and gone, she still had a presence in that suite, not only for Mrs. March but, after a while, also for me, wearing her clothes, using her things, and seeing her pictures, her face constantly in mine. I couldn't help but lie awake nights and think of her there, wondering what her thoughts were like when she realized how sick she was. Did she cry? Was she angry? Was she simply afraid all the time? From the way Mr. and Mrs. March had described her, none of that seemed to be true. I knew that all parents saw their children as angels when they were so young and innocent, but maybe Alena really was angelic. Maybe she had been helping me find my way. Maybe, even now, she felt sorry for her sister and wished that somehow, some way, I could have changed her the way she had pretended to change.

Forgive me, Alena, both for failing and for wishing harm to Kiera, I thought, and I continued to the end of my school day.

Neither Mr. nor Mrs. March was home when I returned. I went directly up to my room. The hallway looked darker than ever, and the room was cold and lonely. I felt like one of those children we read about in class, the ones locked in the Tower of London. Like them, I was left to wither and die. For the first time since I had been brought to the March mansion, even in the beginning, when Kiera was so mean to me, I considered running away. I had survived in the streets before, so why not now? It was more than a passing thought. I considered what I would take with me and what I had that I could pawn to raise money. I still had the two watches Kiera had given me so nonchalantly. If she wasn't lying about those being real diamonds in them, I might have enough to get along for a while.

But then the reality of a girl my age trying to get by sank in. What hotel would rent me a room, even some of the fleabag ones I knew were out there? What would I do when the money ran out? Who would hire me to work, and what could I sell on the boardwalks now? The chances that the police would leave me alone without an adult were far lower, too. Running away was no answer.

Depressed, I lay down and soon fell asleep. I woke when I heard knocking on my door and saw Mrs. March standing there.

"Are you ill?" she asked.

"No, just a little tired."

"Mr. March called to tell me he's arranged a meeting for you with Social Services next week. I believe it's on Monday. They'll find a suitable new home for you," she said, and then pressed her lips together as if to hold back sobs. "I'm sorry, Sasha. I wish it would have worked out for you here. I truly do."

"Thank you," I said.

"Mrs. Duval has your dinner ready," she added, and left.

I heard her footsteps dying away in the corridor, disappearing like my advantageous and hopeful future.

I rose, washed, and went down to dinner. Since the new arrangements had begun, I felt as if everyone around me was mute or deaf. The long silence hung in the air. Faces were averted from mine. Everything was done mechanically and as quickly as possible. It occurred to me, of course, that they had all been told Kiera's story and believed everything bad about me, too. The only friend I had left in the house was the imaginary friend I had in Alena. It seemed appropriate that I would be close only to the dead now.

I didn't linger downstairs after dinner. I went up the grand stairway slowly, walking like someone going to her execution, and went to my room. Doing my homework seemed pointless, as was practicing the clarinet. I wouldn't be finishing school there after all, it seemed. Nevertheless, out of either sadness or a need to keep up my connection with Alena, I did play the clarinet.

After that, I watched some television. I wanted to keep myself awake as long as possible so I would fall asleep faster and not toss and turn, worrying, reliving the pain and misery. It was close to midnight when I finally turned the television off. I was about to get ready for bed when I heard what sounded like quite a commotion, so I went out to the hallway to listen closer. It was coming from the wing of the house where Kiera's and the Marches' bedrooms were. Mrs. March was screaming something. I walked toward the noise slowly and then walked faster, almost running. She was heading toward the stairway when I saw her. She was buttoning her jacket. She stopped when she saw me.

"What's happening?" I asked.

"It's Kiera," she said. "She's being rushed to the hospital from her party. Something about . . . a drug overdose. She's in a coma," she muttered. "My husband . . ."

"What?"

"He's not been notified yet. He can't be reached. He's flying back from a meeting in San Francisco. I have to get to the hospital." She turned again to descend the stairway. She looked so small and frightened.

"Can I come with you?" I asked, rushing to the stairs. "I won't be in your way. I'll be there just to be with you." I wanted to add, *If Alena were here, you'd surely take her.* Perhaps she heard my thoughts, or perhaps Alena spoke to her.

"Yes," she said. "Thank you. Come."

I hurried down to join her, and without another word spoken between us, we got into her car.

"I knew this day would come," she said in a voice barely above a whisper. "I felt it inside me, the way people can feel the rain. The dark clouds were always on Kiera's horizon just waiting to be invited in. I try to blame it all on Donald, on his permissiveness, his blindness, his indifference, but I'm just as guilty."

I didn't tell her, but as we drove on through the night, I felt guilty, too.

I had wished hard for something like this. I had wanted it so much that I had almost tasted it. Was I going along with her now to gloat or to give her comfort?

Was I Alena, or was I Sasha Porter?

It wouldn't be long before I knew.

32

Hospital

They were all there in the emergency room. Every one of them looked frightened, but when they saw me with Mrs. March, their looks of fear changed to surprise. Ricky looked up last. He was sitting, holding his head in his hands. Mrs. March didn't ask any of them anything, nor did she say anything to any of them. She went directly to the nurses' station and introduced herself. At almost the same moment, a doctor was at her side. He said something to her and then led her down a corridor.

Deidre was the first to speak to me. She approached me slowly. The shock of seeing me was replaced by confusion. "Why are you here?" she asked, loudly enough for the others to hear.

"Mrs. March needed someone with her," I said. After I said it, I realized I should have said "my aunt." "My uncle is on his way back from San Francisco and is on an airplane."

She lost her look of confusion, but then, in the tone of a confession, she said, "He's not your uncle. Everyone here knows the truth now. Kiera lost control of her tongue before anything else."

I looked at the others, all sitting there, their gazes now fixed on me.

To my surprise, Deidre added, "It was still very nice of you to come along with her. You can sit and wait with us," she said, indicating a chair next to her.

"Thanks. I'll sit here," I said, and sat.

She didn't look upset. She nodded, understanding, and returned to her seat. I looked at them all. I really hated them for what they had done to me, but they looked pathetic, more like terrified little children now, especially Ricky. In fact, he looked as if he had been crying. He turned away to avoid my gaze.

Two uniformed policemen arrived and went to the nurses' desk. She spoke to them for a while, and while she did, Kiera's friends were all like stone. The policemen turned and looked at them, and then the nurse nodded in the direction of the corridor and they walked down it.

Deidre stared at me thoughtfully. Finally, she got up again and walked over to Ricky. She spoke to him, and they both looked at me. He nodded and got up. I felt my body tighten as he walked toward me.

"Can I talk to you?" he asked.

"What do you want?"

"Let's just go outside for a minute. Please," he added when I didn't move. The others all stared at us.

I got up and walked out to the parking area. He followed, and then I stopped and turned abruptly to him.

"What?" I said.

"I don't expect you to accept any apologies. I just wanted to tell you something about the pills Kiera gave you. She asked me to get them."

"So?"

"She wanted fertility pills. You know, pills for women who have trouble getting pregnant."

"I know what fertility pills are, Ricky."

"I got her pills and told her they were fertility pills, but they were only what we call placebos. There was nothing in them to make it easier for you to get pregnant."

"But thanks to you, I can still get pregnant, right?"

"I hope not. I don't expect it," he said.

"Why not?"

"Right afterward, without Kiera knowing, I had you drink some water and take another pill. It's called the morning-after pill. I wasn't going to be the father of anyone's baby at my age. Anyway," he said, looking back again and then at me, "whatever happens here, it's a wake-up call, at least for me. I'm probably going to be in a great deal of trouble."

"What happened to her?"

"She took something called G. I got it through someone I know. It's like the flavor of the week these days, you know? Everyone's always looking for a new kick. Kiera keeps up with this stuff more than anyone else. I didn't know what dosage people should take. This guy told me you take a shot like whiskey, but she took three. I warned her to go slowly, but it was pretty clear she had gone too far when she collapsed. She fell into a coma. We couldn't revive her, so we had to call for an ambulance. I had to tell them what it was. The police will be out here soon looking for me."

"How could you give her something like that? I guess I shouldn't ask. Look what you gave me."

"You're right. It was a terrible thing to do."

"You didn't seem sorry when I saw you this week."

"I was, but I was afraid to show it."

"Your friends mean too much to you," I said.

He almost smiled. "You're pretty smart, Sasha. I wasn't with you just to do what Kiera wanted."

"It doesn't matter now," I said. "How seriously ill is she?"

"I don't know. Bad, I guess. They said she was having trouble breathing."

"Why was she so reckless?"

"She was just intent on having the best time ever. Actually, I thought she was doing the drugs to try to break out of a depression, not to have a great time. She was acting weird to start with, so I was nervous, and then this happened. Luckily, no one else went for any of the G before she had her reaction, but they would have, I'm sure. We all could be in there," he said, looking down and shaking his head. "Damn."

He looked up at me. "I didn't know the truth about you until tonight. No one except Deidre did, I guess. When Kiera told us about your mother and the accident . . . well, I think what she did bothers her more than she'd ever admit, which is another reason I think she went so heavily for the G. Of course, the others, like me, were surprised to hear the details about you. It made me feel pretty lousy. All this time, I thought you were just another spoiled relative of Kiera's. It's a poor excuse, I know, but I just wanted to say it. If the police ask you anything, you can tell them whatever you want. I won't deny it. Sorry," he said again, and walked back into the emergency waiting room.

I remained outside for a while, just pacing. When I looked through the glass doors, I saw the two policemen talking to Kiera's friends. Ricky stood up and walked out with them. He glanced my way as they led him to the patrol car. After he got into the rear, they drove off. When I turned back to the emergency room, I saw the rest of them at the door. They had been watching, too. They parted to make way for me when I entered, which was just when Mrs. March came out, too.

"Donald's here," she told me. "He came in through the main entrance and was brought to Kiera. He's with her now. We're going to wait for a specialist in a different lounge. If you want to go home, I'll get a taxi."

"No, I'd rather wait with you, if that's all right."

She looked at Kiera's friends, and they all turned away. "I've very disappointed in you, Deidre. In all of you," she added.

Deidre started to cry.

"I'm getting this in bits and pieces," she said, turning back to me, "but I have a feeling you've been misjudged. Come along."

I looked back at the others. They were like people in a desert craving some water. No one was going to talk to them to tell them anything about Kiera. I went over to Deidre.

"Mr. March is here. They're expecting a specialist to examine Kiera."

"Thank you," she said. "We were told to stay here. Two other patrol cars are coming to get us, and our parents are being informed. I'm sorry about what we did to you," she added.

I didn't say thank you. I didn't say she should be. I simply nodded and hurried after Mrs. March. Someone from the hospital brought us to a private room outside the hospital administrator's office. He offered us something to drink and went off to get it.

"Donald and I make big contributions to this hospital," Mrs. March told me as a way of explaining our VIP treatment. "We'll soon see what good that does us." The man returned with some coffee for her and a soft drink for me. "Please let my husband know we're up here," she said, and he left.

As I looked at her now, I thought back to when I had first seen her in the hospital ward. She was so elegant, impressive, and powerful. I'd had no idea who she was and why she was there, but I had sensed that she had the power to get things done. Now, sipping her coffee and curling herself in the corner of the sofa, she looked so much smaller and as pathetic as some of the homeless women Mama and I had known as regulars on the streets. When I had gotten to know some of them, I often felt sorrier for them than I did for us. Many had children who had disowned them, or they had lost children, husbands, and all their friends. We were all hobos looking for a handout of love.

Just as I felt Mrs. March was now. It struck me that neither she nor Mr. March ever talked much about relatives. Their money and their power had lifted them into another realm, and if I did hear Mr. March talk about cousins and uncles, it was always in reference to some fear that they would be asking for money. I had never fully realized until now how lonely the three of them really were. They barely had each other, and now it was possible that after losing their younger daughter, they would lose their older one, too. As miserable as Kiera could be, she still filled some of the empty places in their lives. Their home was too kind to tragic memories. It welcomed them. They would never go away. They could live forever in the dark, empty hallways and rooms. Every shadow would protect a ghost, and there were already too many there.

"She'll be all right," I said.

Mrs. March nodded softly. "Why does she have to go to drugs for a good time? Why could she never see how dangerous it is?"

I didn't know what to say to her. We both sat sipping our drinks and waiting. At one point, she looked as if she had fallen asleep. I was very tired, too, but I wouldn't close my eyes.

I lost track of time, but finally, Mr. March, looking exhausted and defeated, that tall, self-confident posture gone, came into the lounge. His face was ashen. She looked up quickly.

"Mat Kindle is examining her," he said. Then he noticed me. "I got Deidre aside before the police returned for her and the others," he said. "What more can you tell us about this?"

"She wasn't there, Donald."

"I know, but she might know something," he said. "Something more. Well?"

I told him all that Ricky had told me about the party. I

used his words to describe why Kiera had wanted the drug. I made a special effort not to sound happy or satisfied.

He nodded. "That's more or less how Deidre described it. She told me the rest, too," he added.

"What rest?" Mrs. March asked.

"It appears Sasha was telling us the truth about it all. They did a very cruel, sick thing to her at Kiera's bidding, I'm afraid." He turned to me. "I'll look into how we can get that tattoo off you."

I saw the mixed feelings in Mrs. March's face. She was happy for me but devastated about Kiera.

"We've got changes to make after this is over," Mr. March said. "Everything got out of hand. It's my fault. You were always right, Jordan. I'm sorry."

She started to cry. He went to her and held her. The two of them looked destroyed. Every part of me wanted to feel good, to feel vindicated and happy about their misery, but I couldn't stop myself from crying, too. Alena was there in me, I thought. I moved over on the sofa and found Mrs. March's hand. Mr. March looked at me, and then the two of them embraced me.

It was the way the doctor found us.

The three of us looked up at him.

"She took a severe dosage of this crap," he began. He was a short, stocky man with a dark brown mustache but a nearly bald head. I thought he looked more like one of those professional wrestlers on television, even in his suit and tie.

"What is it, exactly?" Mr. March asked.

"Technically, gamma-hydroxybutyric acid, known on

the street as GHB or just G. It looks like plain water, but if you tasted it, you'd immediately know it wasn't. So there's no chance it was a mistake unless someone snuck it into a drink. That happens, but I don't think so this time."

"No, it didn't. You're right, Mat," Mr. March said.

"Why do they take it?" Mrs. March asked.

Dr. Kindle laughed. "You have a few days to hear the sociological and psychological explanations for the drug culture? Kids are taking it because it makes them feel energetic, sensual, intoxicated. They grow talkative, high. They even call it Liquid Ecstasy. People who take it often pass out. That's not unusual with this junk. In street talk, that's 'carpeting out' or 'scooping out.' It has a dramatic effect on respiration. If they hadn't gotten Kiera here quickly, she would most surely have died."

"How is she now?" Mrs. March asked in a soft, frightened voice.

"We have her breathing stabilized. I can't tell you exactly how much longer she'll remain in this coma, but it's usually not for days or weeks. In most cases, it's hours. We're moving her to a private room, and I have a private nurse there already, Donald. We'll need to do a full evaluation of her, of course, and see if there has been any other organ damage. This is one of those drugs there are not enough statistics on, because it leaves the body after twelve hours. More people have probably died from it than has been reported. Young people," he added.

"Thanks, Mat," Mr. March said, rising. "What room is she in?"

"Three-forty. I'll be up in a little while, too," he said.

Mrs. March stood up and took her husband's hand. Then she turned to me and held out her other hand for me. I rose quickly, took it, and walked with them to the elevator.

Our lives really do move in circles, I thought as we went up to Kiera's room. My life with the Marches had begun with my being in a hospital, and there I was again in a hospital with not much more time before my life with them would end.

Although they had both already seen Kiera, the sight of her in the hospital bed with her body connected to the monitors froze them. When I looked at her, I thought she had begun to fade away. Her rich complexion was washed out. Her skin looked grayer. Her hair was still beautiful, but the loose strands on the pillow reflected the havoc that surely had preceded all of this in the ambulance and the emergency room. Caught in the frenzy to save her life, she had been poked and prodded, tossed and turned, and attached to machinery. She seemed more like a doll that had been violently shaken until parts of it were beginning to detach themselves.

I still wanted to harden my heart against her, but Alena was pushing me forward. I could almost hear her pleading, *Help her. Help her.*

I went to the side of her bed. Her nurse stood back, and the Marches stood at the foot of the bed. I pulled a chair to the bed and sat, and then I reached for her hand.

"I know the truth about you, Kiera," I said. "I know you are in more pain than anger, and all you did to me and now have done to yourself was your way of covering up that pain. Don't be afraid of it anymore. It's there to clean away your guilt so you can live. Live for your parents. Live for the people who are waiting to love you. And live for Alena."

I let go of her hand, stood up, and put the chair back.

"I'll wait for you downstairs, Mrs. March," I said. I was sure they wanted to be alone with their daughter.

Neither of them said anything to me. They watched me leave. I fell asleep for a while in the waiting room. Mrs. March woke me, and for a few moments, I really didn't know where I was.

"She's coming out of it," she said, smiling through happy tears. "She has to be fully evaluated yet, but Dr. Kindle thinks the worst might be over."

"Good," I said, and got up.

"Donald's waiting for us in the parking lot. He's leaving his car here. He wants us to go home together."

I saw him standing by the car. He got in when he saw us and started the engine. I got into the rear quickly, and Mrs. March got in beside him. No one spoke for the longest time. I nearly fell asleep again, but when we reached the gate and it opened, Mr. March did not drive in. Instead, he turned to look at me.

"Thank you for what you said to Kiera in there, Sasha. You are a remarkable young lady after all. I apologize for the things I said to you."

I didn't know what to say. He was still staring at me, and we weren't moving. The gate remained wide open, and the March mansion loomed ahead, many lights on. I imagined that Mrs. Duval and Mrs. Caro and the others were all waiting for news.

"Maybe Mrs. March was right," he continued. "Maybe

you are the daughter we lost. Maybe in an ironic and terribly painful way for us all, Kiera brought you here. I know this," he said as he turned around to drive in. "You're not leaving until you're old enough to say good-bye and be on your own."

Smiling, Mrs. March reached back for my hand. I took hers, and the three of us drove up the grand driveway to the waiting mansion.

And for the first time since I had arrived there, I felt that I was really coming home.

Epilogue

I had no idea what Kiera would be like when she came home from the hospital. Mrs. March said that when her husband told Kiera I was going to remain with them, she wasn't upset.

"I wouldn't tell you she was overjoyed with the news," Mrs. March told me, "but she looked relieved. Right now, that might simply be because she's not being blamed for something more. I don't know. I always had trouble understanding Kiera and expect I will continue to have trouble. I'll need your help."

"We'll have to help each other with that," I said, and she laughed.

I was moved back into Alena's suite. For me, it was like renewing an old friendship. I hadn't realized how much the suite and everything in it had become part of me. I shared it with the memory of Alena, but I felt it was more mine now, too.

My schoolwork improved considerably over the next

week. Mr. Denacio even took time out in instrumental class to have me demonstrate what real practice could do. What I enjoyed most was the expressions on the faces of my classmates. Why, they surely wondered, was I so buoyant and energetic, as well as happy, after all that had happened? They knew how much trouble Ricky and Kiera's other friends were in because of what had happened to her. Perhaps they were friendlier to me because they were hungry for more details. Once I had felt as if I had celebrity status because I was friends with seniors and did things with seniors. Now I had it because I was simply an exciting person to get to know.

Of course, I gave them little information, but that just made them more determined to talk to me, be with me, and invite me to their homes. It all made me feel much better about myself. Why, Lisa Dirk even told me I looked as if I was limping less and less.

On Friday, they brought Kiera home. She was still confined to bed rest. All of her meals were brought to her, which was nothing new to her, I guessed. When I arrived home, Mrs. March told me she was upstairs and getting better. She knew that because Kiera was complaining.

"However, I think she's still a bit stunned," she said. "Dr. Kindle said psychological problems often follow such an event, so I wouldn't be upset about anything she might say or do right now."

I knew she was trying to prepare me for anything Kiera might say or do to me, but I had a new sense of power and strength. I was no longer afraid of Kiera. Her friends had practically crawled underground. They were meek mice in school now. Ricky's disposition remained unknown. If his parents hadn't had money and influence, he wouldn't even have been attending Pacifica. The few times I saw him, he said nothing to me, and I said nothing to him.

It was impossible to avoid seeing Kiera, so I thought it would be best if I simply went directly up to her suite. The door was open, and she was propped up on big pillows in her bed.

"How are you?" I asked.

She stared at me as if we had never met. "Terrible," she finally replied. "They want me to stay in bed another three days or so. I haven't been able to wash my hair, put on any makeup, or anything. Look at what I look like."

"Look at what you almost did," I told her.

"Another goody two-shoes." She looked away and then back at me. "Deidre called me in the hospital and told me what was going on with Ricky. I heard he told you things."

"He did."

"Are you happy now?"

"More than I was last week, yes," I said.

She smirked. "It looks like I'm going to have to live with you."

"Looks like it."

"Why would you want to stay here after all you went through? They'd probably give you lots of money and place you in a comfortable new home."

"Probably."

"So?"

"I'm staying for Alena. I'm not *becoming* Alena," I quickly added, "but I'm staying because of her. Besides, someone has to look after you."

"Very funny." She paused, her eyes narrowing a little. *Here it comes,* I thought. "I'm not going to say I'm sorry, if that's what you're waiting to hear."

"That's all right. I can wait. Someday you will."

"How did you get so arrogant?"

"I had a good teacher," I said.

I saw her fighting a smile. "I don't want to like you," she said defiantly.

"You will, eventually."

"And I suppose you'll like me, is that it?"

"Maybe. Eventually."

"Eventually, eventually. Everything's 'eventually.'"

"Everything is. When my mother and I were living in the streets, I used to wonder if we'd ever get off them, get back into a home, into a life. If I asked her, she'd always say 'soon.' *Soon's* a great word. It's full of promise and hope."

"Is it?"

"Sure. Soon you'll get out of this bed, and soon you'll go to school. Soon you'll graduate and go to college, and soon you'll meet someone you can love, who can love you, and soon you'll get married and have a daughter maybe just like you, too."

"Please. You sound like my mother now."

"We all get to sound like our mothers."

"She's not yours."

"No, but she knows where to stand, when to smile, when to laugh and comfort me."

"You're giving me a headache."

"Okay." I turned and started out.

"Hey."

"What?"

"I don't like you yet, but I don't hate you anymore. Don't ask me why not. And don't say I hate myself more or anything stupid like that."

"Okay."

"They moved you back next door?"

"Yes."

"Come back later, maybe eat in here. If you can stand it."

"I think I can. I lived in the streets once, remember?"

Now she laughed.

I would eat with her, but before I did anything else, I asked Mrs. March for a favor, and she called Grover to bring the car around.

He drove me out to the cemetery where Mama was buried. It was one of those wonderful California late afternoons when the shadows from some scattered clouds were refreshing and the air cleaned out by the sea wind was sharp and fresh. When I entered the cemetery, the aroma of freshly cut grass surrounded me. It was a scent that spoke of life and renewal, even in a cemetery.

All week, I had felt guilty about being happy again. It was the old fear that by accepting the Marches' generosity and affection, I was betraying Mama. I was at the cemetery to ask for her forgiveness again, but I thought I would do it a different sort of way. When I reached her grave, I set down the case and took out the clarinet. Then I sat close to her tombstone and began to play.

And before I was finished, I was certain in my heart that wherever she was, she was smiling.

Integrated Working with Children and Young People

Supporting Development from Birth to Nineteen

Edited by

Nadia Edmond and Mark Price

Los Angeles | London | New Delhi
Singapore | Washington DC

First published 2012

SAGE Publications Ltd
1 Oliver's Yard
55 City Road
London EC1Y 1SP

SAGE Publications Inc.
2455 Teller Road
Thousand Oaks, California 91320

SAGE Publications India Pvt Ltd
B 1/I 1 Mohan Cooperative Industrial Area
Mathura Road
New Delhi 110 044

SAGE Publications Asia-Pacific Pte Ltd
3 Church Street
#10-04 Samsung Hub
Singapore 049483

Library of Congress Control Number: 2011936590

British Library Cataloguing in Publication data

A catalogue record for this book is available from the British Library

ISBN 978-0-85702-781-8
ISBN 978-0-85702-782-5 (pbk)

Typeset by C&M Digitals (P) Ltd, Chennai, India
Printed in MPG Books Group, Bodmin, Cornwall
Printed on paper from sustainable resources

For our colleagues and students in the School of Education at the University of Brighton. Their belief in, and commitment to, higher education in the professional learning of those working with children and young people has provided constant support and inspiration.

Particular thanks are due to Jessica Hamlin and Lindsay Macpherson for always excellent and unfailingly good natured editorial support.

Contents

List of Figures and Tables

Figures

Tables

About the Editors and Contributors

The editors

Nadia Edmond is Assistant Head of the School of Education at the University of Brighton and initiated the Foundation Degree Professional Studies in Primary Education for primary teaching assistants. She has a background in teaching in adult and further education and her research interests include professionalism, professional learning and identity.

Mark Price originally trained as a playworker, secondary school teacher, youth worker and psychotherapist. Mark is now a Principal Lecturer in the School of Education at the University of Brighton, where he leads on economic and social engagement and workforce development. His main teaching and research interests are in reflective practice, professional identity formation and narrative enquiry.

The contributors

Erica Evans is currently working for the University of Brighton as Programme Leader for the Early Years Professional Status and as an Associate Lecturer for the Open University on the Foundation Degree in Early Years. Her previous experience includes working as a class teacher, registered childminder, childminding network co-ordinator and adult education tutor.

Denise Kingston is a qualified educational psychologist and teacher. She has worked for many different local authorities as a teacher, educational psychologist, portage supervisor, advisor, consultant and Early Years Development and Childcare Partnership senior manager.

She is now Senior Lecturer in the School of Education at the University of Brighton and is particularly interested in the links that can be made between inclusion and quality improvement.

Jane Melvin has been in the field of youth work for over 25 years. During this time, she has worked within centre-based and residential contexts, moving from direct face-to-face contact with young people, through training and development, to senior management. She is now Route Leader for the FdA Working with Young People and BA (Hons) Youth Work at the University of Brighton.

Deborah Price has worked with children and young people for thirty years. She has worked as a primary teacher, OFSTED inspector and playworker and is now a Senior Lecturer at the University of Brighton and is the Route Leader for the Foundation Degree in Playwork. Her other professional roles are as Lecturer in children's literature for The Open University, manager of 'Childcare Training' and as a freelance trainer for 'Working With Others'.

Sarah Wilkins has been a social worker for over 20 years, working as a practitioner and manager with children and young people in care and leaving care. Prior to this she completed a Degree in drama, theatre and television, which has always allowed her to think creatively about her work. Alongside her ongoing role in social work, she is also now a Lecturer in the School of Education at the University of Brighton, where she contributes to the Foundation Degree and other practice-based programmes.

Preface

How this book came about

The *Every Child Matters* policy agenda has had a major impact on the children and young people's workforce. Existing roles such as early years practitioners, teaching assistants, playworkers and youth workers and new roles such as learning mentors and parent support advisors require increasingly high standards of professional development and qualification. Much of this professional development and qualification has been provided by Higher Education programmes (predominantly Foundation Degrees) in Further and Higher Education institutions.

The authors of this book are a programme team that have been involved in the development and delivery of a range of Foundation Degrees across the children and young people's workforce since their introduction in 2002. Initially these were separate courses but since 2008, the team have worked together to develop a common curriculum across the different awards. We recognise the need for professionally distinct content for different groups of workers within the children and young people's workforce, yet increasingly, effectiveness in any role depends not just on specific professional expertise but on the capacity to communicate and collaborate with a range of other professions. We saw the need for programmes which include professionally distinct content but also acknowledge and make the commonalities explicit. This thinking has informed the development of core content for courses in the children and young people's workforce – the basic understandings we all need to share.

In this book, we have aimed to provide an accessible foundation to working with children and young people which is of relevance to all those undertaking professional development in their role, particularly through a Foundation Degree. Its interdisciplinary perspective is designed specifically to support the development of practitioners as effective contributors to integrated working through multi-disciplinary teams. It clearly identifies the skills and knowledge which cross the occupational boundaries and aims to support better communication between those working with children and young people and transitions between associated roles. Whether readers are employed and studying part-time or on a full-time programme which includes periods of placement working with children and/or young people, they will welcome the practical focus of this book, which relates key ideas to practice in the workplace.

Who is this book for?

The book arises directly out of teaching common aspects of Foundation and Undergraduate Degrees for the Children and Young People's workforce in an interdisciplinary way at the University of Brighton, where the authors work together, teaching across five Foundation Degrees and two BA Degrees. This kind of teaching for common modules of Foundation and Undergraduate Degrees and the development of generic programmes in working with children and young people is becoming increasingly widespread within Higher Education.

As a tutor team we experienced the need for a core text which would support the teaching and learning of common themes in working with children and young people in an interdisciplinary and multi-agency context. Having worked on developing teaching materials to support our students, we wanted to develop these as a book to make the resources, activities and ideas available to a wider audience. In particular, we know from colleagues working in local authorities and a range of children and young people settings that there is a need for materials to contribute to an interdisciplinary perspective on continuing professional development (CPD). This book, therefore, is for anyone working with children and/or young people who is interested in developing a more informed critical perspective on their practice and thinking about how their particular role relates to the others in the children and young people's workforce. The book offers exciting new perspectives on professional roles and puts multi-disciplinary working into practice from the very start.

What does the book cover?

The book addresses issues common to all those working with children and young people. The introduction provides an overview to two theoretical perspectives fundamental to the whole book. Thereafter, the book is organised into three sections.

In Section 1, 'Professionalism in the Children and Young People's Workforce', four chapters address the policy context and issues for working with children and young people. These chapters look at policy trends and themes, debates around and strategies for evaluating 'effectiveness' and 'quality', the nature of professionalism and professional relationships and leadership, and the challenges presented by multi-agency and inter-professional working.

Section 2, 'Supporting Children and Young People's Development' is aimed at helping students understand children and young people's development from a range of perspectives. Three chapters address physical development, cognitive development and social and emotional development.

In Section 3, 'Effective Communication and Engagement', the five chapters focus on professional relationships with children and young people, with families, on promoting the well-being and safeguarding of children, supporting transitions, and promoting equality and inclusion.

Finally a conclusion encourages readers to review their learning and plan for ongoing professional development.

How to use this book: Guidance for students

This book is designed to be read by busy students and professionals. We have worked hard to make it engaging and accessible and recognise that readers will want to be able to dip in and out, depending on their particular interests or concerns. Each chapter includes:

- a *chapter overview*

- illustrative *case studies*

- *Reflection points*, at which you will be challenged to think about how what you are reading relates to your practice

- *Workplace activities*, which will support you in taking your thinking about your practice forward and/or broaden your perspective on particular issues

- *Further reading* to guide you in developing the ideas further.

To get the most from reading this book, it is important that you engage with the case studies, reflection points and activities as these will help you build on your experience at work or on placement to develop as critically reflective professionals. The inter-professional perspective will help you to engage with this important aspect of current practice in the children and young people's workforce.

Introduction

Nadia Edmond

The role of theory in this book

This book is not intended to be a 'how to' manual – rather, on the principle that, as the educational theorist Kurt Lewin argued, there is nothing so practical as a good theory (Lewin, 1951: 169), it introduces the reader to ideas which will allow them to develop thinking about practice. For us, the value of higher education in professional development is that the skills of research and critical engagement with a subject learnt in higher education make for more thoughtful, critical and better informed practitioners. Theory informs all the sections of the book and you will encounter a number of key ideas to help you think more deeply about your practice in all of the chapters. In this introduction, we explore two fundamental ideas which influence the whole book.

The first fundamental idea is that factors influencing learning and development are interconnected. This idea is captured in 'ecological models' of human development.

Ecological models of human development

According to this model, children and young people's development can only be understood as embedded within and influenced by the totality of their context. When we talk about 'ecology' we are referring to the complex inter-relationships and interdependencies in nature, the way everything is connected to everything else in the 'web of life'. A similar idea can be applied to understanding human development, that is, all the different aspects of our lives interact and interconnect to influence our development.

> Ecological models encompass an evolving body of theory and research concerned with the processes and conditions that govern the lifelong course of human development in the actual environments in which human beings live. (Bronfenbrenner, 1994: 37)

Bronfenbrenner puts forward two propositions in his ecological model. The first is that human development takes place through enduring (regular and/or repeated over an extended period of time) forms of interaction between the individual and their immediate environment (he calls these 'proximal processes'). Examples of such 'proximal process' interactions might be those between parent and child, or group or solitary play: essentially anything that comes to form part of the child's pattern of experiences. Bronfenbrenner goes on to propose that the form, power, content and direction of these proximal processes will depend on the characteristics of the individual, their environment and the development outcome under consideration, and suggests that it is possible to investigate this.

According to Bronfenbrenner, an example of such an investigation is a study by Drillien (1963) which looked at factors affecting the

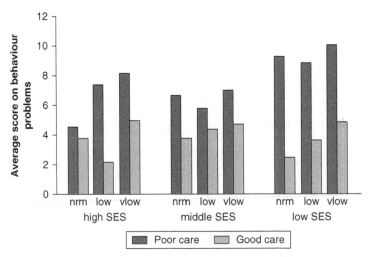

nrm = normal birth rate; low = between normal and 5.5 lbs; vlow = 5.5lbs or less

Figure I.1   Problem behaviour at age four (by birth weight, mother's care and social class)

Source: Brofenbrenner (1994: 39)

development of children of low birth weight compared to those of normal weight. Drillien looked at problem behaviour observed at age four by birth weight, quality of mother–infant interaction at age four and social class. What the study showed was that the proximal interaction (the mother–infant interaction) was the most powerful predictor of developmental outcome; in all instances high quality mother–child interaction reduced substantially the degree of behavioural disturbance observed in the child. But it also showed that there was a systematic relationship between the impact of this proximal process and characteristics of the individual (in this case birth weight), and characteristics of the environmental context (in this case social class).

If we want to understand child behaviour we cannot only look at parenting, for example, but need to recognise the complex relationship and interactions between the child and the different levels of their 'ecological environment'. Bronfenbrenner sees this as a set of nested structures, each inside the other, like a set of Russian dolls, as shown in Figure I.2.

Microsystem
A pattern of activities, social roles and interpersonal relations experienced by the individual in a given face-to-face setting which inhibit or enable sustained interactions with and in the immediate environment. Examples include such settings as family, school, peer group and workplace.

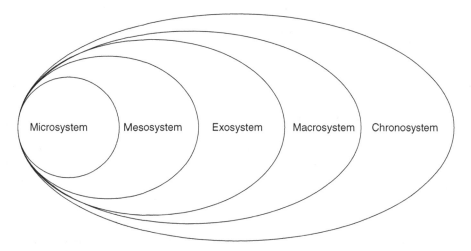

Figure I.2 Brofenbrenner's model of ecological environments

Mesosystem

The mesosystem comprises the linkages and processes taking place between two or more settings – for example the relationship between school and home.

Exosystem

The exosystem comprises the linkages and processes taking place between two or more settings, at least one of which does not contain the developing person but in which events occur that indirectly influence processes within the individual's immediate setting. An example for a child would be the relation between the home and the parent's workplace.

Macrosystem

The macrosystem consists of the overarching pattern of micro- meso- and exosystems characteristic of a given culture or subculture, with particular reference to the belief systems, bodies of knowledge, material resources, customs, lifestyles and life course options embedded in this overarching system. Examples of 'macrosystems' would include social class.

Chronosystem

In the study of human development, the passage of time has traditionally been treated as synonymous with chronological age. A chronosystem encompasses change or consistency over time, not only in the characteristics of the person, but also of the environment in which they live. Studies wanting to identify the impact of the chronosystem might focus on the impact of particular historical circumstances, such as the Great Depression of the 1930s in the USA (Elder, 1974).

The ecological model of human development emphasises the interconnectedness and interdependency of all these systems. It suggests that whilst we may want to concentrate on one system (for example, as practitioners we may want to focus on the microsystem of the setting in which we work with children or young people), we must acknowledge the links with, and impact of, all the other systems on the individual and the microsystem.

The ecological model of human development also provides a theoretical framework from which to consider what has been termed the 'nature–nurture' debate in human nature. There are essentially two factors that can affect the way in which individuals 'turn out' (biologists refer to this as the 'phenotype'). One is our genotype (our genetic makeup), sometimes referred to as 'nature' (because our genetic makeup is determined by biology), and the other is our environment or 'nurture' (because our environment is primarily controlled by other people). The 'nature–nurture' debate is the general debate about the relative importance of these factors in human development. The ecological model suggests that our phenotype is best understood as a complex interaction and interdependency of these factors rather than the simple dominance of one over the other.

Reflection point

What are the implications of the ecological model for how you might think about your practice?

Which of the various systems would you say is your primary concern?

Which other systems do you acknowledge through your practice and how?

Focusing on a case study child or young person, write a paragraph about them from each of these system perspectives identifying the connections between them.

Microsystem: what are the proximal processes that are most significant in your work with this child or young person? What are the other proximal processes influencing them and how?

Mesosystem: what are the relationships between your professional setting and other microsystems? How are these fostered and/or managed? What impact does this relationship have on the children/young people you work with?

Exosystem: how does the relationship between the home and the parent's workplace or other systems, of which the child/young person is not directly a part, impact on their learning and development?

Macrosystem: how would you categorise the social group of which the child/young person is a part? How does membership of this group impact on their learning and development?

Chronosystem: this is inevitably more speculative, but how do you think the particular characteristics of the time in which the child/young person is developing (for example, recession, high unemployment) may impact on them?

Postmodernism: Certainty and scepticism in knowing about learning and development

Postmodernism is the second fundamental idea that influences this book.

The idea that the world is knowable and can be subject to rational enquiry seems self-evident and obvious to us now but it was not always so. Willis (2008), for example, has tracked the development of the philosophy of science from the middle ages (330–1450), when uncritical application of the thinking of Greek and Roman philosophers and adherence to Christian values and beliefs dominated our understanding of the source and authority of knowledge. The idea of knowledge arising out of science and rational enquiry was the result of a major shift in the way we think about the world in Europe around the 17th century. The 'Enlightenment', also sometimes called 'the Age of Reason', was the era in European intellectual, scientific and cultural life in which reason came to challenge religion, tradition and superstition as the primary source of legitimacy and authority of knowledge.

The Enlightenment grew out the social and economic transformations which characterised the transition from the medieval period, into the Renaissance, and on to what has been termed the 'modern era'. It was the emphasis on rationality within the Enlightenment which enabled the growth of science and technology and a view of the world as knowable and ordered, and of humans as rational beings. The 'modernist project' arising out of the Enlightenment has been characterised as applying thought and intellect to improving human existence and is associated with a belief in the capacity of science to establish reliable, value-neutral truths, to make consistent predictions about the world and to provide solutions to problems of human existence. 'Positivism' (the belief that the best way to come to know the world is through the 'scientific method' consisting of systematic observation, measurement and experiment, and the formulation and testing of hypotheses) and 'empiricism' (the belief that knowledge of the world comes through our senses and our experience provides evidence of the nature of the world) have been hugely successful and came, and continue, to dominate what we understand as a valid source of knowledge.

From the early 20th century, this view, and the whole 'modernist project', has come to be challenged by an alternative world view – 'postmodernism'. In opposition to the certainty provided by the scientific method, a great deal of postmodernist theory depends on the maintenance of a sceptical attitude. A figure head of the postmodernist movement, Lyotard (1984), argued that we now live in an era in which legitimising 'master narratives' (overarching accounts which frame how we understand the world) are in crisis and decline. One of these 'narratives' is that of the 'triumph of science', in which science is presented as the provider of solutions to all our problems (rather than, as many increasingly argue, the source of all our problems!). 'Simplifying to the extreme, I define postmodern as incredulity towards metanarratives' (Lyotard, 1984: xxiii). This 'incredulity' has been particularly pronounced in the social sciences, where the certainties about the natural world offered by the scientific method have remained elusive. Three reasons are proposed. The first is that the dynamism and complexity of the social world means that we can never achieve reliable predictions about it – there are always too many variables to consider. So, for example, poverty is linked to poor educational attainment but we can't reliably predict a child's educational attainment only from the income of their parents. The second reason is that any research and interpretation of a social phenomenon inevitably reflects the observer/researcher's perspective. The third reason arises out of the postmodern claim that there is no certainty or universal understanding that exists outside history or society; instead all of us, including the children and young people with whom we work, influence our world and our understanding of it. We make sense of the world in terms of our historical and social context, including our language. Realisation of this has led to the 'linguistic turn' in the social sciences, recognising the role of language in shaping and constructing our understanding of the world through 'discourse'.

Discourse is language (and other cultural mediators, such as signs and images) that works to make particular sets of ideas obvious, common-sensical and self-evidently 'true'. 'Discourses mobilise truth claims and constitute rather than simply reflect social reality' (Ball, 2008: 5) and through discourses 'Language is deployed in the attempt to produce certain meanings and effects' (Edwards et al., 1999: 620).

What this means for practitioners is that critical, informed practice requires a healthy scepticism and a consideration of the way in which understanding of what is 'true' in the field of children and young people's learning and development is shaped by various discourses which exist to present this particular version of the truth. Examples of such discourses, which we address in later chapters, are policy discourses and the discourses around the concept of 'quality' and 'professionalism'.

> ᔌᔌ **Reflection point**
>
> These ideas are quite challenging because they require us to iden-
> tify and question our assumptions. A good starting point for getting
> to grips with this is to think about something which you believed
> to be an obvious 'self-evident' truth in relation to your practice and
> about which you have changed your mind or which you now see
> differently. What was the 'discourse' (the way in which this issue
> was presented) and the characteristics of that discourse which
> made it seem so obvious, so 'right'? What was the counter-
> discourse (the way in which the alternative perspective was pre-
> sented) and the characteristics of that discourse which made you
> change your mind?

Further reading

Bronfenbrenner, U. (2004) *Making Human Beings Human: Bio-ecological Perspectives on Human Development*. London: Sage. This most recent book by a figure in the field of human development shows the historical development of the bio-ecological model and the ecology of human development.

Butler, C. (2002) *Postmodernism: A Very Short Introduction*. Oxford: Oxford University Press. This books provides a brief and accessible introduction to the key ideas of postmodernism.

http://www.infed.org/biblio/b-postmd.htm An entry on postmodernism from the excellent *infed* (the informal education homepage and encyclopaedia of informal education). This was established in 1995 as an open and not-for-profit site which aims to provide a space for people to explore the theory and practice of informal education, social action and lifelong learning and provides a wide range of articles of general interest. http://www.infed.org/

References

Ball, S.J. (2008) *The Education Debate: Policy and Politics in the Twenty-first Century*. Bristol: The Policy Press.

Bronfenbrenner, U. (1994) 'Ecological models of human development', in *International Encyclopedia of Education*, Vol. 3 (2nd edn). Oxford: Elsevier. Reprinted in M. Gauvain and M. Cole (eds), *Readings on the Development of Children* (2nd edn) (1993, pp. 37–43). New York: Freeman.

Drillien, C.M. (1963) 'Obstetric hazard, mental retardation and behaviour disturbance in primary school', *Developmental Medicine and Child Neurology*, 5: 3–13.

Edwards, R., Nicoll, K. and Tait, A. (1999) 'Migrating metaphors: The globalization of flexibility in policy', *Journal of Education Policy*, 14(6): 619–30.

Elder, G.H., Jr. (1974) *Children of the Great Depression: Social Change in the Life Experience*. Chicago, IL: University of Chicago Press.

Lewin, K. (1951) *Field Theory in Social Science: Selected Theoretical Papers*, D. Cartwright (ed.). New York: Harper & Row.

Lyotard, J.F. (1984) *The Postmodern Condition: A Report on Knowledge*. Manchester: Manchester University Press.

Willis, J. (2008) *Foundations of Qualitative Research: Interpretive and Critical Approaches*. London: Sage.

Section 1

Professionalism in the Children and Young People's Workforce

1

Children and Young People's Services in Context

Mark Price and Nadia Edmond

Chapter Overview

This chapter examines the concept of policy and discusses how national social and educational policy impacts on the shape and direction of the work done with children and young people, with a particular focus on recent years. The chapter aims to provide an overview of current policy and its impact on service provision as well as providing an introduction to the understanding and critiquing of policy discourse. Overall themes and trends, such as the move towards targeted and integrated services, are also considered.

By reading and engaging with the activities in this chapter, you will:

- become aware of the range of policies and service development initiatives which have shaped children and young people's services in recent years;
- develop your understanding on how these policies and service developments reflect values, priorities and thinking about children and young people;
- reflect on possible future developments in children and young people's services, especially related to learning and development, and the likely impact on delivery of provision.

What is policy?

Policy is a plan or course of action defined by a government, political party, or organisation, intended to influence and determine decisions and actions. Policy refers to organisational or governmental statements of vision and intent which seek to provide a direction, framework and impetus for practice. Policy may be:

- **aspirational** – presenting a statement of intent or planned direction; these are often presented as 'green papers' (a preliminary report of government proposals to stimulate discussion). Green papers may be followed by 'white papers' (an authoritative report or guide that seeks to solve a problem and which serves as a prelude to legislation);

- **strategic** – setting out a series of planned actions, including (possibly) funding commitments, e.g. *Aiming High for Young People* (DCSF, 2007);

- **legislative** – law enshrined in an Act of Parliament, e.g. Education Reform Act, 1988.

The policies which governments use for education, health, welfare and social care to direct the practice and provision of a range of institutions and social arrangements, have come together to form what is termed 'the welfare state'. In thinking about how policy directs our practice, a good starting point would be the emergence of the welfare state during war-time Britain in the 1940s, the key architect of which was the economist William Beveridge. The Beveridge Report (1942) identified 'five evils' it wished to address in British society – *squalor, ignorance, want, idleness* and *disease* – and the creation of the welfare state was a contribution to building a fairer, more equitable society in Britain in the post-war years.

Much social policy and welfare provision continues to aim to address the impacts of social inequality. This is not just because of moral arguments related to the principle of social justice but because, increasingly, social inequality is recognised as being associated with, if not the cause of, social problems. Wilkinson and Pickett (2009), for example, have shown that societies which are more unequal (in terms of income and wealth distribution) tend to have not just more poverty, but less social mobility and poorer educational attainment, amongst other social ills. However, whilst welfare provision is often targeted at the poor to provide a 'safety net', it does not necessarily make society more 'equal'. For example, the recent Hills report (National Equality Panel, 2010) showed that income inequality in the UK declined steadily from the 1930s to the mid-1970s but since then has increased, and is now back to levels comparable to the 1930s. There also continues to be systematic differences in educational attainment across social groups.

The main inequalities in society (relevant to those working with children and young people) identified by a number of analysts (e.g. Cole, 2006) relate to gender, 'race' and ethnicity, disability, sexual orientation and social class. The recent Equality Act (2010) brings many of these together under a single overarching legislative framework for businesses and public services. The associated Equality Duty came into effect in 2011 replacing the three previous duties on race, disability and gender, now extended to include sexual orientation, religion or belief, and gender reassignment.

Policy does not just exist at a national, governmental level. International policy-makers, such as UNICEF, can be seen to directly influence our work with children and young people, through the United Nations Convention on the Rights of the Child (UNCRC) (1989). The UNCRC, via 54 articles and two optional protocols, sets out a global framework to protect the fundamental rights of all children and young people to survival; to develop to their full potential; to protection from harmful influences, abuse and exploitation; and to participate fully in family, cultural and social life. At the time of writing, every country in the world has ratified or acceded to this legally binding Convention, with the exception of Somalia and the United States of America.

The UNCRC influences work with children and young people in Britain. For example, Article 12 states 'When adults are making decisions that affect children, children have the right to say what they think should happen and have their opinions taken into account'. This article supports and reinforces practices relating to children and young people's voice and participation, from school councils and the UK Youth Parliament, through to representation on policy formation and staff appointment processes and related procedures now followed by many employers.

Why is policy important?

Think for a moment about the working policies and practices we have taken for granted in recent years – the National Curriculum, Sure Start, *Every Child Matters*, etc. These have become embedded in education, learning and development provision, but they too will change and be replaced by newer policy initiatives, for example, academies and free schools, 'the Big Society', all of which will have a direct impact on practice.

Individual nurseries, schools, play organisations and youth services will have their own policies which relate to an individual organisation's own vision, priorities and services and/or reflect or interpret broader government policy. For example, the Equality Act (2010) places a duty on public bodies to eliminate discrimination on the grounds of race, disability, gender, age, sexual orientation, religion or belief, pregnancy and maternity, and gender reassignment. An individual school or local authority will then have its own policies relating directly to its localised responses to this duty.

Understanding policy is helped by having some understanding of its historical development, and some key points of policy affecting children and young people over the last 30 years are outlined in the chronology below.

A chronology of policy relating to children and young people 1981–2011

Conservative government: 1979–1997

Prime Ministers: Margaret Thatcher (1979–1990); John Major (1990–1997)

> **1981**   The **1981 Education Act** sets the first duty of LEAs to educate disabled children in mainstream schools, taking account of parents' wishes and establishing three conditions that were to be met before it could happen. These conditions are: that the disabled child can be educated in the ordinary school; that other children's education will not be adversely affected; and that there is an efficient use of resources.
>
> The Act comes into force in April 1983 and one of the direct consequences of this legislation is the increasing use of teaching assistants and learning

support assistants to support the learning of children with special educational needs in mainstream schools.

1988   The **Education Reform Act 1988** restates the functions of LEAs in respect of Further and Higher Education. It introduces the National Curriculum, intended to be in operation in all schools by September 1992. Four age-related Key Stages are defined, incorporating all pupils of a particular age at the beginning of each academic year. Citizenship is designated as one of a set of five 'cross-curricular themes'. Parents have the right to vote a school out of local authority control. The Act provides for greater delegation of budgets to newly constituted governing bodies for FE colleges that from 1989 become corporate bodies.

The **Youth Training Guarantee** is introduced. It decrees that no sixteen/seventeen-year-old is to be without education, employment or training.

1989   The **1989 Children Act** gives every child the right to protection from abuse and exploitation and the right to inquiries to safeguard their welfare. Its central tenet is that children are usually best looked after within their family. The Act comes into force in England and Wales in 1991 and (with some differences) in Northern Ireland in 1996.

The **United Nations Convention on the Rights of the Child** (UNCRC) spells out the basic human rights that children everywhere should have: the right to survival; to develop to the fullest; to protection from harmful influences, abuse and exploitation; and to participate fully in family, cultural and social life. The four core principles of the Convention are: non-discrimination; devotion to the best interests of the child; the right to life, survival and development; and respect for the views of the child. The Convention protects children's rights by setting standards in health care, education, and legal, civil and social services.

1991   The **Parents' Charter** gives parents the right to information about the school and its performance (updated in 1994). This leads to the introduction of **school league tables** in 1992 with the stated aim to give parents the consumer information they need to create a free market in school choice. Staff guidance on working together under the **Children Act** require **Area Child Protection Committees and Child Protection Panels** (ACPCs) to conduct an investigation to establish whether child protection procedures were followed when child abuse is suspected or confirmed to be the cause of a child's death.

The **UK ratifies the Convention on the Rights of the Child** (UNCRC), accepting responsibility for the obligations in it.

1992   Concern about variable local inspection regimes leads government to introduce a national scheme of inspections though a reconstituted Her Majesty's Inspectorale (HMI), This becomes known as the **Office for Standards in Education (Ofsted)**. Schools judged by Ofsted to be failing can be put in 'special measures' or closed if they fail to improve.

1996   The **1996 Education Act** consolidates all the Education Acts concerning schools since 1944. Under the legislation for a National Curriculum, children are entitled to an education which is broad and balanced and which prepares them for further education (FE) and training or the job market. Compulsory school starting age is defined at five years, as amended by the Education Act 1997. The Act also restates the principle that pupils are to be educated in accordance with the wishes of their parents and provides for parental choice of school.

Labour government: 1997–2010

Prime Ministers: Tony Blair (1997–2007); Gordon Brown (2007–2010)

1998   The **National Childcare Strategy** green paper, 'Meeting the Childcare Challenge', is launched while the Nursery Education Voucher scheme is abolished. **Early Years Development and Childcare Partnerships (EYDCP)** are introduced, composed of the key local groups in the early years and childcare with a remit of planning early years provision. Over 150 Partnerships in England are now in operation.

Sure Start local programmes are introduced but these are limited to disadvantaged areas. Initial districts for Sure Start development are selected 'according to the levels of deprivation within their areas'. **Sure Start** is set up as a cross-departmental strategy to improve services for younger children and families based on the government's belief that investment in early childhood can help later performance at school, prevent truancy and reduce the risk of unemployment, drug abuse and crime. Its goal will be to ensure that all children are ready to learn when they arrive at school. It is targeted at children under four and their families in areas of need.

Education Action Zones are launched. These are geographical areas in which group of schools work together to meet educational targets for improvement. They receive extra funding for three to five years and are run not by the LEA, but by a forum including businesses, parents and community organisations (in 2005 these become 'Excellence Clusters').

1999   The **Protection of Children Act 1999** is passed, aiming to prevent paedophiles from working with children. It requires childcare organisations in England and Wales to inform the Department of Health about anyone known to them who is suspected of harming children or putting them at risk.

2000   The **Learning and Skills Act** 2000 introduces 'city academies' (later termed 'academies') which are publicly funded with some private sponsorship and independent of LEA control.

2001   The first wave of **Connexions** partnerships begins with the aim of every young person aged thirteen to nineteen having access to the Connexions service by 2004. The role of **Personal Adviser** is created.

In September 2001, **HMI and Ofsted** become responsible for the registration and **inspection of day care and childminding in England** (previously this had been done by local authorities).

In November 2001, a new **Special Educational Needs Code of Practice** (DE, 2001) replaces the previous Code of Practice (1994). It reflects legislation introduced early in the year in the form of the Special Educational Needs and Disability Act (2001) and redefines assessment processes and provision of support.

2002   Citizenship becomes a **Foundation Subject of the National Curriculum** in secondary schools, giving Citizenship statutory status for the first time. The Department for Education and Skills (DfES) begins to actively promote the concept of '**extended schools**', initially through some demonstration projects and then by sponsoring 25 LEAs to develop extended schools pathfinder projects.

The Department for Education and Skills publishes **Transforming Youth Work: Resourcing Excellent Youth Services**, designed to inform Ofsted's Inspection Framework for Youth Work. The specification states that local youth services must develop a curriculum related to the overall goals of the Connexions service.

2003   Lord Laming's report into the death of child abuse victim Victoria Climbié, finds that health, police and social services missed numerous opportunities to save her. This gives impetus for the government green paper, **Every Child Matters**. The paper proposes an electronic tracking system for England's children; the creation of 150 children's trusts to be set up by 2006, amalgamating health, education and social services; a children's director to oversee local services; statutory local safeguarding children boards; and a children's commissioner for England.

A **national agreement on raising standards and tackling workload** is signed by government, employers and school workforce unions. The agreement acknowledges the pressure on schools to raise standards and tackle teacher workload, and introduces a series of significant changes to teachers' conditions of service. This leads to the establishment of **higher level teaching assistants (HLTA)** (and associated standards). The agreement also helps create other new roles that support teachers' work and pupils' learning and wider workforce reform.

2004   The **Children Act 2004**, which pushes forward the main proposals of the *Every Child Matters* green paper is passed by parliament. It allows local authorities more flexibility in organising their children's services, with the amalgamation of education and social services not mandatory. Councils are given two years to set up children's trusts. It introduces switch from Sure Start local programmes to Sure Start Children's Centres, controlled by local authorities, and provided not just in the most disadvantaged areas.

'**Extended schools**' becomes a manifestation of the 'joined-up' work of children's trusts. The desire that all schools become extended schools forms part of the government's **Five Year Strategy for Children and Learners** (DfES, 2004a).

2005   England's first children's commissioner (Professor Al Aynsley Green) is appointed. The **Children's Workforce Development Council** (CWDC) is created to support the implementation of the government's *Every Child Matters* strategy. Amongst other things, the CWDC is responsible for introducing Early Years Professional Status, as part of the government's aim to professionalise the early years workforce.

The CWDC steers through the development of the Common Core of Skills and Knowledge for the Children's Workforce (DfES, 2005), a framework later revised in 2010, aimed at enabling all professionals, practitioners and volunteers working with children, young people and their carers and families to develop a shared language and understanding across services and provision and so facilitate inter-professional and multi-agency working.

2006   The **Parent Support Adviser** (PSA) pilot is introduced. This is a government-funded initiative to support 20 local authorities (LAs) to introduce PSAs into their workforce in over 600 schools.

2007   Early Years Professional Status is introduced. It is the government's aim to have an early years professional in every daycare setting by 2015 (DfES, 2007c). This will require 20,000 EYPs.

Ofsted is merged with the **Adult Learning Inspectorate** (ALI) to provide an inspection service which includes all *post-16 government funded education* (except *Higher Education Institutes and Universities*). Ofsted also takes on responsibility for the registration and inspection of social care services for children, and the welfare inspection of independent and maintained boarding schools to become the Office for Standards in Education, Children's Services and Skills.

Aiming High for Young People: A Ten-year Strategy for Positive Activities is published (DCSF, 2007). The strategy includes 55 commitments intended to increase young people's participation in constructive leisure-time activities and includes the proposed creation of 'Youth Professional Status' (with associated degree qualification requirement).

Every Parent Matters (DfES, 2007a) introduces a number of initiatives to support parenting, including models of good practice in early intervention and preventative support for parents developed in the Parent Support Advisor pilot.

2008   Statutory framework for the **Early Years Foundation Stage** becomes mandatory for all schools and early years providers in Ofsted registered settings attended by young children (0–5 years). An Early Years Register of childcare providers registered with Ofsted is established.

As part of the commitment from the Children's Plan, the **National Play Strategy** (DCSF, 2008) is launched in which the government sets out a plan and a budget to improve play opportunities for children and young people.

2010   The **Equality Act (2010)** enters the statute book in the last weeks of the Labour government. It harmonises a range of existing legislation relating to specific employer responsibilities and duties under a single legislative framework and also seeks to strengthen protection and rights against discrimination and harassment.

Conservative–Liberal Democrat Coalition government 2010–?

Prime Minister: David Cameron (2010–?); Deputy Prime Minister: Nick Clegg (2010– ?)

2010   **The Big Society** is the flagship policy of the Conservative–Liberal Democrat Coalition Agreement. The stated priorities are: to give communities more powers (localism and devolution); to encourage people to take an active role in their communities (volunteerism); to transfer power from central to local government; to support co-operatives, mutuals, charities and social enterprises; and to promote open/transparent government.

National Citizen Service (NCS) is introduced. This is a two-month summer programme for sixteen-year-olds, involving both residential and at-home components, to be delivered by independent charities, social enterprises and businesses.

The Coalition government's policy agenda is dominated by the aim of cutting public sector spending and the 2010 **Comprehensive Spending Review** represents the largest sustained fall in public expenditure since 1922. It affects many bodies associated with children and young people (for example, the Children's Workforce Development Council, the Training and Development Agency for Schools, the Young People's Learning Agency), with significant cuts in budgets.

The tight financial settlement also includes significant cuts to Local Authority Grants, resulting in **cuts to local public sector jobs and services**.

The Department for Children, Schools and Families is renamed the **Department for Education**.

The **Academies Act** enables more schools in England to become academies funded at a comparable level to maintained schools but able to get the share of central funding that local authorities used to spend on their behalf. Schools that apply to become academies will be allowed to keep any surplus balances that they hold.

2011   **The Education Act** provides for the introduction of targeted free early years care for children under compulsory school age; makes changes to provisions on school discipline and places restrictions on the public reporting of allegations made against teachers; makes changes to the arrangements for setting up new schools; and amends the Academies Act 2010 to make provision for sixteen to nineteen academies and alternative provision academies.

Early indications are that **youth services and children's centres are worst hit** by local authority spending cuts (Higgs, 2011).

The **Special Educational Needs green paper** ('Support and Aspiration: A New Approach to Special Educational Needs and Disability') proposes that a simplified assessment process is introduced resulting in an *Education, Health and Care Plan* and re-introduces an emphasis on special schools as an alternative to mainstream school inclusion.

The **Tickell Review** (2011) of the Early Years Foundation Phase seeks to reinforce developments in early years provision by emphasising the role of parents and carers as partners in their children's learning, and simplifying and streamlining early learning goals.

Workplace activity

What are the workplace policies which govern your practice? How do they relate to government policy? Can you find examples of workplace policies which are clearly about implementing government policy? Discuss with colleagues how the national policy changes outlined have impacted on you and your setting?

What does this chronology tell us? What conclusions can we draw from it? Bear in mind that it only presents a selection of policy relating to children and young people over this period. Clearly, in this time, as Paul Spicker (2010) has argued:

> Education has been particularly significant as an instrument of social policy, in the sense not only of policies for welfare but also as policies intended to deal with the structure of society.

Spicker (2010) is careful to clarify here that:

> 'Education' is principally identified with schooling, though in theory it extends far beyond this, being concerned with intellectual and social development. The main emphasis is on children, though there is clearly scope for education for all and 'lifelong learning'.

Spicker goes on to say that the aims of education include:

- Liberal education: the development of each individual intellectually and socially to that person's fullest potential.

- Socialisation: education is a method of transmission of social norms and values. This is also sometimes seen as a form of social control.

- Education as 'handmaiden': the education system serves the industrial process and the economy by producing a trained workforce, and by providing childminding services.

- Social change (or 'social engineering'). The education system has been seen as a means of bringing about social change. (Spicker, 2010)

We can see these different aims for education present in the policies outlined in the chronology. But although there may be consensus that the purpose of social policy is to help to create the 'good society' and to 'fix' perceived social problems, there are differences of opinion as to what constitutes the 'good society' and even less agreement as to the best ways of achieving it.

There are also differences in beliefs about the causes of social problems and therefore how these can be fixed. Such beliefs are often based on 'ideology' (an overarching general view of how the world functions and how the world should be) and thus the distinction can be made between ideological policy-making and 'evidence-based' policy-making. John Maynard Keynes, a very influential economist, once famously quipped, 'There is nothing a government hates more than to be well-informed; for it makes the process of arriving at decisions much more complicated and difficult' (Keynes, 1937, cited in Skidelski, 1992: 630).

Evidence-based policy has been defined as an approach that 'helps people make well informed decisions about policies, programmes and projects by putting the best available evidence from research at the heart of policy development and implementation' (Davies, 2004: 3). This approach is now well established in the UK (see, for example, The Evidence for Policy and Practice Information and Co-ordinating Centre (EPPI-Centre), part of the Social Science Research Unit at the Institute of Education, University of London). However, there are problems with the notion of evidence-based policy-making. It may pose problems for policy in very new areas in which an evidence base has not been developed. The proof sought for evidence-based policy is modelled on the medical evidence base of big randomised trials. Yet as we saw in the Introduction, this scientific approach to research into social issues is problematic and the evidence base, in terms of research data, may be weak or contradictory.

For this reason, opinions and beliefs remain central to policy-making. We can see social problems and solutions to those problems as articulated within 'narratives' or 'discourse' which policy-makers adopt.

Understanding policy discourse

The idea of 'narrative' or 'discourse' relates not just to the surface of what is said but to the underlying assumptions and beliefs. For example, a dominant discourse adopted by both the previous Conservative and Labour governments over the past 30 years, relates to the idea of a dangerous 'moral underclass' within society – unruly and dysfunctional families living in areas of high deprivation – being the source of social unrest and challenging the notion of good 'citizenship'. This narrative is reflected in key policies, such as the Crime and Disorder Act, 1998, which saw the introduction of Anti-Social Behaviour Orders or ASBOs. An alternative narrative or discourse of the 'underclass' (itself, a contested term) could be one that is underpinned by analysis of the impact of poverty and which sees the poor as victims of such disadvantage. In contrast to the 'control' policy response outlined above, such a discourse leads to and justifies policies designed to provide support to disadvantaged communities. An example of such policy is the Sure Start programme which was introduced in 1998 and aimed to reduce child poverty.

Ball (2008: 5) described the way that such narratives may become accepted 'truths', suggesting that governments:

> organise their own specific rationalities, making particular sets of ideas obvious, common sense and 'true'... the ways in which policies are spoken and spoken about, their vocabularies, are part of the creation of their conditions of acceptance and enactment. They construct the inevitable and the necessary.

We can see this very clearly in the 'there is no alternative' (to budgetary restraint and public sector spending cuts) discourse of the 2010 Coalition government. Gee (1996: 10) has observed that: 'Discourses create "social positions" (perspectives) from which people are "invited" ("summoned") to speak, listen, act, read and write, think, feel, believe and value'.

For example, a policy discourse may create or confirm the social position or category of 'benefit scrounger' or 'school refuser'. These terms present reality in a particular way, people on benefit are (often) lazy, feckless and fiddling the system for their own gain, the persistent truant is choosing to opt out of education. Both of these imply that the problem is with the individual and exclude consideration of the way in which economic and social factors (in the case of 'benefit scroungers') and school, family, and other social factors (in the case of the 'school refuser') are contributing to the issue. Identifying the way in which discourse shapes the particular view of reality is termed 'discourse analysis'.

An approach to discourse analysis which summarises this is exemplified by Ruth Levitas (2005), who developed a useful framework for interrogating New Labour's social exclusion policy. Levitas identified three broad narratives in relation to the Labour government's policies to address social exclusion:

- the **redistribution discourse** ('RED') – where the cause of exclusion is seen to relate to poverty, and so to address this, resources and funding should be redistributed to areas of need (an example of such a policy was the Sure Start programme);

- the **social integration discourse** ('SID') – where the cause of exclusion relates to lack of paid work and the way to support social integration is through engagement in the mechanisms of employment and steps towards it provided by education and training (an example of such a policy was the Connexions strategy for young people);

- the **moral underclass discourse** ('MUD') – where the cause of social exclusion relates to the actions and behaviour of particular groups, such as workless, criminally active young men and lone parents, and the policy response based on this discourse tends to involve controlling the behaviour of these groups (an example of which was the introduction of ASBOs).

In considering Levitas's model, it is important to note that policy can encompass different discourses, emphasising issues of both individual moral and social responsibility, and at the same time acknowledging wider social, community and collective issues.

Policy discourse and narrative, especially that of political parties, contribute to what Antonio Gramsci, the Italian political theorist, referred to as 'hegemony' – the way that dominant ideology goes unchallenged and results in conformity through uncritical consensus. In the next chapter we look at professionalism, which we argue includes a critical perspective on policy and a recognition of the difference between what a policy claims to do and its real impact.

In the chronology, we can see the individual policies in terms of key trends which have emerged over this period. One key trend has been the changing role of the state from provider to commissioner of services through the creation of 'markets' for and privatisation of services. Associated with this has been increasing differentiation of provision and a shift from universal provision to targeted provision. In relation to the children and young people's workforce, another trend has been increasing managerialism, auditing and accountability of professional roles, as well as the 'modernisation' of the workforce, creating many new 'associate professional' roles.

Reflection point

Think about a local or national policy which relates directly to your everyday practice: what is the nature of the 'issue' or in some cases 'problem' that the policy seeks to address? What does the policy tell us about how the government regards the underpinning issues and factors – what is the discourse?

Do you think the overall conception of the policy is reasonable and is it likely to be successful?

Summary

In this chapter we have provided a chronology of some of the key policy developments relating to children and young people of the last 30 years. This is not an exhaustive list but clearly shows the importance of this area for government policy. We have argued that policy needs to be seen as arising out of fundamental understandings of social problems and have related this to notions of policy discourse. Ultimately, all policies are subject to change and practitioners have an important role to play in the implementation and evaluation of policies which can inform such change.

Further reading

Action For Children (2008) *As Long As It Takes: A New Politics for Children.* London: Action for Children. This comprehensive report examines 21 years of policy affecting vulnerable children and young people in the UK.

Children and Young People Now: http://www.cypnow.co.uk/go/policywatch_england/ Includes a useful 'Policy watch' page through which you can keep up to date with policy relating to children and young people.

EPPI-Centre: http://eppi.ioe.ac.uk/cms/Default.aspx?tabid=63&language=en-US The EPPI-Centre conducts systematic reviews of the evidence available across a range of topics including: Education, Health Promotion, Employment, Social Care, Crime and Justice.

Spicker, P. (2010) 'An introduction to social policy', Aberdeen, The Robert Gordon University: http://www2.rgu.ac.uk/publicpolicy/introduction This website provides an accessible and comprehensive introduction to the topic of social policy.

UNICEF: Convention on the Rights of the Child: http://www.unicef.org/crc/ This website provides excellent background information and discussion of the Convention on the Rights of the Child.

References

The Academies Bill 2010. London: HMSO.

Ball, S.J. (2008) *The Education Debate: Policy and Politics in the Twenty-First Century*. Bristol: Policy Press.

Beveridge, W. (1942) *Social Insurance and Allied Services*. London: HMSO.

The Children Act 1989. London: HMSO.

The Children Act 2004. London: HMSO.

Children's Workforce Development Council (2010) *Common Core of Skills and Knowledge for the Children's Workforce: At the Heart of What You Do*. Leeds: CWDC. Available online at: http://www.cwdcouncil.org.uk/common-core (accessed 21.07.11).

Cole, M. (ed.) (2006) *Education, Equality and Human Rights* (2nd edn). London: RoutledgeFalmer.

Crime and Disorder Act 1998. London: HMSO.

Davies, P.T. (1999) 'What is evidence-based education?', *British Journal of Educational Studies*, 47(2): 108–21.

Davies, P.T. (2004) 'Is evidence based government possible?' Jerry Lee Lecture, presented at the 4th annual Campbell Collaberation Colloquium, Washington D.C.

Department for Children, Schools and Families (DCSF) (2007) *Aiming High for Young People: A Ten-Year Strategy*. London: HM Treasury.

Department for Children, Schools and Families (DCSF) (2008) *The Play Strategy*. Available online at: www.sustrans.org.uk/assets/files/AT/APTTO/PlayStrategy%20DCSF.pdf (accessed 17.05.11).

Department for Education (1991) *The Parent's Charter: You and Your Child's Education*. London: HMSO.

Department for Education (1998) *Meeting the Childcare Challenge: A Framework and Consultation Document*. London: DfE.

Department for Education (2001) *Special Educational Needs Code of Practice*. London: HMSO.

Department for Education (2011) *Special Educational Needs Green Paper*. London: HMSO.

Department for Education and Skills (2002) *Transforming Youth Work: Resourcing Excellent Youth Services*. Nottingham: DfES.

Department for Education and Skills (2003) *The Government's Response to the Health Committee's sixth Report of Session 2002–03 on the Victoria Climbié Inquiry Report*. London: The Stationery Office.

Department for Education and Skills (2004a) *Five Year Strategy for Children and Learners*. London: DfES.

Department for Education and Skills (2004b) *Putting the World into World-Class Education*. London: DfES.

Department for Education and Skills (2005) *Common Core of Skills and Knowledge for the Children's Workforce*. Nottingham: DfES. Available online at: https://www.education.gov.uk/publications/standard/publicationDetail/Page1/DfES%20 1189%202005 (accessed 21.07.11).

Department for Education and Skills (2007a) *Every Parent Matters: Helping You Help Your Child*. London: DfES.

Department for Education and Skills (2007b) *Youth Matters: Next Steps*. London: DfES.

Department for Education and Skills (2007c) *Children's Workforce Strategy Update, Spring 2007: Building a World-class Workforce for Children, Young People and Families*. London: DFES. Available online at: www.education.gov.uk/publications/standard/childrensworkforce/page3/DFES-00087-2007

Education Act 1944. London: HMSO.

Education Act 1981. London: HMSO.

Education Act 1996. London: HMSO.

Education Act 2011. London: HMSO.

Education Reform Act 1988. London: HMSO.

Equality Act 2010. London: HMSO.

Gee, J.P. (1996) *Social Linguistics and Literacies: Ideology in Discourses*. London: Routledge/Falmer.

Higgs, L. (2011) 'Exclusive survey: youth services and children's centres worst hit as cuts average 13 per cent in one year', *Children and Young People Now*. Available online at: http://www.cypnow.co.uk/news/1050883/Exclusive-survey-youth-services-childrens-centres-worst-hit-cuts-average-13-per-cent-one-year/ (accessed 17.05.11).

HM Treasury (2003) *Every Child Matters*. London: The Stationery Office.

HM Treasury (2010) *Spending Review 2010*. London: The Stationery Office.

Laming, Lord (2003) *The Victoria Climbié Inquiry: Report of an Inquiry by Lord Laming*. London: HMSO.

Learning and Skills Act 2000. London: HMSO.

Levitas, R.A. (2005) *The Inclusive Society? Social Exclusion and New Labour* (2nd edn). London: Palgrave Macmillan.

National Equality Panel (2010) *An Anatomy of Economic Inequality in the UK: Report of the National Equality Panel*. London: Government Equalities Office.

Protection of Children Act (1999). London: HMSO.

Skidelsky, R. (1992) *John Maynard Keynes: A Biography. Vol. 2: The Economist as Saviour, 1920–1937*. London: Macmillan.

Special Educational Needs and Disability Act 2001. London: HMSO.

Spicker, P. (2010) 'An introduction to social policy: Education and Social Policy, Aberdeen, The Robert Gordon University. Available online at: http://www2.rgu.ac.uk/publicpolicy/introduction/education.htm#UK (accessed 17.05.11).

Tickell, C. (2011) *The Early Years: Foundations for Life, Health and Learning – An Independent Report on the Early Years Foundation Stage to Her Majesty's Government*. London: HMSO.

UNCRC (Office of the United Nations High Commissioner for Human Rights) (1989) *United Nations Convention on the Rights of the Child*. New York: OUNHCHR.

Wilkinson, R. and Pickett, K. (2009) *The Spirit Level*. London: Allen Lane.

2

Professionalism in the Children and Young People's Workforce

Nadia Edmond and Mark Price

Chapter Overview

This chapter explores the nature of professionalism and inter-professionalism and the concept of 'informed critical practice' in the children and young people's workforce. We explore how fundamental beliefs about human nature shape and inform our professional understanding of childhood and youth and the role of adults. We discuss childhood and youth as social constructs with different understandings dominant in different social and professional contexts.

By reading and engaging with the activities in this chapter, you will:

- develop your understanding of the concept of professionalism and informed critical practice and how this relates to roles and contexts in the children and young people's workforce;
- consider the commonalities and differences between different professional groups engaged in integrated working with children and young people; and
- familiarise yourself with different perspectives on childhood and youth and how these inform practice in your own and other contexts.

Professionalism, 'para-professionalism' and inter-professionalism

Development and reform in public services in recent years has seen rising expectations of standards of performance in the children and young people's workforce. These have been linked to rising expectations and requirements of professional development, as well as the emergence of new roles for those working with children and young people. A feature of many of these new roles is that they work alongside professionals in 'associate professional' or 'para-professional' roles and share some of the characteristics and functions of professionals working in the setting. A key distinction is often that the professional will have the formal or legal responsibility for outcomes but practitioners in a range of 'associate professional' roles will have some discretion over what they do on a day-to-day basis.

What, exactly, do we mean by the term 'professional'? Here is the term used in a number of different contexts.

- As a successful professional football player, Wayne Rooney can expect to retire a millionaire.

- Although she had done all the decorating herself, Mary was really pleased with the professional result.

- John was utterly reliable and trustworthy, his colleagues considered him the consummate professional.

The term has different meanings but these tend to be the result of the particular emphasis given to different key aspects of professionalism: status and pay, expertise and standards, values and ethics. A professional is someone who is paid for the service they provide (we see this most clearly in the distinction between amateur and professional in sport), while in employment, remuneration often reflects the relatively high status of certain professions (think of medicine and the law). A professional is also someone who has a particular (not generally available) skill or knowledge, and as a consequence can perform to a higher standard than someone who doesn't. Finally, a professional is someone who shares a set of values with other professionals and abides by a (explicit or implicit) code of ethics (this is the aspect of professionalism we are focusing on when we talk about people being 'unprofessional').

As we saw in Chapter 1, a key aspect of the *Every Child Matters* policy agenda (DfES, 2004) has been the reform of the children's workforce, including greater emphasis on inter-professional and integrated working. The requirement for co-operation with the children and young people's workforce has been embedded in integrated processes and structures such as the Common Assessment Framework (CAF), 'Team Around the Child' (TAC), Lead Professional (LP) and information sharing.

A review of the evidence of the effectiveness of integrated working in the children and young people's workforce (Oliver et al., 2010: 5,6) concluded that there is strong evidence that high-quality pre-school provision which integrates childcare and education is associated with improved cognitive and behavioural outcomes for children, and that school-based integrated working can bring about improvements in school attendance and academic attainment. Additional perceived benefits included improvements in children's behaviour, well-being and family relationships. However, initiatives taking a multi-agency approach to reduce youth offending and anti-social behaviour showed mixed results, although promising evidence was reported of a positive impact on school attendance, alcohol consumption and anti-social behaviour. Studies considering the impacts of integrated working on children with disabilities or mental health difficulties have overall reported positive results with improved outcomes for children and parents.

In terms of the impact on practitioners, the research showed that integrated working was associated with a range of positive outcomes, including improved enjoyment and well-being at work and enhanced knowledge and understanding of other professional roles and the needs of families. However, an increase in workload appeared to be more likely. Evidence also indicated that integrated working can produce confusion about professional identity, and risk of some roles being marginalised in some settings. There was also evidence of variability in progress towards embedding integrated working in practice. Some negative impacts of integrated working were identified, including greater fragmentation, a lack of specialist support and poor co-ordination of services (Oliver et al., 2010: 6).

Workplace activity

Having thought about your own view of professionalism in your practice, talk to colleagues about their perspective. What has been their experience of training, professional development and qualification for their role? How do they regard what it means to be 'professional' and 'professionally qualified'? If you have the opportunity, talk to members of other professional groups with whom you work. What are their perspectives?

What has been your experience of inter-professional working? What positives and negatives would you and your colleagues identify?

Case study: Developing professionalism and inter-professionalism in youth work

Nazeem is 31 and in 2007 he completed a Foundation Degree in Youth Work. This was a three-year programme at his local university which he attended for one day a week. While he was working, his local authority employer paid his course fees and released him from his work with young people to undertake his studies.

Upon completing his Foundation Degree, Nazeem was 'professionally qualified' as a youth worker and is now eligible to apply for youth work roles which are described as being open only to 'JNC qualified' applicants. The Joint Negotiating Committee (JNC) for Youth and Community Workers is the national body which agrees the salary scales, yearly pay increases and other terms and conditions of service for youth workers. Nazeem's employer is committed to the JNC agreement and he received a pay rise in recognition of his professional status.

In September 2010, the level of courses for JNC recognition was raised from Foundation Degree (or equivalent) to an Honours Degree or Postgraduate qualification. Nazeem's Foundation Degree is still valid as a professional qualification, but he is now considering returning to university to 'top up' to an Honours Degree, as this would give him graduate professional status, equivalent to that of teachers and social workers.

In addition to managing the local youth centre, Nazeem also undertakes targeted work with young carers. He works very closely with the local secondary school, especially with the inclusion team, and supports young people for whom social and emotional issues play a part in their behaviour and attendance. Here, he works alongside teachers and teaching assistants and regularly attends multi-disciplinary team meetings with social workers and the school counsellor.

The issue of a professional register and associated licence to practise for youth workers has been considered by previous governments but there are no measures currently to introduce this. Nazeem has mixed feelings about this. On the one hand, he recognises that people are employed as youth workers at many different levels, from voluntary work through to paid, professional roles, but he also would like more formal and wider recognition of the professional status he worked hard for and is justifiably proud of. Nazeem feels a professional register and licence to practise would provide this.

How important do you feel graduate-level study is to professional practice? To professional status? Why?

How important do you feel a professional register and licence to practise is to professional status? Why?

∿ Reflection point

Are you a professional? How would you justify your answer with reference to your context?

Perhaps the issue is not whether you are a 'professional' but whether you behave 'professionally' in your practice. What does this mean to you in your context?

Do you work with people in different professional groups? If so, how do they see their professional status? What is your perspective of the benefits and limitations of integrated working?

Becoming professional

An important idea at the heart of professionalism is that of professional judgements; professionals, and perhaps to a lesser extent 'associate professionals', tend to be characterised by unpredictable work contexts in which they have some autonomy to exercise judgement about the appropriate course of action at any time. For this reason, professional practice needs to be 'informed critical practice' in which practitioners can draw on sound and current knowledge and explicit values and ethics in reaching and justifying judgements.

Expertise and specialist knowledge: *informed* critical practice

Professional knowledge enables practitioners to take those 'everyday' decisions about 'what is the right thing to do in this moment' from an informed, critical perspective. This is what defines professional autonomy. Gaining expertise and specialist knowledge involves a number of processes: identifying learning and development needs, meeting these through formal and informal learning, and keeping up to date. We will look at each of these in turn.

Part of being professional is being aware of the limitations of our current knowledge – knowing what we don't know! A popular model used to consider this is the *conscious competence* ladder or matrix. The origins of this model are unclear – some attribute it to Abraham Maslow, whereas others claim it originates from the California-based Gordon Training Organisation in the early 1970s. The central idea is that, in professional development, we move through four stages:

- **Unconscious incompetence** – we don't know what it is we don't know! This is usually the stage of 'blissful ignorance' before embarking on a process of professional development.

- **Conscious incompetence** – in the early stages of professional development we get an insight into the journey ahead and the knowledge, skills and values we need to acquire. This process can be daunting and when people drop out of professional development programmes in the early stages, it is often because they have hit the conscious incompetence 'wall'.

- **Conscious competence** – here the required knowledge, skills and values have been acquired but we still have to think carefully about how we undertake professional tasks.

- **Unconscious competence** – this is where those 'competences' (the professional knowledge, skills and values) have become thoroughly embedded in our practice and we know what to do 'in the moment'. The challenge here is not to slip back to unconscious incompetence!

We can make a link between this model and the Johari window of self-awareness (Luft and Ingham, 1955) (see Figure 2.1).

The 'open' or' public' window in the diagram contains those aspects of ourselves we choose to share, whilst the hidden or private window

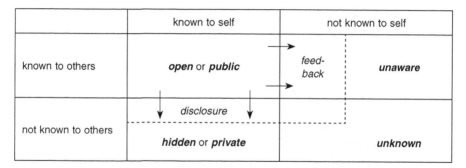

	known to self		not known to self
known to others	*open* or *public*	*feed-back*	*unaware*
not known to others	*disclosure* *hidden* or *private*		*unknown*

Figure 2.1 Johari window. Adapted from Luft, J. and Ingham, H. (1955) 'The Johari window: a graphic model of interpersonal awareness'. *Proceedings of the Western Training Laboratory in Group Development.* Los Angeles: UCLA.

contains those things we choose to hide or not declare. Through disclosing personal information, we can make the open or public window wider. We may be unaware of aspects of ourselves which are clear to others. By receiving feedback from others, especially those we trust, we can reduce the 'unaware' window. The 'unknown' window refers to those aspects of ourselves which we might also refer to as being our 'unconscious' selves. Sometimes, this window opens when we encounter new challenges and are placed in unfamiliar situations – we discover things about ourselves.

The important link between these two models is that within the context of professional development, we make a commitment to learning and development of self-awareness – to ask ourselves difficult questions and to be open to feedback from others. For example, it is important to acknowledge that our perspectives on childhood and youth are influenced by cultural and other personal values and we may be challenged on things we take for granted. As practitioners and professionals, we need to be prepared to be challenged, knowing that at times this may feel uncomfortable.

~~~ Reflection point

Using the competence matrix above, can you position yourself in terms of where you are in your own professional development? What are the implications of this?

In terms of the Johari window shown in Figure 2.1, can you identify anything you have learned about yourself from the feedback of others? How did you respond?

Professional knowledge can be organised within disciplines and two important disciplines for practitioners working with children and young people are psychology and sociology. Psychology aims to understand behaviour and mental processes. From a psychological perspective, we tend to regard children and young people primarily as individuals. Different theoretical perspectives within psychology inform our view of how they learn and develop. We look at this perspective in more detail in Chapter 6.

Sociology is the study of society and seeks to understand the behaviour of individuals and groups in society. From this perspective, we are much more interested in the way we interact and behave socially and how groups such as families, friendships or communities influence behaviour and development. This perspective informs the discussion in Chapters 7 and 12.

The ecological model, outlined in the introduction, highlights the inter-relationship of psychological and social factors and the impact of this on children and young people's development. The two disciplines of psychology and sociology can be helpful in providing contrasting views of certain processes in development. For example, Ellen is 15 and wants to have her nose pierced. We can understand this behaviour from the psychological perspective as Ellen is making an individual choice reflecting her identity development as an *adolescent* (itself, a psychological construct). By contrast, from a sociological perspective in terms of specific *youth cultures* (a sociological construct), the act of body piercing relates to establishing a sense of belonging to specific peer and social groupings. Each perspective gives a different view of the same phenomenon.

Different professional groups will also have different perspectives on their work with children and young people. Integrated working can bring these different perspectives together to provide a more complete picture of the child or young person or they can be the cause of difficulties in communication between different professionals. To support the former and avoid the latter it is important to recognise the distinct contribution and the common values and ethics of different professional groups – we return to values and ethics later in this chapter.

Professional development in the children and young people's workforce draws significantly on part-time and work-based programmes. In these programmes, there has been a growing recognition that the workplace is not just a context in which to apply learning done at college or university, but an important source of learning in its own right.

The idea that we learn from our experiences and from practice has a long pedigree in educational theory but the idea of 'reflective practice' as an important process in professional development was introduced in *The Reflective Practitioner* by Donald Schön (1983). Reflective practice is now widely accepted and through the use of tools such as learning logs and journals, many professional development programmes seek to encourage and support reflection. As Boud et al. have argued:

> Reflection is an important human activity in which people recapture their experience, think about it, mull it over and evaluate it. It is this working with experience that is important in learning. (Boud et al., 1985: 19)

But engagement in practice does not just provide experiences that we can reflect on (and through that reflection learn). Lave and Wenger (1991) have argued that becoming a professional is the result of participating in 'communities of practice' as newcomers and being supported in becoming full members of that community. This is why, for many practitioners in the children and young people's workforce, there are 'mentoring' or 'supervision' arrangements with an experienced colleague whose role is to support trainees learning from work. They will also discuss with them when they are ready to take on more challenging activities, for example, as well as helping them to reflect on and think critically about their practice.

As well as formal and informal learning opportunities through work, professional development includes continuous research and keeping abreast of new and emerging policy and practice. Professional publications and websites are a crucial source of information, and an important skill for modern professionals is the discriminating use of the internet to ensure the quality and currency of the information accessed.

📁 Case study: Developing professionalism as a teaching assistant – Higher Level Teaching Assistant (HLTA) status

Here Jane talks about her professional development as a teaching assistant (TA). 'I started like lots of TAs with helping out in school, and I just really liked the atmosphere. When my youngest started school I thought about going back to my previous job, but it just didn't seem that rewarding after working in school. When a post of part-time TA came up, I jumped at it. When I started, it was helping

(Continued)

(Continued)

the teacher, setting up the classroom for activities and clearing away and that sort of thing. I did listen to some of the children reading and I found that I really liked working with the kids that were struggling a bit. Gradually I started taking small groups of children for remedial programmes on my own. Then the head teacher suggested that I go for HLTA. I wasn't sure at first, going to university to do the Foundation Degree was very scary – the scariest thing was realising how much I didn't know! I got a lot of support from my tutor and the teacher I was working with – they both helped me see what I was already good at and where I needed to develop so I stuck with it and developed a much better understanding of my job. I became much more confident and able to contribute suggestions in school and take on new activities and challenges. I learnt a lot from that and was able to prove myself to others. I got the HLTA status and the Foundation Degree and I feel much more on a par with the teachers now. I work with a new teacher now and right from the start it has been a partnership. She's got overall responsibility but I have a lot of say and I contribute ideas and I'm trusted to take the class on my own at times. I wouldn't want to be a teacher, but I really enjoy my role supporting children's learning. I love the fact that you are never standing still. I'm always learning new things. Just recently a boy with autism spectrum disorder joined the class – I've been booked onto a course but in the meantime I've been able to do a lot of research and find out a lot for myself. The work is always interesting.'

In the above, what would you see as evidence of 'professionalism' in Jane's practice?

What other indications might you look for?

Reflection point

How are formal learning, informal learning and reading and research contributing to your professional development? How might you enhance and develop the learning opportunities open to you?

Think of an example of where you have had to make some decisions at work – what knowledge did you use to help you make the decision? How did you develop that knowledge?

Values and ethics: informed critical practice

Questions of professional practice are often not just about how to do things right but how to do the right thing and it is here that values and ethics play an important role.

Extract 1: from *The Black Papers*, Cox and Boyson (1975)

Children are not naturally good. They need firm, tactful discipline from parents and teachers with clear standards. Too much freedom for children breeds selfishness, vandalism and personal unhappiness.

Extract 2: from *Autobiographical Notes*, Albert Einstein (1979)

It is, in fact, nothing short of a miracle that the modern methods of instruction have not yet entirely strangled the holy curiosity of inquiry; for this delicate little plant, aside from stimulation, stands mainly in need of freedom; without this it goes to wrack and ruin without fail. It is a very grave mistake to think that the enjoyment of seeing and searching can be promoted by means of coercion and a sense of duty.

Extract 3: from *Hard Times*, Charles Dickens (1854)

'NOW, what I want is, Facts. Teach these boys and girls nothing but Facts. Facts alone are wanted in life. Plant nothing else, and root out everything else. You can only form the minds of reasoning animals upon Facts: nothing else will ever be of any service to them. This is the principle on which I bring up my own children, and this is the principle on which I bring up these children. Stick to Facts, sir!' ...

The speaker, and the schoolmaster, and the third grown person present, all backed a little, and swept with their eyes the inclined plane of little vessels then and there arranged in order, ready to have imperial gallons of facts poured into them until they were full to the brim.

As the above examples illustrate, views of what children and young people are like and what they need are contested. The views expressed relate to fundamental philosophical views about human nature. For example, the 17th-century philosopher Thomas Hobbes argued that humans have natural desires they wish to satisfy and suggested that the rule of law is necessary to avoid the inevitable conflict of individuals seeking their own ends. From this perspective, working with children and young people plays an important role in 'taming' them. On the other hand, for the 18th-century philosopher Jean-Jacques Rousseau, humans are naturally 'good' and learning and development should be about individual development and fulfilment.

The beliefs expressed in the extracts above would lead to very different practices. An emphasis on the view expressed in extract 1 would lead to a focus on control and discipline in practice, while an emphasis on the view expressed in extract 2 would lead to practice which seeks to minimise control and maximise freedom and choice. Most people would agree that in working with children and young people there is a need for some control, and some flexibility and freedom, and that adults have a degree of responsibility for imparting knowledge. Just as individuals will differ in the priority they give these different aspects, so will different professional groups.

Reflection point

How would you respond to each of these extracts and how do your beliefs translate to your practice?

Think about the children or young people you work with. How do you view *them*? What are your priorities in terms of your work with them? Discuss your ideas with colleagues or fellow students.

In the introduction, we argued that certainty in social sciences is problematic and in Chapter 1 that policy reflects particular discourse. Both suggest that a healthy scepticism is a useful quality in professional practice and we should aim to challenge assumptions and justify our actions. In practice, what is right is not simply a question of the individual's personal beliefs. Consensus about what is right and desirable in professional practice is encapsulated in professional bodies' codes of practice and in statements of 'professional standards'. Integrated working will be supported by an understanding of shared values.

In 2008, the General Social Care Council (GSCC), the General Teaching Council for England (GTC) and the Nursing and Midwifery

Council (NMC) produced this joint statement which sets out the values and dispositions underpinning effective inter-professional work with children and young people (GSCC, 2008).

Key attributes

Children and young people value practitioners who enjoy working with them, who treat them with respect and who are good at communicating with them.

Children's practitioners place the interests of children at the heart of their work. They share responsibility for a range of outcomes. They are committed to ensuring all children have the chance to: be healthy, stay safe, enjoy and achieve, make a positive contribution, and experience economic well-being. They recognise children's fundamental right to be safe, in order to reach other goals.

Practitioners concern themselves with the whole child, whatever their specialism. Although their own involvement with specific children may be short-term, children's practitioners work to develop the potential and capacities of children for the longer term.

Children's practitioners are committed to equality of opportunity for all children, and actively combat discrimination and its effects through their work. They respond positively and creatively to diversity among children and families, and colleagues...

Practitioners recognise that respect, patience, honesty, reliability, resilience and integrity are valued by children, families and colleagues. By demonstrating these qualities in their work they help to nurture them in others.

Work with children and young people, parents, carers and families

Children's practitioners recognise and uphold children's rights. They involve children and young people in decisions that effect them and take account of their views and preferences taking account of their capacities. They recognise that childhood and early adulthood are times of change, and that they need to respond to changes in children's views, capabilities and circumstances.

Practitioners recognise the fundamental role played by parents in their children's well-being and development, and strive to work in partnership with them.

Practitioners are committed to engaging children, young people and families fully in identifying goals, assessing options, making decisions and reviewing outcomes. They support children's and families' involvement in issues that matter to them, including through involvement in the development and evaluation of children's services.

Children's practitioners appreciate that their work will present dilemmas to be resolved particularly between sharing information and maintaining confidentiality. They understand that their duty to safeguard children and young people comes first, but otherwise respect the right of children, young people and families to confidentiality, and are always clear about information they are obliged to share.

Integrated work with a range of colleagues

Children's practitioners value the contribution that a range of colleagues make to children and young people's lives, and they form effective relationships across the children's workforce. Their integrated practice is based on a willingness to bring their own expertise to bear on the pursuit of shared goals for children, and a respect for the expertise of others.

Practitioners recognise that children, young people, families, and colleagues, value transparency and reliability, and strive to make sure that processes, roles, goals and resources are clear.

Practitioners involved in integrated work recognise the need to be clear about lines of communication, management and accountability as these may be more complex than in their specialist setting.

They uphold the standards, and values of their own professions in their inter-professional work. They understand that sharing responsibility for children's outcomes does not mean acting beyond their competence or responsibilities.

They are committed to taking action if safety or standards are compromised, whether that means alerting their own manager/employer or another appropriate authority.

Children's practitioners understand that the knowledge, understanding and skills [for] integrated work may differ from those in their own specialism. They are committed to reflecting on and improving their inter-professional practice, and to engaging with relevant research and other evidence.

Work with children and young people is stimulating and rewarding. It can also be emotionally demanding, and children's practitioners are sensitive to and supportive of each others' well being.

∿ Reflection point

What do you make of these statements? It is likely that you will agree with them – after all they were written to capture the common values of those working with children and young people, but which do you think are the most important? Which would you prioritise in your professional role? How might this differ for different practitioners?

Whilst there may be agreement around these values, it is also likely that practitioners with different occupational roles in the children's workforce will prioritise them differently. For example, early years practitioners may view relationships with parents differently from youth workers. Additionally, upholding the standards and values of your own profession in your inter-professional work may sometimes result in tension when you are dealing with other practitioners with different professional standards and values. For Nazeem (case study), tensions relating to different professional perspectives arise when exploring the cases of individual young people in the school inclusion unit. This may be at the level of information sharing and professional perspectives of 'confidentiality', whilst it might also relate to what different professionals see as being in the 'best interests' of a young person. The specific professional language or 'jargon' used by different practitioners can also be challenging.

In professional practice, professional knowledge is necessary to inform action and 'reflective practice' is a process by which we develop professional knowledge through reflecting on practice. In Lave and Wenger's (1991) terms, professional knowledge is not something we acquire but something in which we participate. The problem with learning from practice, whether through reflection or in terms of participation, is that it raises the question: where does improvement in practice come from? If we are not going to replicate what could, after all, be poor practice in a setting, we need an external reference point, an authoritative source of professional knowledge (such as a university or college) and a clear sense of what constitutes 'good practice'.

Values and ethics help us identify 'right action'. One feature of professionalism which has been proposed as a defining characteristic (see e.g. Johnson, 1972; Sims et al., 1993; Frost, 2001) is that of altruistic service – doing good for society and its individuals. Hence the moral and ethical codes of professions give boundaries and constraints to their membership (think about doctors being 'struck off' for malpractice). The notion of 'right action' has also been linked to the concept of 'praxis' – the tight and mutually dependent relationship of theory and practice. Mark Smith suggests praxis is:

> not simply action based on reflection. It is action which embodies certain qualities. These include a commitment to human well being and the search for truth, and respect for others. It is the action of people who are free, who are able to act for themselves. Moreover, *praxis* is always risky. (Smith, 1999)

This reflects the thinking of Paolo Freire, the Brazilian educationalist who described praxis as 'reflection and action upon the world in order to transform it' (Freire, 1972: 73). Professionalism can also be seen as embodying praxis, in that our work is underpinned at all times by an altruistic commitment to support and improve children and young people's education, health and well-being.

Summary

In this chapter we have looked at the issue of professionalism and the professionalisation of the children and young people's workforce. Professional development not only depends on courses and formal learning; work-based support, individual research and keeping up to date are also important components. In working with other professionals we not only need to be aware of the commonalities in our concerns and values, but also of the differences. Different perspectives coming together can provide challenges but, engaged with constructively, can ensure better provision for children and young people.

Further reading

Professionalism

Cunningham, B. (ed.) (2208) *Exploring Professionalism*. London: Bedford Way Papers. This edited collection provides a good introduction and current overview of issues of professional knowledge, institutions, work patterns and identities.

Miller, L. and Cable, C. (2011) *Professionalization, Leadership and Management in the Early Years*. London: Sage. This book considers professionalisation in the sector, what this means in practice and brings a critical perspective to the developing knowledge and understanding of early years practitioners at various stages of their professional development.

Inter-professional and integrated working

There is a wealth of information on inter-professional and integrated working – the following portals and websites provide some useful starting points for research:

Centre for the Advancement of Interprofessional Education: http://www.caipe.org.uk/

Children's Workforce Development Council: http://www.cwdcouncil.org.uk/

European Interprofessional Education Network: http://www.eipen.org/

Learning in and for Interagency Working (Teaching and Learning Research Programme): http://www.tlrp.org/proj/phase111/daniels.htm

Social Care Institute for Excellence: http://www.scie.org.uk/

Foley, P. and Rixon, A. (eds) (2008) *Changing Children's Services: Working and Learning Together*. Bristol: The Policy Press. Explores in detail the practice of multi-disciplinary and integrated working.

References

Boud, D., Keogh, R. and Walker, D. (1985) *Reflection, Turning Experience into Learning*. London: Routledge.

Cox, C.B. and Boyson, R. (eds) (1975) *The Black Paper*. Worthing: Littlehampton Book Services Ltd.

DfES (2004) *Every Child Matters: Change for Children*. London: HMSO. Available online at: www.education.gov.uk/publications/standard/publication Detail/Page1/DfES/1081/2004

Dickens, Charles (1854/1984) *Hard Times*. London: Penguin.

Einstein, Albert (1979) *Autobiographical Notes*, by Paul Arthur Schilpp (Centennial ed.). Chicago: Open Court.

Freire, P. (1972) *Pedagogy of the Oppressed*. London: Penguin.

Frost, N. (2001) 'Professionalism, change and the politics of lifelong learning', *Studies in Continuing Education*, 23(1): 5–17.

GSCC (2008) *Values for Integrated Working with Children and Young People*. Available online at: http://www.gscc.org.uk/cmsFiles/Publications/GSCC_Children_And_Young_People_Values.pdf (accessed 27.07.11).

Johnson, T. (1972) *Professionals and Power*. London: Macmillan.

Lave, J. and Wenger, E. (1991) *Situated Learning: Legitimate Peripheral Participation*. Cambridge: Cambridge University Press.

Luft, J. and Ingham, H. (1955) 'The Johari window: A graphic model of interpersonal awareness'. *Proceedings of the Western Training Laboratory in Group Development*. Los Angeles: UCLA.

Oliver, C. and Mooney, A. with Statham, J. (2010) *Integrated Working: A Review of the Evidence*. London: Thomas Coram Research Unit, Institute of Education. Available online at: http://www.cwdcouncil.org.uk/assets/0001/0545/Integrated_Working_A_Review_of_the_Evidence_report.pdf

Schön, D. (1983) *The Reflective Practitioner: How Professionals Think in Action*. New York: Basic Books.

Sims, D., Fineman, S. and Gabriel, Y. (1993) *Organising and Organisations: An Introduction*. London: Sage.

Smith, M.K. (1999) 'Praxis', *Infed – the Encyclopaedia of Informal Education*. Available online at: http://www.infed.org/biblio/b-praxis.htm

3

Professional Relationships and Leadership in the Children and Young People's Workforce

Jane Melvin, Deborah Price and Nadia Edmond

Chapter Overview

This chapter will help you to reflect on leadership and management and effective working relationships within the childcare workforce as well as on how to develop appropriate skills and understandings.

By reading and engaging with the activities in this chapter, you will:

- examine the concepts of leadership and management;
- reflect on conditions for effective professional relationships;
- consider issues of professional relationships in integrated working with children and young people.

Leadership and management

Of the various reasons people have for working with children and young people, working relationships with other adults does not feature widely. Yet, if we took a straw poll of managers of preschools, nurseries, childminders, teaching assistants, after school club managers and youth workers, and asked them which part of their job causes them the most anxiety, it is very likely to be relationships with other staff rather than working directly with children and young people. Even those working on a part-time basis might have to manage a team of colleagues and may not feel confident about their abilities to do this effectively. This may be compounded by the fact that training often looks closely at the skills, knowledge and experience that are needed to provide a good service to the children and young people, but often provides less input on leadership, or the skills needed to manage and motivate a team of people.

It is important to define what we mean by 'leadership' and 'management' as they are terms that are often used together and/or interchangeably. However, they do mean different things. The focus of management is the present and the effective and efficient implementation of policy, whilst the focus of leadership is the future and response to or initiation of change.

These different focuses are apparent in Northouse's (2004) summary of the differences between leadership and management (see Figure 3.1).

What Figure 3.1 shows is that any organisation or setting requires elements of both. All organisations require management for the day-to-day smooth functioning of the setting, for example, devising staff rotas, ordering and allocating resources, supporting staff and monitoring performance. Organisations also need to respond to change, and create a vision and sense of purpose for the setting whilst ensuring that staff understand, support and adhere to this.

There is a tendency to see both leadership and management as aspects of managers' roles but they are distinct. An important difference

Management focus – order and consistency	Leadership focus – change and movement
Planning/budgeting • Establish agendas • Set timetables • Allocate resources	Establishing direction • Create a vision • Clarify the 'big picture' • Set strategies
Organising/staffing • Provide structure • Allocate staff • Establish and implement rules and procedures	Aligning people • Communicate goals • Seek commitment • Build teams and coalitions
Controlling/problem solving • Develop incentives • Generate creative solutions • Take corrective action	Motivating and inspiring • Inspire and energise • Empower subordinates • Satisfy unmet needs

Figure 3.1 Differences between leadership and management

Source: Northouse (2004: 9)

between them is the source of the manager's or leader's power. Managers are defined by their position in a management structure and their authority and power derives from this. Leaders, on the other hand, are defined by the extent to which they influence people, initiate change and take people with them. Not all managers are leaders and not all leaders are managers. Belbin (1997: 98) has suggested that 'leadership is not part of the job but a quality that can be brought to a job ... the work that leadership encompasses in the context clearly is not assigned but comes about spontaneously'. This means that whatever your position within an organisation, even where you have no management responsibility, you may have some potential for leadership. As we saw in Chapter 2, an important dimension of professionalism, whether in a professional or para-professional role, is the ability to make judgements about the appropriate course of action in unpredictable work contexts. This will often mean influencing people (colleagues, parents, children and young people) to get agreement and 'buy in' to the course of action.

The notion of a course of action with desired outcomes and the necessity to achieve engagement by others relates to two dimensions of leadership identified by Blake and Mouton (1964, 1985). These are: concern for tasks and outcomes and concern for people and relationships (Figure 3.2). Leaders can rate their concerns for these two aspects as high or low, resulting in different 'types' of leaders.

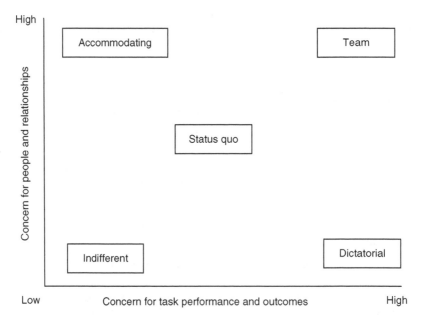

Figure 3.2 Different leadership styles

Source: adapted from Blake and Mouton (1985)

Where managers/leaders have little concern for either task outcomes or relationships with people, their main concern may be preservation of their position, to 'play safe.' This may lead to less innovation and change.

Where managers/leaders have a high level of concern for relationships with people but little for task outcomes, staff morale may be high and relationships good but the setting may not be very effective in achieving outcomes. Such leaders may be less adept at using disciplinary procedures through fear of being seen as authoritarian and this can impact negatively on relationships.

A high concern for task outcomes and low concern for relationships will often be associated with an autocratic style of command rather than dialogue, and the use of monetary incentives and/or rules and punishments to achieve goals. This style is often characteristic of crisis management.

Blake and Mouton (1985) argue that high levels of concern for both people and outcomes lead to managers encouraging teamwork and valuing contributions. High levels of performance are ensured by staff commitment and a sense of mutual responsibility and accountability as well as recognition. A great deal of management study and theory has sought to provide definitive answers to management problems and there has been an aspiration to develop a 'science' of management. As Hassard and Parker have argued:

> ... modernism has advanced in concert with faith in the notion of progress and our absorption in the machine metaphor. These various assumptions remain central to Western culture and have left a lasting impression on our theories of organizations. (1993: 6)

In the late 19th century, Frederick Taylor introduced 'scientific management' (or Taylorism) which sought to identify systems for maximising economic efficiency, particularly labour productivity. This was done, in large part, through the specification of how work should be carried out, thus removing much autonomy from workers. As a distinct theory, Taylorism has been superseded but its legacy is evident in much management practice, for example the standardisation of best practice, as we saw in the specification of professional standards in the previous chapter.

Since the 1980s, the influence of postmodernism and the ideas we encountered in the introduction have also been felt in the area of management and leadership. Management and leadership need to work within the bounds of complexity, fluidity and constant change, which are characteristics of many organisations. In particular, McKimm and Phillips suggest that 'the ideas enshrined in post-modern leadership can be helpful when we are thinking of rapidly changing and shifting services or when taking into account complex systems involving multiple stakeholders' (McKimm and Phillips, 2009: 11).

The importance of language and how language is used to 'construct' a shared understanding of the organisational context and purpose is apparent in the focus on 'vision' and 'mission statements' and the development of 'transformational' or 'distributed' leadership, both of which have been a feature of management and leadership in recent years. So called 'transformational' leaders engage with colleagues and stakeholders, successfully conveying their vision of the future so that it becomes a shared goal. The idea of 'distributed leadership' proposes that all levels within an organisation are enabled to lead in ways to achieve the shared goal.

The particular quality of the leader in prioritising achievement of a shared goal over individual power or status is at the heart of Greenleaf's concept of 'servant leadership', which 'begins with the natural feeling that one wants to serve, to serve first. Then conscious choice brings one to aspire to lead ...' (Greenleaf, 1977: 13). The very idea of 'public service' incorporates fundamental concepts around the altruistic nature of the care or education provided. Professionals who work in public services are 'duty bound' to work within ethical frameworks and values, all of which prioritise the patient, client or learner rather than the needs of the organisation or the state.

∿ Reflection point

Plot your own leadership style or your experience of being led/managed on the grid presented in Figure 3.2. Which style or styles would you say are most effective under which conditions and why?

Who do you consider to be leaders in your setting (you might include yourself)? What characteristics define them as leaders?

What do you make of the concept of 'servant leadership'? Is this something you recognise? Can you identify examples of it in your setting?

Have you experienced any tension between the needs of the children/young people you work with and the needs of the organisation? How can such tensions be resolved?

Effective professional relationships

Figure 3.2 above emphasised the importance of a high and balanced concern for both tasks and outcomes as well as concern for people and relationships. This concern needs to be supported by the ability to develop and sustain effective professional relationships. This ability has been associated with the notion of 'emotional intelligence'. A number of theorists have contributed to the development of this concept, including Howard Gardner (1983), who proposed a model of 'multiple intelligences' including 'intrapersonal intelligence' (capacity for self-awareness and understanding) and 'interpersonal intelligence' (capacity for understanding the intentions, motivations and desires of other people). Salovey and Mayer (1990) coined the term 'emotional intelligence', which was popularised by Daniel Goleman (2001), to describe the ability to '...monitor one's own and others' feelings and emotions, to discriminate among them and to use this information to guide one's thinking and actions' (Salovey and Mayer, 1990: 189). Effective professional relationships depend on colleagues understanding each other and require high levels of emotional intelligence. Goleman's adaptation of the concept includes five basic competences (2001: 318):

- **Self-awareness**: knowing and understanding your own feelings and making a realistic assessment of your own abilities;

- **Self-regulation**: managing emotions to facilitate rather than interfere with the task at hand;

- **Motivation**: using your aims to take the initiative and persevering in the face of setbacks;

- **Empathy**: ability to understand a broad diversity of people;

- **Social skills**: interacting smoothly through effective communication.

We look in more detail at communication skills in Chapters 8 and 9 where we discuss effective communication with children and young people and effective communication and engagement with families. Here we focus on two key components of effective communication which contribute not only to our relationships with children and young people but also with colleagues and other adults. These components are active listening and assertive communication.

Active listening

In conversation, and especially in a busy work context, much of our attention may be on other things; we may assume we know what the person is saying or going to say, we may be distracted or already thinking about our response. Active listening aims to improve communication and mutual understanding through a structured form of listening and responding that focuses the attention on the speaker. It requires the listener to attend fully and then feed back to the speaker what they have understood from the communication – this can be both in terms of the content of what was said and also the feelings behind it. The speaker then has the opportunity to clarify if they feel they have been misunderstood. The benefits of active listening are that it requires attentiveness, it avoids misunderstandings and it encourages open communication and conflict resolution.

Case study

Jilly runs a small preschool that has a team of three full-time staff and two part-timers who help at lunchtime and if children need special assistance. The staff team have worked together for many years and all socialise regularly. Liz and Bernice have teenage children (Ella is Liz's daughter and Jo is Bernice's) who were friends but have now fallen out with each other. Liz and Bernice have subsequently let this affect their relationship. Jilly decides to speak to Liz and, using active listening techniques, does not make judgements about the situation but is able to feed back to her: 'So, Jo has really hurt Ella and you are clearly very upset by that but feel that Bernice is just shrugging it off and not taking it seriously?' Liz basically agrees with this but hearing it from Jilly makes her question her interpretation of Bernice's behaviour and look again at her own. Maybe Bernice is embarrassed or feels guilty. Perhaps Liz is blaming Bernice for something which is really between the two girls. She decides to talk to Bernice and the next day both Liz and Bernice come to see Jilly together to reassure her that they have resolved the situation.

Can you think of situations where the presence or absence of active listening has contributed to conflict resolution?

Assertive communication

The desired outcome of an assertive interaction is a 'win:win' situation, where both parties leave feeling satisfied. Assertiveness is defined as knowing what you want, and being able to state it clearly whilst appreciating the point of view of the other person. Assertive communication might be facilitated by the following techniques:

- Summarise the situation or recap on what has brought you to this point. In this way you are setting the scene for the interaction and making it clear what is going to be discussed. For example: 'I notice that you arrived late for work today and did not let us know. This is the third time in two weeks and I think we need a conversation about this'.

- Say how you feel about the situation and how it impacts on yourself and others. This makes it clear what you are feeling, and that you are sharing this information openly. For example: 'I have already mentioned how difficult this is for your colleagues, including me, and it bothers me that you seem to be ignoring this'.

- Be clear about how you would like things to be in the future. For example: 'As a team, we need to be able to rely on you being here when you are due to be and you must let us know if that is not going to be possible'.

The person you are dealing with can choose not to respond to this but you have made your position clear and started a process of negotiation that can then continue. Being specific is important; it is not enough to say 'I want things to be different'. For example, to say 'I would like you to talk to me privately if you disagree with me and not in front of the children/young people' is much clearer and less confrontational than 'Don't embarrass me like that again'.

Assertive communication requires participants not to be diverted by emotional responses, excuses or attempts to blame others. This can be helped by active listening, acknowledging what the other person is saying and steering the conversation back to the item on your agenda. Difficult situations tend not to resolve themselves and instead have a tendency to get worse. It can be tempting to hope things improve but this is unlikely to be an effective strategy.

If the discussion results in tears, then give the person a moment to compose themselves and if necessary end the discussion, but on the understanding that it will be resumed in the very near future. Conflict and differences of opinion are not inherently bad; on the contrary, they can be the basis for dynamism and change but they do need to be dealt with in a professional and respectful manner.

Role playing some situations in advance will give you a chance to try some of these strategies and feel more comfortable with them. Further practical training in assertiveness will be time well spent by you in order to deal with difficult situations effectively.

Case study

Dave runs an open access adventure playground for children aged seven to fifteen. There is high unemployment in the area and there are no other facilities for older children. Because of this, a lot of young people continue to come to the playground even when they have left school, mainly because there is nothing else to do and they have built up good relationships with each other and the staff team. Dave finds this difficult at times as the older and younger people have different needs and the older people's presence sometimes intimidates the younger ones. However, he finds it hard to say that they cannot come in as he has such a strong relationship with them. The core staff team in the adventure playground is increased during the busy summer holidays with temporary staff, many of whom are students from a local university. This means that the age difference between the young people at the club and some of the staff is minimal. Dave has become aware through gossip that one of the male students, who is nineteen, has struck up a relationship with one of the girls, who is sixteen, and has been seen out and about with her at the local shopping mall.

How should Dave approach this situation? Who should he speak to and what should he say to them? Is there anything he should change about the practice in the setting as a result of this incident?

Workplace activity

Think about all the adults that you work with during a typical week and make a list of them. On a piece of A4 paper, make a mark at the centre of the paper to represent yourself. Then place the adults you have listed on to the page according to how much contact you have with them. So someone you see every day would be near to you and someone you only see once a week would be further away. Next, rank them in terms of the quality of the relationship that you have with them, with one being a very conflicted and difficult relationship and ten being a friendly and supportive one. You can now clearly reflect on the quality of the relationships you have with your colleagues. Is there a correlation between frequency of contact and quality of relationship? Is this because you have not put time into establishing a good relationship? Or are the people you have most contact with the lowest in terms of relationship quality because you are in conflict with them regularly? What are the implications for inter-professional relationships where you might have infrequent contact? Is there anything that you could do to improve the quality of the relationships that you have ranked lowest? Take one of these and think about three things that you could do to make the relationship work more effectively.

Inter-agency and partnership working

As we saw in Chapter 1, one of the trends that has characterised policy developments of the last 20 years has been increasing recognition of the need for professionals to collaborate to improve the quality of services to children and young people. Promoting children's well-being and safeguarding them from significant harm depends crucially upon effective information-sharing, collaboration and understanding between agencies and professionals.

 Workplace activity

With colleagues at work consider the following questions:

How does inter-agency working impact on your professional context? Which other agencies and professionals do you come into contact with and to what purpose? How effective is this inter-professional working?

What is the experience of the children and young people you work with of different agencies? What are their views of the different agencies and professionals with which they come into contact?

Issues and challenges of inter-agency and partnership working

A great deal of research has been carried out relating to effectiveness in partnership working and practice (see e.g. Anning et al., 2009). Anning et al. (2009) identified different dilemmas that need to be resolved in individual examples of multi-agency team participation. These are: structural, ideological, procedural and inter-professional.

- The **structural dilemmas** relate to the decisions that need to be taken with respect to team membership, management and organisational structures and location of team activities.

- In terms of the **ideological dilemmas**, inter-professional teams need to acknowledge and deal with the issue of different professional cultures, areas of expertise and ways of working, and the creation of new inter-professional knowledge and practice.

- **Procedural dilemmas** refer to the decisions that inter-professional teams have to make regarding the creation of common protocols/ procedures and documentation.

- Finally, **inter-professional dilemmas** relate to the ways in which inter-professional teams respond to threats to professional identity, status and agency.

We can see these different dilemmas illustrated in the following case study.

Case study: Inter-professional practice

Janet is manager of a children's centre in a deprived area. The centre serves a local population of about 3,000 people, including about 700 under-fives. The centre has recently been built, adjacent to a local primary school. A medical centre is also due to be built on the site soon. The centre provides a range of services, including early years learning and childcare, play facilities, speech and language therapy, health care support and advice, and family support and parental outreach. The structural and procedural dilemmas were addressed by having a core team and managing many of the

services through service-level agreements with
The centre also hosts a range of other agencies
a base for delivering community services, for
long learning team and teenage pregnancy service
ment has presented challenges in terms of integrated w
regular centre user meetings have been instituted. The team in
a monitoring officer who manages the Common Assessmen
Framework database to monitor which families are receiving support from which agencies.

For Janet, these informal links have been a key feature of addressing ideological and inter-professional dilemmas. It is important
that all members of inter-professional teams within the centre
recognise each other's areas of expertise and different ways of
working, as well as valuing the particular contribution that each
can make. An important dimension of practice within the centre
is the common use of a staffroom, which has helped to forge
links. Regular conversations over lunch or coffee have helped
break down barriers of language with colleagues sharing and
explaining jargon.

In terms of inter-professional working within your own context, how
do you think the various dilemmas of inter-professional working
have been addressed? Where do you see room for improvement?

Effective inter-professional and multi-agency working requires
change to existing and established ways of working; change is not
easy for organisations or individuals. Kotter (1996) has identified
what he believes are the critical differences between organisations
that are successful in their change effort and those that are not.
He has identified 'lessons from success' which are summarised in
Table 3.1.

Reflection point

Thinking about your own context, how would you rate progress
towards integrated working in terms of these steps?

Put yourself in the role of leading a group or team where you have
the role of co-ordinating a joint project.

Table 3.1 Eight steps to successful change for integrated working

Step	Lessons from success
Step 1 Increase urgency	This is about inspiring people to act now by making objectives real and relevant. It involves engaging all members of multi-agency teams and building on their strengths, styles and experiences.
Step 2 Build the guiding team	This is probably one of the greatest challenges within a multi-agency context as it involves trying to get the best people in the room with the right commitment and motivation, and the best combination of expertise and skills. Managers are often faced with having to work with people who are nominated, sent or volunteered into the process. Initial groundwork spent agreeing on roles, actions and commitment is usually time well spent but is also a stage in group development that is often skipped due to the pressure of time and workload.
Step 3 Get the vision right	Another phase that is often skipped or rushed through is that of developing and building ownership for the project amongst all participants. Some of the issues already described in relation to motivation and the identification of the best people to participate can be worked through within this aspect, which is about facilitating the team to create and agree on a joint vision and strategy that focuses on the emotional and creative aspects as well as the process necessary to attain the outcomes.
Step 4 Communicate for buy-in	The first three steps can be seriously undermined if participants then feel that they are not included or kept updated in follow-up processes. Additionally, for a multi-agency project to be successful there needs to be confidence that the same message will be delivered to all outside partners. Clarity and vision can only be communicated to others in a consistent way if there is agreement and ownership by the group in relation to the vision and objectives.
Step 5 Empower action	Successful and effective multi-agency partnerships are those that work hard to create ownership and their own working culture, and often this culture is about the group working together to remove obstacles and enable constructive feedback about progress, which is combined with support and backing from leaders. Linked back to step 4, an effective communication strategy is a way of ensuring support from leadership as well as providing a mechanism to reward and recognise progress and achievements.
Step 6 Create short-term wins	This involves ensuring that set aims and objectives are achievable, that those responsible for contributing to them are identified and accountable, and that achievements are recognised and credit is given.
Step 7 Don't let up	An approach that has engendered ownership and empowerment will also support and encourage determination and persistence. How does the group cope with failure or a change of plan? Does the ownership created give it a mandate to not give up but to try a different approach? A process that is centred and directed totally by the 'leader' means that the group can apportion blame and also absolve themselves of responsibility.
Step 8 Make change stick	Some multi-agency partnerships work brilliantly and some are really dysfunctional, focusing only on in-fighting and organisational jealousies. Ensuring that good practice is demonstrated, evidenced and communicated is an important part of role-modelling good practice and weaving change into existing culture.

Source: adapted from Kotter (1996)

Summary

Michael Hart, the director of Ofsted, has stated that 'Effective leaders know what they are doing well and what contributes to this. They are frank about their weaknesses and use their self-evaluation to improve' (Ofsted, 2008). In this chapter, we have provided you with some starting points for such self-evaluation by discussing the concepts of a leadership and management and differentiating between them. We have also discussed how to use emotional intelligence as a framework for reflecting on effective professional relationships and considering the dilemmas and change processes associated with integrated working with children and young people.

Further reading

Harrison, R., Benjamin, C., Curran, S. and Hunter, R. (2007) *Leading Work with Young People*. London: Sage. This accessible text examines the leadership roles which practitioners take on as members of teams, organisations and inter-agency partnerships.

References

Anning, A., Cottrell, D.M., Frost, N., Green, J. and Robinson, M. (2009) *Developing Multiprofessional Teamwork for Integrated Children's Services: Research, Policy and Practice*. Maidenhead: Open University Press.

Belbin, R.M. (1997) *Changing the Way We Work*. Oxford: Butterworth-Heinneman.

Blake, R. and Mouton, J. (1964) *The Managerial Grid: The Key to Leadership Excellence*. Houston, TX: Gulf Publishing Co.

Blake, R. and Mouton, J. (1985) *The Managerial Grid 3: The Key to Leadership Excellence*. Houston, TX: Gulf Publishing Co.

Gardner, H. (1983) *Frames of Mind: The Theory of Multiple Intelligences*. New York: Basic Books.

Goleman, D. (2001) *The Emotionally Intelligent Workplace*. San Francisco, CA: Jossey-Bass.

Greenleaf, R.K. (1977) *Servant Leadership: A Journey into the Nature of Legitimate Power and Greatness*. Mahwah, NJ: Paulist Press.

Hassard, J. and Parker, M. (1993) *Postmodernism and Organizations*. London: Sage.

Kotter, J. (1996) *Leading Change*. Boston, MA: Harvard Business School Press.

McKimm, J. and Phillips, K. (eds) (2009) *Leadership and Management in Integrated Services*. Exeter: Learning Matters.

Northouse, P.G. (2004) *Leadership, Theory and Practice* (3rd edn). London: Sage.

Ofsted (2008) *Early Years: Leading to Excellence*. London: Ofsted.

Salovey, P. and Mayer, J.D. (1990) 'Emotional intelligence', *Imagination, Cognition and Personality*, 9(3): 185–211.

4

Quality and Effectiveness in Working with Children and Young People

Denise Kingston and Jane Melvin

Chapter Overview

This chapter examines how the terms 'quality' and 'effectiveness' are used in different professional contexts. Different perspectives and 'discourses' of quality are discussed and the chapter provides both an analysis of, and guide to, effectiveness and quality, and how they can be meaningful to practitioners. Finally, it gives examples of some systems of internal quality audit.

By reading and engaging with the activities in this chapter, you will:

- engage in debate around the existence of quality;
- explore principles and practice relating to quality;
- consider current models of quality;
- reflect on current quality processes and their impact within
  your own setting;
- consider quality and multi-disciplinary practice.

What is quality?

As practitioners, we are urged to constantly improve quality, whether we work within the private, voluntary or independent sector, a maintained setting or for a local authority (LA). In order to monitor and evaluate quality, different bodies (e.g. Ofsted) have been created. However, monitoring and evaluation practices are contested and many practitioners report feeling uncomfortable about processes associated with quality (Jones, 2010). This can be for a great many reasons, including concern about being judged and what those judgements mean, but it undoubtedly also reflects the issue that quality is a very difficult concept to agree upon.

Quality judgements are made within our settings as we appraise staff, the environment, resources and so on, both as part of our natural daily practice and also as part of our more formal quality assurance procedures. In addition, formal quality judgements are made of us by external agents, such as LA advisors and Ofsted, and less formal judgements are made by others, including visiting professionals and parents. As critically reflective practitioners we will often need to consider and question our practice and reflect upon different views from our own.

 Reflection point

What does the term 'quality' mean for you in relation to your setting/practice? How is the quality of your setting currently measured and for what purpose? What are the characteristics or 'quality indicators' that you would identify as indicating quality?

What evidence do you have that these indicators help the setting/ you achieve its/your aims? How would you know which are the most important or which have the greatest effect?

How might a list of quality indicators look if it was compiled by all of the staff in your setting or by another stakeholder group, for example the children and young people, the parents, etc.? Do parents look for and value the same things as staff?

Do you consider all of your stakeholders to have an equal voice? Have you ever had a disagreement about quality with one of your stakeholders and, if so, how was that resolved?

Think about a setting that you consider to be of low quality, on what basis do you make that judgement? How might they be made aware of their inadequacies, be encouraged to improve or shut?

Does quality exist?

Despite the large-scale use of the term 'quality', and the wide-ranging quality judgements made both internally and externally in our setting, there is a current and important debate considering its existence and usefulness. Siraj-Blatchford and Wong (1999) crystallised the current debate in terms of the objectivist and relativist views of quality. The two views of quality relate to the philosophical underpinnings of the term and to historical and political changes and demands. The term 'quality' has existed in its present form since the beginning of the 20th century and, according to Dahlberg et al. (1999), it was and remains influenced by the modernist perspective (see Introduction) and the objectivist belief that it is possible to measure the world 'scientifically'. This, however, has been countered by the relativist view of quality. These two views of quality are considered in turn.

The objectivist view

The objectivist view suggests that quality can be impartially measured and quantified according to a set of identified criteria. Stephen Covey, in his book *The Seven Habits of Highly Effective People*, talks about the concept of 'beginning with the end in mind' (Covey, 1989: 95), which implies knowing exactly what we are trying to achieve from the outset. The outcomes that are sought will vary across settings and can often be found, at the general level, in 'settings', 'mission statements' or 'visions', or, at the specific level, in a set of aims and objectives relating to a session or project. In early years, proposed outcomes are likely to include enhanced children's social, emotional and cognitive development, whilst in play or youth services they might include improved personal relationships, greater self-confidence and/or crime reduction.

From an objectivist perspective, the quality of a setting is the extent to which characteristics (often called 'quality indicators') of the setting contribute to children and young people attaining the specified outcomes. These characteristics might include the ratio of adults to children or young people, the qualification levels of the staff, the variety of activities on offer, the relationships and interactions between the children, young people and adults, the spaces and resources available, and so on. Having qualification levels of the staff as one of these characteristics, for example, reflects the expectation that more highly qualified staff will better enable the settings to meet its aims. This expectation can be based on evidence – for example that children progress better in settings where the staff are more qualified (Sylva et al., 2004).

The current list (or rather lists) of quality indicators or characteristics used today have been developed through research and judgements (usually of professionals) on the value of certain characteristics of settings. They tend to be used universally across the various settings and within the sectors for which they have been compiled. For example, what Ofsted looks for in one setting would be the same set of characteristics that they are looking at in all similar settings. Some sets of characteristics are thought to apply internationally as well as nationally (e.g. the Early Childhood Environment Rating Scales; Harms et al., 2005).

From this perspective, assessing or measuring quality is a process of comparing the observable and measurable characteristics of a particular setting against a set of pre-determined, planned and agreed quality indicators expressed as requirements and expectations. The more the characteristics of the setting conform to these requirements and expectations, the higher quality it is judged to be and, conversely, the less the characteristics of the setting meet the requirements and expectations, the lower its quality.

Figure 4.1 illustrates some aspects common to the quality discourse found across the children and young people's workforce. Consider the objectivist's view in the terminology (be specific, be measurable, etc.), the standards (external requirements) and the underlying assumptions of the observable nature of quality.

There are a number of objections to this approach. The first objection relates to the characteristics which have been identified as important to quality. In the UK, the staff–child ratio is often considered to be an important element of quality. However, the Effective Provision of Pre-school Education (EPPE) project (Sylva et al., 2004) suggested that other characteristics, such as the qualification level of the practitioners, were far more important indicators of quality, and in other countries staff–child ratios are not seen as a

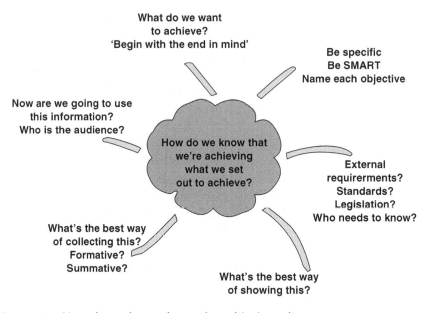

Figure 4.1   How do we know that we're achieving what we set out to achieve?

characteristic of quality at all. For example, the Reggio Emilia approach has an international reputation for providing high-quality provision for early years and has staff–child ratios which would not be allowed in the UK.

A second objection relates to the overall aims, 'missions' or 'visions' of settings and whether what is considered to be high quality in one context is necessarily high quality in another. This argument is relevant both within the UK and beyond. In the UK, child-centred approaches, in which practitioners recognise and support children's interests, and where children and young people are encouraged to develop independence and autonomy, are seen as an aspect of high-quality provision. Other countries, however, including many Asian countries, adopt more formal approaches to supporting learning and development, and place greater impor-tance on community and community values, responsibilities and decision-making (Kashima et al., 2005). It seems unlikely, given such different philosophies, practices and views on learning and development, that a single agreed universal definition of quality could be found.

Ultimately, a fundamental objection to the objectivist view is that assessing quality is not like measuring physical characteristics of an object where there is very little scope for interpretation. In the case of quality, making judgements depends on interpretation – quality is in the eye of the beholder!

The relativist view

The response to these objections, and presenting an alternative perspective, is the relativists' view, which is related to postmodernism (see Introduction). According to this view, quality is a dynamic and context-specific concept and therefore comparisons between settings are impossible. Relativists would argue that it is not possible to have a general view of what constitutes quality as it is dependent on the context, culture, values and beliefs of the stakeholders in the setting. Assessment of quality is subjective and complex and will depend on whose views are included and what measures are used (Mooney et al., 2003). Relativists argue that there cannot be a universal set of characteristics to determine quality. Therefore, existing quality improvement tools, targets and goals set by government agencies such as Ofsted, and the associated quality assurance processes, are inappropriate and unhelpful. From this perspective, if quality is to be considered at all, it should involve a process of negotiation between, and reflect the views of, all the stakeholders in the setting.

Relativists would argue that all of the systems that surround the child or young person need to be considered (consistent with the ecological model of human development presented in the Introduction). At the setting level, assessing quality would involve seeking the views of practitioners, parents, management, the surrounding community and of course the children and/or young people. As the stakeholders change over time, it may be that what constitutes quality within the setting may also change.

Consulting all stakeholders would be exceptional practice – however, we would also need to consider how to reconcile differences in stakeholder perspectives. Mitchell et al. (1997) talk about the necessity of analysing whether stakeholders have 'power' in relation to being able to influence practice, procedures and the concept of quality. Some stakeholders are seen as very powerful while others are not; some stakeholders have power over certain aspects of the setting and not over others. Consider, for example, strong 'parent-power' – this might have a positive or negative effect on the work of a setting, depending on the issues. In the maintained sector, parents might have a lot of power in relation to challenging a local authority decision to close a facility, but might be powerless in relation to government policy stating that services must be delivered in a specific way. Consider also the power of children and young people's voices; are they able to influence decisions about quality when factors such as funding, staffing and health and safety also have to be considered? Mitchell et al. (1997) also discuss the 'legitimacy' and 'urgency' of the stakeholders. They talk about stakeholders' rights over or authority to influence the quality of the work (legitimacy), and the speed with which they want to see change happen (urgency). In practice, different stakeholder groups are seen to possess different levels of 'legitimacy' and 'urgency'.

The relativist view suggests that quality has a subjectivity and dynamism that precludes the development of local and national standards and associated comparisons between settings. One serious implication of this view of quality is, according to the objectivists, that the resulting variations may leave some settings with unacceptable standards and inappropriate and ineffective practice. It has been the absence of quality standards in many of the areas of work with children and young people which is thought to have led to inappropriate and ineffective practice being tolerated. The government, having recognised this, suggested that it was imperative that 'essential standards of provision are in place' (DCSF, 2008: 10).

Rejecting the term 'quality' as redundant, as Dahlberg et al. (1999) amongst others suggest, would not be an easy solution. Quality is fundamental to our settings and services, and research (e.g. Sylva et al., 2004) has consistently shown the value of the concept. However, the relativist view encourages us to view simplistic, universally applied quality measures critically, and recognise that such approaches, particularly if used without reflection or recognition of the context, are likely to be inadequate. They urge instead that practitioners engage in quality processes and adopt different and varied ways of capturing quality; and that such processes include the judgements of all stakeholders.

Workplace activity

Consider the statements in Figure 4.2. Which are allied to an objectivist approach to quality?

1. Measuring the quality of a setting or service allows us to compare it with others

2. Quality is too complex and too varied and changing to be a useful concept

3. Quality changes over time and is dependent upon who you ask

4. Understanding quality helps practitioners to understand what they should do and how they should do it

5. Quality is an outdated concept and is harmful because it can mean that we concentrate on unimportant aspects of practice

6. Research can help us identify quality by looking for characteristics in a setting that support children and young people in the way society agrees is right

7. Measuring quality ensures minimum standards and safeguards our children and young people

8. Quality measures can help us ensure that our children and young people are well cared for and that we fulfil our objectives/vision statements

9. If we are to get a useful view of quality, then we first need to ask all of our stakeholders what they think quality is, so what you measure will change each time you do it

10. Quality can be measured by considering a pre-determined set of characteristics

11. Quality measures support practitioners monitor and evaluate their practice

12. Everyone has their own view of quality, so one true measure does not exist

13. For all stakeholders' views to be taken into account they must be given equal worth to the professionals and researchers in this area, even if they give contradictory views

14. What constitutes quality in a setting one week may be different the next

Figure 4.2 Views of quality

Now look at these statements again. Which do you agree with yourself?

Objectivists are likely to agree with statements 1, 4, 6, 7, 8, 10 and 11. Statement 13 may have also been noted, as although this is a relativist viewpoint some objectivists might also recognise its importance – it is respectful practice but often difficult to achieve. In reality, people are not typically either objectivist or relativist and many people agree with elements of both. A pluralist (see Hinman, 2003) would agree with aspects of both the objectivist and relativist views. Pluralists believe that no single explanation or view of reality can account for all of nature. They acknowledge diversity and recognise that neither the objectivist nor relativist view can account for or give the answer to all of the questions that surround quality.

Quality and effectiveness

In practice, 'quality' is often seen as synonymous with 'effectiveness' so we need to consider both these terms, as they are often used interchangeably. It is important to be clear about the differences and similarities in meaning, as, whilst a particular practice might be effective, it might not necessarily represent quality or 'good practice'.

〰️ Reflection point

Consider Table 4.1 and decide whether each of the situations could be described as either quality or effective practice, or both.

Whilst some of the practices highlighted in Table 4.1 might be considered both effective and high quality, and we can see clear links between these terms, other practices may be considered effective but not high quality. They are effective because they are likely to meet the desired target or goal and so possibly support measurable outcomes; however they are not high quality as they do not represent the beliefs and values which we associate with quality. For example, strapping a toddler to a chair in an effort to prevent running indoors would not support the child learning how to behave in the setting and could be seen as very punitive. Excluding 'disruptive children' from school may support the school's focus on preventing disruptive behaviour within that setting but is unlikely to support the child or young person in their understanding of what is expected behaviour in school, and may just move the problem into the community and even exacerbate it.

Table 4.1 Quality or effective practice?

Target or goal	Example of practice
Prevent children from running indoors and hurting themselves and others	Restraining a toddler in a high chair
Prevent binge drinking in teenagers	Setting a curfew on Friday/Saturday nights for 13–18 year olds
Encourage children not to graffiti illegally	Creating a graffiti board in the play centre
Preventing teenage pregnancy	Inviting a teenage mother with her baby to come and talk to young people about parenthood
Helping children to concentrate and keep on task in class	Prescribing Ritalin to children diagnosed with ADHD
Preventing disruptive behaviour	Excluding disruptive children from school
Supporting healthy eating	Only providing nutritionally balanced school lunches
Supporting children's attendance	Excluding children for non attendance
Supporting children's transition to nursery, school, etc. and reducing crying and upset in the mornings	Distracting a child who has separation anxiety, while her mother leaves

Quality practice is about considering the values and beliefs within the setting and, amongst other elements, it is about supporting learning and development, respecting individual needs and recognising the impact of our work on the wider society. We need to consider why we do the things we do and what the children and young people are likely to learn from our practice. However we interpret the concept of quality, working to enhance the quality of provision requires us to engage with 'quality management', a concept rooted in the objectivists' view of quality.

Quality management

Quality management includes all the activities that organisations use to direct, control and co-ordinate quality. These activities include formulating a quality policy and setting quality objectives. They also include quality planning, quality control, quality assurance and quality improvement.

To manage quality, it is important to be clear about the specific purpose of the setting or service (its mission or vision), and how this is going to be achieved (the strategy). In addition, a clear plan needs to be formulated about how the judgements on what constitutes quality will be made and how evidence of quality delivery will be collected. As part of this process, there needs to be clear guidance on how staff, service users, volunteers, etc. will report on issues relating to quality. The final element is how feedback on quality will be built into the planning and development of service delivery and how it will be published and disseminated externally.

Different approaches to quality management

Different contexts have resulted in the development of differing approaches to quality management and we explore three here – quality control, total quality management (TQM) and quality assurance (QA).

Quality control

Quality control is a set of activities intended to ensure that quality requirements are actually being met. Quality control is one part of quality management and 'requires the setting of standards and is essentially a process of inspection, rejection and correction. Quality control is a widely-used method for ensuring quality' (Bone, 1991, as cited by Ford et al., 2002: 167).

An example of this approach is the Ofsted inspection. Ofsted, in their publication *Raising Standards, Improving Lives* (2009: 3), state:

> Inspection entails assessing a service against a published framework and criteria. It involves close observation by trained and experienced inspectors with knowledge of the sector concerned, informed by a range of data, and dialogue with staff and users of services. The output of inspection is normally the publication of judgements set out in a report.

Over the years, Ofsted has increasingly been reliant on information and evidence relating to the impact of services, which they collect primarily from service users. For example: what difference has attending this play centre or youth project made to you? What is the benefit to your child of attending this provision? The intention behind such inspection is to identify when quality standards are not being met.

Total quality management (TQM)

TQM is a more wide-ranging and holistic approach to quality because it relies on all staff in an organisation interacting with each other to meet the expressed goal of continual improvement; this is done by constantly monitoring and evaluating their own work, rather than being inspected or audited (Murgatroyd and Morgan, 1994). West-Burnham (1997) also comments that staff need to be passionate about this way of working, as well as systematically following the principles through.

The Japanese word 'kaizen' has become associated with the term 'continuous improvement', which is at the heart of the TQM model, and this was based on Deming's 14 Points theory (1982) which was key in relation to the transformation of American and Japanese post-war manufacturing industries. Deming maintained that leadership was as important as ownership and that the manufacturing process should be seen as a whole system, rather than discrete, separate parts.

The starting point of the principle of *kaizen* is that everything can be improved and that no day should go by without some improvement being made. It encourages staff to imagine the ultimate service user experience and then think how to improve it, instead of thinking why it cannot be improved. It challenges staff to find ways of making things work better, even if something is working well, by thinking beyond common-sense solutions. This is sometimes described as 'blue sky thinking' or 'thinking outside the box'. *Kaizen* sees problem-solving as a cross-functional systematic process involving all staff in a collaborative approach.

Deming (1982) took these principles and converted them into a cycle of PLAN (establish objectives and define methods to reach them), DO (implement what you have planned), CHECK (measure and compare results obtained against results expected) and ACT (take action to improve what you have implemented). These simple steps were designed to encourage organisations to work in a planned yet adaptable way that accepts and flexes to the constant improvement agenda.

Quality assurance (QA)

Quality assurance is a process that sits somewhere between quality control and TQM. QA processes are based on prevention not cure, and work on the principle of getting it right in the first place, rather than getting things wrong and then putting them right. It involves the development of a structure where everyone agrees on the standards to be reached, by enabling all involved to discuss, understand, own and embed the standards. Leadership and management are then tasked with the following: ensuring that appropriate action is taken, and that processes and procedures for action-planning, reflection, review and evaluation are in place and accessible to all.

Quality assurance relates to an agreed set of activities that are intended to monitor that quality requirements are being met, and quality improvement refers to anything that enhances an organisation's ability to meet the identified quality requirements. Both elements form part of an overall quality management strategy.

Quality improvement or self-evaluation/assessment is the process that is conducted within and for the setting. If it forms part of team development and is conducted in collaboration with all of the stakeholders, it can be a powerful and empowering process. Quality improvement is linked to effective practice and as such is encouraged by many government agencies. The Self-Evaluation Form (SEF) used in the Ofsted inspection has been developed to encourage and evidence this approach.

 Workplace activity

In your setting, find out how quality is managed as it relates to both individual practitioners and the setting as a whole. What are the internal quality management processes and those externally imposed?

Do you recognise any of the approaches to quality management outlined in this chapter (quality control, TQM and quality assurance) in your setting? Can you give examples of them? Which do you think are most effective in ensuring quality?

Is a combination of different approaches important in enhancing quality of provision? Why/why not?

Multi-disciplinary work

In this chapter, we have explored some of the tensions and contrasting perspectives relating to quality and effectiveness in working with children and young people. These can be compounded when working across different professional practices and cultures. No one can deny the aspirations of integrated working and when multi-agency working is successful it undoubtedly improves the quality of experience and services for the children, young people and families with whom we work. However, it is being increasingly recognised that there are many challenges to ensuring the quality of such work.

A particular challenge to multi-disciplinary work relates to the structures and leadership within the team. A disparity of structures (in management and strategic planning), pay and conditions within different organisations can lead to arbitrary judgements around this, including an imposed hierarchical structure of practitioners according to perceived power outside the team, rather than an agreed one within it, or alternatively leave the team with no structure at all. As we are aware (see Chapter 3), effective leadership is vital in order to drive a clear vision in any team and it is particularly important within multi-agency and integrated teams where typically we find more diverse and complex challenges.

Governments, locally and nationally, have introduced frameworks for monitoring and evaluating quality across multi-disciplinary and integrated teams. In fact the *Common Core of Skills and Knowledge* (DfES, 2005; CWDC, 2010) might be seen as defining indicators of quality and effectiveness in children and young people's services from the perspective of working practices.

From a more formalised inspectorate position, the Education and Inspections Act (2006) brought together inspections of schools, education provision and social care under a unified framework, reflecting the move towards integration of services at all levels. The following year, Ofsted (2007) published their first report reviewing inspections and Joint Area Reviews undertaken as part of this move towards integrated inspections. This report highlights the

> importance of councils and their partners having a high level of self-awareness and the ability to undertake accurate self-review, based on good use of data. This enables mapping and analysis of need to be undertaken at a strategic level, and effective multi-disciplinary assessment of need at a service level. (Ofsted, 2007: 8)

An outcomes-focused framework for inspection is also present in the Scottish guide (HM Inspectorate of Education, 2007) to evaluating services using quality indicators, which poses six 'high level' questions:

1   What key outcomes have we achieved?

2   How well do we meet the needs of our stakeholders?

3 How good is our delivery of services for children and young people?

4 How good is our management?

5 How good is our leadership?

6 What is our capacity for improvement? (HM Inspectorate of Education, 2007: 1)

Research reveals differing routes to quality improvement in relation to multi-disciplinary working, including the importance of joint training and sharing ideas and values (Tomlinson, 2003). In addition there is a need for key understandings of the different roles and responsibilities different sectors have (Frost, 2005) and the importance of learning together and establishing a strong learning community (Whalley et al., 2004).

Finally, Messenger (2010) tells us that the key to effective multi-agency working lies in the personal qualities necessary to engage with this type of work. She extols the virtues of individual and shared reflection and calls for it to be integrated into all professionals' training. She believes that shared reflection will build upon this to support skills, develop knowledge and impact on quality. She warns that without this

> we are in danger of once again attempting to base multi-agency working around roles and demarcated responsibilities, a practice we know does not support the needs of often the most vulnerable children and families in our society. (Messenger, 2010: 137)

Summary

During this chapter we have explored some of the current thoughts about quality, including concerns about the universal use of the term and its close association with effectiveness. We support the notion that standard approaches towards quality and quality improvement should be viewed with caution, and that external universal measures may not be able to reflect and capture the unique quality aspects of each of the settings or organisations that they are designed to measure. However, we also recognise the need for practical guidance and for all settings to meet at least minimal standards in order to ensure the safety and protection of the children and young people they serve. Internal systems of quality assurance, which are owned and led by the practitioners within their settings and involve all stakeholders where possible, can provide a useful and supportive measure of quality when they are guided by evidence-based research and external agencies.

Further reading

Aiming High – Kids Club Network and the PQASSO Approach: Available online at: http://www.ces-vol.org.uk/index.cfm?pg=42&gclid=CKOpwseO26gCFdFX4Qo djjsJ_w (accessed 09.05.11). A framework for developing quality services within third-sector organisations.

Children's Workforce Development Council (2011) 'Raising Quality and Consistency'. Available online at: https://sharestreet.cwdcouncil.org.uk/ CaseStudyDocument.aspx?ID=470 (accessed 20.07.11). A case study looking at raising quality and consistency.

Confederation of Heads of Young People's Services (CHYPS) (2009) *Demonstrating High Quality Youth Work*. Available online at: http://www.chyps.org.uk/assets/ Demonstrating High Quality Youth Work March 091.pdf (accessed 05.05.11). This statement aims to present a framework for judging 'quality' aligned to Ofsted inspection.

Department for Education (2011) *The National Strategies*. Available online at: http://webarchive.nationalarchives.gov.uk/20110202093118/http://national-strategies.standards.dcsf.gov.uk/ (accessed 17/07/11). This is an archive for many of the ideas, strategies and information developed by the National Strategies as they supported early years, primary and secondary schools with their quality improvement processes.

Haynes, P. (2003) *Managing Complexity in the Public Services*. Maidenhead: Open University Press. Chapter 4 looks at performance and quality issues within the public sector.

Siraj-Blatchford, I. and Wong, Y. (1999) 'Defining and evaluating "quality" early childhood education in an international context: Dilemmas and possibilities', *Early Years*, 20(1): 7–18. This article expands on the ideas of the objectivist and relativist approach to quality.

The National Quality Improvement Network. Available online at: http://webarchive. nationalarchives.gov.uk/20100202100434/dcsf.gov.uk/everychildmatters/strat-egy/improvingquality/guidance/nationalquality/nqin/ (accessed 09.05.11). This website gives access to the principles and practices of quality improvement that have been considered key within government in early years.

Zeithaml, V.A., Parasuraman, A. and Barry, L.L. (1990) *Delivering Quality Service: Balancing Customer Perceptions and Expectations*. Oxford: Free Press. A look at quality from a customer-oriented or client-centred focus, predominantly aimed at service industries.

References

Children's Workforce Development Council (CWDC) (2010) *Common Core of Skills and Knowledge for the Children's Workforce: At the Heart of What You Do*. Leeds: CWDC. Available online at: http://www.cwdcouncil.org.uk/common-core (accessed 21.07.11).

Covey, S. (1989) *The Seven Habits of Highly Effective People*. London: Simon & Schuster.

Dahlberg, G., Moss, P. and Pence, A. (1999) *Theoretical Perspectives: Modernity and Postmodernity, Power and Ethics*. London: Routledge.

Deming, W.E. (1982) *Out of the Crisis: Quality, Productivity and Competitive Position*. Cambridge: Cambridge University Press.

Department for Children, Schools and Families (DCSF) (2008) *Statutory Framework for the Early Years Foundation Stage*. Nottingham: DCSF.

Department for Education and Skills (2005) *Common Core of Skills and Knowledge for the Children's Workforce*. Nottingham: DfES. Available at: https://www.education.gov.uk/publications/standard/publicationDetail/Page1/DfES%201189%202005 (accessed 21.07.11).

Education and Inspections Act 2006. London: HMSO.

Ford, K., Hunter, R., Merton, B. and Waller, D. (2002) *Transforming Youth Work Management Programme: Course Reader*. Leicester: FPM.

Frost, N. (2005) *Professionalism, Partnership and Joined-up Thinking: A Research Review of Front Line Working with Children and Families*. Dartington: Research in Practice.

Harms, T., Clifford, R.M. and Cryer, D. (2005) *Early Childhood Environment Rating Scale*. London: Teachers College Press.

Hinman, L.M. (2003) *Ethics: A Pluralistic Approach to Moral Theory* (3rd edn). London: Thompson Learning.

HM Inspectorate of Education [Education Scotland] (2007) *A Guide to Evaluating Services for Children and Young People Using Quality Indicators*. Available online at: http://www.hmie.gov.uk/documents/publication/Evaluating%20Services.pdf.pdf (accessed 21.07.11).

Jones, C. (2010) 'Inspecting and evaluating the quality and standards of early years and childcare provision', in Pugh, G. and Duffy, B. (eds) *Contemporary Issues in Early Years* (5th edn). London: Sage.

Kashima, Y., Kashima, J., Chiu, C., Farsides, T., Gelfand, M., Hong, Y., Kim, U., Strack, F., Werth, L., Yuki, M. and Yzerbyt, V. (2005) 'Culture, essentialism and agency: Are individuals universally believed to be more real entities than groups?', *European Journal of Social Psychology*, 35: 147–69.

Messenger, W. (2010) 'Managing multi-agency working', in Reed, M. and Canning, N. (eds) *Reflective Practice in the Early Years*. London: Sage.

Mitchell, R., Agle, B. and Wood, D. (1997) 'Towards a theory of stakeholder identification and salience: Defining the principle of who and what really counts', *Academy of Management Review*, 22(4): 853–86.

Mooney, A., Cameron, C., Candappa, M., McQuail, S., Moss, P. and Petrie, P. (2003) *Early Years and Childcare International Evidence Project: Quality*. London: DfES.

Murgatroyd, S. and Morgan, C. (1994) *Total Quality Management in the Public Sector*. Buckingham: Open University Press.

Ofsted (2007) *Narrowing the Gap: The Inspection of Children's Services*. London: Ofsted. Available online at: http://www.ofsted.gov.uk/resources/Narrowing-gap-inspection-of-childrens-services

Ofsted (2009) *Raising Standards, Improving Lives*. Available online at: www.ofsted.gov.uk/node/1940.

Siraj-Blatchford, I. and Wong, Y. (1999) 'Defining and evaluating "quality" early childhood education in an international context: Dilemmas and possibilities', *Early Years*, 20(1): 7–18.

Sylva, K., Melhuish, E., Sammons, P., Siraj-Blatchford, I. and Taggart, B. (2004) *The Effective Provision of Pre-school Education (EPPE) Project: Final Report*. Nottingham: DfES.

Tomlinson, K. (2003) *Effective Interagency Working: A Review of the Literature and Examples of Practice*: LGA Research Report 40. Swindon: NFER.

West-Burnham, J. (1997) *Managing Quality in Schools*. London: Pitman.

Whalley, M., Whitaker, P., Fletcher, C., Thorpe, S., John, K. and Leisten, R. (2004) *NPQICL Induction Programme: Pen Green Research Development Training Base and Leadership Centre*. Nottingham: NCSL.

Section 2

Supporting Children and Young People's Development

5

Children and Young People's Physical Development

Jane Melvin and Erica Evans

Chapter Overview

In this chapter we examine growth and motor development and the associated concepts of normative and dynamic development. This chapter also considers the process of physical development and how this impacts on children and young people's overall development, for example the relationship between motor development and cognitive development and the relationship between physical development and body image.

By reading and engaging with the activities in this chapter, readers will:

- develop an awareness of key terms and concepts such as 'growth', 'maturation', and 'motor development';
- develop an understanding of the normative and dynamic process of physical development;
- consider a range of influences on physical development – the relationship between cognitive, physical and social development and how these domains of learning impact on one another;
- critically reflect on how considering physical development can impact on professional roles.

Physical development

Physical development relates to physical growth, maturation and the development of gross and fine motor skills. Human growth begins at conception and refers to the continuous increase in the size of a human being. Children pass through relatively predictable stages of physical development; however the rate of growth will vary from child to child. There are identifiable periods of rapid physical development throughout childhood, during which time children and young people will experience growth spurts.

In the 15–20 years following birth, individuals grow from the average size of a newborn (3.5 kg and 50 cm) to their full adult size. This growth is also associated with a change in proportions: from the newborn's relatively large head and small torso and limbs, to the relatively small head and long torso and limbs of the adult. Children experience four periods of physical growth; two periods of slow growth and two of rapid growth. The first period of rapid physical growth, from conception to the age of six months, gradually slows during the toddler and preschool periods. The second period of rapid growth is during puberty, and starts in the years of pre-adolescence. This then slows again as adolescence progresses until puberty is completed and adult growth is achieved.

Maturation refers to the child's physical development as pre-determined by their genetic code. However, physical development is more than maturation, as we saw in the Introduction (p. 5). How we 'turn out', including our physical makeup, is our 'phenotype' and is best understood as a complex interaction and interdependency of these factors rather than the simple dominance of one over the other. Children concurrently develop a range of abilities across physical, cognitive and social and emotional domains of learning and these interact with each other. As with other domains of learning, physical development must be considered in terms of the whole of the child or young person's 'ecosystem'. Family, friends, schools and communities, as well as the wider society, all have a part to play in supporting physical development.

〰 **Reflection point**

Thinking about the children and young people you work with, can you identify the range of influences on their physical development?

What impact does the quality of the environment of your setting have on physical development?

What evidence have you seen, from your professional practice, that development is holistic?

In considering the physical development of children and young people, we can think in terms of normative and dynamic development:

Normative development describes the typical capabilities that most children and young people of a given age within a specified cultural group, can and cannot be expected to do and learn. This includes physical development, but will also involve the development of cognitive and social and emotional skills.

Although such measures may be useful in supporting health professionals, parents and practitioners to identify specific additional needs, it is also prudent to be cautious about normative views of development. Each child is unique, with individual strengths, interests and needs. Babies, children and young people will develop at varying rates and it is important for practitioners to understand the differing needs of individuals in order to provide appropriate support to foster development. Valuing and celebrating difference enables practitioners to challenge ideas of 'normality'. Prioritising beliefs about 'normal' patterns of development may lead to practice which attempts to categorise and divide children and young people according to a hierarchy of values about what is considered to be 'normal'. This approach may prevent practitioners from fully appreciating the abilities and potential of individual children. A commitment to truly inclusive practice, which recognises the unique capabilities of all children and young people, can support an environment that enables each individual to reach their potential (Booth and Ainscow, 2011).

Dynamic development is about the sequence and physical changes that occur when growing from baby to child to adolescent to adult, taking into account not only age but also learning and experience. It involves an appreciation of the interaction of physical skills gained through practice and experience, and an interest in the mastery and improvement of learned skills.

A specific directional pattern can be seen in the physical development of a child and young person's body. It is important to understand this principle of directional growth and to have appropriate expectations of the children and young people we work with, in relation to their physical abilities. Physical development proceeds from:

- **Large- to small-muscle development**. This means that the large muscles in the neck, trunk, arms and legs develop before the small muscles in the fingers, hands and wrists, for example. Strong muscles in the shoulders and upper arms support the development of fine motor skills in the fingers. Young children need plenty of opportunities for big movement play, which lays the foundations for skills such as writing and drawing.

- **Head to toe or top to bottom**. This means that a child's muscles develop from head to toe and babies can hold up their heads or sit up, before they can walk.

- **Inside to outside or centre to outside**. A child's muscles develop centrally first and then towards the outside of the body. A child is able to hold up their head and sit up before they can walk as muscles around the trunk of the body develop earlier and are stronger than the muscles in the legs and feet.

- **General to specific growth**. Large-muscle movement begins with babies waving their arms and legs, and then develops to where a child can make more deliberate movements such as walking and drawing. Compare the dancing ability of a five-year-old in comparison to a fifteen-year-old street dancer, and you can see that muscle growth begins with more general abilities and becomes more defined, controlled and specific as children and young people get older.

Variation occurs naturally in the way that children develop their physical abilities. However, recognition of normative development and discontinuous changes in specific physical and mental abilities (such as walking and understanding language) in children's development has led to the concept of developmental milestones.

Milestones of development

Arnold Gesell (1880–1961), psychologist and paediatrician, was particularly interested in the impact of the environment on differences between an individual's physical growth and development, and was one of the first scientists to undertake studies of identical twins.

Gesell realised that identical twins were similar in many ways, including the rate at which they developed and perfected motor skills, so he conducted a study starting with 46-week-old twins who had not yet mastered the skill of climbing stairs. One twin was encouraged and trained to climb stairs, whilst the other was not exposed to stairs at all. Six weeks into the study, the first twin could climb stairs whilst the other could not. However, once exposed to the challenge of climbing stairs, within a short period time the second twin could climb as competently as the first. From this and many other studies, Gesell concluded that in relation to these motor skills, training might enable a child to perform a new skill earlier, but that untrained children would still catch up within a short period of time.

Gesell put forward the theory that motor development in children is maturational, that is, it is pre-programmed genetically, and motor skills will develop whether or not specific elements are taught or given emphasis. He argued that children develop the same types of skills at roughly the same age, regardless of environment or training, and proposed that it is our biological makeup that provides the momentum for change to occur. Whilst it is each child's unique genetic blueprint that will determine exactly when new growth or development will start to take place, it is the evolutionary blueprint of humans as a species that shapes the sequence and order. In children, growth generally tries to fulfil the potential that it is programmed to reach. If growth is slowed for any reason, for example malnutrition, the body will try to catch up when it is able to do so.

An example of this is 'sequential growth' where different areas of a child's body will grow at different times. These changes are usually orderly and occur in a pattern. For example, children must be able to stand before they can walk, even if they move from crawling to walking in a relatively short period of time. Patterns are evident in a number of other ways, such as rolling over before sitting up, sitting up before crawling and crawling before walking. Children from Romanian orphanages during the Ceaușescu regime in the 1980s who were prevented from walking because they were kept tethered in cots, were able to develop those skills and develop normally once their terrible living conditions were exposed and changed (Rutter and the ERA Study Team, 1998).

The term 'milestones of development' is attributed to Gesell and these milestones are still used worldwide today as a way of measuring the physical development of children. In the UK, the development of young children is monitored by Health Visitors and developmental milestones are recorded in the Child Health Record or 'red book'. Figure 5.1 shows some examples of the developmental milestones that are identified.

'Testing' young children against a set of developmental milestones can provide a snapshot perspective of an individual's capabilities. However, practitioners and parents who interact with children on a daily basis will be well aware of the value and importance of detailed observations which can provide a richer source of information to assess needs and abilities. When asked to perform a set task by a stranger, a young child may not be successful and this might be an indication of a delay. However, there may be other factors to consider. For example, a child may feel uncomfortable with an adult with whom they have not developed a strong and trusting bond. Similarly, a child may not understand the instructions, or may not be interested in carrying out the given task. There might also be cultural or language barriers which prevent a child from successfully completing an assessment task. In order to develop a secure and detailed understanding of a child's capabilities, practitioners must invest time; time to develop a relationship of trust, and time to gather reliable data, through careful and objective observation.

The concept of milestones of development is primarily used for young children, where changes and development can be seen occurring at a rapid pace, and where it is also more apparent when a child does not achieve a specified stage. A child is said to be 'developmentally delayed' when he or she is not progressing as expected in one or more area of development, and this delay may be temporary or permanent. Delay in all areas is referred to as 'global development delay'. Although we focus on physical development here, key milestones also relate to language development (see Figure 5.1) and we refer to this in Chapter 6.

Challenging the maturational perspective, a number of factors have been found to influence motor development. Examples include socioeconomic status, the mother's educational level, the existence of siblings, socio-cultural rearing practices (Venetsanou and Kambas, 2010) and social disadvantage (McPhillips and Jordan-Black, 2007). Younger siblings may have the opportunity to hone some motor skills earlier than older siblings because they are exposed to opportunities that the older ones did not have. For example, older children

Your child's developmental firsts

Babies want to explore the world around them. Your baby grows and learns faster in the first year than at any other time. There are many things that all babies and young children do, but not always at the same age or in the same order. Use these pages to note down when your child does things for the first time.

Finding out about moving...

Lifts head clear of ground,
aged:................

Rolls over,
aged:................

Sits with support,
aged:................

Sits alone,
aged:................

Crawls,
aged:................
and/or
Bottom shuffles,
aged:................

Stands holding on,
aged:................

Stands alone,
aged:................

Walks holding on,
aged:................

Walks alone,
aged:................

First outdoor walk,
aged:................

See *Birth to Five* for more information on children's development.

Finding out about words...

Smiles,
aged:................

Laughs,
aged:................

Babbles,
aged:................

Copies noises,
aged:................

Says "mama" – to anyone,
aged:................

Says recognisable word,
aged:................

Joins two recognisable words,
aged:................

Helps turn pages in a book,
aged:................

Speaks in sentences,
aged:................

See *Birth to Five* for more information on children's development.

Figure 5.1   Example of developmental milestones from the NHS Personal Child Health Record

kicking a football around the garden or swinging on a swing will expose the younger ones to those activities, who may then want to copy and join in. A culture where girls are not encouraged to do sports because of conventional roles or traditional dress restrictions might mean that girls do not have the opportunity to develop hand–eye co-ordination in the same way that girls from a different culture, who are encouraged to get involved in sport, do.

> ∿ Reflection point
>
> What differences do you notice in relation to the children and young people you work with in your setting? Are there differences between boys and girls? Have you noticed differences in relation to social class or culture?
>
> How do you differentiate activities and experiences in order to support the motor development of all the children and young people you work with?

Motor and physical development: Age related aspects

Early years

Gallahue and Ozmun (2005) have identified age-related phases of motor development. In the early years these are:

- **Reflexive Movement Phase**. From conception to the end of the first year of life, babies use reflexive movements to engage with their environment and other humans. Reflexive movements are involuntary reactions that the infant has to certain stimuli. For example, newborns exhibit reflexes such as rooting and sucking which enable them to feed.

- **Rudimentary Movement Phase**. The second stage of motor development occurs in early childhood, from birth until about the age of two. These are the first forms of voluntary movement, which can be observed alongside the reflexive movements in infancy. Rudimentary movements are used to gain control and manipulation. For example, babies begin to develop control over their heads and are able to reach for objects. Creeping and

crawling are important movements involving cross-lateral movement of the arms and legs which support hand–eye co-ordination
and horizontal and vertical eye-tracking. These movements lay
fundamental foundations for later learning.

Babies need plenty of 'tummy time' where they will learn how to
control their movements and strengthen their muscles. Research
undertaken by Goddard Blyth suggests that babies who do not have
sufficient experience in creeping and crawling may later demonstrate
problems with reading and writing (Goddard Blyth, 2009). Crawling
is a particularly important activity for babies as it helps to:

• develop muscle strength and co-ordination;

• co-ordinate both sides of the body;

• promote spatial awareness;

• support hand–eye co-ordination;

• integrate both the left and right side of the brain, thus promoting
  positive brain development.

Early development is reliant on sensory experiences. Infants and
young children develop their understanding of the world around
them through the use of their senses:

• touch (haptic perception);

• taste (gustatory perception);

• smell (olfactory perception);

• hearing (auditory perception);

• sight (visual perception), including depth perception.

Physical interaction with an environment which is rich in sensory
experiences will support positive development. Proprioception,
which is sometimes referred to as the sixth sense, is 'the internal
sense the body has of position and balance, movement and posture,
and which gives us an awareness of where our body is and what it is
doing' (Doherty and Hughes, 2009: 472). Along with proprioception,
the vestibular system supports children to develop spatial awareness

and motor co-ordination. The vestibular system is located in the inner ear and controls balance and movement. It is important for the acquisition of movement skills such as crawling. The vestibular system has great importance for hand–eye co-ordination, eye-tracking, and fine motor control. Hannaford (1995) suggests that when young children move they are stimulating this system, which then improves learning. Once again we can see the very close relationship between movement and cognitive development.

Childhood

In the **Fundamental Movement Phase**, between the ages of two and seven, children will actively experiment with movement skills and develop greater control over their bodies. These skills can be divided into three overarching types of movement:

- **Stability skills**, such as balancing, pushing, pulling and stretching. This type of movement helps to develop co-ordination and balance.

- **Locomotive skills**, such as running, climbing and jumping. This type of movement helps to develop large muscle and gross motor skills.

- **Manipulation skills**, such as throwing, catching and kicking. This type of movement helps to develop fine motor skills and hand–eye co-ordination.

Although some fundamental movement skills will occur through maturation, it is evident that the environment has a part to play in supporting children to acquire and perfect new movement skills. Gallahue and Ozmun (2005) argue that the environment can influence the development of fundamental movement skills and that children must be provided with sufficient encouragement to develop and master key skills. Additionally, children require the appropriate apparatus, encouragement and opportunities to practise skills.

This is followed by the **Specialised Movement Phase**. Between the ages of seven and eleven children master fundamental movement skills and begins to develop the ability to refine and combine movements to perform specific activities, such as team sports. Between the ages of eleven and thirteen children move into the application stage of the specialised movement phase and develop greater control and accuracy over combined movement skills. This is also a time when children begin to develop a sense of who they are and they begin to define themselves in terms of their interests (this is further explored in Chapter 7), and become more involved in activities of their choosing. For example, some children will seek opportunities for team-related sports activities, whilst others might prefer dance or individual athletic activities. Once again we recognise the influence that relationships and culture have on shaping children's experiences. Offering children a range of experiences enables them to make choices. This links to Bronfenbrenner's (1994) ecological model (see Introduction) which highlights the influence of cultural context on development. The lifelong utilisation stage is the final stage of the specialised movement phase and takes children from adolescence to adulthood. Experiences during the previous stage will influence movement capabilities and interests throughout life. For example, young people who engage in sports-related activity are more likely to continue to take part in recreational sports in adulthood.

The benefits of physical education and school sport have been researched and there is some agreement that opportunities for physical activity promote the development of motor competence, the development of positive social relationships, and increased academic performance (Bailey et al., 2009). Worryingly, with the emerging emphasis on literacy and numeracy in the primary curriculum, there has been a decline in the status of physical education. Indeed, there is some evidence to suggest that the marginalisation of physical education is a global problem (Hardman, 2008).

Adolescence

The adolescence period of development begins with puberty which can be defined as a series of physiological changes which make a human being capable of reproduction – nearly every organ and body function is impacted during this time. Although what happens during puberty is generally the same for each person, the timing can vary widely. Research has shown that puberty is linked to body weight and body mass index (Lee et al., 2007) and the increased rates of obesity in children means that puberty can start at a younger age, sometimes as young as nine years old.

The key challenge that children and young people face during puberty is adapting to the changes in their bodies. Co-ordination and physical skills have to be adjusted as weight, height and strength changes. Adolescents are sometimes described as clumsy and unco-ordinated, and this can be attributed to physical growth and a change in spatial awareness. For example, rapid height growth in a young man means that they have to get used to the new height and change in leg length, and may not be as adept at moving their body appropriately as they were previously. Young men's shoulder width also becomes broader, meaning that they have to learn to operate a body that has become longer and wider in what might seem to be a quite short period of time. These changes must also be integrated into their emerging self-image and identity, and this can cause uncertainty and conflict. As adolescents look more like adults, they can be expected to behave and perform like adults regardless of their physical ability, emotional, intellectual or social maturity.

As the purpose of puberty is to prepare the body for reproduction, young people are faced with a new or increased interest in sexual activity, relationships and image. Many adolescents will regularly masturbate and will start to experiment sexually. Any increase in sexual activity brings in new dynamics, such as possible conflict with parents/carers, competition amongst peer groups, homophobic bullying, pregnancy, and sexually transmitted diseases. Some of the professional challenges in dealing with these areas of risk are discussed further in Chapter 10.

Entering puberty much earlier or later than your peers can be problematic for young people. Studies (see e.g., Peskin, 1967; Simmons and Dale, 1987) have found that maturing early could be a real advantage for boys. However, this has been disputed in more recent research which found that boys who were more physically developed at twelve (compared with their less physically developed peers), manifested more externalised hostile feelings and internalised distress symptoms between thirteen and sixteen (Ge et al., 2001). There is consensus that early onset puberty can be difficult for girls because the physical changes taking place in their bodies are more obvious, and their friends and classmates do not experience the same emotions associated with the start of puberty. Children starting puberty early, in particular girls, may need substantial support to understand what is taking place, whilst those entering puberty late will need support in coping with situations that a more emotionally mature and physically stronger person would handle easily.

There is growing understanding about the importance of nutrition, in all age phases, on growth and physical development. Understanding about nutrition has vastly improved over the last one hundred years and as a result, more children are now receiving better nutrition. However, there has also been a growth in childhood obesity, which is now considered to be a worldwide epidemic (Wang and Lobstein, 2006). Whilst there is some evidence to demonstrate that obesity is hereditary, there is also an understanding that social and environmental factors can have an impact on weight gain. The acceptance that nutrition and lifestyle are important factors in positive physical development can be seen through various government initiatives over the past ten years. The Healthy Schools programme has been developed as a way of promoting healthy lifestyles within school. This initiative recognises that schools play an important part in working with families to promote healthy lifestyles.

It has also been argued that nutrition can be a significant issue for adolescents (Stang and Story, 2005) as adolescents' dramatic physical growth and development during puberty appreciably increases their nutritional requirements. This, combined with increased autonomy when making food choices and immature cognitive abilities, alongside social pressures, can place adolescents at nutritional risk (Stang and Story, 2005: 1).

Workplace activity

How is motor development supported and encouraged in your setting?

To what extent do these activities respond to the phase of motor development of the children and/or young people you work with?

Reflecting on this and in discussion with colleagues, how do you think this aspect of the setting could be improved?

Motor development and cognitive development

A growing body of research has contributed to our understanding of the relationship between motor development and cognitive development (Diamond, 2000). Studies which have examined conditions such as ADHD and dyslexia have provided evidence that motor and cognitive development are linked (Viholainen et al., 2002; Klimkeit et al., 2004). The development of mind and body are supported by one another. In early childhood, children require plentiful opportunities to experiment with movement play. This helps to lay the foundations for positive motor and cognitive development.

Brain development is influenced by both biological and environmental factors. Current research suggests that the brain is a flexible organ which is able to react to experiences throughout life. During infancy and early childhood it is particularly important to ensure that the brain is exposed to rich and stimulating interactions and experiences (Gerhardt, 2004).

At birth a human brain weighs about 450 grams and will grow to about 1,500 grams by adulthood. A stunning amount of brain development happens within the first three years of life, during which time the brain will achieve three-quarters of its fully developed size. Experiences in infancy and early childhood have a tremendous impact on the positive development of the brain. Within each brain there are about 100 billion brain cells, called neurons, which are present at birth. These neurons are the nerve cells which communicate messages around the brain. Neurons have axons, which send messages, and dendrites which receive messages. Dendrites appear like branches at the top of each neuron (see Figure 5.2). As the brain

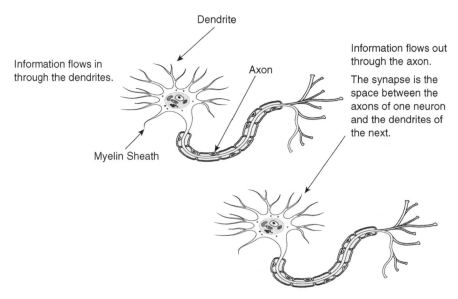

Figure 5.2   Features and functions of brain neurons

Source: Sprenger (2008)

develops, and in response to stimulation, more dendrites are formed. The more dendrites at a neuron's head or axons at the bottom of the neuron, the more connections with other neurons can be made. Signals travel easier and faster where neurons are covered in myelin. Connections used regularly become stronger and more complex while connections that are not used are considered non-essential, and the brain eventually prunes them away to increase efficiency, in a process known as synaptic pruning.

Recent research, which has explored the relationship between neuroscience and developmental psychology, has found that social experiences in early infancy have a direct impact on brain development (Gerhardt, 2004). A lack of stimulating interactions in early childhood directly influences the growth of dendrites, which then weakens the ability of the brain to form strong neurological connections. We understand that the more a developing brain is stimulated, the stronger and more powerful it becomes.

Case study

Lianne is a two and half year old girl. She was born at 28 weeks with hip problems. This necessitated operations and hip casts holding her legs in a 'froggy' position until she was 18 months old. When she was first brought home she developed sleeping problems which have continued until now. She has a loving relationship with both of her parents and she babbles conversationally but as yet has no words. She is interested in the people and things around her but frustrated by being unable to move and explore her environment independently. From the happy little girl of her first two years, she has become, according to her mother, a 'constant grizzler', needing a pacifier nearly all the time.

Lianne's mother and father compare her development to that of her eleven-month-old brother, who is also babbling in a conversational way. He is crawling and is beginning to pull himself to standing. She is immobile and has a favoured position of sitting. When she is placed on her stomach she cries and becomes frustrated until she is removed from the floor.

The speech and language clinic Lianne attends fortnightly have advised her parents to remove the pacifier at all times to support

(Continued)

(Continued)

her language development. Removing Lianne's pacifier is especially difficult in the evenings and at night as she grizzles and cries constantly, leaving little time for good quality family interactions.

Lianne sees a physiotherapist weekly who has suggested daily exercises which require three adults to perform and throughout which Lianne screams. She has also suggested that Lianne needs plenty of time on her tummy to strengthen muscles ready for crawling and that she should be discouraged from bottom shuffling. The exercises are difficult both in practical and emotional terms.

A Portage worker (a volunteer from their community) visits weekly and talks to the family about enjoyable activities to support Lianne's development. She has noticed that Lianne is 'shuffling about' on her bottom while sitting and suggests putting a tea tray under her bottom, thus reducing friction, so that Lianne can begin to move by bottom shuffling and actively to explore her environment, which may calm her and improve her sleeping. After discussing the speech and language clinic advice about the pacifier, she suggests that they follow her advice during the day but not in the evenings or at night.

How would you advise Lianne's parents given the different advice they have received? What actions would you suggest they take?

How would you ensure that mixed messages from different agencies are avoided in the future?

There are some general principles which might be useful to consider here. The importance of:

- **seeing the child as part of their family** (see the Introduction regarding Bronfenbrenner and the important influence of the microsystem on the developing child);

- **viewing development holistically** While separating development into categories such as physical and cognitive and social and emotional can be useful, it is also artificial and limited;

- **working in a multi-agency way** which will not only support us in understanding others' roles, for example physiotherapist and speech and language therapist, but allow us to appreciate the child as a whole and the competing demands that services inadvertently place on families.

Think about your setting and the children/young people you work with. Can you identify a child or young person whose physical development is impacting on them? Are there different professionals involved? How is this inter-professional working being co-ordinated to ensure consistency?

Summary

In this chapter we have explored physical and motor development and have highlighted the influence of early experiences. The inter-relationship between physical development and other areas of development has also been identified. We have considered the concept of maturation and the extent to which stages of development are pre-determined and linked to our unique genetic code. However, we have also appreciated other influences on development and how environmental factors and social interactions influence opportunities for positive motor development. An important consideration for all practitioners in the children and young people's workforce is the way in which they can support physical development.

Further reading

Coleman, J.C. (2011) *The Nature of Adolescence* (4th edn). Hove: Routledge. The latest edition of an important text on the nature of adolescence, which covers issues of physical development as well as other related areas.

Gallahue, D.L. and Ozmun, J.C. (1998) *Understanding Motor Development: Infants, Children, Adolescents, Adults* (6th edn). Boston, MA: McGraw-Hill. This book explores motor development throughout life and considers the relationship between motor development and other domains of learning.

Goddard Blythe, S., Consultant in Neuro-Developmental Education. Visit Sally Goddard Blythe's blog at: http://www.sallygoddardblythe.co.uk/index.php (accessed 20.05.11). This website provides up-to-date research and commentary on neuro-development. Goddard Blythe explores the relationship between brain development, motor development and learning difficulties, and how practitioners and parents can support positive development.

Play England: Making Spaces for Play: http://www.playengland.org.uk/ This organisation promotes opportunities for children to play and helps to raise awareness about the value and importance of play in the lives of young children.

References

Bailey R., Armour K., Kirk D., Jess M., Pickup I., Sandford R., et al. (2009) 'The educational benefits claimed for physical education and school sport: An academic review', *Research Papers in Education*, 24: 1–27.

Booth, T. and Ainscow, M. (2011) *Index for Inclusion: Developing Learning and Participation in Schools* (3rd edn). Bristol: Centre for Studies on Inclusive Education.

Bronfenbrenner, U. (1994) 'Ecological models of human development', in *International Encyclopaedia of Education 3* (2nd edn). Oxford: Elsevier.

Doherty, J. and Hughes, M. (2009) *Child Development: Theory and Practice 0–11.* Harlow: Pearson Education Ltd.

Diamond, A. (2000) 'Close interrelation of motor development and cognitive development and of the cerebellum and prefrontal cortex', *Child Development*, 71(1): 44–56.

Gallahue, D.L. and Ozmun, J.C. (2005) *Understanding Motor Development: Infants, Children, Adolescents, Adults* (6th edn). Boston, MA: McGraw-Hill.

Ge, X., Conger, R.D. and Elder, G.H. (2001) 'The relation between puberty and psychological distress in adolescent boys', *Journal of Research on Adolescence*, 11(1): 49–70.

Gerhardt, S. (2004) *Why Love Matters*. London: Routledge.

Goddard Blythe, S. (2009) *Attention, Balance and Coordination: The A.B.C. of Learning Success*. London: Wiley-Blackwell.

Hannaford, C. (1995) *Smart Moves: Why Learning Is Not All in Your Head*. Arlington, VA: Great Ocean Publishers.

Hardman, K. (2008) 'Physical education in schools: A global perspective', *Kinesiology*, 40: 1–28.

Klimkeit, E.I., Sheppard, D.M., Lee, P. and Bradshaw, J.L. (2004) 'Bimanual coordination deficits in attention deficit/hyperactivity disorder (ADHD)', *Journal of Clinical and Experimental Neuropsychology*, 26: 999–1010.

Lee, J.M., Appugliese, D., Kaciroti, N., Corwyn, R.F., Bradley, R.H. and Lumeng, J.C. (2007) 'Weight status in young girls and the onset of puberty', *Pediatrics*, 119(3): 624–30.

McPhillips, M. and Jordan-Black, J. (2007) 'The effect of social disadvantage on motor development in young children: A comparative study', *Journal of Child Psychology and Psychiatry*, 48(12): 1214–22.

Peskin, H. (1967) 'Pubertal onset and ego functioning', *Journal of Abnormal Psychology*, 72: 1–15.

Rutter, M. and the English and Romanian Adoptees (ERA) Study Team (1998) 'Developmental catch-up, and deficit, following adoption after severe global early privation', *Journal of Child Psychology and Psychiatry*, 39(4): 465–76.

Simmons, R. and Dale, B. (1987) *Moving into Adolescence: The Impact of Pubertal Change and School Context*. Hawthorn, NY: Aldine de Gruyter.

Sprenger, M. (2008) *The Developing Brain: Birth to Age Eight*. Thousand Oaks, CA: Corwin Press.

Stang, J. and Story, M. (eds) (2005) *Guidelines for Adolescent Nutrition Services*. Minneapolis, MN: Center for Leadership, Education and Training in Maternal and Child Nutrition, Division of Epidemiology and Community Health, School of Public Health, University of Minnesota.

Venetsanou, F. and Kambas, A. (2010) 'Environmental factors affecting preschoolers' motor development', *Early Childhood Education Journal*, 37: 319–27.

Viholainen, H., Ahonen, T., Cantell, M., Lyytinen, P. and Lyytinen, H. (2002) 'Development of early motor skills and language in children at risk of early familial dyslexia', *Developmental Medicine and Child Neurology*, 44: 761–69.

Wang, Y. and Lobstein, T. (2006) 'Worldwide trends in childhood overweight and obesity', *International Journal of Paediatric Obesity*, 1: 11–25.

6

Children and Young People's Cognitive Development

Nadia Edmond and Erica Evans

Chapter Overview

This chapter explores theories of learning as they apply to children and young people. It highlights some of the key ideas about child and adolescent learning and development and will support readers in thinking about the role of adults in supporting learning and development in their own contexts. Alongside this, it will provide an understanding of the commonalities in thinking about children and young people's learning across a range of contexts. This thinking is informed by the theories of behaviourism, constructivism and social constructivism, which will be outlined. Readers will also be encouraged to think critically about the way theories and perspectives on learning and cognitive development impact on their own professional role. In addition, the inter-relationship between all domains of learning in the development of the whole child/young person is considered.

By reading and engaging with the activities in this chapter, readers will:

- develop an understanding of some of the key theories of child and adolescent learning and development;
- consider the role of adults in supporting learning and development;
- critically reflect on the way theories and perspectives on learning and development impact professional roles;
- explore the relationship between cognitive, physical and social development and how these domains of learning impact on one another.

Thinking about learning

📁 Case study: Karen

'I am 29 years old and I have just passed my driving test! It was probably the toughest test I have ever done. The thing was, I had started to learn when I was eighteen with my dad and it was terrible, I was so scatty then I couldn't keep anything in my head and my dad just shouted at me and made me cry and in the end I couldn't get behind the driving wheel without feeling sick so I just gave up. But more recently I had to learn to drive for my job so I had to give it another go. My driving instructor, Sue, was great. In the beginning Sue took me out and showed me how to work the gears and clutch. It took me ages to get the hang of it, but with lots of positive encouragement from Sue I started to feel more confident. I also gave myself a goal. I wanted to pass the test before my 30th birthday and so I promised that I would buy myself a special treat if I did. That gave me lots of motivation to keep going. Before I got the hang of driving, I would watch my husband do a hill start and I would think how impossible it looked! But just having a go myself, getting used to the feel of it and having plenty of time to practise really helped. My husband was great. He was really patient and took me out to practise. He was very good at hiding his worry and would just give me gentle reminders if it looked like I was going to crash! I am so proud of myself that I have finally learned how to drive!'

In the case study above, Karen describes the process of learning a new skill as an adult. She highlights some of the strategies that supported her to successfully pass her driving test, for example, she found it helpful that her driving instructor gave her lots of positive encouragement. She also commented on the fact that she needed plenty of time to practise the skills herself. Karen also received help from her husband, an experienced driver, who was able to support her during her practice sessions.

〰️ Reflection point

Think of a recent learning event in your own life. An example could be when you learnt how to use a new piece of technology, or how you developed a new skill, such as knitting. Perhaps you used some

(Continued)

(Continued)

new equipment at the gym, or got to grips with a new concept you have been learning about whilst studying. What process did you go through to enable you to successfully develop your new knowledge or skill? What kind of support did you receive? Did you learn on your own, or with the support of other people? Were there any incentives to help you to be successful?

The process of learning is certainly a complex one! Some of the ideas to consider are:

- Learning can be inhibited by negative associations.

- Learning is supported when the learner is given positive encouragement.

- The motivation for learning can be increased when the learner is given rewards.

- Learning requires a great deal of practice and experimentation.

- We can learn from observing others.

- Learning happens when people work together and share ideas.

- Effective learning happens when the learner is supported by another more experienced or more able person.

- How individuals think and learn is different at different ages and changes over time.

- To understand the process of learning we need to understand not just the individual but their social context.

In this chapter we explore key ideas about learning and relate them to some of the theories which underpin our understanding of child and adolescent learning and development. We also explore the ways this can be related to both examining our own learning and that of the children and young people with whom we work.

Key ideas about learning 1: Learning results from the making of associations between our behaviours and the external world

The observations that learning is inhibited by negative associations, that learning is supported when the learner is given positive encouragement and that motivation for learning can be increased when the learner is given rewards, all relate to the key idea that learning results from the making of associations between our behaviours and the external world. In the example above we saw how Karen's learning was first inhibited and then supported by the link she made between her behaviour and the reactions of her teachers and the promise of a reward.

This key idea was the contribution of 'behaviourism' as a theoretical model of learning. As the name suggests, 'behaviourists' were concerned with the behavioural manifestations of learning. The behaviour can be involuntary (or reflex) and result from an association with a stimulus that precedes it. A famous example is that of Pavlov's dogs. They heard a bell just before they were given food and came to associate the ringing of a bell with the presentation of food, so much so that whenever they heard the bell ring they would begin to salivate (this is the phenomenon that came to be known as 'classical conditioning') (Pavlov, 1927).

Classical conditioning is significant in understanding learned emotional reactions which are so important in the learning process. In our example, Karen came to associate getting behind the wheel of a car with negative feelings of hurt and humiliation and to avoid those feelings, she removed herself from the learning situation that gave rise to them.

Other behaviourists, such as Skinner (1953), focused on the associations between voluntary behaviours (or 'operations') and their consequences. When an association is made between behaviour and a positive consequence then the behaviour is repeated and increases. Conversely, when the association is made between behaviour and a negative consequence the behaviour decreases. Increases in behaviour can be the result of an association between the behaviour and a pleasant or desired outcome (positive reinforcement) or an association between the behaviour and the removal or reduction of an unpleasant or unwanted outcome (negative reinforcement). In Skinner's experiment, this could be a pellet of food (positive reinforcer) or the stopping of a loud unpleasant noise (negative reinforcer), for example.

The negative consequences which lead to a decrease in the behaviour are known as 'punishers' and these too can be positive or negative. The terms 'positive' and 'negative' can be somewhat confusing in this context and it can be helpful to think of them as referring to either adding or taking something away – a positive reinforcer is something that is added and a negative reinforcer is something that is taken away but both result in an increase in the behaviour. In the kinds of experiments Skinner and other behaviourists have undertaken with animals, a positive punisher might be an electric shock whilst a negative punisher might be the removal of a food bowl.

Just as associations can be made, they can be lost. A pigeon which is rewarded by a food pellet every time it pecks a particular pad in its cage will make the association between pecking that pad and receiving food and will consequently peck at it more. If the pecking stops being rewarded, the pigeon will lose the association and will eventually peck at the pad no more than at any other part of its cage. The behaviour is then said to have been 'extinguished'.

The early behaviourists focused on the learning and behaviours of animals (Skinner worked primarily with rats and pigeons) and we can question how relevant behaviourist principles are to helping us understand the learning and behaviour of children and young people. The insight that behaviourism offers us is that patterns of behaviour are the result of the consequences of those behaviours for the individual. Even what we might consider 'problem' behaviours persist because they are being reinforced in some way.

When thinking about what may be reinforcing the behaviours in children and young people we need to extend the range of 'reinforcers' to include:

- **Attention** – for example, a child bangs blocks on the floor to get his mother's attention (if the behaviour results in attention being paid, even if it is to be told to stop, the behaviour will persist, especially if the child is not given attention when being 'good').

- **Escape or avoidance** – if the behaviour enables the child to escape or avoid a situation they find unpleasant, this too will reinforce the behaviour. So a child may misbehave to be kept in at play time if this will enable her to avoid being teased or bullied at play time.

- **Automatic reinforcement** – sometimes the behaviour is its own reinforcer, for example, when a child flaps or hums loudly in order to release some of the tension s/he is feeling or for sensory stimulation. Self-harming behaviours are often associated with temporary feelings of relief, of being in control and/or calm or feeling alive and/or able to function, all of which can be seen as reinforcing the behaviour.

Some reinforcers are obvious and common, and this informs what we consider to be 'rewards'. However, reinforcers can sometimes be much less obvious and individual, and require careful observation before they can be identified. The value of behaviourism is that it has provided very powerful ways of analysing behaviour so that it can be managed. Applied Behaviour Analysis provides a framework for analysing behaviour which, with reference to a particular behaviour, identifies its antecedents and its consequence.

Albert Bandura introduced the idea that learning from the antecedents and consequences of actions should be extended to observational learning of the antecedents and consequence of the behaviour of others (this view was called 'social learning theory'). In a very famous study (Bandura, 1965) he showed that preschool children who were shown a film of children playing aggressively with a blow up doll were more likely to replicate this type of play if the children in the film were rewarded rather than punished.

The following scenario can be analysed in terms of behaviourist principles. Try to identify examples of classical conditioning and operant conditioning, positive reinforcement, and think about what observational learning may be happening.

Case study: Claire

Claire is a teaching assistant and Chris the teacher in a Year 5 class. The children are working in groups on posters for a history project and Chris (teacher) is moving around the tables helping

(Continued)

(Continued)

and supervising. Chris is sitting at a table with a group of children and notices that Jerzy, who is normally very reticent, has contributed some drawing and written a few sentences for his group's poster. Chris is keen to encourage him: 'That's great Jerzy, you can read that bit out to the class when your group shows their poster'. As Chris moves on to another table, Claire notices that Jerzy has started to look very uncomfortable and is squirming in his seat. He has stopped working and is fiddling with his neighbour's pens and pencils. When she asks him to stop, he shoves her, knocking her off her chair. There is the inevitable disruption to the class and Chris reprimands Jerzy, telling him that she is very disappointed in him and he will have to spend the rest of the lesson sitting quietly at the back and she will talk to him at break time. To the rest of the class she says 'you have until break to finish your posters, if you haven't finished you will have to stay in over the break to finish it. After the break we will have our poster exhibition you've been looking forward to. We will be able to vote for the best poster and the winners will get these wonderful sticker books! So off you go – I want to see everybody working hard!' While the children are working, Claire shares her observations with Chris and they agree that Jerzy's behaviour may have been avoidance of presenting to the class and that inadvertently, Chris has reinforced his behaviour.

Can you identify examples of possible learned emotional response, positive reinforcement, negative reinforcement, positive punishment, negative punishment?

Workplace activity

Think about how the behaviour of children or young people is managed in your context. What might be examples of positive and negative reinforcers and positive or negative punishers? What do you see as the ethical issues associated with these different ways of managing behaviour?

Thinking back to 'classical conditioning', can the concept of 'learned emotional reactions' help you make sense of the behaviour of a child or young person you work with? What are the implications for you in your practice?

Key ideas about learning 2: We learn from practice and experimentation and our capacity to learn changes and develops through our life

The behaviourist perspective is useful when we want to understand behaviour but less useful when we want to understand how learners develop their understanding and knowledge. 'Cognition' is the term for our capacity to know, think and understand. An insight provided by cognitive theories is that we actively make sense or 'construct' our understanding of the world (so these perspectives are also called 'constructivist'). Whilst behaviourists are interested in how the external world impacts on an individual's behaviour, cognitive psychologists are interested in how we make internal representations of the external world. Cognitive psychologists are interested in our innate tendency to organise our thinking into 'cognitive structures'. These are ways of making sense of experience through organised systems of actions or thought that allow us to mentally represent or 'think about' our experiences.

A particularly influential cognitive theorist was Piaget (1896–1980), who was interested in the development of cognition from babyhood to adolescence. Piaget gave the name of 'schemas' to these cognitive structures and was interested in their development (Piaget, 1954). Very young infants, for example, can either look at or grasp an object when it comes into contact with their hand, and they can 'make sense' of the object either in terms of how it looks or how it feels. As they develop, infants integrate these 'schemas' into a more sophisticated schema of looking at, reaching for and grasping objects and making sense of the object both in terms of how it looks and how it feels.

Piaget suggested that schemas develop as the result of *adaptation* to our experiences of the world around us. This ensures a balance between our schemas and our experiences of the world (*equilibration*) and we aim for a state of equilibrium between the two. New experiences can lead to disequilibrium and we need to go through a process of adaptation (of our schemas) to return to equilibrium. New information can be incorporated within existing schemas (*assimilation*) or may require the development of new schema (*accommodation*). For example, a child may have developed a schema for 'dog' from her experience of her grandmother's bad-tempered, old Yorkshire Terrier (her schema constructs the concept of 'dog' in terms of characteristics such as small, yappy, unfriendly). When she encounters her friend's Pekinese (who is also small, yappy and unfriendly) she can *assimilate* this new information into her existing schema (altering it slightly to include both Yorkies and Pekes). Yet when she comes across her cousin's Great Dane (who is large, quiet and very friendly) she has to alter her 'dog' schema to accommodate this new information and will have a more developed and sophisticated schema for 'dog' as a result. The implication of this view is that the key element required to support cognitive development is varied and stimulating experiences which generate adaptation of schemas through *assimilation* or *accommodation*.

For Piaget, the development of schemas, and of cognition more generally, was also the result of 'maturation' (naturally occurring genetically programmed changes over time). This suggests that the development of cognition is not just the gradual and cumulative effect of adaptation, but also the progression through distinct stages in which ways of thinking are qualitatively different (Table 6.1).

Piaget's ideas have been very influential – his schema theory has been developed and extended in a number of ways – but it is important to recognise that they have been subject to criticism and that the idea of separate stages is flawed. The model can also lead to children's abilities being undervalued and it underestimates the key role of the child's cultural and social context.

It is also important to recognise that others have put forward alternative models of the key idea that we learn from practice and experimentation and that our capacity to learn will also change and develop through our life. For example, Bruner (1966), proposed three modes of representation: enactive representation (action-based); iconic representation (image-based); and symbolic representation (language-based). Rather than neatly delineated stages, the modes of representation are integrated and only loosely sequential. Some have argued (e.g. Knowles, 1970, 1990) for the concept of 'andragogy' (the processes involved in enabling and supporting the learning of adults) as separate and different from pedagogy (the processes involved in enabling and supporting the learning of children). Others (e.g. Kidd, 1978; Tennant, 1988/1996) have argued that it is not helpful to think of the learning of adults as fundamentally different from the learning of younger age groups.

Table 6.1 Piaget's stages of cognitive development

Stage	Age	Characteristics	Commentary
Sensory-motor	0–2	Begins to make use of imitation, memory and thought. Develops 'object permanence'. Moves from reflex actions to goal-directed activity.	'Sensory-motor' because the child's thinking involves seeing and touching, etc. The development of 'object permanence' (the understanding that objects have a separate permanent existence) is important in developing an ability to construct a mental representation.
Pre-operational	2–7	Gradually develops use of language and ability to think in symbolic form. Able to think operations through logically in one direction only (non-reversibility). Has difficulties seeing another person's point of view (egocentrism) and believes that inanimate objects are capable of actions and have lifelike qualities (animism).	This stage is called 'pre-operational' because the child has not yet mastered the ability to think separately from action through logical mental operations, but the development of the 'semiotic function' (the ability to use language and symbols to represent actions or objects mentally) is emerging. Between the ages of two and four, most children enlarge their vocabulary from 200 to 2,000 words.
Concrete operational	7–11	Understands laws of conservation and is able to classify and put things into a series. Understands reversibility and is able to focus on more than one aspect of objects.	Concrete operational because the child is able to solve logical problems through concrete interaction (e.g. hands on) with the problem. Understanding reversibility (being able to think backwards from the end of a process to the beginning) and conservation (recognising that volume or number is constant through changes in shape or arrangement) are key to more sophisticated thinking. At this stage, children become decentered and so are able to appreciate that others have different experiences of the world.
Formal operational	11–adult	Able to solve abstract problems in logical fashion. Becomes more scientific in thinking. Develops concerns about social issues and identity. They show naïve idealism.	Through formal operations children, young people and adults are able to mentally manipulate abstract and hypothetical ideas and concepts in their reasoning. Adolescents may be prone to 'adolescent egocentrism' – they may recognise that others have different experiences and perspectives but become focused on thinking about and analysing themselves and assume that others are also focused on them. They use their new and powerful capacity for abstract thought to create an ideal world which they then compare to the real world. Unfortunately the real world often falls short.

Source: adapted from Woolfolk et al. (2008: 40)

> ### Case study
>
> A teenager of divorced parents who lives with one parent suddenly decides that she would like to live with the other parent. At the same time she joins an organisation which supports animal rights and becomes sexually active. When urged to take care not to break the law and also to take precautions to avoid pregnancy, she replies 'I just don't see myself getting into trouble or getting pregnant, so I cannot see the point'.
>
> How would Piaget explain this?
>
> A teenager is likely to show naive idealism and construct an ideal world for themselves. They are then likely to decide that the real world does not meet the expectations or live up to their ideal world. So they will be looking for an alternative better world and may try out different political and/or religious organisations and make alternative choices. A different life with an alternative parent may therefore become very appealing. If they then see themselves as inhabiting a new and ideal world, they perceive that nothing bad is likely to happen to them and so they are more likely to take risks. At this stage of development they also show adolescent egocentrism and so assume that others will share their views on what is right in the world and focus on and agree with their views. If they perceive themselves as always right what could possible go wrong?

Key ideas about learning 3: Learning happens when you work with other people and share ideas. Effective learning happens when the learner is supported by another more experienced or more able person

If we think about Karen and the process she went through whilst learning to drive, we can see that an important element in her learning was the support she received from her driving instructor and husband. When we consider how children learn and develop, we must recognise the importance of the cultural context and the role that other people play in supporting and extending learning.

The social constructivist theory of learning is constructivist in that it focuses on how we make sense of the world. Yet (unlike Piaget), it sees learning as a social process embedded in a cultural context in which effective learning happens when the learner is supported by another more experienced or more able person. Social constructivist theories of learning originated in the 1920s and 1930s with Russian psychologists such as Vygotsky (1896–1934). His work was translated and became available in the West, and has subsequently been developed (e.g. Rogoff, 1990). From this theoretical perspective, children are viewed as social beings, immersed in their culture. Unlike constructivism, which predominantly views children as 'lone scientists' on a journey of learning through independent discovery, social constructivists argue that children learn through their social and cultural experiences and interactions, and that the role of other people in supporting that learning is vital.

The role of the adult, or more knowledgeable other, is not simply one of ensuring that an appropriate learning environment is created for children. Rather, it is through the promotion of quality interactions that effective learning is supported. Vygotsky (1993) believed that a greater level of understanding can be achieved when the learner is being supported by someone more knowledgeable. He accepted that there may be a limit to what a child can understand and achieve on their own, but argued that when working with an expert, a child may be able to extend their ability.

At any point in our learning we will encounter things which we already know, problems we can already solve and those issues which are completely beyond our current capability, even if they are explained to us and we have assistance. In between these two are those things we can learn and those problems we can solve if we have help. Vygotsky spoke about this as the zone of proximal development (ZPD), which he described as

> the distance between actual developmental level as determined by independent problem solving and the level of potential development as determined through problem solving under adult guidance or in collaboration with more capable peers. (Vygotsky, 1978: 86)

In other words, the zone of proximal development is the difference between what a child can do independently and what they are able to achieve with support. Vygotsky believed that the 'level of actual development' was the measure of what a child can successfully achieve without support. However, he argued that children have varying capabilities and that whilst children may display a certain level of development, this may not provide the full picture. For example, two children may be given a test where mathematical concepts are assessed and score equally. Both children may demonstrate some understanding of these concepts in their independent responses to the test questions, but when working through the problems with support, one may be able to demonstrate a much higher level of understanding and/or performance than the other. They therefore have different zones of proximal development.

This view of learning places an emphasis on the role of joint problem-solving. The learner is supported in extending their understanding by an adult or another child who has already acquired a higher level of understanding. This perspective suggests that learning is first a process of social interaction in which understanding is 'co-constructed' and then internalised. Children are not viewed as passive recipients of knowledge, as their active involvement is a vital ingredient in the learning process.

Theorists have explored the role of 'scaffolding' in supporting children's emerging abilities. The concept of 'scaffolding' describes the interactions of the adult in supporting the learner. Scaffolding requires more than simple demonstration. It is a complex process of joint problem-solving where the practitioner employs a wide range of strategies to support the child to work within their zone of proximal development. Research carried out by Wood, Bruner and Ross (1976) examined the nature of effective scaffolding. They found that scaffolding strategies used in asymmetrical relationships are complex and require the adult to be in tune with the needs of the individual, altering behaviour in response to their observed needs. Effective scaffolding can only occur when the practitioner has a clear understanding of the needs and abilities of the learner. It is through the use of effective observation and assessment that this knowledge is acquired.

The social constructivist view of learning places an emphasis on the role of language in the development of knowledge and understanding. Cognitive development is acquired through social interactions and it is language which supports quality interactions and provides the means for complex thought. Language enables children to engage in joint problem-solving and it is through this interaction that children extend and develop understanding. Vygotsky believed that language is a vital cognitive tool used by children to support their developing understanding of the world around them. For Vygotsky, language enables thought and supports cognitive development, whilst for Piaget, language follows cognitive development. In other words, for Piaget we need to have the concept before applying a linguistic label to it, whilst for Vygotsky it is having the linguistic label which enables us to develop the concept.

Young children (3–7 years old) can often be heard providing a commentary, or monologue, to accompany their actions, which Vygotsky saw as the use of language to support the planning and organisation of their actions and thoughts. As they become older (7–9 years old), this speech becomes internalised. Vygotsky believed that this *inner speech* becomes the mechanism used to support internal dialogue and understanding. For Vygotsky, the role of language is key to the process of thought and learning.

Talk, dialogue and conversations are central to all learning but are particularly important to informal learning contexts. In this environment, they are the way in which both learner and educator can engage in a process of learning from the context of the everyday, as well as being the way in which educators support learning.

Case study: Sue

Sue is a childminder. She currently cares for two children each day: Ahmed who is 23 months old and Emily who is three and a half years old.

Sue has observed that Emily enjoys playing with the wooden train set. This is always the first toy she wants to get out and play with every day. Emily's dad is a train driver. Sue recognises that Emily enjoys putting the train set together independently. Quite often she will put the set together in different ways and create different paths for the trains. Sometimes Sue understands that she needs to support Emily by helping her to fit the pieces together successfully. A few months ago Sue bought a new tunnel and bridge for the train set. Emily was thrilled with this and wanted to use it straight away. Sue let her explore and try out the new pieces. Emily was able to fit the tunnel to the existing set without support but found the bridge more difficult. Sue sensitively intervened to help her understand how the bridge works. Together they looked at the pictures which came with the bridge and then worked together to get it to fit with the rest of the set. Over time, with Sue's gentle support, Emily has learned how to fit all of the different bridges, crossings and junctions together. Ahmed has just started to take an interest in the train set. Sue has noticed that, on several occasions, Emily has helped Ahmed by turning pieces over so that they will fit together. Sue enjoys watching the children create different pathways with the train set. Sometimes she will support their play by providing a

(Continued)

(Continued)

commentary of what they are doing. For example, 'That train is going to go right over the bridge! Will it crash into the other train?' She will also provide challenges for the children. For example 'How can we connect this part of the track with the section over there?'

Which important aspects of learning do you think are illustrated by this case study?

- Learning is supported through collaboration.

- Learning happens through positive social interactions.

- Scaffolding is a way of extending understanding.

- Observation is a tool used to know when and how to employ scaffolding strategies.

- Learning is an active process.

- Language is used to support problem-solving and enhance learning.

Reflection point

Think about a recent event in your professional practice where you supported a child or young person to move their learning forward. What role did you have in supporting that learning? Were other children/young people involved? How? What potential can you see for extending peer support in your learning and teaching context?

Summary

In this chapter we have looked at some key theories of learning and development and considered how they relate to real learning situations involving children and young people, both through case studies and reflection on practice. We have provided a brief overview of these theories and readers may want to find out more about all or some of them (as well as some others!) by looking at the 'Further reading' below.

We have focused on theories which seek to explain children and young people's thinking and learning, but it is important to recognise that children and young people's development is holistic, that is, children and young people develop. Whilst we can focus on aspects of this development, this focus should not lead us to think of these different aspects as separate from each other. Cognitive development is one aspect of overall development, which also includes the aspects of physical and social and emotional development, and each is closely linked to the other. Our cognition develops from experience but what we experience and how we experience it is influenced by our physical and social and emotional state.

Further reading

Batsleer, J.R. (2008) *Informal Learning in Youth Work*. London: Sage. This book focuses on the context of informal learning in youth work and the author places particular emphasis on conversation as a key means of promoting informal learning and engaging effectively with young people.

Kearney, A.J. (2008) *Understanding Applied Behaviour Analysis*. London: Jessica Kingsley. A clear and user-friendly introduction to behaviour analysis and how it can be effectively applied to real-life behaviour management situations.

Lindon, J. (2010) *Understanding Child Development: Linking Theory and Practice* (2nd edn). London: Hodder Education. This book provides a clear, readable and user-friendly text which covers the main theoretical approaches and the key concepts that have shaped good practice in early years.

McLeod, S.A. (2007) *Simply Psychology:* http://www.simplypsychology.org/ Simply Psychology is a website designed specifically to help A level psychology course students and provides a good range of resources on learning theory.

Woolfolk, A., Hughes, M. and Walkup, V. (2008) *Psychology in Education*. Harlow: Pearson Longman. This book is focused very much on teachers and schools but provides a comprehensive overview of psychology applied to understanding learning and development.

References

Bandura, A. (1965) 'Influence of models' reinforcement contingencies on the acquisition of imitative responses', *Journal of Personality and Social Psychology*, 1: 589–95.

Bruner, J.S. (1966) *Toward a Theory of Instruction*. Cambridge, MA: Belknap Press.

Kidd, J.R. (1978) *How Adults Learn* (3rd edn). Englewood Cliffs, NJ: Prentice-Hall Regents.

Knowles, M.S. (1970) *The Modern Practice of Adult Education: Andragogy versus Pedagogy*. New York: Association Press.

Knowles, M.S. (1990) *The Adult Learner: A Neglected Species* (4th edn). Houston, TX: Gulf Publishing.

Pavlov, I.P. (1927) *Conditioned Reflexes: An Investigation of the Physiological Activity of the Cerebral Cortex*. Translated and edited by G.V. Anrep. London: Oxford University Press. Available at: http://psychclassics.yorku.ca/Pavlov/

Piaget, J. (1954) *The Construction of Reality in the Child*. Translated by M. Cook New York: Basic Books.

Rogoff, B. (1990) *Apprenticeship in Thinking: Cognitive Development in Social Context.* New York: Oxford University Press.

Skinner, B.F. (1953) *Science and Human Behaviour.* New York: Macmillan.

Tennant, M. (1988/1996) *Psychology and Adult Learning.* London: Routledge.

Vygotsky, L.S. (1978) *Mind and Society: The Development of Higher Psychological Processes.* Cambridge, MA: Harvard University Press.

Vygotsky, L.S. (1993) *The Collected Works of L.S. Vygotsky.* Translated by J. Knox and C. Stevens. New York: Plenum.

Wood, D., Bruner, J. and Ross, S. (1976) 'The role of tutoring in problem solving', *British Journal of Psychology,* 66: 181–91.

Woolfolk, A., Hughes, M. and Walkup, V. (2008) *Psychology in Education.* Harlow: Pearson Longman.

7

Children and Young People's Social and Emotional Development

Erica Evans and Mark Price

Chapter Overview

This chapter explores the nature and key aspects of social and emotional development in children and young people. It considers the importance of effective relationships and the impact of these on learning and development. Consideration is also given to the role of adults and other children and young people in supporting social and emotional development. In particular, issues of attachment, identity and resilience are explored.

By reading and engaging with the activities in this chapter, you will:

- develop your understanding of the nature of social and emotional development in children and young people;
- become familiar with concepts such as attachment, resilience, identity and self-esteem, and how these influence children's personal and social development;
- reflect on the role of the practitioner in promoting positive social and emotional development.

Children and young people as social beings

The way we live our lives and interact with each other in the early 21st century is very different from 100 years ago, 50 years ago or even ten years ago. However, the place of social relationships and communication with family, friends and those with whom we work, study or share an interest remains at the heart of our lives as social beings.

From the earliest moment of life, our lives are experienced through relationships and in social contexts. An unborn baby develops a relationship with its biological mother, whose own life experiences will influence the baby's development from the outset. The earliest experience of relationships that a child has, with their mother and/or others closely involved in the care process, is recognised as setting down a template for relationships to be developed in later life. This concept of 'attachment' will be explored in more depth later in this chapter.

As the child develops, the relationships they forge with other children (for example, siblings or others with whom the child has contact in early years and other social settings) enable them to develop a palette of social skills. These are then taken into school and developed within the context of a more formalised, educational curriculum and the social learning space school provides.

The child's identity and sense of self becomes more individualised as they step further into the world, separating from parents and primary carers. How they 'feel' about themselves becomes increasingly important as the child heads towards adolescence, and, as a teenager, the 'self' and associated issues of self concept and self-esteem come to the fore even more. Whilst commonly (but not necessarily), a time of stress, the young person negotiates an increasingly challenging and complex set of social relationships and associated demands and dilemmas through their adolescence. Risk taking too becomes part of the social learning process, as does responding to stress and the development of resilience in adversity, which we return to later in this chapter.

As practitioners, we have an important role as a contributory influence and point of reference for a child or young person's social and emotional development. For most practitioners working in play, learning and development contexts, issues of social and emotional learning are now firmly established as being of significant influence on broader issues of learning, welfare and well-being. This is evidenced by the inclusion of social and emotional development as a core element of the Early Years Foundation Stage (EYFS) (DfES, 2007). Similarly, SEAL (Social and Emotional Aspects of Learning) (DfES, 2005) has become embedded in the personal, social and health education school curriculum, whilst social interactions form the basis of free play and personal and social development and is at the heart of the youth work process.

As practitioners, we may also come into contact with other professionals – particularly those from social services, Child and Adolescent Mental Health Services (CAMHS) and counsellors and psychotherapists. An awareness of the multi-professional dimension of supporting children and young people's social and emotional development is important.

A social constructivist view (see Chapter 6) suggests that children are social beings whose development is supported by relationships and interactions with other children and adults. From this perspective, the context of those relationships – cultural traditions, social customs, parental behaviours and aspirations – may also be seen as a factor in development. Therefore, when exploring child development it is important to consider the cultural background of the child and family.

Attachment

Reflection point

What ideas come to mind when you think of the term 'attachment'? Is the concept of 'bonding' familiar to you, in relation to close personal relationships? Thinking back over your life, who are the significant people that you feel you have developed a strong bond with? How did this bond develop?

Attachment can be defined as the strong emotional bond which exists between individuals. Research examining attachment relationships has considered the process and motivation of attachment and the importance of early attachment relationships on personal, social and emotional development (Schaffer, 1996). Bowlby (1969, 1973, 1980) developed the concept of attachment as a biological process which can be universally adopted to explore the close personal relationship between a child and mother. Bowlby saw attachment as a maturational process which occurs in order to maintain survival. The biological motivation of the child is to remain close to the mother, both for reasons of safety and to have their basic needs met in order to survive. At the same time, the child has a natural instinct to explore and learn through first-hand experiences. Bowlby suggested that the process of attachment occurs as a way of balancing the need for proximity to the mother with the need for independent exploration in order to support development and understanding. Although the primary attachment figure is likely to be the mother, Bowlby argued that secondary attachment figures, such as fathers and grandparents (Bowlby, J. cited in Bowlby, R., 2007) are equally important.

Soon after birth, babies will begin to develop an awareness of the power of their voice and how actions such as crying or smiling will elicit certain responses from the adults close to them. As babies grow, the responsiveness of close adults will determine the development of secure attachments. Through very close, face-to-face interactions, babies soon learn that communication involves turn-taking. When adults respond to this and engage in preverbal exchanges with babies, it supports the development of strong attachment. From about seven or eight months, babies demonstrate anxiety when separated from their primary care giver, most commonly the mother, indicating that by this stage, a strong and enduring attachment relationship has been formed (Schaffer, 2004).

The **Strange Situation**, developed by Ainsworth et al. (1978), has been used as the main experimental tool to assess the quality of attachment between mother and child. Ainsworth devised the Strange Situation following studies carried out in America and Uganda where she observed similarities in the attachment behaviours of infants from both cultural groups. Using the Strange Situation as a universal measure of attachment, Ainsworth was able to study and compare the attachment-related behaviours of infants from diverse cultural backgrounds (Ainsworth, 1967; Ainsworth et al., 1978).

The Strange Situation involves a process of seven episodes whereby a child's reactions to different situations, such as the introduction of a stranger, separation from mother and reunion with mother, are measured. Ainsworth (Ainsworth et al., 1978) used this research scenario to establish the level of attachment, identifying three classifications of attachment: **secure, insecure/avoidant, and insecure/resistant.** According to Ainsworth, securely attached children are able to explore new surroundings independently without the need to continually seek reassurance from their mother. They are upset at separation from their mother but are easily comforted upon reunion. The insecure/avoidant child demonstrates little concern when left with a stranger and is reluctant to accept comfort from the mother upon her return. The insecure/resistant child displays a much greater level of anxiety in new surroundings, is reluctant to explore and is very upset when left by the mother. The child is also difficult to console on reunion with the mother. Securely attached children have the foundations in place to become confident, independent learners. This supports the view put forward by Bowlby, who argues that strong early attachments are necessary for long-term psychological well-being.

Based on the work of Mary Main and others (Main and Solomon, 1986, Main and Cassidy, 1988; Main and Hesse, 1990) **disorganised** attachment has been added as a fourth classification. Children with disorganised attachment may display a contradictory or chaotic combination of avoidant and resistant behaviours, appearing unable to adopt a coherent coping strategy, often as a result of abuse.

More recently, the disciplines of neuroscience and developmental psychology combined to analyse the impact of attachment on early brain development (Gerhardt, 2004; Hardy 2007; Kemph and Voeller 2007). What has emerged from this body of research is an understanding that brain development is directly influenced by the quality of early interactions between babies and adults. As we saw in Chapter 5, babies are born with all of their neurons but require a wealth of positive experiences and interactions with carers in order to connect the neurons and enable them to use all areas of the brain effectively. There are now clear indications that attachment is a central aspect of development and that 'one's early attachment experiences serve not only as templates for a person's holistic development, but are also the hub around which a person's life revolves' (Ebbeck and Yim, 2009: 900).

Strong attachment relationships between children and parents are clearly important. However, very young babies and children can also be cared for in early years childcare settings and this certainly has implications for practitioners. Concern has been raised about the impact of childcare on the development of secure attachments (Goldberg, 2000; Belsky, 2001; Bowlby 2007). There has been some agreement that the *quality* of the childcare must be considered and that high-quality childcare can foster and support positive social and emotional development (NICHD, 1996; Dettling et al., 2000).

As practitioners and policy-makers have begun to develop their understanding of attachment theory, this has led to the promotion of identified 'key persons' in early years childcare settings. This approach is advocated by the EYFS in the UK (DfES, 2007) and in related strategies in Australia (DECS, 2001) and in the USA (HighScope, 2010). Such frameworks promote the development of strong attachments with one primary care giver (the key person) which will support positive social and emotional development.

The EYFS defines the key person as the practitioner who 'has special responsibilities for working with a small number of children, giving them the reassurance to feel safe and cared for and building relationships with their parents' (DfES, 2007: 15). The framework suggests that the key person approach enables children to develop secure attachment relationships, which then impact positively on personal, social and emotional development.

> ### 🗀 Case study: Sandra
>
> Sandra is an early years practitioner working in a preschool setting with children aged two to five. New children to the setting are allocated a special 'key person' practitioner who is the first point of contact for the family. Each key person in the setting is responsible for five children. Key person responsibilities include: settling the child and family into the setting, ensuring regular observations and assessments are carried out for each child, keeping records for each child up to date, liaising with parents and carers, and developing and maintaining strong relationships with their key children.
>
> Over the last three years the practitioners have met to discuss the success of the key person approach and how it might be improved. Sandra raised an important point at a recent team meeting which has now instigated a change in the way that the key person is allocated.

Sandra had noticed that children sometimes seem to 'bond' more naturally with practitioners who have not been allocated as their key person. She suggested that the setting use the settling in period to observe children before the key person is allocated. The allocation could then be informed by the child's choice of which practitioner they feel most comfortable with and naturally migrate towards. The preschool is now trialling this approach.

Thinking about a setting you either work in or have contact with, how are supportive relationships between children and practitioners promoted in this setting? How appropriate is a 'key person' approach?

There has been interest recently in attachment theory and how it might explain relationships and behaviours throughout life. There is some evidence to suggest that insecure attachments in infancy may impact on an individual's ability to form successful relationships in adolescence and adulthood (Hardy, 2007; Kemph and Voeller, 2007). Reactive Attachment Disorder (RAD) has been used to describe conditions where secure attachments have not successfully formed in infancy. RAD is diagnosed when an individual experiences 'a pattern of disturbed and developmentally inappropriate social relationships prior to age five' (Hardy, 2007: 30). Young people who are diagnosed with RAD commonly demonstrate an inability to form successful relationships with peers and adults, suggesting that established patterns of behaviour in early childhood lay the foundations for life.

The experiences of children in orphanages in Romania have been well documented and provide some evidence of the impact of social deprivation and poorly developed attachment in infancy (Rutter et al., 1998, 1999). Evidence from this research suggests that children who experience prolonged episodes of social deprivation and neglect are more likely to display characteristics of disturbed attachment. However, Rutter and his colleagues found that Romanian orphans who were adopted prior to the age of two were often able to catch up. The research findings suggest that some children appear to be more resilient, and upon receiving treatment and being placed within a supportive adoptive family, were able to display normal levels of cognitive and social development by the age of six.

As practitioners working with children and young people, it is important to recognise the influence that early attachment relationships have on cognitive and affective development. Supporting parents and carers to foster strong, enduring bonds with their children is a key part of promoting positive social and emotional development. Secondary attachments with key people also help to lay the foundations for emotionally confident children and young people. For social workers and those in the care system for children, young people and their families, issues of attachment underpin much of everyday practice but are also of relevance to everyone working with children and young people.

Stop here !!

Self and identity

The phrases 'self', 'self concept' and 'self-esteem' are often used to refer to how children and young people create a view of themselves as developing individuals. This sense of self may be developed both through internalised reflection and though interaction with others in socially and culturally mediated contexts.

The American sociologist James Cooley developed the concept of 'the looking-glass self', an elaboration of earlier thinking by the psychologist and philosopher William James. James' work encompassed much of what frames current thinking about self and identity – the place of emotions, free will and personal truth, etc. Cooley's 'looking-glass self' (1902) embodied key concepts which are relevant here: that we recognise that others perceive us as individuals, that we imagine how we are perceived by others and that this recognition and imagination produces a response (e.g. pride, shame, etc.) in us. Thus the notion of 'self concept' is socially constructed.

Jung (1978) differentiated between the everyday self or 'ego' and the Self (with a capital S), which referred to the totality of an individual's conscious and unconscious psyche. Jung considered that a major driving force throughout an individual's life is the journey towards individuation, or what Maslow (1954) later referred to as 'self-actualisation' – the process of reaching our potential, becoming fulfilled and integrated as individuals.

Whilst being fulfilled and reaching our potential may be seen as a developmental goal, it is also important to acknowledge that we may not always feel good about ourselves along the way. We might feel we have a poor 'self concept' (i.e. we see ourselves in negative terms with respect to our abilities or attributes) or that we have low 'self-esteem' (i.e. we see ourselves as being of low worth or value). These issues are clearly important in considering children and young people's overall learning and development.

Issues of self-esteem can be very significant in terms of the impact on an individual's learning and behaviour. Such issues can be problematic if the individual's view of themselves and their self-worth then becomes part of a 'life script' or 'self-fulfilling prophecy' (e.g. 'I'm never going to learn to swim – you might as well give up on me now').

Case study: Jemima

Jemima is ten years old and is in Year 6, her final year at primary school. Her mum is concerned that Jemima has always seemed to have had friendship and peer group problems, and that at times she appears to be 'excluded' from the group of girls she's part of. Jemima works hard at school and always tries her best – in her work, with her friends and at home – but is often anxious and feels that her best isn't quite 'good enough', especially when it comes to fitting in with her friends. Her anxiety manifests itself in her plucking her eye lashes out. Jemima then feels that she looks ugly, which in turn compounds her view that she's not good enough.

How might you intervene in this situation to help Jemima develop a more positive self-image and avoid a negative 'life script'?

Smith (2009) considers four models which link selfhood with identity:

- **The self as a bounded container**: we carry our individual self within us.

- **Looking to the whole – people in community**: we can only really understand ourselves in relation to the wider community, family and cultural networks we belong to.

- **Interaction – the dialogical self**: we continually create and re-create ourselves and our identities through conversations, dialogues and interactions with others.

- **The postmodern self**: our multiple selves and identities are influenced and determined by the discourse and narratives open to us.

A key issue here, particularly when thinking about the social and emotional development of children and young people, is how much of one's sense of self and developing identity might be experienced and defined by the individual (the issue of self-identification and 'agency' – being your own person), and how much by the wider social network, including the 'media' in its widest context (being defined by others).

Erikson (1968) identified eight stages of psychosocial development, with each stage representing a point of challenge to be encountered, the resolution of which would impact on psychosocial development (Table 7.1).

Table 7.1 Erikson's eight stages of psychosocial development

Stage	Challenge
Baby 0–12/18months	If cared for with dependable affection, the child's developing view of the world will be one based on trust. If the care provided is inconsistent or abusive, the child will experience and regard the world as unreliable and dangerous
Toddler 18 months–3 years	If the care provided encourages self sufficiency this will lead to autonomy in the child. However, if carers have unreasonable expectations or the child is ridiculed at early stages of developing autonomy, the child then may experience doubt or anticipate failure
Preschool 3–6 years	In the preschool years the challenge is to develop initiative. Overly critical carers and blaming for mistakes may burden them with a sense of guilt
Childhood 6–12 years	Here the challenge is for the child to find what they are 'good at' and develop competence. If not allowed to discover own talents in their own time, children will develop low self-esteem, and low motivation
Adolescence 12–18 years	The challenge for the adolescent is to develop a sense of their own identity. Time and space is needed to explore their own sense of self and not to become overwhelmed with others' expectations
Young adulthood 19–40 years	For young adults the challenge is to make long-term commitments to others. If unable to experience intimacy, a sense of isolation and regard for relationships as threatening or painful may result
Middle adulthood 40–65 years	The challenge in middle age is to be productive and recognise success and achievement. Failure to do so may result in a growing sense of dissatisfaction and stagnation
Late adulthood 65 years onwards	At this stage, the challenge is to look back on your life with the wisdom which comes from a sense of what has been achieved and learned. Despair and bitterness may follow from a sense of futility and unachieved goals

Adapted from Erikson, E. (1968) *Identity: Youth and Crisis*. New York: W. W. Norton & Co

Erikson argued that each of these processes occurs throughout the lifetime in one form or another, and emphasised the stages as periods when the conflicts become most prominent.

In very early childhood, babies and toddlers begin to develop a concept of themselves as independent individuals. Lewis and Brooks-Gunn (1979) worked with mothers and their infants to gather evidence about the age at which babies begin to recognise their own faces in a mirror. Babies between the ages of nine and 24 months had a red spot placed on their noses and were put in front of a mirror. Younger babies did not react to the red sport but by the age of 18 to 24 months the majority of the infants were reaching for their own noses to remove the red spot, thus demonstrating that they had developed a concept of self.

As young children grow, they begin to ascribe characteristics to themselves, developing a sense of their own identify. Initially, self-awareness is primarily focused on physical characteristics, such as hair colour or external behaviours. Children will talk about what they look like or what they like to do – 'I have curly hair', 'I like to play with Lego'. As they progress through later childhood, self concept becomes more complex; children continue to identify themselves through associated activities and interests, but are also able to identify subtle personality attributes and the qualities which make them unique.

James Marcia (1966, 1980) refined Erikson's stage of 'identity crisis' encountered during adolescence by proposing four stages of identify formation:

- **Identity diffusion** – here, the child has yet to explore their own identity *per se*, but rather is defined through their activity or interests.

- **Identity foreclosure** – here, the young adolescent has not actively explored their identity on their own terms, but rather has accepted or is conforming to the identity given to them by others (e.g. family, school, culture, etc.).

- **Identity moratorium** – here, the young person is actively exploring their own identity, their choices and who they are for themselves, on their terms. However, they have yet to make a commitment to these identities, which may be fluid.

- **Identity achievement** – here, the young adult has made some commitment to an identity for themselves; this may reflect familial and cultural expectations or some of these may have been rejected.

⌇ Reflection point

Think back to your own adolescence. How much did you experiment with your identity? Did you change your name – for example, from Shereen to Shez or Mark to Marc? Perhaps you dyed your hair or got your first piercing or tattoo? Maybe you did this to be part of a gang or youth culture? How much of this experimentation stayed with you into adulthood as part of your identity today?

When working with children and young people who are wrestling with such issues as 'what defines me' and 'how I feel about myself', it is important to acknowledge that every one of us has a unique self-defining experience which impacts on our learning and development, our relationships and our behaviour.

Feelings and emotions

From very early childhood, babies are able to demonstrate emotional responses such as contentment or distress. Emotion is displayed through facial expression and there is some agreement that very young babies are able to use a range of facial movements to communicate feelings such as anger, sadness and surprise (Lewis et al., 1990; Schaffer, 2004).

Although the ability to feel emotion and use facial expression to display emotion may be innate, there is no doubt that emotional development is influenced by social and cultural factors. Children learn about the complexity of emotions through interactions with peers and adults. Close personal relationships help children to understand their own emotions and the emotions and feelings of others. Emotions can be confusing for young children and they need support in labelling and understanding them. Through socialisation, children begin to understand how to control emotions and the appropriate reactions to these feelings. Children begin to develop emotional competence – the ability to deal with their own emotions and accept and understand the emotions of others (Schaffer, 2004).

Supporting children to manage and understand feelings is deeply rooted in family customs, practices and beliefs. There is strong evidence to suggest that cultural differences exist in the acceptance of expression of emotions. Various studies have explored cross-cultural differences in relation to emotional development (Chagnon, 1968; LeVine et al., 1994). Findings suggest that emotional socialisation occurs within the cultural context and children therefore learn about the socially acceptable expression of emotion through interactions with close family members, peers and adults within their community. Jean Briggs (1970, cited in Schaffer, 2004) is an anthropologist who has carried out close observations of the Utku Eskimo community. Within this culture it is unacceptable to display any feelings of anger and Utku children are socialised to suppress emotions of anger. Consequently, displays of aggression are rarely observed. It is evident that humans experience wide-ranging emotions, but how these feelings are managed and expressed is directly influenced by cultural context.

An understanding of different attitudes towards emotional expression has relevance for practitioners who work with children from a wide range of cultural backgrounds. Western 'norms' may not easily blend with diverse cultural experiences, and therefore practitioners have a responsibility to develop an understanding of the unique cultural context within which children are raised.

〰 Reflection point

Think about your own childhood. Was the demonstration of emotion acceptable within your family? How did your parents react to your own displays of anger, sadness, fear or happiness? Were feelings and emotions discussed within your family? How has this influenced you as an adult? Do you find it easy to talk about emotions and feelings?

Talking to children about the feelings that they express will help them to develop an understanding of emotions. Children begin to talk about their own feelings around the age of two, and the ability to use more sophisticated language to describe feelings develops throughout early childhood. By the age of three children are able to comment on the feelings of others, recognising and understanding facial expressions and how these relate to emotions. Developing the language of emotion is an important part of social and emotional development. It allows children to express their inner feelings and thoughts, enabling them to develop an awareness of the feelings of others, which supports the development of positive interpersonal relationships.

The capacity to feel empathy for other human beings is a crucial aspect of social and emotional development. Empathy can be defined as the ability to respond to the emotions and feelings of others. As with the development of other emotions, empathy is partly an innate response which exists in all humans, but is equally reliant on effective cognitive development and socialisation. Hoffman (1993) suggests that all human beings are capable of feeling empathy as it has a neurological basis. However, he argues that this innate ability is fostered through external, social experiences. Whilst cognitive development theorists such as Piaget (1965) suggest that children are egocentric beings, incapable of appreciating the views of others until later childhood (age 7–11), more recent research has found that much younger children, within the second year of life, are able to demonstrate feelings of empathy (Zahn-Waxler et al., 1992).

Barnett (1987) argues that the development of empathy in young children is fostered in an environment where the child's emotional needs are met but where excessive self-concern is discouraged. This enables children to develop an awareness of the emotional state of others. However, research evidence has also suggested that distressing childhood experiences can actually lead to higher levels of empathy in adulthood (Barnett and McCoy, 1989). Research continues to contribute towards our understanding of empathy and why some people appear to have highly developed empathetic feelings whilst others demonstrate little concern for the feelings of others. Baron-Cohen (2011) argues that there is a spectrum of empathetic ability – some people are able to demonstrate high levels of empathy whilst others have low levels of empathy. He believes that the 'empathy circuit' lies within the brain and that whilst social experiences may influence the development of empathy, there are also genetic pre-dispositions. Further to this, Wilkinson (2004) proposes that neural pathways can be reinforced and that the brain can essentially be 're-wired' (particularly during adolescence) as a direct result of emotional and relational contact between individuals, supporting 'the emotional scaffolding necessary for the emergence of reflective function' (2004: 83).

Resilience

When we use the word 'resilient' or 'resilience' in everyday language, we usually refer to the ability to withstand stress or 'bounce back' following significant set-backs or trauma. In terms of working with children and young people, we focus on supporting resilience as a quality or attribute to be acquired and fostered as they play, learn and develop. Such a disposition or set of resources or life skills can be seen to be beneficial, not only to the learning and developmental process through childhood and adolescence, but also in managing the inevitable change, stress and trauma those children and young people may experience in their later lives. Newman and Blackburn (2004: 1) comment that 'resilient children are better equipped to resist stress and adversity, cope with change and uncertainty, and to recover faster and more completely from traumatic events or episodes'.

The nature of the stress and uncertainty, trauma and change is clearly important here. For example, we might acknowledge differences between what might be regarded as 'everyday' stresses and uncertainty (the challenges at school and among friendship groups, for example) and those of a more uncommon or unreasonable nature (e.g. being bullied or abused). Similarly, we can distinguish between stresses of an *acute* nature – a single event or episode (moving home, for example) – and chronic or ongoing stresses and challenges (e.g. being a carer for a parent or sibling).

In observing children at risk, Masten et al. (1990) identified different examples of resilience:

- children who do not succumb to adversities, despite their high-risk status, for example babies of low birth-weight;

- children who develop coping strategies in situations of chronic stress, for example the children of drug-using or alcoholic parents;

- children who have suffered extreme trauma, for example through disasters, sudden loss of a close relative, or abuse, and who have recovered and prospered.

Hart et al. (2007) differentiate between **popular** resilience – an everyday ability/capacity to overcome difficulties – and what they refer to as **real** resilience – where the child or young person has major vulnerabilities and few assets and resources, but experiences better outcomes than might be expected. They also acknowledge the place of **inoculated** resilience – where vulnerabilities are seen as resources; through exposure, a child or young person develops the capacity to turn adversity into success.

Case study

Ed is fifteen. He is diabetic and since the age of nine he has had to inject himself with insulin every day. Most of the time, Ed manages this and accepts that it is just part of who he is, yet at times he feels angry and resentful. Ed's mum worries about him, particularly now that Ed has started spending a lot of time at the local park with friends, and going to parties where certainly alcohol and possibly even drugs will be taken. Ed is actually very sensible about this, but sometimes he wishes he could really 'go for it' like some of his friends. Ed's big passion is basketball and he sees this as his way of getting the best out of his body. His coach recognises this and has become an informal mentor for Ed, keeping an eye on his mood swings and talking in a matter-of-fact way about Ed's diabetes. Like most teenagers, Ed struggles with balancing friendships, school and home life. He has realised, though, that in a strange kind of way, his diabetes and his basketball are what make him who his is.

What do you think are the key factors contributing to Ed's resilience?

For us as practitioners, what are the qualities, skills, attributes, relationships and other environmental factors which are important in building resilience? In particular, what can we do to support and foster resilience?

In their model of Resilient Therapy, Hart et al. (2007) suggest five key factors:

- **Basics** – core environmental conditions;

- **Belonging** – contexts, relationships and activities;

- **Learning** – factors relating to organisation, engagement and achievement at school and in other learning contexts;

- **Coping** – strategies to withstand stress and trauma;

- **Core self** – issues of self-awareness, emotional competency, agency and social skills.

In working to foster and support the development of these, Hart et al. (2007) suggest there are four **noble truths** which underpin our practice: **accepting** the child and young person for who they are; **conserving**, holding and containing the boundaries and focus of professional relationship; providing **commitment** to the child or young person in working with them and their family; and **enlisting** the support of others (family, professionals and others in the child or young person's world).

 Workplace activity

With colleagues in your setting, identify young people or children you work with who have had to withstand adversity or cope with significant stress. How did they cope? How effectively were they able to 'bounce back'? What contributed to this? Were there earlier adversity or stresses that helped prepare them and develop their resilience? What could you collectively do to foster resilience? How might you enlist the collaboration of other professionals and/or family members?

Mental health

For some children or young people, their level of anxiety, grief or feeling troubled is such that they need more specialist help than an 'everyday' practitioner can provide. In such cases, the child might be referred (or refer themselves if they are old enough) to a counsellor or Child and Adolescent Mental Health Service (CAMHS) professional. CAMHS professionals include those working with predominantly 'talking therapies' (e.g. Cognitive Behavioural Therapy) or more active, creative or play therapies. In some cases, where medication is also considered to benefit the child or young person, the CAMHS practitioner will be a child psychiatrist. These specialist practitioners work specifically to support mental health and emotional well-being (we return to this issue in Chapter 10).

Summary

This chapter has explored some of the key ideas in relation to personal, social and emotional development. As with other areas of development, the importance of key relationships in childhood has been considered. We have also considered some of the research which has contributed to our understanding of emotional development. It is evident that the formation of strong bonds between babies and their primary carers will lay the foundations for positive social and emotional development. Throughout childhood and adolescence, children will continue to learn about feelings and emotions through close personal relationships with peers and adults. The ability to draw upon support from within family, social groups and communities, together with a positive and accurate sense of self and agency or self-efficacy is central to the development of identity formation and resilience building. It is clear that practitioners play a key role in promoting social and emotional development, through modelling effective interactions and supporting children to form positive relationships, and engaging in activities and opportunities which challenge, stretch and develop self-worth and self-esteem.

Further reading

Bomber, L.M. (2007) *Inside I'm Hurting: Practical Strategies for Supporting Children with Attachment Difficulties in Schools*. London: Worth. This book provides a clear introduction to working with attachment issues.

Coleman, J.C. (2011) *The Nature of Adolescence* (4th edn). Hove: Routledge. The sections on self, identity, stress and risk are especially relevant here.

Gerhardt, S. (2004) *Why Love Matters*. London: Routledge. This book explores the relationship between 'nature' and 'nurture' in relation to development. Gerhardt considers the vital influence that early positive relationships have on brain development, bringing together research findings from neuroscience and psychology.

Luxmoore, N. (2000) *Listening to Young People in School, Youth Work and Counselling*. London: Jessica Kingsley. A really excellent and readable account of supporting young people's social and emotional development.

Wilkinson, M. (2006) *Coming into Mind*. Hove: Routledge. An insightful exploration of mind–brain relationship and the emergent self from a Jungian perspective.

References

Ainsworth, M. (1967) *Infancy in Uganda*. Baltimore, MD: Johns Hopkins University Press.

Ainsworth, M.D.S., Blehar, M.C., Waters, E. and Wahl, S. (1978) *Patterns of Attachment*. Hillsdale, NJ: Lawrence Erlbaum Associates.

Barnett, M.A. (1987) 'Empathy and related responses in children', in N. Eisenberg and J. Strayer (eds), *Empathy and its Development*. Cambridge: Cambridge University Press. pp. 146–62.

Barnett, M.A. and McCoy, S.J. (1989) 'The relation of distressful childhood experiences and empathy in college undergraduates', *The Journal of Genetic Psychology*, 150(4): 417–26.

Baron-Cohen, S. (2011) *Zero Degrees of Empathy: A New Theory of Human Cruelty*. London: Allen Lane.

Belsky, J. (2001) 'Developmental risk (still) associated with early child care', *Journal of Child Psychology and Psychiatry*, 42: 845–60.

Bowlby, J. (1969) *Attachment and Loss. Vol. 1: Attachment*. London: Hogarth Press.

Bowlby, J. (1973) *Attachment and Loss. Vol. 2: Separation: Anxiety and Anger*. London: Hogarth Press.

Bowlby, J. (1980) *Attachment and Loss. Vol. 3: Loss, Sadness and Depression*. London: Hogarth Press.

Bowlby, R. (2007) 'Babies and toddlers in non-parental daycare can avoid stress and anxiety if they develop a lasting secondary attachment bond with one carer who is consistently accessible to them', *Attachment & Human Development*, 9(4): 307–19.

Chagnon, N.A. (1968) *Yanomamö: The Fierce People*. New York: Holt, Rinehart and Winston.

Cooley, C.H. (1902) *Human Nature and the Social Order*. New York: Charles Scribner's Sons.

Department of Education and Children's Services (DECS) (2001) *South Australian Curriculum Standards and Accountability Framework*. Available online at: http://www.sacsa.sa.edu.au/index_fsrc.asp?t=LA (accessed 21.05.11).

Department for Children, Schools and Families (DCSF) (2008) *Social and Emotional Aspects of Development: Guidance for EYFS Practitioners*. Available online at: http://www.teachfind.com/national-strategies/early-years-foundation-stage-personal-social-and-emotional-development (accessed 02.01.12).

Department for Education and Skills (DfES) (2005) *Social and Emotional Aspects of Learning (SEAL): Improving Behaviour, Improving Learning*. Available online at: http://nsonline.org.uk/node/87009/ (accessed 02.01.12).

Department for Education and Skills (DfES) (2007) *Practice Guidance for the Early Years Foundation Stage: Setting the Standards for Learning, Development and Care for Children from Birth to Five*. London: DfES.

Dettling, A.C., Parker, S.W., Lane, S.K., Sebanc, A.M. and Gunnar, M.R. (2000) 'Quality of care and temperament determine whether cortisol levels rise over the day for children in full-day child care', *Psychoneuroendocrinology*, 25: 819–36.

Ebbeck, M. and Yim, H.Y.B. (2009) 'Rethinking attachment: Fostering positive relationships between infants, toddlers and their primary caregivers', *Early Child Development and Care*, 179(7): 899–909.

Erikson, E. (1968) *Identity: Youth and Crisis*. New York: W.W. Norton & Co.

Gerhardt, S. (2004) *Why Love Matters*. London: Routledge.

Goldberg, S. (2000) *Attachment and Development*. London: Arnold.

Hardy, L.T. (2007) 'Attachment theory and reactive attachment disorder: Theoretical perspectives and treatment implications', *Journal of Child & Adolescent Psychiatric Nursing*, 20(1): 27–39.

Hart, A., Blincow, D. with Thomas, H. (2007) *Resilient Therapy: Working with Children and Families*. Routledge: London.

HighScope (2010) *Curriculum>Infants and Toddlers>Teaching Practices>Daily Schedules*. Available online at: http://www.highscope.org/Content.asp?ContentId=300 (accessed 20.05.11).

Hoffman, M.L. (1993) 'Empathy, social cognition, and moral education', in A. Garrod (ed.), *Approaches to Moral Development: New Research and Emerging Themes*. New York: Teachers College Press.

Jung, C.G. (ed.) (1978) *Man and His Symbols*. London: Picador.

Kemph, J.P. and Voeller, K.K.S. (2007) 'Reactive attachment disorder in adolescence', *Adolescent Psychiatry*, 30: 159–78.

LeVine, R.A., Dixon, S., LeVine, S., Richman, A., Leiderman, P.H., Keefer, C.H. and Brazelton, T.B. (1994) *Child Care and Culture: Lessons from Africa*. New York: Cambridge University Press.

Lewis, M., Alessandri, S.M. and Sullivan, M.W. (1990) 'Violations of expectancy, loss of control and anger expressions in young infants', *Developmental Psychology*, 26(5): 745–51.

Lewis, M. and Brooks-Gunn, J. (1979) *Social Cognition and the Acquisition of Self*. New York: Plenum Press.

Main, M. and Cassidy, J. (1988) 'Categories of response to reunion with the parent at age 6: Predictable from infant attachment classifications and stable over a 1-month period', *Developmental Psychology*, 24: 415–26.

Main, M. and Hesse, E. (1990) 'Parents' unresolved traumatic experiences are related to infant disorganized attachment status: Is frightened/frightening parental behavior the linking mechanism?', in M.T. Greenberg, D. Cicchetti and E.M. Cummings (eds), *Attachment in the Preschool Years: Theory, Research, and Intervention*. Chicago, IL: University of Chicago Press. pp. 161–82.

Main, M. and Solomon, J. (1986) 'Discovery of a new, insecure-disorganized/disoriented attachment pattern', in T.B. Brazelton and M. Yogman (eds), *Affective Development in Infancy*. Norwood, NJ: Ablex. pp. 95–124.

Marcia, J.E. (1966) 'Development and validation of ego identity status', *Journal of Personality and Social Psychology*, 3: 551–8.

Marcia, J.E. (1980) 'Identity in adolescence', in J. Adelson (ed.) *Handbook of Adolescent Psychology*. New York: Wiley.

Maslow, A. (1954) *Motivation and Personality*. New York: Harper.

Masten, A.S., Best, K.M. and Garmezy, N. (1990) 'Resilience and development: Contributions from the study of children who overcome adversity', *Development and Psychopathology*, 2: 425–44.

Newman, T. and Blackburn, S. (2004) *Transitions in the Lives of Children and Young People: Resilience Factors*. Edinburgh: Scottish Executive Educational Department.

NICHD Early Child Care Research Network (1996) 'Characteristics of infant child care: Factors contributing to positive caregiving', *Early Childhood Research Quarterly*, 11: 269–306.

Piaget, J. (1965) *The Moral Judgment of the Child*. New York: Harcourt Brace & World. (Original work published in 1932.)

Rutter, M. and the English and Romanian Adoptees (ERA) team (1998) 'Developmental catch-up and deficit following adoption after severe global early privation', *Journal of Child Psychology and Psychiatry*, 39: 465–76.

Rutter, M., Anderson-Wood, L., Beckett, C., Bredenkamp, D., Castle, J., Groothues, C., Kreppner, J., Keaveney, L., Lord, C. and O'Connor, T.G. (1999) 'Quasi-autistic patterns following severe early privation', *Journal of Child Psychology and Psychiatry*, 40: 537–49.

Schaffer, H.R. (1996) *Social Development*. Oxford: Blackwell.

Schaffer, H.R. (2004) *Introducing Child Psychology*. Oxford: Blackwell.

Smith, M.K. (2009) 'Selfhood', in *The Encyclopaedia of Informal Education*. Available online at: www.infed.org/biblio/b-self.htm (accessed 20.05.11).

Wilkinson, M. (2004) 'The mind–brain relationship: The emergent self', *Journal of Analytical Psychology*, 49: 83–101.

Zahn-Waxler, C., Radke-Yarrow, M., Wagner, E. and Chapman, M. (1992) 'Development of concern for others', *Developmental Psychology*, 28(1): 126–36.

Section 3

Effective Communication and Engagement

8

Effective Communication and Engagement with Children and Young People

Mark Price, Deborah Price and Erica Evans

Chapter Overview

This chapter considers the importance of effective communication and engagement across a range of settings. It supports the practitioner's awareness of the importance of building trusting relationships, including the value of knowing the child or young person well. Empowering and supporting children and young people's independence and autonomy and the importance of the child's voice within the setting are key elements here, and consideration of the process of communication itself, as well as the rationale and reasons for it, are covered.

By reading and engaging with the activities in this chapter, you will:

- develop your understanding of supporting effective engagement with children and young people;
- develop your understanding of children and young people's choice, autonomy and responsibility and how best to foster these;
- explore the different dimensions of relationship building, including parameters of trust, disclosure and boundary setting;
- consider how to manage endings effectively.

Communication and interaction

Rather than being viewed as a time when young people are preparing for adulthood, childhood is now considered an important phase of life in its own right. The perspectives of children and young people are valued and there is an increasing acknowledgement of children as experts in their own lives. This is reflected in Article 12 of the United Nations Convention on the Rights of the Child, which UNICEF (2011) summarises as 'When adults are making decisions that affect children, children have the right to say what they think should happen and have their opinions taken into account'. UNICEF (2011) goes on to acknowledge 'that the level of a child's participation in decisions must be appropriate to the child's level of maturity'. Consequently, in this chapter, issues of communication and interaction with children and young people are related to supporting this right and the child's or young person's developing voice, autonomy and independence.

From the most 'everyday' greetings and acknowledgements, through to more complex interactions and professional interventions, we communicate in different ways and with different purposes and intentions. It is commonly reported (see Mehrabian, 1972) that our response to others' communication is based not just on the content but on other factors, such as the person's tone of voice and their non-verbal communication, or 'body language'. Cultural differences may be very significant here. For example, the place of eye-to-eye contact within communication varies considerably within different cultures, as does the use of hand gestures, and degrees of appropriate, permissible personal 'body space'.

John Heron (1975, 2001) proposed two generalised categories of intervention for those working in education, health and social care contexts, with each broad category broken down further into three dimensions of suggested intervention:

- **Authoritative:** prescriptive (giving directions or advice), informative (giving information), confronting (challenging or giving feedback);

- **Facilitative:** cathartic (exploring feelings), catalytic (exploring options or change), supportive (affirming and encouraging) (adapted from Heron, 1975, 2001).

These categories are useful in helping us to analyse the communication and interactions, but also in helping us thi. developing our communication 'palette' – the range of commu. tion styles we can draw upon, appropriate to our professional roi. and to the particular needs of the children and young people with whom we work.

Another tool we might use in thinking about the way we communicate is that which is provided by Transactional Analysis (TA). Eric Berne (1964) suggested that, in communicating with others, we draw upon three internalised 'ego states' – a combination of our behaviours, thoughts and feelings:

- **Parent** – relating to our internalised experience of our actual parents or other authoritative figures. Communication relating to the Parent ego state might be either *nurturing* (supporting and affirming self-worth) or *structuring* (providing boundaries and limits to activity and behaviour).

- **Adult** – relating to a neutral, logical and objective appraisal of situations, contexts and experiences.

- **Child** – relating to our internalised experience of childhood and both playful and adaptive behaviours. Communication relating to the Child ego state might involve a spontaneous *natural* or *free* playfulness as a well as being *adapted*, complying with or reacting to others' expectations and norms.

For both the Parent and Child ego states, it is also possible to identify positive and negative aspects of communication and behaviour. For example, in our *nurturing* communication from the Parent ego state, we might offer empowering, supportive encouragement. Alternatively, our feedback might be experienced as punitive or harsh. Similarly, our communication in *free* or *natural* Child mode might be playful and creative or it could be lacking in boundaries and irresponsible.

Berne went on to consider how we respond to and interact with communication from others – for example, how behaviour from a Child ego state in one person may be invoked by another's communication from a Parent ego state.

〰 **Reflection point**

Think about the last time someone spoke to you in the following 'modes':

- Gave you supportive encouragement

- Scolded you for getting something wrong

- Gave you instructions

- Encouraged you to do something playful or spontaneous

- Asked you to join in their 'rebellion' against something.

According to TA, from which ego state do you think the person was communicating with you? How did you respond, from which ego state?

Teaching assistant theory and practice goes far beyond this analysis of communication (see e.g. Stewart and Joines, 1987), but even this simplified model is useful in helping us think though how our own ego states and associated behaviours and feelings can impact on our interactions with others. To what extent, for example, are we giving rise to Child ego state responses by our Parent ego state communication?

How we communicate will reflect the nature of the relationship we have with the child or young person. Different professional relationships may have different styles of communication. For example, our 'titles', how we are addressed as well as the extent of physical contact are aspects of communication subject to professional norms. At work, a teacher or teaching assistant would usually be referred to as Ms, Miss, Mrs or Mr Price, whereas a practitioner working in a playwork or youth work context would almost certainly be referred to as Deb or Mark. In the same way, the extent to which a practitioner might have physical contact with a child or young person will be dependent on roles and/or circumstances. Practitioners need to consider the needs of the child or young person, the organisational and professional guidance in place, and the cultural norms or expectation in the given context. Gender and age are important factors here too. An understanding of different practices across different roles in the children and young people's workforce is important to effective integrated and inter-professional working.

> ## Workplace activity
>
> Think about your own professional role and context. What expectations or 'norms' are there about the use of names and titles and limits of physical contact between practitioners and children/young people? What do you and your colleagues think of them?
>
> If you were a parent or carer of children or young people in your setting, what expectations would you have of practitioners? Explore these issues with colleagues or a supervisor/manager.

Trust and relationship building and development

In early years practice, a relationship is made with the child and, as importantly, with the parents or carers. As the child gets older, practitioners may see the primary relationship as being with the child/young person, with the relationship with parents and carers becoming secondary (although often remaining very important). We look at effective communication and engagement with families in the next chapter.

In early years settings, the key worker is part of a group of people who will influence the way that the child will learn to communicate and form relationships with others in the future. By modelling trust and clear communication – for example, eye contact, using the child's name and listening closely to the child and valuing what they are saying, both verbally and non-verbally – the early years worker will be a role model of healthy interactions for that child.

The potential of practitioners to provide positive role models continues throughout the child's/young person's contact with professionals such as teachers, teaching assistants, playworkers and youth workers as they get older. This is especially important if such role models are limited or absent in the child or young person's home or extended family and social environment.

Modelling positive relationships and effective communication extends beyond interaction with the individual child or young person. Children and young people will also be taking in messages from the way that they see the adults in their life interacting with each other and with other children and young people. They therefore need to see practitioners treating each other with respect and consideration and valuing each other's opinions (this was explored in more detail in Chapter 3).

〰 **Reflection point**

Think about the relationships you have with the children and young people with whom you interact. Do you think that they are affected by the expectations that you may have of children and young people in terms of behaviour, attitude, learning ability, etc.? If you have these expectations, then where do you think they came from?

Consider the phrase 'children should be seen and not heard' and think about how that expectation of behaviour would influence the relationship that existed between an adult and a child or young person.

In all settings, the relationship that practitioners have with children or young people will be influenced by employer and stakeholder expectations as well as working arrangements. So in schools, relationships with pupils will be influenced by expectations of achievement in SATs or GCSEs, for example, and the delivery of the curriculum dominates most child–practitioner interactions. In the early years, the EYFS curriculum is delivered through play, and the emphasis on educational achievement may not be so marked. Playworkers are not charged with 'delivering' a curriculum, instead they are an adult in the child's life, who will create opportunities for play and can provide a positive model of an adult who plays.

Youth workers and those who work with young people in more informal learning and development contexts aim to establish and build relationships at a pace which puts the young person in the 'driving seat'; the youth work 'curriculum' focuses on this process (DfES, 2005). Particular activities may provide an initial focus for relationship building, but youth work and related work with young people aim to put the relationship between practitioner and the young person at the heart of the learning process. Indeed, one of the challenges for current practitioners is to maintain the focus of a relationship developed over time, whilst often being driven in terms of policy and organisational strategy, towards achieving identifiable outcomes.

Youth workers sometimes describe this as managing the tension between 'product' and 'process'.

Another challenge for those who work with teenagers is to maintain professional boundaries and communication, whilst working at what might sometimes be seen as the 'edges' of everyday practices in other professional fields. For example, youth workers will often exchange mobile phone numbers and communicate by text and other social network media with young people. But even here, it is important to maintain some personal privacy and ensure the young person regards their youth worker as a 'professional' friend. Communication and trust need to be built on a foundation of professional ethics and values.

Practitioners in education, learning and development contexts often refer to themselves as child- or person-'centred' in their communication and relationships with children and young people. The work of Carl Rogers (1961) and Abraham Maslow (1954) underpins this approach. Humanistic psychology, particularly associated with the work of Carl Rogers, is underpinned by a set of principles:

- People are motivated by the wish to grow and fulfil their potential.

- People can choose what they want to be, and know what is best for them.

- We are influenced by how we feel about ourselves, which in turn results from how we are treated by others.

- The aim of humanistic psychology is to help people choose what they want and help them fulfil their potential (Jarvis, 2000).

According to these principles, all practitioners working with children and young people have a contribution to make to their personal growth. In particular, we need to consider how our interactions with the children and young people we work with may influence how they feel about themselves. Self-esteem was a very important concept for Rogers, who believed that a high level of self-esteem is necessary to be motivated to grow. Levels of self-esteem depend on the extent to which we receive what Rogers called 'unconditional positive regard'. By this he meant relationships and interactions which provide us with acceptance, respect and affection for our essential self. He contrasted this with relationships which don't provide this acceptance, respect and affection, or make these things contingent on meeting certain conditions (conditional positive regard). If I am not shown acceptance, respect and affection, I will believe I am not worthy of them. If I am only shown acceptance, respect or affection when I do as I am told, I will believe that it is my behaviour that is worthy of them, rather than myself.

It is important to realise that 'unconditional positive regard' does not mean approval of everything a child or young person does. Rather it means that even when we disapprove of their behaviour we are able to communicate this whilst also communicating continued acceptance of and respect and affection for them. We can do this, for example, by distinguishing between the child and their behaviour; an individual is always more than their behaviour and we can make it clear that it is the behaviour, not the child, that is being judged.

In addition to 'unconditional positive regard', Rogers proposed two more 'core conditions' for communication and relationship building to support someone in fulfilling their potential:

- **Congruence**: being genuine and communicating authentically. We can't pretend to have unconditional positive regard; it has to be genuine.

- **Empathy**: understanding the world and experience from the child or young person's perspective. To really accept someone, we have to understand them and empathy is necessary for this understanding.

These conditions sometime provide a challenge for practitioners, but they provide useful 'touchstones' in considering the basis of communication and relationship formation.

Case study

Callum is fourteen. He's clearly a bright lad – sharp-witted – but has a reputation that 'goes before him'. He gets bored easily and feels that much of his school experience is pointless. His father is a painter and decorator and sanctions frequent school absences when he needs Callum to give him a hand on a job. This of course interrupts any chance of learning for Callum, although teachers are often relieved when he's not in school as he is a disruptive influence in many classes.

However, Callum does have a reasonably good relationship with Samina, who works in the school's inclusion unit, to which Callum is often referred. Samina gives Callum attention. She's able to talk with him without rising to his jibes, but at the same time managing to be 'straight' with him. She lets him blow off steam when he's wound up. She's also managed to get him talking about the one thing he's proud of – fishing.

One thing Samina does is to tell Callum if he's 'out of line' and what the consequences will be. She manages to do this in a fairly direct way, whilst not appearing to be 'having a go'.

As a template, she uses the **SET** model (Richardson, 2001) in a lot of her work with students like Callum:

- She communicates her **S**upport for Callum.

- She **E**mpathises or validates Callum's position (without condoning his behaviour).

- She reinforces the reality or the **T**ruth of the situation.

Callum is smart enough to almost anticipate how Samina will react to him now, because their relationship has built up over a period of time. This is also a sign that Callum has developed his own self-awareness. It doesn't always stop him getting into trouble with some teachers and other authority figures though!

In your own context, can you think about how you might apply the SET model?

Trust provides the bedrock for the building of relationships over time. We cannot *demand* trust from children and young people, some of whom may already have plenty of experience of damaged or broken trust with adults. Neither can we hope to create it in an instant. Rather, as practitioners, we seek to foster the conditions in which trust is nurtured over time. At the heart of these conditions are the principles of consistency and integrity – being there for children and young people, keeping our word and honouring our professional commitment to them in all our communication. Combined with maintaining warmth and compassion – being human – the trust process has to begin with us.

An aspect of this process, which can be a challenge for practitioners, is letting go of the need to be liked by the children and young people we work with. Most of us want approval from others – as we've seen, our self-esteem depends on being accepted for who we are. But as a practitioner, if this desire to be liked by the children and young people we work with drives our communication and relationship development, it will distort our interactions and 'interventions' (the action and responses we undertake with a particular focus or intention in mind). We need to be driven by meeting the child's or young person's needs, rather than our own.

As children and young people develop trust in us as practitioners, through our consistency and commitment to them, they may begin to disclose more and more personal information about themselves – their hopes, fears, worries and 'secrets'. These are 'gifts' to us and we must honour them and not treat them lightly. At the same time we need to be clear about when and how such disclosures need to be acted on. We look at this issue in Chapter 10 on safeguarding and promoting well-being, particularly relating to child protection. Children and young people may also be inquisitive and ask practitioners quite personal information in return. This is a quite a common process in relationship and trust building but one that, as practitioners, we need to consider carefully.

Case study

Owen has been working with Cheri (13 years) on a summer activity programme for the last four weeks. They get on well together and Cheri has begun to open up to Owen, telling him about her younger brother, whom she has to look after most days, and how she feels her parents never recognise how fast she's growing up (she's recently started going out with a boy who is also on the activity programme).

On Monday morning, Cheri rushes over to Owen saying 'I saw you in town on Saturday night – you were with this really fit looking man – is he your boyfriend?'

What's behind Cheri's question? How do you think Owen should respond?

What aspects of your personal life would you consider possibly appropriate to share with children and young people and which aspects would you consider being 'off limits'? Under what circumstances would you share such personal information? What might the impact be of sharing this information with the children and young people, on them and on colleagues with whom you work?

Effective communication and engagement with children and young people also requires us to think about how we help children and young people establish effective communication between each other. A number of initiatives are designed to support practitioners in this, a good example being the Working with Others project (Ota, 2010).

Facilitating choice, autonomy and responsibility

The relationship that the practitioner develops with the child or young person should have the principle of facilitating choice and fostering autonomy and responsibility in the child at its core. In the early years, this starts with perhaps giving the child options of objects to grab and play with, and choices of food and drink. It continues with the adult encouraging the child to perform tasks themselves, such as dressing, toileting and getting up and putting resources away. In this way the relationship between the practitioner and the child moves away from one where the adult has all of the power and makes all of the decisions to one where there is mutual respect and consideration, and the child is consulted and given choices. This needs the adult to listen carefully to the child and respect their decisions.

Reflection point

Maria Montessori believed that the child and the adult had a mutually complementing relationship, 'therefore it is not only the adult who must help the child, but also the child who must help the adult' (in Standing, 1998: 81). Are there instances that you can think of where your relationship with a child or young person has been a two-way process of learning?

Workplace activity

Think of your setting and your workplace practices. Are there activities or tasks that you carry out that could be done by the children or young people you work with? Examples are (dependant on age range) putting outdoor clothes on, 'tidy up time', choosing resources and activities, preparing and putting up displays, deciding how money allocated for resources is spent and writing policy documents.

Following on from this idea of extending the young person's autonomy is the concept of *play cues* developed by playworkers Gordon Sturrock and Perry Else (1998). Play cues relate to the idea that a child will give a clear signal to an adult to join their play and that an adult should not attempt to do this until they receive this indication. Rennie (2003: 25) comments that a play cue

> is a signal that anticipates a response within a fairly small range. At the very least it anticipates a response. It is a demand for engagement and comes in various forms and strength levels.

Hence, the practitioner's role here is to be alert and to recognise the play cue when it comes, as it may be in a subtle form. It could be a direct 'do you want to play?' from the child, or it could be a look or a gesture that asks the adult to take part. The more subtle the cue, the more worried a child may be at having that cue rejected by the adult.

Sometimes children will not give a play cue as they are happy to explore resources on their own or with a friend without an adult's input. The play environment can contain its own play cues in this instance and the adult needs to recognise when a child is playing and when they want to be left to play on their own or with their friends. The adult's role here is to enable the child to experience their play, rather than to direct or control their play. If a play cue is given, then the adult's knowledge of the child and their understanding of the play will inform them as to the correct response and their next step.

Workplace activity

In your observations of workplace practice, both your own and that of your colleagues, be extra vigilant around play cues. How do children give play cues? Do you see adults taking part in children's play without being invited?

It is not uncommon, for example, for an adult to move into the role play area in a nursery and, unintentionally, direct what is happening – for example 'Oh, are you having a picnic? That's nice, can someone make me a cup of tea?', or for a playworker or youth worker to ask to join in a game of football. This can be done with the best intentions and children and young people will often respond obligingly to adults' suggestions and include them, but essentially it is altering the dynamic of the children or young people's interactions and play. Adults may feel that they are operating at a child's level and want to be included in their play and that this is part of their role – this can be a common occurrence amongst playworkers – but practitioners need to consider that ultimately children will regard them as the adults 'in charge'. Hence practitioners need to keep this in mind and notice the way that this role will affect their relationships with the children and the dynamics of their play and interactions.

Adults may feel that it is part of their role to take an active part in children's play and other activities and that colleagues and parents may be critical if they seem to be 'just' standing and watching. In fact this can be a valuable thing to do as it is letting children's play or experiences develop at its own pace. In a classroom, a practitioner may constantly ask children if they need help or correct them, thus stopping the child reaching their own conclusion. For older children, the urge to take part in conversations between two young people or engage without being invited can be prevalent in some practitioners. The relationship with the child or young person needs to be centred on, where possible, letting them take the lead, and recognising the value of play cues is a way of doing this.

As children get older, we can expect them to take more responsibility for their own play, learning and development. Hart's 'ladder of participation' (1997) usefully describes eight stages or 'rungs' of progressive involvement and empowerment of children and young people in processes that relate directly to their lives (Figure 8.1). These processes may be either directly within the setting within which practitioners engage with children or young people, or at a wider community, society or governmental level.

Hart saw the first three rungs on the ladder to be 'non-participation', with real participation not starting until rung four. It is also important to remember that children and young people need experience of the lower rungs before they can climb to the higher rungs.

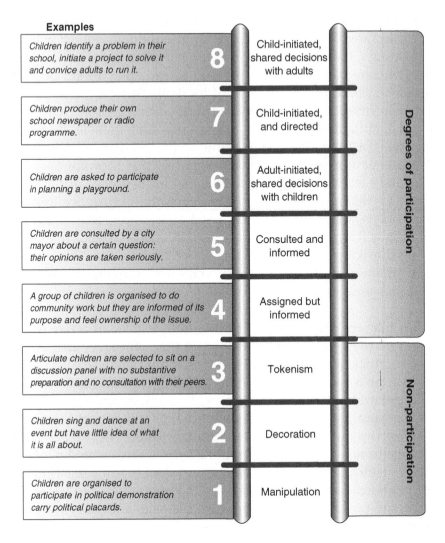

Figure 8.1 The ladder of participation

Source: Flowers et al. (2009: 255)

Within schools, support for 'pupil voice' and other mechanisms for children and young peoples' participation and decision-making has echoed the development of youth cabinets and a youth parliament, locally and nationally, reflecting Article 12 of the UN Convention on the Rights of the Child (OUNHCHR, 1989) and supported by the children's commissioner's guidance for Children's Services (11 MILLION, 2009):

> Children and young people will actively be involved in shaping all decisions that affect their lives, are supported to achieve their full potential through the

provision of appropriate services, and will live in homes and communities where their rights are respected and they are loved, safe and enjoy life. (11 MILLION, 2009: 2)

Williamson (1995) described the process of *social action* youth work which sets out a framework for: (i) supporting groups of young people in identifying which issues are important to them; (ii) exploring with them why these issues are important; (iii) considering what difference they want to make in respect of the issues; (iv) supporting action to be taken by the young people; and (v) young people reflecting on their experiencing.

📁 Case study

The Just 4 Girls (J4G) group provides a female environment that allows young women to overcome the cultural barriers that can prohibit them from attending other leisure activities. Members of the group formed a Girls' Forum in order to develop the range of activities on offer; in particular they wanted the opportunity to go climbing. They applied for a 'Here to HELP' award and this has helped with employing female-only climbing instructors. As a result, the J4G group are now able to take part in non-traditional sporting activities and continue to steer the delivery of the sessions (NYA, 2011).

In your own context, how might children or young people be supported in taking the initiative?

The benefits of promoting meaningful participation have been explored in a recent study carried out by Sebba and Robinson (2010). This study followed a three-year evaluation of the Rights Respecting Schools Award. In order for schools to achieve this award they must demonstrate that they are promoting children's rights, as stated in the UNCRC. The aim of the study was to evaluate the impact of the award on the 'well-being and achievement' of children within the schools (Sebba and Robinson, 2010: 3). The study found that participating schools were overwhelmed by the positive impact the initiative had on relationships and well-being within the school communities. When children were actively made aware of their rights, they were more likely to display positive behaviour; they felt empowered; demonstrated positive attitudes with regards to issues around diversity and inclusion; participated actively in school decision-making processes;

and had higher levels of engagement in learning. This study clearly demonstrates the positive benefits to promoting practice which respects the rights of children. When children are given a voice and made aware of their rights they are more likely to demonstrate positive, active participation.

The extent to which meaningful participation has been achieved can be held up to scrutiny. Whilst it is true that legislation and policy have promoted participation, it is less clear whether participation at the highest level has been achieved. Sinclair (2004) suggests that there are clear examples of initiatives which have included consultation with children. However, some may have involved children in a very passive role. For example, children may be representatives in a school council and may be encouraged to express opinions about the policies and practices within the school. But to what extent do the children impact on change? Are their views taken seriously and do their opinions act as anything more than a tokenistic nod to participation? Sinclair (2004) argues that participation can only be meaningful when adults understand why they are seeking the views of children. In identifying the extent to which children share the power, adults need to be honest about the expectations they have of the joint working.

Enabling the 'voice' of very young children to be heard presents unique challenges to practitioners and parents. Very young children, under the age of six, may not have fully mature verbal communication skills to engage in dialogue with adults when exploring their perspectives. However, this does not mean that young children have no views about their lives. Indeed, young children have a great deal to say about what is important to them (Clark and Moss, 2001; Einarsdottir, 2005; Sumsion et al., 2011).

Clark and Moss (2001, 2005) have developed the 'Mosaic Approach' as a participatory framework for 'listening' to the perspectives of young children. They argue that young children have important things to say about their lives and that it is the responsibility of adults to search for effective methods which will facilitate participation. Listening is not simply about using verbal communication, but rather relates to the ability to 'hear' what the child has to say through a wide range of methods. This builds on the views of Malaguzzi, an educationalist from Reggio Emilia in Italy, who developed the idea of the 'hundred languages of children' (Edwards et al., 1998). This perspective of childhood promotes the belief that children use a wide range of methods to communicate, not simply through speech, and that it is the responsibility of adults to seek opportunities to 'listen' to children through whatever means they use.

The opinions, aspirations, perspectives and views of young children are unique and valuable. Children are undoubtedly the true experts in relation to their own life experiences. If adults are to understand children, they must seek opportunities for their voices to be heard. Listening to children enables adults to see the world from a child's perspective, developing an understanding of what the world is like for the youngest members of society. Promoting a participatory approach may help adults to improve the quality of life experiences for young children. It will also help to lay the foundations for children to become thoughtful, reflective, strong and competent citizens.

Ending relationships

Working with children and young people is punctuated by transitions (see Chapter 11) and these include times when the child or young person leaves the service or provision that we work in and moves on.

The role of the practitioner includes managing these endings and transitions so that they are seen as part of the natural rhythm of life, rather than a traumatic, unresolved close to a relationship. In facilitating this ending, the practitioner is preparing the child to be autonomous and to have a level of self-awareness and esteem that they carry within themselves through the transitions yet to come in their life. It also gives the child or young person the skills to manage these partings and endings of relationships effectively and healthily.

If there are partings and endings in the child or young person's life outside the setting, then the secure relationship that they have built up with the practitioner can help them to manage the grief and loss they may feel during this time. The setting and the relationships that they maintain there could be the only secure place for the child or young person during a difficult and painful time in their life.

Acknowledging endings and partings is vital, as is recognising that the child or young person may have previously had difficulties in dealing with such endings. 'Acting out' or poor behaviour, especially directed at the practitioner or the setting, may not be 'personal' but rather is the child or young person's way of dealing with the remembered trauma of previous endings.

Planning endings with children and young people is crucial, as is 'letting go' ourselves as practitioners and allowing the children and young people to leave on their terms, rather than ours.

Summary

The relationship between the practitioner and the child or young person is at the heart of every setting and is an essential component of good practice throughout the children and young people's workforce. Practitioners ultimately need to be 'professional' (see Chapter 2) but without warm, effective and affirming communication and engagement the learning environment is sterile.

Relationship, communication and engagement are practitioners' gifts to the children and young people they work with. They enhance and enrich children and young people's lives and provide a positive 'template' that children and young people can refer to when making decisions about the way that they want to interact with their peers, family, employers and partners in the future. It is the responsibility of practitioners to promote positive communication with children and young people. Adults who understand the complexities of effective communication, and demonstrate a commitment to creating environments which foster positive communication, will enable children to become confident individuals who are able to express their own views, whilst appreciating the perspectives of others.

Further reading

Bonel, P. and Lindon, J. (1996) *Good Practice in Playwork*. Cheltenham: Stanley Thornes. This is a useful overview of playwork and also contains a chapter on positive relationships. There are lots of practical activities to try out.

Hear by Right: http://www.nya.org.uk/quality/hear-by-right A National Youth Agency initiative which aims to promote the voice of young people and includes the Hear by Right Award Scheme.

Kilvington, J. and Wood, A. (2010) *Reflective Playwork, for All Who Work with Children*. London: Continuum. This book is a thoughtful look at play and there are sections on practice and relationships.

Luxmoore, N. (2000) *Listening to Young People in School, Youth Work and Counselling*. London: Jessica Kingsley. Nick Luxmoore's work is accessible and provides insight into the everyday interactions and relationships developed in working with young people.

Rinaldi, C. (2005) *In Dialogue with Reggio Emilia: Contextualising, Interpreting and Evaluating Early Childhood Education*. London: Routledge. This book explores the early years pedagogical approach in Reggio Emilia in Italy. The concept of the child as a strong, independent learner is highlighted, with a focus on respectful practice which promotes a listening ethos.

Taylor, A.M. (2003) *Responding to Adolescents*. Lyme Regis: Russell House. A good overview of working with young people, going into more depth than is possible in this chapter.

Wheal, A. (2006) *Adolescence: Positive Approaches for Working with Young People* (2nd edn). Lyme Regis: Russell House. Another good overview, again providing more in-depth analysis of working with young people.

References

11 MILLION (2009) *Statutory Guidance: The Roles and Responsibilities of the Lead Members for Children's Services and the Director of Children's Services*. Available online at: www.childrenscommissioner.gov.uk/content/publications/content_379 (accessed 18.05.11).

Berne, E. (1964) *Games People Play: The Basic Handbook of Transactional Analysis*. New York: Ballantine Books.

Clark, A. and Moss, P. (2001) *Listening to Young Children: The Mosaic Approach*. London: National Children's Bureau.

Clark, A. and Moss, P. (2005) *Spaces to Play: More Listening to Young Children Using the Mosaic Approach*. London: National Children's Bureau.

Department for Education and Skills (DfES) (2005) *Youth Matters*. London: DfES.

Edwards, C., Gandini, L. and Foreman, G. (eds) (1998) *The Hundred Languages of Children: The Reggio Emilia Approach to Early Childhood Education* (2nd edn). Norwood, NJ: Ablex.

Einarsdottir, J. (2005) 'Playschool in pictures: Children's photographs as a research method', *Early Chid Development and Care*, 175(6): 523–41.

Flowers, N., Brederode, M.E., Claeys, J., Fazah, R., Schneider, A. and Szelenyi, Z. (2009) *Compasito: Manual on Human Rights Education for Children* (2nd edn). Budapest: Council of Europe. Available online at: http://www.eycb.coe.int/compasito/pdf/Compasito%20EN.pdf

Hart, R. (1997) *Children's Participation: The Theory and Practice of Involving Young Citizens in Community Development and Environmental Care*. London: Earthscan.

Heron, J. (1975) *Six Category Intervention Analysis*. Guildford: University of Surrey.

Heron, J. (2001) *Helping the Client* (5th edn). London: Sage.

Jarvis, M. (2000) *Theoretical Approaches in Psychology*. London: Routledge.

Maslow, A. (1954) *Motivation and Personality*. New York: Harper.

Mehrabian, A. (1972) *Nonverbal Communication*. Chicago: Aldine-Atherton.

NYA (2011) *Just for Girls*. Available online at: http://www.nya.org.uk/quality/hear-by-right/what-s-changed/just-4-girls (accessed 18.05.11).

Office of the United Nations High Commissioner for Human Rights (OUNHCHR) (1989) *Convention on the Rights of the Child*. Geneva: Office of the United Nations. Available online at: http://www2.ohchr.org/english/law/crc.htm (accessed 19.05.11).

Ota, C. (2010) *Working with Others*. Available online at: http://www.cathyota. com/content/working-others (accessed 18.05.11). This project website provides a good example of the kind of support available to practitioners who want to help children and young people develop effective communication and group working skills.

Rennie, S. (2003) 'Making play work: The fundamental role of play in the development of social relationship skills', in F. Brown (ed.), *Playwork Theory and Practice*. Buckingham: Open University Press.

Richardson, B. (2001) *Working with Challenging Youth: Lesson Learned Along the Way*. New York: Brunner Routledge.

Rogers, C. (1961) *On Becoming a Person: A Therapist's View of Psychotherapy*. London: Constable.

Sebba, J. and Robinson, C. (2010) *Evaluation of Unicef's UK's Rights Respecting Schools Awards*. Available online at: http://www.sussex.ac.uk/research/news? id=5781 (accessed 02.11.10).

Sinclair, R (2004) 'Participation in practice: Making it meaningful, effective and sustainable', *Children & Society*, 18: 106–18.

Standing, E.M. (1998) *Maria Montessori: Her Life and Work*. New York: Penguin.

Stewart, I. and Joines, V. (1987) *TA Today: A New Introduction to Transactional Analysis*. Melton Mowbray, UK: Lifespan Publishing.

Sturrock, G. and Else, P. (1998) *The Playground as Therapeutic Space: Playwork as Healing. 'The Colorado Paper'*, IPA/USA Triennial National Conference. Available online at: http://www.ludemos.co.uk/COLFULLa4%20final%2007.pdf (accessed 18.05.11).

Sumison, J., Harrison, L.J., Press, F., McLeod, S., Goodfellow, J. and Bradley, B.S. (2011) 'Researching infants' experiences of early childhood education and care', in D. Harcourt, B. Perry and T. Waller (eds), *Researching Young Children's Perspectives: Developing Ethics and Dilemmas of Educational Research with Children* (pp. 113–127). Abingdon, Oxon: Routledge.

UNICEF (2011) 'Understanding the Convention on the Rights of the Child'. Available online at: http://www.unicef.org/crc/index_understanding.html (accessed 13.07.11).

Williamson, H. (1995) *Social Action for Young People: Accounts of SCF Youth Work Practice*. Lyme Regis: Russell House.

9

Effective Communication and Engagement with Families

Deborah Price, Sarah Wilkins and Nadia Edmond

Chapter Overview

In this chapter we look at the different ways practitioners work with families and the challenges that this brings. We also examine the benefits of maintaining good relationships and ways to do this. The nature and quality of relationships with parents, carers and families is very much related to the age of the child or young person and we look at these changing relationships from birth to adolescence. The term 'parent' is used to refer to parents and carers, including foster carers. We also look at vulnerable families and families coping with difficulties and the ways in which we can help and support them.

By reading and engaging with the activities in this chapter, you will:

- consider how the concept of the 'family' is not fixed but a social construction that takes many forms;
- explore some of the different issues associated with working with families in different contexts;
- examine ideas for communicating and engaging with children and young people's parents and carers.

The concept of 'family'

In terms of the ecological systems theory we encountered in the introduction, families (however constituted or constructed) provide perhaps the most influential microsystem for children. As practitioners working with children and young people, we are inevitably, either directly or indirectly, also working with their parents, carers and families. Even where practitioners have relatively little contact with home, having an understanding of the child or young person's family context and how this impacts upon them is an important aspect of understanding and engaging with the child or young person. We also need to remember that some of the young people we work with may be young parents themselves or have other caring responsibilities. Families have always taken and continue to take many different forms.

So, when we talk about a child or young person's family, who do we include? The difficulty with the concept of family is that despite the importance of family in people's everyday lives, there is no absolute consensus on what constitutes a family. Attempts at definition of the concept in the social sciences can be categorised in terms of three general perspectives, 'structural', 'functional' and 'transactional' (Koerner and Fitzpatrick, 2004). 'Structural' definitions of families are based on the presence or absence of certain family members and definitions within this perspective include the presence of people related through blood or marriage or civil partnership. It is in this context that the term 'nuclear family' was coined and defined as:

> A social group characterized by common residence, economic cooperation, and reproduction. It includes adults of both sexes, at least two of whom maintain a socially approved sexual relationship and one or more children, own or adopted, of the sexually cohabiting adults. (Murdock, 1949: 1)

The problem with this view is that families may be recognisable as families even though they may not be made up of people who fit the structural definition. 'Functional' perspectives on family focus on the role of the family in performing necessary societal functions, such as socialising children, providing material and emotional support and care of its members. The issue here is that some families may be recognisable as families (albeit dysfunctional) even though they do not fulfil some or all of these functions. 'Transactional' perspectives define families as groups who 'through their behaviour generate a sense of family identity with emotional ties and an experience of a history and a future' (Koerner and Fitzpatrick, 2004: 177). There is, of course, a tautological problem here as this essentially says that a family is any group in which people feel and behave as though they belong to a family.

Hence, the difficulty with trying to define the family is that the concept is potentially fluid and varied and one definition may not encompass the multitude of families. For this reason, some theorists (e.g. Bernades, 1999) have argued that it is more useful to recognise this fluidity and focus on how people use the concept in their everyday lives. This perspective suggests that individuals create an individual and personal conception of family.

～～ Reflection point

When you think of your own family, who do you include? When you think about the family of a child or young person you work with, how would you define their family? What are the important characteristics of families for you? How might your conception of family differ from those of the children or young people you work with and their parents/carers and other professionals?

There has been increasing recognition of the wide variety of family arrangements within which children and young people live. For example, the government policy document *Every Parent Matters* (DfES, 2007) explicitly acknowledges that there is variety in family structures and relationships. It is important, therefore, for settings and practitioners to strive to acknowledge and respect the wide variety of family structures they may encounter.

Workplace activity

The influential *Index for Inclusion: Developing Play, Learning and Participation in Early Years and Childcare* (Booth et al., 2006) includes 'practitioners and parents/carers collaborate' as one of the indicators of inclusive practice. The index includes sets of questions to help you think about how well settings collaborate with parents/carers, for example, 'Is respect shown for all families, including lone parents/carers, same-sex parents/carers, dual and multiple heritage families, large and small families?'. Check your setting and practice against the questions associated with that indicator. Where appropriate, how could you improve your practice?

How practitioners work with parents, carers and families will need to be responsive to the different conceptions of family that exist. How we conceive of a child or young person's family and how we work with them will depend on the nature of the setting and the age of the child or young person. This is reflected in the organisation of this chapter which looks at communicating and engaging with families of children in terms of three broad age phases: the early years, child-hood and adolescence.

The early years

Relationships with parents and carers may be important across the age range but are fundamental to working with children in the early years. It has been argued that parents are the child's first and most enduring educators (QCA, 2000). The Early Years Foundation Stage (EYFS) (Childcare Act 2006 s39) calls for practitioners to work in partnership with parents and carers. A review of the EYFS in 2011 recommended that a greater emphasis be given in the EYFS to the role of parents and carers as partners in their children's learning (Tickell, 2011: 5).

As we saw in Chapter 7, in early years settings, children will be allocated a 'key worker' who liaises with the parents and is a point of contact. That key worker's engagement and communication with parents/carers is crucial in gaining the child's trust and overcoming any fears as well as gaining the respect, confidence and trust of the parents and carers. Indeed, some practitioners have commented that the 'settling in' of the parents/carers can be more difficult than getting the child accustomed to new routines and people.

The relationship with a very young baby can be very intense and, consequently, the practitioner is normally a key worker for no more than three babies or children under two years. There is a dual dynamic here, with the practitioner providing a service for the parent/carer as well as caring for the child. Maintaining professional boundaries and relationships with the child and their parents/carers, whilst consulting with parents/carers on all aspects of the child's care in order to include them, respect their wishes and acknowledge them as the main carer of the child, is at the heart of this professional relationship.

📁 **Case study**

Pamela works in a baby unit with three children – all of them just approaching twelve months. She has been their key worker since they were roughly three months old. Today the oldest one pulled herself up on a piece of equipment and then took her hands off and balanced for a second on her own. This was the first time she had done this and Pamela was thrilled. When her father came to collect the child, Pamela told him in a rush of excitement, but to her surprise the father was upset and said that he would rather the child had done this at home. He asked Pamela not to tell the mother when she came the next morning. Pamela relayed all of this to her manager who told Pamela that she should have let the parents discover this crucial milestone for themselves.

Thinking about Pamela, was the manager right? What would you have done if you had been Pamela? Are there some milestones that you would share and others that you would not?

As practitioners, we may have expertise in how young children learn but parents/carers will know their individual child best. Unless there is a sharing of information and respect between practitioners and parents/carers, a child's needs will be not be fully understood or met, and relationships of trust will not emerge.

Keyes (2002) has commented on the different roles and perspectives of early years practitioners and parents/carers. In order for these to avoid becoming a point of conflict between the family and the practitioner, Keyes suggests that there is a need for each to understand and complement the other's role. Also essential is effective communication between parents/carers and practitioners to assist each role in 'enlightening' the other (Keyes, 2002: 184). Building such professional relationships can be particularly challenging for childminders who work in their own home setting.

As professionals, we have to be aware that a family who has a complex set of needs may have a number of professionals working with them, for example a health visitor with a baby, a playlink visitor with a toddler, educational psychologists, teachers and teaching assistants, with the school age children, and social workers with the young people and adults in the family. These professionals could have a variety of ways and styles of communicating with the family and could also potentially be giving them different messages about their lifestyles and parenting, and ways to manage both.

The cornerstone of effective relationships with children and their families is taking the time to get to know them. This process can be aided by regular ongoing contact and collecting and recording information about the child and family so that the setting is aware of personal information such as birthdays, and family members and pets living with the child. Also important are the other people that are significant to a child's life. Similarly, knowledge of any religious beliefs and information about cultural background is necessary to help practitioners understand the child and their family more fully.

〰 Reflection point

Some nurseries have a system where parents can log on and see live footage of the nursery and see what their child is doing – what do you think of this? Is it a good system or one that is fraught with difficulties – a way of promoting trust or evidence of lack of trust? Think about your own setting and how this would affect the practices there. What could be the positive benefits and what could be the disadvantages?

The middle years of childhood

Staff/child ratios in school are much lower than in early years settings, and relationships and communication between staff and parents/carers are inevitably different. The *Index for Inclusion* (Booth and Ainscow, 2002) includes the indicator 'There is a partnership between staff and parents/carers' and a set of questions for schools to examine their practice. One of the issues, which is raised in these questions, is that parents' own experiences of school may make them wary or otherwise uncomfortable about coming into school and meeting staff. Parents/carers will have their own memories of school days and these may not all be positive. It may be that they are reluctant to engage with the teaching assistant or the teacher, recalling times when children were left at the school gates with very limited interaction with the teacher. Another obstacle to communication with and engagement of parents in school activities may be language and/or different cultural expectations.

These obstacles are acknowledged in examples of good practice in supporting families in early years settings and schools outlined in *Every Parent Matters* (DfES, 2007). Some schools and settings, for example, have been successful in engaging parents in their children's learning and development through family learning programmes. Such schools and settings 'boost parents' involvement in their children's learning, encourage parents to go on to further training and can also re-connect them with schools they might previously have been wary of' (DfES, 2007: 11). As Knowles (2009) has argued, many settings and schools have adopted successful practices from Children's Centres, particularly through developing the role of an outreach or community liaison worker to build relationships. Family or Parent Support Workers can offer such support, spanning the roles of social worker and learning mentor.

Schools and settings may find it frustrating that in spite of their perceived best efforts, engagement and participation by some groups of parents remains limited. It can be tempting to conclude that some parents/carers 'just aren't interested'. This is very unlikely to be the case and it is much more likely that parents/carers lack confidence and are wary of being judged negatively. The challenge for schools and settings, then, is to find activities in which parents can feel their contribution is valued.

📁 Case study

Blackhurst Primary School is in a large council estate on the edge of town. It is an area of disadvantage and after struggling with a range of problems was put in 'special measures'. The strategy for turning the school around adopted by the senior management team included developing much more effective communication with, and engagement of, parents/carers at the school. Attendance at parents' evenings and sports days and interaction with teachers was very poor and almost non-existent in the case of fathers. The development of play areas and gardens in the large school field provided the opportunity to invite parents to volunteer to help create these areas and many parents, including fathers and other male carers, came forward. Being able to contribute in this very direct and tangible way was appealing to many parents who had not previously interacted much with the school. As a result, relationships were

(Continued)

(Continued)

built between parents/carers and, most importantly, between parents/carers and school staff. Once the first phase of play areas and garden developments was complete, the school held a summer fête which was well attended by parents and has become a regular feature of the school year. A number of parent volunteers continue to contribute to the maintenance of the play areas and gardens through after-school activities with the children.

How do you engage parents in your setting? What activities might promote the involvement of parents who are not currently involved?

We have focused primarily on the relationships between schools and parents/carers, but communication and engagement with parents can be an issue in other settings in which we work with children. For example, a playworker has a particular relationship with a child that is developed in an after school club or play scheme. He or she is not a parent and their role is not to facilitate formal education but to encourage and provide play experiences. Convincing parents/carers of the value of play and of the benefits for their child of participating in a play setting and of the value of the play setting as more than a childcare service can be challenging. The playworker will want to provide experiences that will encourage risk taking and creativity, and this may result in tension with the parent/carer whose priority may be that the child is kept clean and safe. Of course risk assessment and maintaining a safe environment is fundamental to playwork provision, but issues of independence and children carrying out their own risk assessments are also crucial to the play experience. Gill (2007) suggests that it is easier to gather quantitative data about the negative effects of risk taking because of the volume of statistics that are recorded and collected when risk taking results in injury. Kilvington and Wood (2010: 52) refer to Gill when considering

the anxieties of some adults related to allowing children to play fight or engage in gun play, as they may be blamed if the children get hurt or other adults may find it unacceptable.

Risk taking and differing views of appropriate levels of risk can be an area of conflict between playworkers and parents/carers and also between different playworkers in a setting.

> ### Case study
>
> Jill, a senior playworker in an adventure playground, organises a barbeque around a fire pit one evening. During the activity one child is closely supervised lighting the fire and the top of the match breaks off and flies off and lands on the child's arm causing a small burn which is treated appropriately. When the parent comes to pick the child up and is informed of the injury she argues with Jill and says that she just expects the children to be kept safe and not end up covered in dirt and with burns. She threatens to sue the council who runs the playground.
>
> What would you say and do in Jill's situation?

The teenage years

The growing maturity of the young people we work with presents a key issue, which is the young person's right to confidentiality in making their own decisions. A framework of guidance for this is provided by the 'Gillick competency' and associated 'Fraser' guidelines (see NSPCC, 2009). These refer to the outcomes of a legal case which looked specifically at whether doctors should be able to give contraceptive advice or treatment to under sixteen-year-olds without parental consent. Since then, this guidance has been widely used to consider whether a young person has the maturity to make their own decisions and to understand the implications of those decisions. In considering such situations, professionals are directed to ensure that the young person should not only understand the nature of the advice which is being given, but that she or he must also have a sufficient maturity to understand what is involved (NSPCC, 2009). Guidance is also given generally on the issue of balancing parents' and children and young people's rights, citing Lord Scarman's ruling:

> Parental right yields to the child's right to make his own decisions when he reaches a sufficient understanding and intelligence to be capable of making up his own mind on the matter requiring decision. (Scarman, 1985, cited in NSPCC, 2009)

In Chapter 7, we considered how part of a young person's identity development during adolescence relates to the process of separation from parents and families. This process will be very dependent on the cultural, social and economic opportunities in the community where the young person is based.

Coleman (2011: 83) has noted the shift in ideas about adolescence over recent decades. In many early developmental studies it was assumed that the most fundamental part of the process of transition for young people was to separate from the parents and family so that the young person could become more detached (and therefore independent). Coleman argues that more recent research has highlighted that the process of 'moving out' or 'moving on' has become more about young people becoming interdependent. This could be about the young person and the parent redefining their relationship and the young person developing themselves and their identity. Alongside this, they may also want to keep a close relationship with the family and parents.

This can be a challenging time for children and their parents, one when young people often start to take risks and experiment with alcohol, drugs, relationships and sex. For some young people, this can be an uncertain and stressful time, while others simply get on with their lives, and are able to cope with a variety of problems and challenges. When working with young people and their parents, it is worth remembering this. It is also important not to make assumptions about what challenges and problems they might be dealing with. Rather than looking at problems and deficits, perhaps we should also consider what is going well for young people. Equally, it is important not to make assumptions about parents, as family relationships can often be complicated and the adults may need the same amount of care and consideration that we give children and young people.

Research from the Trust for the Study of Adolescence (Roker and Coleman, 2007), identified some interesting prompts in relation to working with parents and carers and thinking and talking to children and young people about alcohol and substance misuse. Parents wanted:

- 'hints and tips' for opening up discussion with children and young people about alcohol and drugs;

- suggestions and ideas about how to monitor and supervise their children and young people;

- accurate information about the legal and health issues and risks/legal issues so they could discuss these and feel informed when talking to their children;

- ideas and strategies that could be practically used to deal with difficult situations related to drugs and alcohol.

📁 Case study

Jordan (15 years) has just moved to a new school. A recent Personal, Social and Health Education (PSHE) lesson has highlighted the risks associated with smoking drugs. Bill, the learning mentor for another pupil in Jordan's class, overhears several of the boys in the class talking about where they can buy 'weed' and thinks he overhears Jordan's name mentioned. Bill mentions this to the class teacher and she asks him to record the incident and remain vigilant (Bill really isn't sure if the name mentioned was 'Jordan').

Three weeks later Bill is at a parents evening and Jordan's mother approaches him. She tells Bill that Jordan has spoken about him and that he really likes him. The following day in school Bill sees Jordan and says hello, and while they are talking he smells what he thinks is strong, sweet-smelling smoke. After further discussion with the class teacher, Bill agrees to be involved in a discussion with the class in the next PSHE lesson, and, if needed, to assist in a meeting with Jordan and his mother.

In terms of the four bullet points above, how should Bill prepare for the meeting?

What are the specific factors and characteristics that relate to the young people you work with that might lead them to take risks?

How might parents' and carers' views differ in relation to this risk-taking behaviour?

Make some notes about how you might discuss the different perspectives of parents with your colleagues and team. What could you put in place to anticipate what issues affect the parents of young people in the community you work in?

Roker and Coleman (2007) suggest that parents often feel reassured when hearing about the experiences of both young people and other parents or carers. The experience of having one's individual experience validated cannot be underestimated. It is also important to consider that engaging young people and their parents in activities or discussion can have a very positive effect. Programmes such as 'Triple P' (Positive Parenting Program®) offer such opportunities and resources for parents to develop positive attitude, skills and behaviour in their children.

Supporting vulnerable families

When social problems stack up, specific strategies are sometimes employed by governments, directly intervening in family contexts, that are aimed at bringing about change. The national network of Family Intervention Projects (FIP) was launched as part of the Respect Action Plan in 2006. The government's intention was to address cycles of anti-social behaviour and homelessness through what has been described as 'an "assertive" and "persistent" style of working to challenge and support families' (DfE, 2011) with 'clear rules, and clear punishments if they don't stick to them' (Brown, 2009).

Nationally, FIPs have targeted the most vulnerable and socially inadequate families, the majority of which have significant learning disabilities and mental health problems. However, the FIPs have been criticised:

> ... in practice, FIPs fail in multiple ways: by targeting the wrong people for the wrong reasons; by targeting false 'causes of ASB' while failing to tackle the real underlying causes in those targeted; by failing to deliver support in key areas like mental health; by failing to deliver sustained changes in family behaviour or reduced ASB in the community. At root, the FIP remains enforcement-led and sanctions-oriented, where someone must be blamed and punished for bad behaviour. This ethos justifies forcing very vulnerable families with mental health problems into projects under threat of eviction, loss of benefits and removal of children into care. (Gregg, 2010: 2)

Hart et al. (2007) propose an alternative discourse of therapy, rather than punishment. They propose a framework of what they call 'ordinary magic', working with parents, carers and the extended home and family to explore how supportive relationships might be fostered to build resilience (see Chapter 7).

This type of systemic approach (i.e. working with the parents and family as a network or 'system' of relationships and social capital) is at the heart of developing good social care.

It is also worth remembering that it is generally agreed that services which are focused on prevention and support are less stigmatising for families, and parents in particular, to work with. These are often community-based projects that seek to build on parents' strengths and skills rather than focus on the deficits and problems in a family. This is probably an ethos that many practitioners also strive to develop with the children and young people they work with. This approach tends to be less threatening to parents and young people. Indeed, if the family has approached a service or project themselves, they are more likely to take advice and support. If a family is referred to a service, there will inevitably be some resistance or feelings of powerlessness that need to be explored.

Working in 'partnership' with parents and other professionals is crucial to developing a working relationship; one which enables parents and young people to feel supported and able to accept support, and develop strategies and skills to manage the changes or challenges they are going through. It is important to think about how you introduce ideas and problem-solving strategies to young people and their parents and it is also essential to consider how you ensure other professionals in the network know and understand your role and the work you are undertaking with a family. Similarly, when working with foster carers or other wider family members (grandparents, aunties or uncles), it is important to consider that many of these adults will bring their own ideas and strategies to the discussion. It is worth remembering, particularly when working with foster carers, that they might be part of a wider support network that you can learn from or they might have a number of professionals giving them differing advice.

Reflection point

Think about a young person and parent or carer that you may be working with. How do you introduce your role and the work you do to them? Think about giving examples of work or projects you have been involved with before and what the outcome was.

What words and ideas will you use to illustrate the strategies or themes you would like the family to consider? Would you consider talking about research or tried-and-tested theory with parents and young people?

Now think about describing or summarising the work for another professional. Would you use the same sort of language? If not, think about what you might do differently and why.

If you are discussing the young person, parent or carer with another professional, make sure that you have checked that the parent, carer or young person is aware that you are going to have this discussion and the sort of things you might be talking about.

Looked after children or children in care

The term 'looked after' was introduced by the Children Act 1989 and refers to children who are subject to care orders and those who are voluntarily accommodated. Wherever possible, the local authority will work in partnership with parents. Many children and young people who become looked after retain strong links with their families and many eventually return home. Since the Children Act 2004 came into force, children who are looked after by the local authority tend to be known as 'children in care'.

Children in care are one of the lowest attaining groups nationally (DCSF, 2009), and the gap between all pupils' attainment and the attainment of young people in care widens further as pupils get older. In 2008 14 per cent of looked after children achieved five or more GCSEs at A*–C, compared to 65 per cent of all children (Lipsett, 2009). The guidance set out in Table 9.1 is based on the evidence obtained from visits to a small sample of primary schools that were recognised as having very effective practice in supporting looked after children and ensuring that they make good progress and achieve appropriate levels of attainment. The guidance summarises the specific actions and approaches adopted by the schools to support their looked after children. Whatever kind of setting you work in, it is worth considering how this guidance may relate to your own work with looked after children.

Foster carers are in the unique position of acting as parent and professional within a wider professional network. This might include social workers, mental health specialists, teachers and others. They are often the key professional in this network as well as being the adult most likely to know the child best. Foster carers are trained and supported by their own social worker and support network. The foster carer will also frequently be the main link to the child's birth family, and are often very skilled in communicating and in the management of conflict and separation issues. However, foster carers can often be overlooked when information is communicated about the child. In many ways, the foster carer should be treated no differently from any parent or carer, but it is important to remember that they are part of an inter-professional team along with other practitioners. This means that the foster carer will be aware of relevant policy and guidance and it could mean they are a vital source of information.

Some foster carers will specialise in emergency care and might be very used to managing and supporting children and young people for a short time or during a crisis period in the child's life. Other foster carers might be offering long-term, permanent care or a short-term 'bridging' placement. The terminology and focus of the foster placement will vary from child to child and place to place. It is worth noting that

Table 9.1   Summary of actions and approaches used to support looked after children

1 Doing the things they do for all children but more so	• Promote personalised learning and a culture where every child does matter • Ensure that specific needs and barriers to learning are identified, recorded in each child's personal education plan and progress is reviewed on a regular basis • Track the children's progress as a special group • Provide proactive support through the designated teacher • Implement a range of intervention strategies to address both social and academic needs
2 Balancing high levels of support with real challenge	• Secure high expectations of involvement in learning, progress and behaviour • Support the children in working productively with others • Regularly review targets • Facilitate the mentoring/support role
3 Skilfully linking each child to a key person they relate well to	• Hand pick an adult to act as a confidant and advocate for the child • Provide opportunities for the child to have regular and easy contact with their key person
4 Making it a priority to know the children well and to build strong relationships	• Put the designated teacher at the centre of communication • When possible allocate the child to an experienced teacher and a class that already has support from a teaching assistant • Provide an induction period for the child so that they can become accustomed to their new surroundings • Show an interest in all aspects of the child's involvement in the school • Look for the signs and intervene early
5 Developing strong partnerships with carers, local authorities and specialist agencies	• Work in genuine partnership with foster carers • Help carers to support their child's learning at home • Ensure purposeful and focused contact with support agencies
6 Making things happen and seeing things through	• Work at building trust • Act as an intermediary to secure support for emotional difficulties
7 Ensuring consistency as well as discrete flexibility	• Signal changes in routine well in advance • Be perceptive to situations which could prove difficult for looked after children • Avoid exclusion
8 Actively extending the horizons of each child	• Look for opportunities to involve the child in a range of activities • Maintain an active interest in the activity and monitor the child's involvement • Engage carers and children in family learning
9 Planning for future transitions	• Carefully manage transition from one class to the next and transfer from one school to the next

Source: DCSF (2009)

some children might be proud of being in care and their foster family, whilst others might want this information kept private, so it always important to ensure we have checked out our assumptions.

Workplace activity

Discuss the issue of children in care with your manager. Find out what mechanisms are in place for liaising with foster carers or social workers for those children and young people. What additional challenges has your setting encountered in working with and supporting looked after children and their foster carers/carers and how have these challenges been met?

Summary

Working with parents and families can be challenging. As professionals, working with children and young people across the age spectrum, we are also working with their parents, carers and families. Some of the young people we work with may also be young parents. Most practitioners working with young people go into the work understandably focusing on direct contact with the children and young people themselves. However, returning once more to the ecological model (see Introduction) we can see how significant the family system is in children and young people's lives and the influence this has on their play, learning and development. It is therefore important to pay close attention to our engagement with the wider family unit.

No two families are alike and we must remember that the modern family structure is a changing dynamic and affected by social and economic change. It is a particular challenge for practitioners to respect and support family structures that may be different from those that they grew up in or are familiar with.

Finally, we need to be respectful of the family as a building block and a microcosm of society. To enter into a child or young person's family context is a privilege and can be a sign of developing trust that we need to acknowledge and respect. However, we also need to be mindful that families are not always happy places. This will be explored further in the next chapter where we will address issues of safeguarding and child protection.

Further reading

Aldgate, J., Jones, D., Rose, W. and Jeffery, C. (eds) (2006) *The Developing World of the Child*. London: Jessica Kingsley. Written for practitioners working in children's services and child protection, this text includes useful chapters on communicating with children, exercising professional judgement, and planning, interventions and outcomes in children's services.

Coleman, J. and Hagell, A. (eds) (2007) *Adolescence, Risk and resilience: Against the odds*. Chichester: John Wiley.

Perry, A. (ed.) (2009) *Teenagers and Attachment: Helping Adolescents Engage with Life and Learning*. London: Worth Publishing. This book considers a range of disadvantages that may impact on adolescents and ways to help this group and their families overcome them.

Promoting the Quality of Life of Looked-after Children and Young People: http://guidance.nice.org.uk/PH28 This joint guidance from NICE and the Social Care Institute for Excellence (SCIE) is for all those who have a role in promoting the quality of life (that is, the physical health, and social, educational and emotional well-being) of looked after children and young people.

Supporting Looked After Learners: http://www.solihull.gov.uk/Attachments/Governor_Guide__Looked_After_Learners123.pdf This practical guide to supporting looked after learners for school governors contains accessible and useful information for anyone working with school-age looked after children.

References

Bernades, J. (1999) 'We must not define "the family"!', *Marriage and Family Review*, 28: 21–44.

Booth, T. and Ainscow, M. (2002) *Index for Inclusion: Developing Learning and Participation in Schools*. Bristol: Centre for Studies in Inclusive Education.

Booth, T., Ainscow, M. and Kingston, D. (2006) *Index for Inclusion: Developing Play, Learning and Participation in Early Years and Childcare*. Bristol: Centre for Studies in Inclusive Education.

Brown, G. (2009) Speech to the Labour Party Conference, 2009.

Childcare Act 2006 (c.21). London: HMSO.

Children Act 1989. London: HMSO.

Children Act 2004 (c.31). London: HMSO.

Coleman, J.C. (2011) *The Nature of Adolescence* (4th edn). London: Routledge.

Department for Children, Schools and Families (DCSF) (2009) *Improving the Attainment of Looked After Children in Primary Schools: Guidance for Schools*. Available online at: https://www.education.gov.uk/publications/standard/SchoolsSo/Page8/DCSF-01047-2009

Department for Education (DfE) (2011) *Family Intervention Projects: An Evaluation of their Design, Set-up and Early Outcomes*. Available online at: https://www.education.gov.uk/publications/standard/publicationdetail/page1/dcsf-rbw047 (accessed 21.05.11).

Department for Education and Skills (DfES) (2007) *Every Parent Matters*. London: DfES.

Gill, T. (2007) *No Fear: Growing Up in a Risk Averse Society*. London: Calouste Gulbenkian Foundation.

Gregg, D. (2010) *Family Intervention Projects: A Classic Case of Policy-based Evidence*. London: Centre for Crime and Justice Studies. Available online at: http://www.crimeandjustice.org.uk/opus1786/Family_intervention_projects.pdf (accessed 21.05.11).

Hart, A., Blincow, D. with Thomas, H. (2007) *Resilient Therapy: Working with Children and Families*. London: Routledge.

Keyes, C. (2002) 'A way of thinking about parents/teacher partnerships for teachers', *International Journal of Early Years Education*, 10(3): 177–91.

Kilvington, J. and Wood, A. (2010) *Reflective Playwork*. London: Continuum.

Knowles, G. (2009) *Ensuring Every Child Matters: A Critical Approach*. London: Sage.

Koerner, A.F. and Fitzpatrick, M.A. (2004) 'Communication in intact families', in A.L. Vangelisti (ed.), *Handbook of Family Communication*. Mahwah, NJ: Lawrence Erlbaum. pp. 177–95.

Lipsett, A. (2009) 'Just 14% of children in care get five good GCSEs', *The Guardian*, 30 April. Available online at: http://www.guardian.co.uk/education/2009/apr/30/children-in-care-gcse-results

Murdock, G.P. (1949) *Social Structure*. New York: Macmillan.

NSPCC (2009) *Gillick Competency and Fraser Guidelines: NSPCC Factsheet*. London: NSPCC. Available online at: http://www.nspcc.org.uk/inform/research/questions/gillick_wda61289.html (accessed 22.07.11).

QCA (2000) *Curriculum Guidance for the Foundation Stage*. London: QCA. Available online at: http://www.smartteachers.co.uk/upload/documents_32.pdf (accessed 21.05.11).

Roker, D. and Coleman, J. (eds) (2007) *Working with Parents of Young People: Research, Policy and Practice*. London: Jessica Kingsley.

Tickell, C. (2011) *The Early Years: Foundations for Life, Health and Learning – An Independent Report on the Early Years Foundation Stage to Her Majesty's Government*. London: HMSO.

Triple P. Available at: http://www.triplep.net/ (accessed 21.05.11).

10

Safeguarding and Promoting Well-being

Sarah Wilkins and Mark Price

Chapter Overview

This chapter outlines how professional concern has progressed from thinking in terms of 'child protection' to thinking which includes, more broadly, notions of safeguarding and promoting well-being in children and young people. It considers the role of practitioners in promoting well-being and also discusses definitions of abuse and neglect, assessment of risk and significant harm, and responses to these issues.

By reading and engaging with the activities in this chapter, you will:

- develop an overview of the development of professional responsibility relating to promoting safeguarding and well-being and issues of working with other professionals in these areas;
- consider the practical implications of professional concern extending beyond 'child protection' to include the promotion of well-being in children and young people;
- explore assessment of risk, the concept of 'significant harm' and how this relates to your practice.

From child protection to safeguarding and promoting well-being

The deaths of children, from Maria Colwell in 1973 to Peter Connelly ('baby Peter') in 2007 will be familiar to us all. These tragic incidents have shocked and influenced both professionals and society and have led to inquiries, recommendations and policy changes aimed at avoiding their repetition. A common theme evident in these official responses has been that poor communication and liaison between agencies has been a causal factor. As early as the 1960s, reports from the Central Advisory Council for Education (1967) (*The Plowden Report*), and *The Seebohm Report* (1968), emphasised the importance of professionals and agencies working together, and this theme has been repeatedly revisited in legislation and policy ever since. More recently, following the deaths of Victoria Climbié in 2000 and Peter Connelly in 2007, this subject has been highlighted once more.

In response to such shocking cases, the focus of child welfare and protection policy in the UK in the second half of the 20th century was that of protecting children from harm. The Children Act (1989) introduced some specifically defined areas, for example of 'children in need' (section 17), and 'duty to investigate' (section 47). A legal threshold for intervention in a family and the power to protect and remove children was also introduced, based on there being 'reasonable cause to suspect that a child ... is suffering, or is likely to suffer, significant harm' (Children Act 1989: 47.1.b). However, 'significant harm' was perhaps not sufficiently clearly defined and this led to inconsistent interpretations across the country (Baginsky, 2008). The Children Act (1989) also highlighted the principle that the child's welfare is paramount, and focused practitioners and agencies on keeping the child and young person central to their work and role. The child-centred approach has now become central to practice.

Protecting children was also the concern of the Bichard Inquiry (Bichard, 2004) into the deaths of Jessica Chapman and Holly Wells, which resulted in the Safeguarding Vulnerable Groups Act (2006), which governs much of the Criminal Record Bureau (CRB) checks in place today. Legislation and policy are under continuous review and development and, as we saw in Chapter 3, it is an important part of practitioners' professionalism that they keep up to date and informed of developments through appropriate journals and websites (see 'Further reading').

One of the consequences of the focus on child protection described above has been the idea of safeguarding and welfare as the domain of social services departments, and over the years, referrals to social services departments have increased, resulting in social services having to raise the *thresholds for intervention* (Baginsky, 2008). This led to the feeling that a preventative or more holistic approach to welfare and well-being was needed.

This concern for a more holistic perspective on children and young people's safety and well-being is apparent in the *Every Child Matters* (ECM) (HM Treasury, 2003) agenda, which identified five key 'well-being' outcomes for children (*being healthy, staying safe, enjoying and achieving, making a positive contribution* and *economic well-being*). ECM placed the promotion of well-being at the centre of policy and clearly signalled this as the responsibility of all who work with children and young people, rather than just social workers. It promotes a shared commitment across agencies to achieving these outcomes and emphasises the importance of professionals working together to achieve them.

It is important to note that there have been criticisms of the ECM agenda. For example, it has been argued that it represents an emergent 'social investment state' (rather than 'welfare state') in which children are seen as citizen-workers of the future (rather than children now) (Lister, 2003, 2004), and in which well-being is expressed in terms of successful integration into the world of adults rather than in terms of children's own priorities, so that achievement is prioritised over enjoyment and education over play (Kelley, 2004). Nevertheless, ECM has become part of the shared language for all childcare professionals. Although professionals may interpret the policy differently, the shared framework of aims and aspirations it sets out has supported greater integration.

ECM's call for integrated children's services represented an unprecedented policy shift in welfare services towards integration at every level, making the promotion of well-being and the safeguarding and protection of children the responsibility of everyone who works, or comes into contact, with children.

〰️ Reflection point

What is your role in relation to the five outcomes of *Every Child Matters*? What is your specific responsibility in relation to safeguarding and promoting well-being and what are some of the key tasks you and other practitioners need to complete when considering safeguarding issues?

It may be helpful to discuss these points with colleagues or a manager in your setting.

Within the ECM policy framework, the Common Assessment Framework (CAF) (CWDC, 2005), was introduced to promote a common language and approach to the assessment of children's needs. The pre-assessment checklist within the CAF system focuses on the ECM five outcomes and asks practitioners to consider whether the child or young person appears to be:

- healthy;

- safe from harm;

- learning and developing;

- having a positive effect on others;

- free from the impact of poverty.

These are key areas to consider and should prompt us to take further action if necessary.

The Department for Education (2011d) describes the CAF as a four-step process whereby practitioners can identify a child's or young person's needs early, and assess those needs holistically in order to deliver co-ordinated services and review progress. The CAF is designed to be used when:

- a practitioner is worried about how well a child or young person is progressing (e.g. concerns about their health, development, welfare, behaviour, progress in learning or any other aspect of their well-being);

- a child or young person, or their parent/carer, raises a concern with a practitioner;

- a child's or young person's needs are unclear, or 1 practitioner's service can address.

The process is voluntary and informed consent is families do not have to engage and if they do, they ca information they want to share. The CAF process is a 'request for services' and should be offered to chilc   ...o have needs additional to those being met by universal services. The CAF is not a *risk assessment* (DfE, 2011a) and if a child or young person reveals they are at risk, the practitioner should refer to the local child protection policy (see safeguarding and protecting, below).

The greater efficiency and effectiveness of integrated services is demonstrated by research, showing that implementation of the CAF results in significant savings (from £5,000 to more than £150,000) (Easton et al., 2011) in terms of the potential savings for practitioners and families that come from successful interventions.

 Workplace activity

Think of a child or young person that you know or have worked with and work through the CAF pre-assessment checklist, deciding whether the answer is 'yes', 'no' or 'don't know':

- Does the child or young person appear to be healthy?

- Does the child or young person appear to be safe from harm?

- Does the child or young person appear to be learning and developing?

- Does the child or young person appear to be having a positive effect on others?

- Does the child or young person appear to be free from the impact of poverty?

Think about what gaps in information you have and how you might deal with these missing areas.

What action should you take now? Consider speaking to your manager or colleagues about the CAF checklist.

Make sure you are clear about the guidelines and training in place to implement the CAF locally. If you or any of your colleagues have not undertaken the training – ask for it!

moting children and young people's well-being

Children's social and emotional well-being is important in its own right as it can affect all aspects of a child and young person's health and development.

> Good social, emotional and psychological health helps protect children and young people against emotional and behavioural problems, violence and crime, teenage pregnancy and the misuse of drugs and alcohol. (NICE, 2009: 5)

∿ Reflection point

What is 'well-being'? Think about a child or young person on his or her own and also as part of a group. What can promote well-being and what can hinder it?

When considering this question also think about wider social issues, such as discrimination and social inequality. How do these issues impact on the child/young person and their well-being?

How might the child or young person's friendship group impact on his or her well-being?

There is no agreed definition of the term 'well-being' but it is used as an over-arching concept relating to the quality of people's lives. It is also 'best thought of as a dynamic process, emerging from the way in which people interact with the world around them' (Michaelson et al., 2009: 9).

There are a number of reasons why understanding and promoting well-being is important and valuable. Most fundamentally, the promotion of the well-being of the population should be a fundamental goal of any society. This view led David Cameron (2006) to state:

> wealth is about so much more than pounds, or euros or dollars can ever measure. It's time we admitted that there's more to life than money, and it's time we focused not just on GDP, but on GWB – general well-being.

Unfortunately, the evidence is that the UK does not compare favourably with other countries in terms of the well-being of its children and young people. In 2007, UNICEF gave the UK the lowest average ranking of 21 developed nations in terms of six dimensions of child well-being (UNICEF, 2007), and Bradshaw and Richardson (2009) reported that the UK was 24th of the 29 countries they studied in terms of the overall well-being of children.

In previous chapters (particularly Chapters 7, 8 and 9) we have encountered some key concepts which relate to 'well-being', attachment and resilience. We have looked at how the quality of children and young people's relationships impact on their self-esteem and how their confidence can be boosted in the areas of problem-solving, learning their limits and reframing their problems and concerns.

Resilience, like attachment, can be difficult to pin down but seems to be strongly linked to the development and promotion of children and young people's well-being. Newman (2004: 79) suggests some key messages and factors promoting resilience, which are useful to consider:

- strong social support networks;

- the presence of at least one unconditionally supportive parent or parent figure;

- a committed mentor or other person from outside the family;

- positive school experiences;

- a belief that one's own efforts can make a difference;

- participation in a range of extra-curricular activities;

- the capacity to re-frame problems so that the benefits as well as problems or deficits can be seen;

- working for the community to 'make a difference';

- not to be sheltered from challenging situations that can provide an opportunity for problem-solving/developing coping skills.

In early 2002, the then Department for Education and Skills (DfES) commissioned Southampton University to undertake a study researching effective approaches to supporting the development of children's emotional and social competence. The subsequent report (Weare and Gray, 2002) identified a number of key themes which paved the way for the introduction of SEAL (Social and Emotional Aspects of Learning), a framework and accompanying resources from Key Stage 1 through to Key Stage 4, designed not only to support an intrinsic sense of well-being, but also to have a positive impact on attendance, behaviour and achievement. At the heart of this strategy was the positive impact well-being has on learning (DfES, 2005).

Whilst SEAL may be regarded as a 'whole school' approach, it is broadly aligned with Personal, Social Health, and Economic education (PSHEe) and Citizenship within the school curriculum, where a combination of intra-personal skills and competences (knowing and understanding yourself) and inter-personal skills and competences (relating to and interacting with others) form the basis of learning.

The focus on supporting social and emotional 'learning', 'competence' and 'literacy' (amongst terms presented in the range of literature and research (see Weare and Gray, 2002)), as stepping stones to well-being, goes beyond the school curriculum. In early years, elements relating to social and emotional development have been strengthened in the Tickell review's (2011) recommendations for the Early Years Foundation Stage, whilst NICE's (2009: 5) guidance for secondary education suggests activities 'to develop and protect their social and emotional wellbeing can only form one element of a broader, multi-agency strategy', pointing towards integration with other professional practices (e.g. youth work).

In addition to generalised work to support children and young people's well-being, services and professions are often called to work together to address specific, 'targeted' issues or groups. For example, the impact of bullying on overall well-being, and on learning and development in particular, is well documented (see e.g. Royal College of Psychiatrists, 2005). Previous government policy and legislation regarding the duty of schools specifically (Education and Inspections Act, 2006) and public services more generally (Equality Act, 2010) to address bullying has been reinforced by the Coalition government (DfE 2011b). Equality and inclusion issues are also reflected here, with racist, disablist and homophobic bullying being the focus of specific concern.

Central to all anti-bullying strategy is the need to acknowledge the extent and impact of bullying at the level of institution, community and society. As practitioners, we must learn to recognise the signs of bullying, be prepared to listen to what children and young people tell us, and be committed to take action to address the causes and impact of bullying. This can be challenging for us both in terms of struggling to understand why children and young people might bully each other, as well as developing strategies to respond effectively, both reactively and proactively.

More recently, the issue of online or cyber bullying has justifiably received increased media attention and it is clear that children and young people's participation in chat rooms, instant messaging and other social networking sites potentially puts them at risk. Government guidance (DCSF, 2007) and national charities such as Kidscape (2010) are being co-ordinated to raise awareness and offer support to children and young people, parents and carers and professionals in this area.

 ## Workplace activity

Do you have an anti-bullying policy in your setting? Talk to colleagues about how you have tackled or would tackle examples of bullying (see *Beat Bullying* in 'Further reading').

Safeguarding and protecting children and young people

It is common for non-social-work practitioners to feel unsure about whether to pass on information to the designated child protection officer or to make a phone call to the police or social services. Yet, one of the main lessons we have learnt in recent years is that information can be known by many separate organisation and professionals, but if this information is not shared, the extent of the problem may be missed and children and young people put at risk. The whole picture of a child, young person and their family can only be explored if all practitioners work together.

The DCSF guidelines on working together to safeguard children (DCSF, 2010) provide clear summaries of the different roles and responsibilities of a range of agencies and practitioners. The fundamental principle is that everyone shares responsibility to promote and safeguard the welfare of children and young people. Agencies such as health professionals, youth services, housing authorities, schools, play services and early years services need to be aware of the local child protection policy and understand risk factors, and all settings are required to have a designated staff member with whom any safeguarding or well-being concerns should be discussed. Much of the broad guidance and principles related to different roles and responsibilities is contained within local child protection procedures and the 'working together to safeguard children' guidelines (DCSF, 2010). It is imperative that all practitioners take some time to become familiar with these documents and consider what the key roles and responsibilities are in their setting.

∿ Reflection point

Consider your role and the tasks you need to carry out each day. How often do you refer to your child protection policy in your setting? Who is the key professional colleague you would approach about a concern or worry about a child?

Write a list of any issues that may have arisen from this chapter so far and decide how you will ensure you are familiar with policy, guidance and legislation. Perhaps you will raise these issues with your colleagues in a team meeting or with your manager in supervision.

The ecological perspective, outlined in the Introduction, takes into account not only the child's or young person's needs and development, but also considers the child or young person within their environment. A practical illustration of how this can be explored is through the 'ecomap'. The ecomap is a drawing of the child or young person within their social environment, as in Figure 10.1. The zig-zagged lines indicate relationships within which there is tension and the straight lines indicate a close, positive relationship (the more lines the stronger the relationship). Billy has a close relationship with his mum but it contains some tension as she is disabled and Billy has a lot of caring responsibility. He is a bit of a loner and doesn't get on well with his classmates, who find him a bit odd. His parents are divorced and he only sees his father very infrequently. He gets on reasonably well with his teacher, but his two closest relationships are with Liz and Amir, his neighbour.

This is a quick, holistic assessment tool, which provides a snapshot that gives us and the child or young person a view of the environment in which they are living and interacting. It also gives an idea of

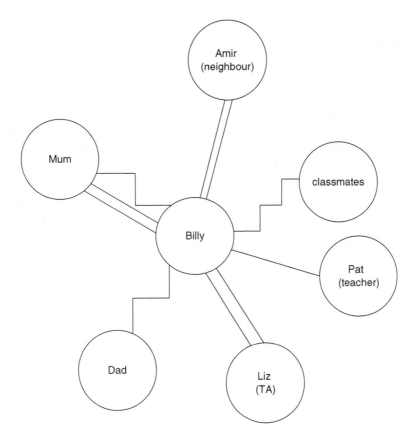

Figure 10.1 Ecomap for Billy

the nature and significance to the child or young person of a number of relationships, with family, friends and organisations.

〰 Reflection point

Start by drawing an 'ecomap' for yourself, putting your own key people in the circles. What does the completed map tell you about yourself? How might it look to somebody else?

Now think about a child or young person you work with and draw an ecomap for them. Sketch out the key people, adults, children, pets and professionals in their life and emphasise the strength or weakness of these relationships. This will give you a 'snap shot' of the situation. Remember that this is your perception of how things are (and the ecomap the child or young person might draw for themselves could look different), and that things are dynamic and the situation and relationships will change.

The child or young person should be encouraged to make the map their own if they wish, and the practitioner might use it as something to be returned to at different times with that child or young person.

As practitioners, it is vital for us to consider our own values and ideas before making judgements and questioning other people and/or their situations. How might our own assumptions make us more or less concerned about children's welfare? For example, a Serious Case Review (SCR) in July 2011 found that three siblings suffered severe and recurring abuse, including frequent episodes of physical abuse, emotional cruelty and neglect over a nine-year period before one child's repeated allegations of mistreatment were finally acted upon. The parents concerned were a research scientist and a chemist and the SCR revealed that the professionals' approach was affected by perceptions and assumptions made regarding the parents' social class, professional status and high academic qualifications (Puffett, 2011).

When thinking about safeguarding children, we therefore always need to be prepared 'to think the unthinkable'. One way of doing this is to consider what we mean by these types of abuse:

- neglect;

- physical abuse;

- sexual abuse;

- emotional abuse.

〰 Reflection point

Take each one of the categories above and think about what these mean to you.

Perhaps discuss with other practitioners the differences between different types of abuse and highlight where they overlap. For example, does emotional abuse feature in all the other types of abuse or does it stand alone as an easily recognisable form of abuse? Are there different forms of neglect which might be more or less difficult to identify?

The assessment of risk involves the weighing up of both positive and negative outcomes for children and their families. Caddick and Watson (2001) have discussed the individual's right to choose to take risks. This is often a discussion that takes place when working with young people, particularly when exploring drug use, alcohol and sexual activity, although taking risks is also a key part of development for younger children. Both children and young people need to learn what their limits are and often the practitioner's role is to support them in exploring this.

However, sometimes the risk at which young people place themselves is unacceptable or a child may be being placed at risk by parents or carers. Professionals other than social workers may not be involved in carrying out full in-depth assessment but will need to make decisions about whether to take their concern to the designated person in their setting, and will benefit from having considered some essential questions, as illustrated in the case study below.

 Case study

The situations below could occur in nursery, play centre, school or youth centre environments. They are not clear and could be open to conjecture and analysis, so consider the final question: what is your overall judgement? This is crucial as rigorous assessment of the problem and examination of any risk or concern needs careful thought.

- Sam is twelve. He tells you that he is worried about his friend Kay who is thirteen. She says that her stepfather has been coming into her room at night and lies on her bed with her, which makes her feel uneasy.

- Joe is three and often plays very rough games, throwing his toys and charging at other children. He has told you that his uncle frightens him at night time.

Consider the following questions when thinking about risk and the case studies above. (These questions are from Eileen Munro's work on risk and child protection (Munro, 2008: 76)):

- What is or might be happening?

- What might happen?

(Continued)

(Continued)

- How likely are these outcomes?

- How undesirable are they?

- What is your overall judgement?

Think of a scenario from your own work context and consider the questions above as a starting point. These are complex questions and you may not be able to answer each of them with a definitive statement, but it is important to explore exactly what your concerns or worries are about a child or young person.

Now consider whether you think the child or young person is at risk of significant harm (see below) and explore with a colleague what you would do next.

In the *Working Together to Safeguard Children* (DCSF, 2010) guidance, significant harm is defined as:

> Sometimes, a single traumatic event may constitute significant harm, for example, a violent assault, suffocation or poisoning. More often, significant harm is a compilation of significant events, both acute and long-standing, which interrupt, change or damage the child's physical and psychological development. (DCSF, 2010: 36)

During the latter half of 2010 and early 2011, Professor Eileen Munro undertook a review of child protection (Munro, 2010; DfE, 2011a). The government's response to this review was published in July 2011 (DfE, 2011c), identifying four main themes:

- valuing professional expertise;

- sharing the responsibility for early help to children and their families;

- developing social work expertise and supporting effective social work practice;

- strengthening accountability and the promotion of learning for all practitioners.

Summary

In this chapter, the core themes of safeguarding and well-being have been explored. The concept of 'significant harm' has been highlighted and issues for practice have been considered, specifically in relation to the assessment of risk, the common assessment framework and other assessment models.

Finally, it is important to remember that we cannot legislate against or protect children and young people from all factors which potentially have a detrimental effect on well-being. However, central to integrated working is the idea that all practitioners can work individually and collectively to promote resilience, and support children's and young persons' lifelong learning and development.

Further reading

Beat Bullying: http://www.beatbullying.org/ An informative and helpful website with examples of projects, resources and training.

Coleman, J. and Hagell, A. (eds) (2007) *Adolescence, Risk and Resilience: Against the Odds*. Chichester: John Wiley. This is a useful book that explores a range of issues such as the role of the family, the experience of young people growing up in care, the experience of disabled young people and risk-taking behaviour and ideas around social exclusion. It is a useful book as it explores many of these issues in great depth and poses some interesting and thought-provoking questions.

Gilligan, R. (2009) *Promoting Resilience: Supporting Children and Young People Who Are in Care, Adopted or in Need*. London: BAAF Adoption and Fostering. A Useful reference to resilience and provides thought-provoking ideas for talking and working with children and young people.

Howe, D. (1999) *Attachment Theory, Child Maltreatment and Family Support: A Practice and Assessment Model*. Basingstoke: Palgrave. Provides a useful exploration of attachment.

NSPCC   http://www.nspcc.org.uk/help-and-advice/leaflets/leaflets-list-wda83843.html The NSPCC produce excellent guidance for children and young people, parents and carers, and professionals.

NSPCC (2010) *Child Protection Factsheet*. Available online at: http://www.nspcc.org.uk/Inform/research/questions/child_protection_legislation_in_the_uk_wda48946.html (accessed 26.07.11).

NSPCC (2011) *Child Homicides: Key Child Protection Statistics*. Available online at: http://www.nspcc.org.uk/Inform/research/statistics/child_homicide_statistics_wda48747.html (accessed 26.07.11).

Munro, E. (2010) 'Learning to reduce risk in child protection', *The British Journal of Social Work*, 40: 1135–51. Very relevant to the changing face of social work.

Perry, A. (ed.) (2009) *Teenagers and Attachment: Helping Adolescents Engage with Life and Learning*. London: Worth Publishing. This is a great book, full of very real examples with a simple 'step-by-step' exploration of what a worker could do to help engage young people.

Protective Behaviours UK: http://www.protectivebehaviours.co.uk/ PBUK are committed to reducing abusive and violent incidents through empowerment and education.

Walker, S. and Thurston, C. (2006) *Safeguarding Children and Young People: A Guide to Integrated Practice*. Lyme Regis: Russell House. A very useful book which explores child protection and safeguarding work, and provides useful exercises and points to consider.

Zwozdiak-Myers, P. (ed.) (2007) *Childhood and Youth Studies*. Exeter: Learning Matters. A challenging read that asks the reader to explore issues such as 'risk' or working with children in need of protection from many different perspectives. The book considers the social construction of risk and poses questions about whether childhood is in crisis.

References

Baginsky, M. (ed.) (2008) *Safeguarding Children and Schools*. London and Philadelphia: Jessica Kingsley.

Bichard, M. (2004) *The Bichard Inquiry*. London: The Stationery Office.

Bradshaw, J. and Richardson, D. (2009) 'An index of child well-being in Europe', *Journal of Child Indicators Research*, 2(3): 319–51.

Caddick, B. and Watson, D. (2001) 'Rehabilitation and the distribution of risk', in P. Parsloe (ed.), *Risk Assessment in Social Care and Social Work*. London: Jessica Kingsley.

Cameron, D. (2006) David Cameron's speech to Google Zeitgeist Europe 2006. Available online at: http://www.guardian.co.uk/politics/2006/may/22/conservatives.davidcameron (accessed 26.07.11).

Central Advisory Council for England (1967) *Children and their Primary Schools: A Report of the Central Advisory Council for Education (England) (The Plowden Report)*. London: Her Majesty's Stationery Office.

Children Act 1989. London: HMSO.

Children's Workforce Development Council (CWDC) (2005) *The Common Assessment Framework for Children and Young People: A Guide for Practitioners*. London: CWDC.

Department for Children, Schools and Families (DCSF) (2007) *Cyberbullying: A Whole-school Community Issue*. Nottingham: DCSF.

Department for Children, Schools and Families (DCSF) (2010) *Working Together to Safeguard Children: A Guide to Inter-agency Working to Safeguard and Promote the welfare of children*. Nottingham: DCSF. Available online at: https://www.education.gov.uk/publications/standard/publicationDetail/Page1/DCSF-00305-2010 (accessed 27.07.11).

Department for Education (DfE) (2011a) *The Munro Report of Child Protection: Final Report – A Child-centred System*. London: The Stationery Office.

Department for Education (DfE) (2011b) *Preventing and Tackling Bullying: Advice for School Leaders, Staff and Governing Bodies*. London: DfE. Available online at: http://www.education.gov.uk/schools/pupilsupport/behaviour/bullying/f0076899/preventing-and-tackling-bullying (accessed 26.07.11).

Department for Education (DfE) (2011c) *A Child-centred System: The Government Response to the Munro Review July 2011*. London: DfE. Available online at: https://www.education.gov.uk/publications/standard/publicationDetail/Page1/DFE-00064-2011 (accessed 27.07.11).

Department for Education (DfE) (2011d) *The Common Assessment Framework (CAF)*. Available online at: http://www.education.gov.uk/childrenandyoungpeople/strategy/integratedworking/caf/a0068957/the-caf-process (accessed 27.07.11).

Department for Education and Skills (DfES) (2005) *Excellence and Enjoyment: Social and Emotional Aspects of Learning (Guidance)*. Nottingham: DfES.

Department of Health and Social Security (1974) *Report of the Committee of Inquiry into the Care and Supervision Provided in Relation to Maria Colwell*. London: HMSO.

Easton, C., Gee, G., Durbin, B. and Teeman, D (2011) *Early Intervention: Using the CAF Process, and its Cost Effectiveness: Findings from LARC3*. Slough: NFER.

Education and Inspections Act 2006. London: HMSO.

Equality Act 2010. London: HMSO.

HM Treasury (2003) *Every Child Matters*. London: The Stationary Office.

Kelley, N. (2004) 'Child's play', *Community Care*, 1–7 July: 34–5.

Kidscape (2010) *Cyber Bullying*. Available online at: http://www.kidscape.org.uk/cyberbullying/cyberbullying.shtml (accessed 26.07.11).

Lister, R. (2003) 'Investing in the citizen-workers of the future: Transformations in citizenship and the state under New Labour', *Social Policy and Administration*, 37(5): 427–43.

Lister, R. (2004) 'The Third Way's social investment state', in J. Lewis and R. Surender (eds), *Welfare State Change: Towards a Third Way?* Oxford: Oxford University Press. pp. 157–81.

Michaelson, J., Abdallah, S., Steuer, N., Thompson, S., Marks, N., Aked, J., Cordon, C. and Potts, R. (2009) *National Accounts of Wellbeing: Bringing Real Wealth onto the Balance Sheet*. London: New economics foundation (nef).

Munro, E. (2008) *Effective Child Protection* (2nd edn). London: Sage.

Munro, E. (2010) *The Munro Review of Child Protection Part One: A System Analysis*. London: Department of Education.

NICE (2009) *Promoting Young People's Social and Emotional Wellbeing in Secondary Education (NICE Public Health Guidance 20)*. London: NICE. Available online at: http://www.nice.org.uk/PH20 (accessed 26.07.11).

Newman, T. (2004) *What Works in Building Resilience?* Ilford: Barnardos.

Puffett, N. (2011) '"Social class" blinded professionals to abuse of siblings', *Children and Young People Now*. Available online at: http://www.cypnow.co.uk/Social_Care/article/1081498/social-class-blinded-professionals-abuse-siblings/?DCMP=EMC-CONCYPNow%20Daily (accessed 26.07.11).

Royal College of Psychiatrists (2005) *The Emotional Cost of Bullying: Factsheet for Parents and Teachers*. Available online at: http://www.rcpsych.ac.uk/mentalhealthinfo/mentalhealthandgrowingup/bullyingandemotion.aspx (accessed 26.07.11).

Safeguarding Vulnerable Groups Act 2006. London: HMSO.

Seebohm, Sir F. (1968) *Report of the Committee on Local Authority and Allied Personal Social Services, Command 3703*. London: HMSO.

UNICEF (2007) *Child Poverty in Perspective: An Overview of Child Well-being in Rich Countries*, Innocenti Report Card 7. Florence: Unicef Innocenti Research Centre.

Tickell, C. (2011) *The Early Years: Foundations for Life, Health and Learning* [The Tickell Review]. Available online at: http://www.education.gov.uk/tickellreview (accessed 26.07.11).

Weare, K. and Gray, G. (2002) *What Works in Developing Children's Emotional and Social Competence and Wellbeing?* Southampton: The Health Education Unit, University of Southampton.

11

Supporting Transitions

Denise Kingston and Mark Price

Chapter Overview

This chapter considers the importance of transitions in different professional contexts and from a number of different perspectives. The term 'transition' incorporates discussion of the following: *physical transitions* or movements within a setting (from one activity to another) and from one setting to another; *key life transitions*, such as moving house and family changes; and *psychological transitions*, including moving towards independence. Readers are invited to consider commonalities between transitions in different settings; this then builds a picture of how transitions link and affect each other and supports a discussion on implications for practice.

In reading and engaging with the activities in this chapter you will:

- reflect on the concept of 'transition' and the importance of transitions in children and young people's play, learning and development;
- consider the transitions that occur within and between settings and how children and young people might be supported to manage these;
- explore the broader life transitions children and young people may experience and the implications for social, psychological and emotional development;
- develop an understanding of how different practitioners might work together to support transitions.

What are transitions?

Transitions are natural occurrences within a child and young person's experience. They include a move from one environment to another, new experiences, changes in relationships, and changes in routine and unexpected events. They occur within all phases of a child and young person's life and can have long-lasting effects.

Earlier chapters have looked at how during our lives we move from being babies to children to becoming adults, with all of the physical changes that this entails (Chapter 5), while others (Chapters 6 and 7) considered cognitive and social and emotional development. These *psychological transitions* support our understanding of how development leads to more complex forms of thought, emotional maturity and greater independence. Information within Chapters 5, 6 and 7 will be drawn upon as a basis for understanding the development of children and young people and how this impacts upon and is affected by the transitions we make.

Another set of important transitions are sometimes referred to as *key life transitions*. These include moving home, perhaps to a different part of the country or even moving between different countries, as well as other significant changes such as changing families and family contexts, resulting from birth, death, separation, divorce, new parental partnerships, all of which may bring upheaval. Such changes within and involving families can have a big impact on the child or young person but so also can changes in other significant relationships. Consider, for example, the potential impact of the loss of a pet, best friend or lifelong companion.

The transitions which currently appear to be producing the most research interest and accompanying literature are *physical transitions*. Typical physical transitions that children and young people make are likely to include moves between different learning and development contexts or settings, for example, as they progress from home to nursery to primary school, then through to secondary school and on to further training, college, university and work. During this time, other physical transitions may be made as well. Whilst spending time in one setting, children often engage with and are involved in other groups and activities. For instance, whilst at school they may attend an after school club. Even though children appear to be in a stable environment, within one location or setting, further physical transitions are likely. In school, for example, children move from one lesson to another or from one activity to another.

Some writers distinguish between these types of transition calling those that happen over time *vertical transitions* and those which occur together or within a close period of time *horizontal transitions* (Kagan, 1991). Vertical transitions are linked to the children's increasing age and the related environmental changes which accompany this. They relate to developmental changes which occur as a child matures and other physical changes, typically associated with location, as they move through the various phases of education. Vertical transitions include moves between settings but also within the setting as the children progress through year groups or move through age associated rooms, clubs and activities. Horizontal transitions tend to happen at roughly the same time and form part of our everyday lives. For example, in one day a child may have a transition from home to school then to after school club or activity and then back to home. Horizontal transitions often involve frequent changes between settings within relatively short time scales.

All types of transition involve a phase of intensified adjustment and accelerated developmental demands which are determined by the particular social situation or series of significant situations or events which constitute the transition. A transition is not complete until the child or young person no longer feels 'like a fish out of water'. Transitions are likely to mean a change in environment and/or status and a feeling of leaving a 'comfort zone' and encountering the unknown. They may include encountering a new culture, place, people, role, rules and identity. They may include unfamiliar sounds, sights, words, new information, new people, larger groups and new routines and 'culture'. As such, they create the potential for anxiety, tiredness, discomfort and bewilderment (Barrett, 1986). However, they can also be seen as new opportunities and an exciting time that involves new people working together and a time for growth and development. Seeing transitions as *processes* like this, rather than one-off events, allows us to see how they may be linked and interconnected and to understand how one transition (and how a child or young person adjusted to that) might impact on how the next one will be approached. It also supports us in understanding how some children and young people might deal with an unanticipated event, such as sudden illness, death or other serious disruption to normal life.

Transitional experiences are important to consider as they may either support a child and young person's development and growth, supporting in particular their resilience, or lead to them becoming more vulnerable in the future (see Chapters 7 and 10). Poor transitions are likely to have an adverse effect on children and young people's learning and development.

Brooker (2008), after considering a number of studies looking at transition to school, estimated that 5 to 10 per cent of children adapted poorly to school life and as a result continued to be at risk of school failure throughout their school careers. She described poorly managed transitions to school as 'creating a huge pool of unhappy children and unfulfilled adults' (2008: 10). Children and young people who have been traumatised by poorly managed transitions in the past may naturally presume that all transitions will be traumatic (Daly et al., 2004). Individuals will generalise from previous experiences, whether they are positive or negative, so that when they enter a new environment during a transition, typically they will apply previously learnt behaviours and skills and continue to use this strategy throughout their lives (Gelfer and McCarthy, 1994). In order to explore these ideas further, two perspectives of the transition experience will be considered in greater depth – the loss and change perspective (Kübler-Ross, 1969; Hopson and Adams, 1976) and the ecological model which we encountered in the Introduction (Bronfenbrenner, 1979).

Transition as loss and change

From the earliest separation from our mother or our primary carer, through to leaving home, transitions involve coping with loss and change – the process of 'letting go' of relationships and belongings. In seeking to explain how individuals deal with transitions, Hopson and Adams (1976) indentified seven key stages:

1 **Immobilisation** – a sense of being frozen, unable to act or understand, this could be seen as similar to shock;

2 **Minimisation** – denial that the change is important or that the change is relevant/happening to them;

3 **Depression** – the emotional impact of the change;

4 **Acceptance** – realisation that there is no going back;

5 **Testing** – trying out new behaviour to cope with the situation;

6 **Seeking meaning** – reflecting on change;

7 **Internalisation** – the new meanings discovered become part of the behaviour and a new identity.

We can see links here to the influential work of Elizabeth Kübler-Ross (1969) and her five stages of grief based on her research with dying patients:

1 **Denial** – *'I don't believe this is happening to me.'*

2 **Anger** – *'It's not fair – why me?'*

3 **Bargaining** – *'If only I could ...'*

4 **Depression** – *'What's the point of going on?'*

5 **Acceptance** – *'It's ok – I can manage this.'*

More broadly, Kübler-Ross's model has been seen as relevant to the process of dealing with loss and change. At a much more 'commonplace' level, for example when we misplace a treasured possession (e.g. a book or favourite item of clothing), we can see echoes of the five stages in our loss process. And at a deeper or more significant level, if a child hears that his or her parents are separating, these five stages might also be anticipated. We can then see that at different times, a child or young person will require different levels of support and intervention. We will all manage such times of loss and change in different ways. Both of these models, though, point to the need to prepare for loss and change when we know it is on the horizon, as well as drawing on coping strategies when change occurs unexpectedly.

 Workplace activity

Consider each of the Hopson and Adams' stages in turn (see above). How would you know that a child or young person was at this stage? What would you be likely to see? How would you support that child or young person on to the next stage of adjustment?

> Remember, it is important to *register* feelings ('Are you feeling sad because Daddy has gone home?'), *recognise* what those feelings are ('Sometimes it is hard when Daddy leaves, isn't it?') and *respond* appropriately ('You know Daddy will be back to collect you for your lunch, don't you?').

Winnicott (1953) introduced the idea of the 'transitional object' which the child uses to span their internalised world and the external world at times of change. At its most fundamental, Winnicott used the term to refer to objects such as a thumb or favourite soft toy or blanket used by the child as comfort and security, substituting for the mother's breast at times of stress and anxiety. Away from this literal interpretation, we can also reflect on the way that we all use transitional objects to support us through transitional processes. For example, a favourite photograph of family members in our wallet, on our mobile phone, or on a desk at work is to remind and reassure us of a loved one when we are apart, or when we move home, the first objects we put in place to help us feel settled in.

We can therefore incorporate the idea of transitional objects into our practice with children and young people; for example, in suggesting that young children bring into nursery or school an object that is important to them in relation to a particular theme. For children in long-term care, it is common to develop 'life story' work, through creating a book (or sometimes a box) of significant events and people in their lives. The child or young person takes this book or box with them as they move between 'placements' (a foster, residential or adoptive home).

Reflection point

Think back to the last time you experienced a big transition in your life (perhaps it was a new job, a new relationship, the end of a relationship, a house move or starting at university?).

How did you feel? How did you prepare yourself for this new phase in your life? How could this transition have been made easier for you?

(Continued)

(Continued)

Consider now the transitions that occur within your setting. If they require a period of adjustment, can you justify them all? Could they be reduced? How are these supported? What preparations are made for children leaving the setting? What strategies are used to involve parents/carers/others in the process, etc.?

Thinking more generally about transitions, should we question the practice of grouping children by age in class, nursery rooms, clubs/ activities and phases of education? What purposes do they serve and whose needs do they meet? How can children and young people be given control and ownership over transitions? How can settings be changed to limit transition difficulties?

The ecological model of transition

Bronfenbrenner (1979) is one of the most influential researchers in the area of transitions. He considered the environment in which children and young people develop to be a major influence on their learning. His description of the settings and relationships which make up the ecological environment of the child can be found in the Introduction. He viewed children and young people not as isolated individuals but as linked to the social world of which they are part. Put simply, he told us that if we want to understand how children develop, we need to view children as belonging to and having links with a range of different interconnected systems, which either directly or indirectly impact on their development. He explained that these links and the interdependency between the systems can change at any level. Such changes he called transitions.

Transitions, such as becoming a parent, the birth of a sibling, starting at school or a club, getting a job or promotion, occur when an individual's position in his or her ecological environment 'is altered as a result of a change in role, setting or both' (Bronfenbrenner, 1979: 26). Bronfenbrenner emphasised the importance of transitions as both a consequence of and the beginning of further developmental processes. He said transitions were fundamental to human development as they require the developing person to change and adapt to their environment. They include alterations to the settings that the children and young people are part of and/or to the roles they hold

in those settings. They expose them to new types of
and new activities. An ecological transition which re
to commute between a primary developmental c
home) to a secondary developmental context (such
about changes in identity, relations and roles.

The application of Bronfenbrenner's model can help us to understand the changes that take place during vertical and horizontal
transitions as well as how they might affect an individual or group of
individuals. Bronfenbrenner's model can support us in developing
good practice by considering the assumptions that underpin his
model and linking those to the transitions we are involved with.

Taking as an example the vertical transition a child makes when they
first leave home (primary developmental context) to attend nursery
or playgroup (secondary developmental context) and linking this to
Bronfenbrenner's ecological environment and his underlying assumptions can be a useful process. The first assumption worth noting is
that the process of adjustment will involve the child in changing to
meet the demands of these two different environments and that they
will interact with each other. The child's ability to adjust to the new
nursery environment will be influenced not only by their own individual characteristics, but by the views of those around them, more
specifically the views of their parents/carers. People who share their
microsystem have a powerful impact on transition. Their views on the
child's readiness, for example, their expectations and beliefs about
what a nursery should offer and what it means to be a child at nursery will all affect the child's adjustment process.

Secondly, Bronfenbrenner reminds us of the importance of the *meso-
systems* within the child's environment, that is, the strength and
nature of the links between the different settings they attend.
Basically, the stronger and better the links between the settings, the
better the outcomes are likely to be. Establishing and maintaining
positive partnerships and links with parents/carers (and others) at
times of transition is important.

Thirdly, at the *exosystems* and *macrosystems* level, we know that all
individuals are affected by decisions and events that take place outside their immediate environment and over which they have little or
no control or knowledge. At the exosystems level, the child's adjustment may be indirectly affected by the demands of a parent/carer's
job, for example. This is a setting that the child does not enter but

...e that may prevent the parent or carer from being able to give all of the time and commitment to supporting the child's induction into the nursery they would like.

At the macrosystems level the child will be influenced by the wider requirements and expectations of the community within which they live, their local authority and the government. These systems affect the individual and their transitions in a number of ways. One example would include the current beliefs and culture within their community, such as the way children are expected to behave and act at particular ages. What is considered a 'normal' reaction will affect how they and others perceive their success or lack of it during any transition. Another example would include the policies and practices that different settings are likely to have, such as the beliefs, values and activities found within the setting, the space and amenities, the staffing and management of the setting. These may be guided by government legislation and/or by local expectations and processes.

Bronfenbrenner's ideas have led to a move away from the traditional view of a transition (especially within the world of education) where the responsibility for its success was seen to lie totally within the child and their readiness for it. This view placed the responsibility for ensuring the child was ready, either on the child or young person themselves or on the adults around them. From this perspective the success of a transition depends on the child's/young person's preparedness or the adults' ability to adequately prepare them. Typically, the adult's role was to prepare the children to 'step up' the educational ladder and ensure that they had acquired 'the requisite academic knowledge and social skills to perform, conform and *learn* in the new setting' (Brooker, 2008: 6). This simplistic view has been replaced by the idea of transition as a process which involves adaptations and changes in roles and identities. Furthermore, these changes in children and young people's lives are seen as experiences which are shared by them, their families, their peers and by the communities in which they live.

〰️ **Reflection point**

Consider the possible changes and development that might result in the following contexts. As you read these statements, reflect on your own experience of any of these changes and of the experience of any children and young people with whom you are working at the moment.

Changes and development within the individual

Transitions from one setting to another typically include a change in role and identity: being a school pupil is different from being a child at nursery, being a secondary school student is different from a primary one, attending a club or outside activity requires the child to respond to another set of rules and expectations. Such changes at this individual level can result in strong positive emotions, such as excitement, anticipation, curiosity and pride, as well as negative emotions, such as anxiety, insecurity and fear. New skills may be learnt in these different settings, such as independence and social and academic skills.

Changes and development with others/interactions

Moving to a new setting will require the development of new relationships with the adults and other children and young people there. It may also impact on existing relationships as moving setting may mean leaving relationships behind as well as signalling the start of new ones. However, even existing and sustained relationships may well change as the expectations of children and young people change as they grow and move from one stage of school and life to the next. Secondary school pupils have different roles from nursery-aged children and they are perceived by those around them, including their parents and siblings, quite differently.

Changes and development at the contextual level

With any transition for one child there is an associated and linked transition for everyone else within their environment. How this is managed has a further effect on the child. Consider the impact that starting school or nursery is likely to have on the rest of a child's family, or how the family of the young person who first starts work or college might feel. The changes here are around the integration of the demands from the two or more settings that the child or young person attends. The family of a child at school needs to reorganise their timetable around school times and terms. They also need to learn to follow and accept the expectations and values within the setting, which might be very different from those at home, if the transition is to be successful.

Bronfenbrenner's ecological view of transition helps us to understand why children and young people's experiences of transitions can be so varied. It also supports us in understanding the importance of recognising and being responsive to the diversity of children and young people's backgrounds, interests, experiences, knowledge and skills. It allows us to make links between the children and young people, their families and the communities within which they live and also to broader society, including relevant current policies and practices. Appreciating the complexity of transition processes ultimately supports us in ensuring that the transitions we are involved with are truly inclusive (see Chapter 12).

Transitions as a trigger for development and learning

Although much of the current research concentrates on identifying the difficulties inherent in transitions, it is important to recognise their potential for supporting growth and development. Many transitions are unavoidable and are a natural part of the maturation process. Others are specifically situated in time, and often associated with age, in order to support the child or young person in their growing independence, knowledge and skills. Although there is continued debate about the age appropriateness of many of these transitions (the age that babies should leave their main carer, the age that formal education should start, etc.), there is no denying that change can be beneficial. Consider, for example, the benefits for young children who spend time away from home and experience new situations and develop new relationships and friendships.

Parents, children and young people themselves recognise the need for change to support growth and development. Parents will, for instance, describe their children as having 'outgrown' their current setting and that they are ready for the challenge of somewhere new as they progress through their educational careers.

Consideration of some of the more recent work on early brain development (see Chapter 5), and in particular the work considering dynamic systems theory, supports these ideas too. Dynamic systems theory tells us that the development of the central nervous system, together with the body's movement capacity, and the goals a child has in mind (for instance, to reach a toy or explore a new part of the room), interact with and are reliant upon the environment that is provided for the child. If this is correct, then ensuring that the environment suits the ability of the developing child is very important. It also explains why children and young people need to move through different environments over time.

There is a growing body of research which links resilience to the experiences children and young people have, and in particular how adversity may be overcome by individuals if they develop sufficient resilience (see Chapters 7 and 10). New situations and experiences can have a 'healing' effect for children if they are experienced as positive events. Children, even when seen as vulnerable, should not be shielded from difficult situations or challenges (Gilligan, 2009). Research is telling us that we should not avoid transitions, even if we could. Instead we should see them as learning experiences and support children and young people successfully through them.

Finally, consideration of the work of famous cognitive developmental theorists, such as Bronfenbrenner (1979) and Piaget (1950) and Vygotsky (1978) (see Chapter 6), support us in understanding the importance of new and novel experiences and situations. Although Piaget and Vygotsky do not use the term, the links to transition within their theories are clear. Piaget tells us that it is the adaptations we make when faced with new information/situations – which enable us to build upon and create more complex schema – that lead us to learning about and understanding our worlds. Vygotsky tells us that support from a 'more able other' in situations which would otherwise confound us, supports and extends our learning through a process of co-construction. Both acknowledge the importance of providing cognitive challenge through the environment.

Transitions, then, are not all bad, and some would say they are necessary for cognitive growth and support the development of resilience. When a child or young person has enjoyed a history of successful transitions they may even use transitions to support and shape their future growth and development towards independence.

Case study

Frankie is sixteen and like other young people in Year 11, she's just about to take her GCSEs. During Years 9 and 10, Frankie went through what her dad calls her 'wild' time. Whilst she didn't go completely 'off the rails', she did row with her parents a lot, used drink and occasionally drugs, stayed out late in the local park and

(Continued)

(Continued)

was excluded once or twice for abusive behaviour towards teachers. During the last few months, though, Frankie has settled down a lot and is determined to go on to college if she can get the grades she needs.

Most of her friends have applied to the local college to continue their studies. However, Frankie has decided she wants a clean break. She doesn't want to lose touch completely with her friends, but she does want to start the next phase of her life without some of the 'baggage' of previous peer group pressures and expectations and so she has applied to go to a college in a nearby town. Frankie is understandably apprehensive about this change – going to college is a big enough deal as it is, but to make a fresh start, making new friends is an added challenge. But facing this challenge has made Frankie even more determined to succeed on her own terms.

Think about children or young people you work with. Can you identify strategies they have adopted to manage transitions?

Examining transitions

In this section we will consider a number of different transitions in more depth in order to recognise some of the general issues, identify some of the difficulties the children and young people may experience, and consider some of the lessons learnt and how these might impact on practice. It would be impossible to consider all transitions that are likely to occur, so we discuss two traditionally recognised transitions across the age phases – that from home to nursery and from primary to secondary school. Understanding these will support us in preparing for transitions if we work within those contexts, but it will also enable us to draw out common issues that support practice within any transition process.

Fabian (2002) describes such transitions as involving three categories of change or discontinuity:

- **Physical changes** – where the physical environment is very different in size, location, number of people, etc.;

- **Social changes** – where the individual's identity changes, as does their social network and the people with whom they interact;

- **Philosophical changes** – where the values, beliefs and approaches to learning and teaching can be very different from those experienced previously.

We will consider the following two key transfers or transitions using Fabian's model.

Transfer from home to nursery/nursery school

Traditionally, the transition from home to the first educational establishment a child attends is regarded as one the most important, and therefore needing the greatest adaptation.

> **Physical changes** Typically, nursery will involve the child becoming familiar with a new, larger environment, with a larger group of children with whom they are expected to interact and generally an even larger group of children within the whole setting.
>
> **Social changes** The social environment in the nursery is usually more complex than the previous home one. It is likely to involve an increase in interactions with peers and a decrease in interactions with adults. Even with small groups and classes, child–adult ratios typically mean that practitioners have less time to respond to the individual needs of the children than their parents at home. In terms of parent–child interactions, this is typically lessened too, as parents have less input in the child's day-to-day activities. Finally, the child begins to see themselves, and is seen by others, as a child who attends nursery, signalling a change in role and identity.
>
> **Philosophical changes** Pianta (2004) describes this transition as one which requires the child to shift and accommodate to new educational demands. Typically, children will be expected to get involved in unfamiliar activities. This is often combined with the recognition that their performance on those tasks will be used to make comparisons between them and others, and possibly also to make future educational decisions. There may also be some changes and adjustments needed regarding beliefs about what education is and any consequent mismatch in expectations. Education might be viewed differently in different nurseries and different homes, with some nurseries seeing independence, choice and play as fundamental for learning, while others prefer a more formal and didactic approach. Such mixed messages will undoubtedly impact on both the child and the parent/carer.

Pianta (2004) summarises the changes for the children within this transition as increasing demands and decreasing support. Perhaps not surprisingly, parents and adults view this transition as requiring the most change for the children – the children typically have to do more 'work' during this transition than anyone else. In other words, the least experienced participants in the transition need to make the most adaptations.

Transfer from primary to secondary school

Although there is some evidence that transfers between primary and secondary schools are improving (Galton et al., 1999), this is still a challenging transition, and one that coincides for many with the onset of puberty and adolescence.

> **Physical changes**   Typically, there are changes in size of school and routines. Pupils might be expected to travel independently to school, and this journey may be longer than the previous one. Pupils often need to become accustomed to moving rooms several times each day. They need to be able to organise their materials, themselves and their time more independently.

> **Social changes**   The social environment in the secondary school is often more complex than in primary school with additional movement between groups, teachers and classrooms throughout the day. Typically, there is a greater concern about, and more reports of, being bullied in secondary schools from both the pupils themselves and their parent/carers (Evangelou et al., 2008). The young person needs to adapt to and take on the role of a secondary school student. This new role is likely to impact on their families, friends and the community within which they live.

> **Philosophical changes**   As the movement is from one educational context to another, the assumption might be that philosophical views of education and how learning is best achieved support the transition. However, this does not appear always to be the case. Secondary school teachers may appear to disregard previous learning and experience so that new students' abilities are underestimated, and secondary school teachers can be critical of their primary school colleagues for not teaching independent learning skills early enough (McGee et al., 2004). It is interesting to note that this transfer is often accompanied by a drop in academic attainment, which may be partly due to the lack of continuity of curriculum between schools.

Evangelou et al. (2008) reports that pupils who considered themselves as feeling comfortable with their new physical environment and the new demands of the routine (described as successful transitions) suggest that pre-start visits, induction days with orienteering activities and relaxed school rules in the early days of attendance are helpful. They also found support with independent learning and writing skills very useful. Further, where schools have supported children early on in developing friendships and have engaged in activities designed to support self-esteem, they have reported positive results (McGee et al., 2004).

The framework used for thinking about the two transitions above can be usefully considered when planning for improvement in any transition process.

> ∿ **Reflection point**
>
> Consider a transition that you have been involved in recently. What were the physical, social and philosophical changes involved? How would/do understanding these support you in developing improved transition processes?

Fortunately, the difficulties most children and young people experience during transitions are temporary. However, for a small number of children this is not the case. McGee et al. (2004) reported that children from ethnic minority backgrounds generally found the transition to secondary school more problematic than those from majority backgrounds, and that the pupils saw these difficulties as lying within the structure and organisation of the school, whereas the teachers perceived these difficulties as resulting from problems the pupils brought with them. The nature and level of family support was linked to successful transition and achievement, and where this was lacking, it had a marked effect. Children from households classified as of low socioeconomic status typically had lower achievements than their peers who benefitted from additional support during transition processes. The gender of children had an effect too, with girls typically valuing education more at transfer and boys being judged by teachers as more demanding and in need of additional support. Particular difficulties for children with Special Educational Needs (SEN) are identified by Evangelou et al. (2008). They found that while academic difficulties were addressed by augmented transition processes, there were still issues with these pupils being bullied more than others.

Such findings are likely to impact on our thoughts around these vertical (over time and linked with age) transitions that children make. However, they are equally valid for the horizontal transitions children and young people make as part of their daily routines. Some children will find the daily transitions they make from home to school to after school club, or even within one setting as they move from one activity to the next, more difficult than others.

Implications for practice

There will always be individual differences and circumstances that need to be taken into account. However, it is possible to pull out some commonly acknowledged good practice with transition processes.

- Transition processes need to be informed by a clear understanding of the 'client' or stakeholder group – the children, young people, families and their communities. An effort should be made to forge links, beyond the setting, with all appropriate stakeholders, including families and communities. The links should be based on respect, which should in turn support the transferral of information both ways and support the development of any additional support mechanisms needed.

- Transition processes need to value and support the continuity of the children and young people's development and learning, including their earlier experiences in other settings and/or at home, together with their relationships and the social expectations they bring. They should encourage children's independence and successful functioning within their setting. Practitioners should reflect on experiences at their setting, noting the physical, social and philosophical changes that may be required by the children and young people. They should ensure an inclusive response to the individuals as well as their local communities.

- Transition processes should ensure that children and young people and their families have clear opportunities to get to know the setting's organisation, rules and structures, and include both formal and informal opportunities to visit and get to know the setting. This should support knowledge of the setting itself, including the social structures within the setting, and allow them the opportunity to make new friendships and relationships, and understand the values and beliefs within the setting.

- Transition processes may need to be adapted to suit the individual or group needs of certain children and young people. Certain groups of children appear to be more vulnerable than others during transitions. Margetts (2007), for example, lists those with developmental delay, from low socioeconomic backgrounds, with English as an additional language, with little previous relevant experience and from diverse cultural groups as likely to be more vulnerable than others. However, it is important to consider each individual as an individual and recognise that additional support may be necessary for some children who do not fall within these groups, and equally some children within these groups will not require additional support. It is also important to consider that such additional support may *just* be good practice and so should be considered for everyone.

There is a growing body of research which concentrates on listening to children and young peoples' views about their experiences during transition (the importance of the child and young person's voice is discussed in Chapter 8). Children and young people undoubtedly have an important part to play in transitions, and by allowing them to be decision-makers and inform the process, the benefits for themselves, for future individuals in transition and for practitioners are undeniable.

For some children and young people, the process of transition can be extended over several years.

 Case study

Mohammed, aged sixteen, remembered his life in Somali as having two separate parts. He remembered the good times when he was surrounded by familiar people and ate good food in the sunshine, when he had friends that he played with and a school he attended. He also remembered the bad times when there was fighting and poverty and it was not safe to play outside or go to school, and when there was a constant feeling of danger and people did not trust one another. He remembered seeing his father killed and how he was so saddened by this that he could not run away. How his mother insisted that they needed to leave their home, take food and travel to the next town. They walked day and night, sleeping in the cover of the woods, until they arrived at the next city. Luckily they found an agent who helped them flee the country. Mohammed recalled the conversation he had with his mother about London while travelling and how she described the UK as a safe and democratic country. He had high hopes for their new lives: they would find a home and get back that sense of belonging and safety they had before the trouble began, a place to make friends, where his mother could work and he could study hard. Mohammed wanted to do well at school and become a doctor, like his father.

The case study above is designed to support us in considering the varied and diverse experiences the children and young people with whom we work may have. Understanding the backgrounds and cultures of the children and young people is the starting point to ensuring inclusive transition practices. However, working with others, those people who inhabit the child's microsystem, including outside agencies, are equally important.

Kohli and Connolly (2009) explain transition from an asylum seeker's perspective as including learning a new language, starting a new school, making new friends, finding a new home, discovering new habits and customs, retrieving and maintaining old behaviours and customs, and developing routines that help to restore ordinary living. Such a transition is likely to involve a deal of adaptation and change. However, alongside this there is often the need to have continued involvement with immigration control and their processes and systems whilst decisions are made regarding asylum being granted. Research suggests that this uncertainty is likely to have adverse implications on both their emotional health and social integration (Children's Society, 2006).

ᙧ Reflection point

Consider the additional support a child with English as an additional language might benefit from, and the value of planning for and making suitable adjustments to the structures within your setting during their transition period.

How would having access to an interpreter support the child/young person in understanding and adapting to their new environment – including understanding the expectations of the adults within the setting, the routines and rituals associated with the setting, as well as supporting the development of those important links with parents/carers/others.

How would not having this support impact on the enormity of the task for such an individual?

☐ Summary

Within this chapter we have considered the many and varied definitions of transitions within children and young people's development. Using case studies and research, we have illustrated some of the commonalities in experiences between and across transitions, and discussed the importance of recognising and valuing the individuality of experiences. We have considered the complexity of the transition process without proposing simple solutions, as we believe there are none, and instead we have invited reflection on the implications that handling such processes have for practice. An understanding of the nature of the transition process and the identified links with culture, community and wider society (mesosytems), which we know will change over time, makes it clear that there is a continuing and ongoing need for research here. This is particularly important given the changing nature of services and where services take new directions and approaches within transitions.

Further reading

Dunlop, A.W. and Fabian, H. (2007) *Informing Transitions in the Early Years: Research, Policy and Practice*. Maidenhead: Open University Press. An interesting selection of articles which consider different aspects of transition and give accounts of transition across various stakeholder groups

Elizabeth Kübler-Ross Foundation: http://www.ekrfoundation.org/ (accessed 24.07.11). This website gives further reading and resources relating to Kübler-Ross's work and implications for practice in supporting people affected by death and bereavement.

Loizou, E. (2010) 'Empowering aspects of transition from kindergarten to first grade through children's voices', *Early Years: An International Journal of Research and Development*, 31(1): 43–55. An in-depth study and close look at one transition and the children's views on it.

Petch, A. (2009) *Managing Transitions: Support for Individuals at Key Points of Change*. Bristol: The Policy Press. This is an interesting collection of articles considering transitions of potentially vulnerable young people and adults, written from a social care perspective.

References

Barrett, G. (1986) *Starting School: An Evaluation of the Experience*. London: AMMA.

Bronfenbrenner, U. (1979) *The Ecology of Human Development*. Cambridge, MA: Harvard University Press.

Brooker, L. (2008) *Supporting Transitions in the Early Years*. Maidenhead: Open University Press.

Children's Society (2006) *Making a New Life in Newham: A Study Investigating the Factors that Facilitate and Prevent Young Refugee Settlement in Newham*. London: The Children's Society.

Daly, M., Byers, E. and Taylor, W. (2004) *Early Years Management in Practice*. Harlow: Pearson Education.

Evangelou, M., Taggart, B., Silva, K., Melhuish, E., Sammons, P. and Siraj-Blatchford, I. (2008) *Effective Pre-school, Primary and Secondary Education 3–14 Project (EPPSE 3–14): What Makes a Successful Transition from Primary to Secondary School*. Nottingham: DCSF.

Fabian, H. (2002) *Children Starting School*. London: Fulton.

Galton, M., Grey, J. and Ruddock, J. (1999) *The Impact of School Transitions and Transfers on Pupil Progress and Attainment*. Research Report RR131. London: DfEE/HMSO.

Gelfer, A. and McCarthy, J. (1994) 'Planning the transition process', *Early Years Development and Care*, 104: 79–84.

Gilligan, R. (2009) *Promoting Resilience: Supporting Children and Young People Who are in Care, Adopted or in Need*. London: BAAF Adoption and Fostering.

Hopson, B. and Adams, J. (1976) 'Towards an understanding of transition', in J. Adams, B. Hopson and H. Hayes (eds), *Transition: Understanding and Managing Personal Change*. London: Martin Robertson.

Kagan, S.L. (1991) 'Moving from here to there: Rethinking continuity and transitions in early care and education', in B. Spodek and N. Saracho (eds), *Yearbook in Early Childhood Education* (Vol. 2). New York: Teachers College Press. pp. 132–51.

Kohli, R.K.S. and Connolly, H. (2009) 'Transitions for young people seeking asylum', in A. Petch (ed.), *Managing Transitions: Support for Individuals at Key Points of Change*. Bristol: The Policy Press.

Kübler-Ross, E. (1969) *On Death and Dying*. London: Routledge.

Margetts, K. (2007) 'Understanding and supporting children: Shaping transition practices', in A.W. Dunlop and H. Fabian (eds), *Informing Transitions in the Early Years: Research, Policy and Practice*. Maidenhead: Open University Press.

McGee, C., Ward, R., Gibbons, J. and Harlow, A. (2004) *Transition to Secondary School: A Literature Review*. Hamilton, NZ: The University of Waikato.

Piaget, J. (1950) *The Psychology of Intelligence*. London: Routledge and Kegan Paul.

Pianta, R. (2004) 'Transitioning to school: Policy, practice, and reality', *The Evaluation Exchange*, 10(2): 5–6.

Vygotsky, L.S. (1978) *Mind and Society: The Development of Higher Psychological Processes*. Cambridge, MA: Harvard University Press.

Winnicott, D. (1953) 'Transitional objects and transitional phenomena: A study of the first not-me possession', *International Journal of Psycho-Analysis*, 34: 89–97.

12

Promoting Equality and Inclusion

Denise Kingston and Mark Price

Chapter Overview

This chapter explores the concepts of equality and inclusion, at both a broad societal level and also more specifically at a setting/practice level, with a view to helping readers consider the extent to which their (and other professionals') practice addresses issues of equality and inclusion. In addition, it considers inequality and explores some of the personal, cultural and structural aspects behind these, with the aim of developing the reader's awareness of how taken-for-granted and implicit understandings of difference leads us to respond in particular ways. Ultimately the chapter seeks to develop thinking and understanding in relation to appropriate practice responses, and in particular examines how practitioners can work to develop an understanding of and commitment to social justice.

By reading and engaging with the activities in this chapter, you will:

- develop your understanding of the concepts of equality and inclusion, particularly in the context of children and young people's learning and development;
- reflect on and consider social, cultural, historical and political issues which have contributed to inequality, discrimination and disadvantage;
- identify aspects and key themes of legislation and governmental policy which seek to direct practice;
- develop skills and professional knowledge which support inclusive practices and service provision.

Inclusion

Despite the numerous frameworks and legislation that have been developed to support inclusion, and the multicultural and diverse nature of society today, inequality persists and blights lives. This poem was written by a fourteen-year-old boy in a school setting:

The Shadow

A lonely figure enters.

He produces a ball.

'Anyone want to play?'

They turn away,

He is different.

'My father told me to stay clear of them sort'.

He moves towards the playground wall.

He knows each red brick almost by name.

The wall is his friend.

He scratches his curly black hair.

'Go back to where you came from!'

The daily chant begins

He closes his ears

And moves on.

School finishes

At the back of the bus queue he stands

Desolate and alone

His expressionless face

Disguises the day's deep damage

Like a veil.

He climbs the stairs to his humble flat,

The lift is out of order

He reaches for his key, enters

He greets his mother and sister

Goes quickly to his room.

He covers his black face

with his black hands

and cries softly into the pillow

which knows his tears so well.

(taken from Brown, 1998: 57)

Promoting equality and being inclusive requires us to be open to change and prepared to challenge the stereotypes and discriminatory views we may hold, as well as those of other practitioners and those found in society more broadly. Consider James Baldwin's words: 'not everything that is faced can be changed, but nothing can be changed until it is faced' (cited in Parker and Fukuyama, 2006: 28).

Understanding inclusion, and inclusive practice, is varied, ranging from only considering children with disabilities or Special Educational Needs, or people identified as belonging to vulnerable groups (examples of these would be disabled people, those from ethnic minority groups and those for whom English is an additional language), through to seeing inclusion as involving everyone within a setting, and finally to seeing inclusion in its broadest sense as a principled approach to education and society (Ainscow et al., 2006).

Different perspectives on promoting equality and inclusion

Some official definitions of inclusion (e.g. DfES, 2004; SkillsActive, 2011) emphasise that inclusion means that all children and young people participate and benefit, whilst others (e.g. DfES, 2003) focus on addressing the needs of specific groups, or do both (DfES, 2005), and yet others stress the importance of promoting positive attitudes to diversity and difference (e.g. DCSF, 2008).

These definitions reflect two perspectives in thinking about equality and inclusion. One is focused on ensuring that groups which have historically been seen as disadvantaged or oppressed are identified and specifically helped to overcome that disadvantage. The other emphasises inclusion as a universal principle applying to all children and young people.

The first of these two perspectives, sometimes called the 'inequalities perspective', can be challenged on a number of grounds. Firstly, an emphasis on vulnerable or 'at risk' might encourage us to view difference as problematic (Nutbrown and Clough, 2007) and reinforce the sentiment that 'everything would be alright if only they were more like us'. Secondly, there is the danger of assuming that all members of particular groups need our support and that there is a set way of supporting them, not recognising the *diversity of circumstances and experiences within groups*. Thirdly, this emphasis on specific groups may lead us to support *only those within such groups* and so fail to address unfairness and exclusion that happens outside those groups. Fourthly, concentrating on specific groups rests on the assumption that membership of a 'disadvantaged' group is unambiguous. It does not recognise that being a member of a group is often part of a subjective judgement, and/or self-identification – whether or not I see myself as belonging to a disadvantaged group will depend on a wide range of personal and social factors. An example of this is the category of (what we now call) Special Educational Needs. Membership of this group has been defined differently across settings, local authorities, countries and time. The term 'Special Educational Needs' and how it is judged or assessed changed between 1994 and 2001 as the Special Educational Needs code of practice was amended.

Countering these criticisms, the inequalities perspective has been driven by the need to recognise and address structural and cultural inequalities prevalent in society through policy and legislation in order to promote equality. For our purposes, the term can be applied to four main areas: equality of opportunity, equality of outcome or conditions, equality before the law, and equality for recognised 'at risk' groups of people.

- **Equality of opportunity** basically refers to everyone having the same opportunities or starting points. It is often contrasted with equality of outcome; equality of opportunity does not necessarily lead to equality of outcome.

- **Equality of outcome or conditions** refers to the degree of equality or inequality between individuals and groups. As we saw in Chapter 1, this is often the focus of policy.

- **Equality before the law** refers to everyone being subject to the same laws regardless of differences such as wealth or social standing. One example would be how the European Convention on

Human Rights (Council of Europe, 1950) regards all people as being equal and therefore being entitled to equal rights and treatment.

- The last aspect of equality links to historically disadvantaged groups, including, for example, **gender equality**, **race equality**, **sexual orientation and realignment equality** and social equality, where past policy and legislation might have supported unfair treatment and inequality but this has subsequently been addressed by more recent policy and legislation to reduce such inequalities.

In each of these areas, the equalities perspectives suggests that it is not until specific barriers to inclusion and equality for socially oppressed groups are removed that true social inclusion (and hence service and institutional inclusion) can occur.

Both the equalities perspective and the perspective of inclusion as a universal principle are important. We need to be committed to inclusion as a universal principle and also be aware of and knowledgeable about how and why certain groups of people and individuals are disadvantaged within society. Without this knowledge we would not necessarily recognise or question our practice at a deep enough level to effect change, as many aspects of inequality can be overlooked because they are seen as natural or routine or appear harmless (see reference to *hegemony* in Chapter 1, p. 25), unless they are truly understood.

Thinking about inequality, discrimination and oppression

Children and young people from black and minority ethnic groups, and children, young people (or their parents and carers) who identify themselves as lesbian, gay or bisexual, as well as children and young people from working-class families or those living in poverty may all experience discrimination and disadvantage which operates at three separate but inter-related levels:

- The individual and *personal* aspirations and prejudices of others (and sometimes themselves), which are embedded in ...

- The *culture* and 'fabric' of society, including the accepted 'norms' or simply the expectations of how everyday lives are lived, which form part of ...

- The *structure* of society (the social, political and economic aspects of the social order) (Thompson, 2003: 17).

The important issue here is that personal prejudices and ill treatment by individuals needs to be considered within the context of the accepted cultural norms of communities and society, and how these influence the values of those who live and work in those communities. In other words, an individual person's racism, sexism or homophobia, for example, needs to be seen as a reflection of the cultural environment in which they live. This is not to excuse these prejudicial and bigoted attitudes and values, but rather to understand how we are all influenced by the generalised cultural norms of the society we live in.

Similarly, such cultural values are influenced by, and in turn influence, structures in society and legislation embodied within government. For example, homophobia has been historically sanctioned through discriminatory legislation, and yet now (through the Equality Act 2010, for example) such discrimination is being challenged, and gay and lesbian relations are more openly accepted than ever before. It is clear, therefore, that such powerful considerations and any remaining prejudicial views or cultural norms (e.g. how many openly gay professional footballers are there?) are bound to impact significantly on any child or young person growing up with gay or lesbian parents, or knowing themselves to be homosexual.

At the personal and cultural level, how are such inequalities supported and perpetuated? One important mechanism is *stereotyping*. This arises from the way we make generalisations about our experiences and the world we encounter. These generalisations or 'yardsticks' are important as we develop frameworks and reference points for making sense of encounters, communication and relationships. We develop sets of perceived common traits or characteristics. For example, we might observe that many boys are interested in machines, mechanical devices and technical details. But it is an easy (and lazy) stereotype to suggest that *all* boys are interested in these, or, in fact, that these are the *only* things that boys are interested in, or that *only* boys are interested in these things. Clearly, not *all boys* or *only boys* are interested in machines and technology – many boys are not, whilst many girls are.

Stereotypes are personal beliefs that the characteristics we see in one person are to be found in all members of the group to which they belong. These beliefs are often supported culturally, through humour and jokes, for example, and through the media more generally. Stereotypes can be conceived as 'good', 'neutral' or 'bad', but all stereotypes do not reflect reality. For example:

- Not all South Asian girls are passive!

- Not all African-Caribbean boys are good at sport!

- Not all gay men are interested in interior design!

Sometimes, when we are unaware of stereotyping, other dimensions of inequality, disadvantage and discrimination can be perpetuated through the language we use. For example, we can discriminate or exclude individuals and groups through *trivialising* or *de-humanising* them. This is sometimes evident at the level of gentle 'banter' ('we were only joking'; 'she knows we don't mean it'; 'isn't this just another case of political correctness gone mad?'), or in the everyday language we use. For example, to refer to women as animals (bird, hen, chick, bitch, etc.), to simply refer to people by their disability ('the Down's boy'), or to make unreal demands ('be a real man – big boys don't cry') can all devalue an individual's identity and self-esteem.

When stereotypes and prejudice are used to make decisions and judgements about people, this is called *discrimination*, and when people or groups of people are treated systematically unfairly within society, this is called *oppression*. It is important to note the importance of power and status here. A feature of discrimination and oppression is the role played by the dominant group or culture in exercising structural and social power over the disadvantaged group or individual.

At the level of culture and structures in society, we might consider how inequalities are driven by the accepted norms and values, and policies, procedures and laws which support them. At the **cultural level**, we can see how history can have far-reaching influences on our values, assumptions and beliefs, and that naturally we tend to look for evidence which supports our beliefs. If this appears to be further endorsed by 'scientific knowledge', as some discriminatory views have in the past, it makes it all the more compelling. One such belief, which was widely accepted in the past but is now acknowledged to be groundless, is that fundamental differences exist between people of different races due to differing biological 'makeup'. This was a common assumption justifying European explorers as they conquered and claimed lands and subjugated people. The treatment of slaves, for example, was justified in terms of biological difference, *nature* rather than *nurture*.

How we explain difference between social groups is often still in terms of nature or nurture. For example, how do we explain why so many of the world's fastest athletes and most successful boxers are black? Possible explanations put forward might include:

- Genetically, people who originate from Africa are biologically, physiologically better equipped to run faster and box more effectively; *or ...*

- Black children and young people are supported and encouraged to engage more in physical activity than in academic study.

In relation to gender, *'nature versus nurture'* arguments also provide contrasting perspectives which account for apparent differences in boys' and girls' behaviour.

The impact of this debate has also been apparent with children and young people who are described as having Special Educational Needs and/or disabilities. Here, looking for medical reasons to account for difference (including genetic defects, abnormality, syndromes and disorders) has dominated practice in the past. This is expressed in the **medical model** of disability, which locates the problem as within the child, who is considered to be 'broken' and in need of 'fixing'. This model leads to practices such as specialist assessments, therapies, procedures and operations and is unfortunately also often accompanied by segregation from peers and communities – the resulting 'treatments' often occur in specialist settings, schools and hospitals. This focus on medical needs means that the child's common human needs – for friendships with the people who live around them, to play, to take risks, to make mistakes and learn from them, and to access all of the things which are available to their peers in their community – can be forgotten.

The **social model** recognises the role of the wider ecosystem of the child and that the problem may be located in society's response to the child and within the interactions that take place between the individual and society. The environment needs to adjust rather than the disabled person.

At the cultural level, discrimination can sometimes result from a group or organisation treating certain people differently from others. This type of discrimination is often known as *institutional discrimination* and is likely to be supported by policy and/or accepted practice within that context or setting. Examples include:

- Children and young people with impairments are not given access to the full range of activities, including outings;

- Meals provided do not meet the dietary requirements of certain religious groups;

- A uniform code does not consider the cultural traditions of certain groups concerning dress.

This kind of discrimination is referred to as *marginalising* individuals and groups. The process of marginalisation can occur through groups being excluded, as in the examples above. Marginalisation can also occur through use of language (e.g. chair*man*) and images which do not represent the range of potential users (e.g. few images of people from black and minority ethnic groups or of gay and lesbian couples/parents). This can lead those from these groups to feel that they are not welcome or the provision is not for them, and this can also reinforce negative stereotypes.

It is easy to miss how powerful the values and attitudes and institutionalised practices of an organisation can be in discriminating against certain groups of children and their families. Institutional discrimination may not necessarily be a conscious policy on the part of the organisation; more often it occurs because of a failure to consider the diversity of the community. Whether conscious or unconscious, institutional discrimination is a powerful and damaging force.

Also, at the **structural level** we find law designed to act against discrimination and as an agent for change. Laws against discrimination cannot necessarily change people's attitudes but they can change people's behaviour, and as there is an inter-relationship between how we behave and how we think, law can have an indirect effect on attitude. Over the past 40 years there has been a considerable advance with regard to addressing aspects of discrimination. There has been a movement away from specific laws designed to protect specific groups of people and towards a more inclusive approach of equality for *all*. This has led to the amalgamation of various government agencies (including those previously responsible for supporting and developing legislation in relation to SEN and disability, gender and race, etc.) – moving to a single Equality and Human Rights Commission and also a single Equality Act (2010).

Reflection point

The relationship between *personal, cultural* and *structural* dimensions of exclusion and oppression is very important. They each influence each other and sometimes it can feel like a set of 'chicken and egg' or 'Russian doll' relationships.

For example, how might ridiculing gay men and lesbians through 'jokes' and TV comedy relate to personal homophobia and the historical legislation against homosexuality?

Why might it then be unsurprising that some lesbian and gay teachers decide that they cannot disclose their sexual identity or young people find it hard to 'come out'?

Can you identify examples of the personal, cultural and structural levels of discrimination relevant to your context?

How might you go about challenging stereotypes in your practice?

Bringing inclusive values and practice together

Equality of opportunity is not equal treatment; it recognises that some people need to be treated differently in order to be able to be included and to participate fully.

Inclusion is about *reducing exclusion and increasing participation.* In schools, and other educational institutions, this exclusion may be linked to some associated behaviour and its impact on the learning of others. Inclusive practice sees the reduction of this type of exclusion and the promotion of the idea of increasing the setting's ability to accept and meet the needs of all children and young people. These ideas link to the rights that children have under the

UNESCO *Salamanca Statement* (1994), which urged all governments to educate all children locally unless there were compelling reasons to do otherwise. Britain's allegiance to the *Salamanca Statement* was reflected in the Green Paper *Excellence for All Children* (DfEE, 1997).

Undoubtedly, within most settings there will be some children or young people who find themselves unable to participate in activities. This more subtle form of exclusion occurs for many reasons and needs careful consideration. Some children and young people may be shunned by others as they do not know how to talk with them, play with them or understand them. If this is the case, we need to develop further our understanding of difference, or exclusion may result from the practices within the setting. Evans (2007) suggests that children and young people may feel isolated from their peers by being withdrawn from sessions for extra help, or from being too closely accompanied by a support worker or teaching assistant, so that other children and young people keep their distance. However this exclusion occurs, the children and young people may or may not recognise it for themselves. If they do, they may be feeling too scared to do anything about it, perhaps because they are being bullied. Being excluded can result in a multitude of negative feelings including depression and anger. These feelings may then result in the child withdrawing or 'acting out', making the situation potentially worse for them.

Recognising the complexity of this area of work, and in order to support the development of inclusive practice within settings, the Centre for Studies on Inclusive Education (CSIE), an independent body working to promote inclusion both nationally and internationally, commissioned a working group to develop a process and set of materials to help schools move forward in their inclusive journeys. This resulted in the *Index for Inclusion* (Booth and Ainscow, 2002). An *Index for Inclusion* was also produced to support early years, clubs and play schemes in reviewing their settings (Booth et al., 2006). The *Indexes* are regularly reviewed and updated and the latest schools' version was published in 2011.

The *Indexes'* (Booth et al., 2006; Booth and Ainscow, 2011) materials are designed to support practitioners in their growing understanding of the knowledge, skills, concepts and understandings required to enable them to empathise with and understand the diverse experiences and backgrounds children and young people may have in their settings. They describe three dimensions which need exploring if inclusive practice is to be considered in detail: *creating inclusive cultures, producing inclusive policies* and *evolving inclusive practices*. Put simply, the dimensions equate to what is in our *hearts* – our attitudes, values and feelings (cultures), in our *minds* – our planning, policies and visions (policies), and in our *hands* – what we do, the activities we offer and how we organise those (practices) within our settings. In order to develop inclusive practice in our settings, the *Index* suggests we engage in a self-review or self-evaluation process. This starts with a period of gathering all stakeholders' views of the setting, followed by the production of a plan, the implementation of that plan, and finally an evaluation, which leads on to another plan and the cycle of improvement continuing.

The materials and ideas within both *Indexes* are underpinned by a series of *inclusive values*. Booth et al. (2006) suggest values such as fairness, participation, sustainability, rights, compassion, and respect for diversity and community are important for truly inclusive settings. When considering society as a whole, other values, such as freedom, honesty and achievement, have been included (Ainscow et al., 2006). The materials are also informed by concepts of fairness and compassion, together with promoting the building of a sense of community and the recognition of how society and others' wishes and needs impact with aspects of legislation, including rights and entitlement.

Although all of these values are important, one in particular warrants further exploration: respect for diversity. Booth and Ainscow (2011: 23) suggest 'diversity includes seen and unseen differences and similarities between people: diversity is about difference within a common humanity'. Put simply, everyone is different from everyone else and what matters is how we view these differences. In relation to race and ethnicity in particular, this respect for diversity and acknowledgement and celebration of difference in terms of social identity is sometimes referred to as **multiculturalism**. Inclusion is about working to meet the needs of the children and young people in the local community. This might mean flexibility to meet differing needs rather than a generalised approach tailored to the majority or dominant group.

Case study: Yusuf

Consider how cultural values, as reflected in the newspapers here, can affect personal attitudes which can then perpetuate stereotypes and unfair treatment and how the structures within schools can fail to protect and support young people such as Yusuf. What are the causes of this vicious cycle of rejection and the resultant inequality of opportunity and outcomes? How might this cycle be avoided?

Early years

When Yusuf was born his parents had high expectations and wanted the best for him. They said he should stand with his 'head held high', proud of who he was.

Three years later, they brought him to England fleeing the unrest and dangers of their homeland in Iran. At the age of three and a half Yusef started nursery. The practitioners found him troublesome as he did not understand the language, played alone and often pushed them away when they tried to get him to join group time.

The newspapers had warned them about such types: 'these asylum seekers who abuse our generous social security system while often embarking on criminal activity'. Hadn't Yusuf already shown his true colours by pushing and refusing to conform? Talking to his parents was difficult too ... shouldn't they have learnt English by now?

Primary school

He moved to school accompanied by a report which clearly outlined his poor language skills and 'difficult' behaviour. Yes, his teachers knew about such children too. They needed to take special care with him. They were a little afraid but knew that they needed to prevent him from becoming uncontrollable and a criminal. They watched him closely and kept him under control. As the adults' unfair attitudes became clear to Yusuf, he began to question them. 'Just because I am always in trouble doesn't mean I did it'. He chose not see himself as the teachers did, someone who was inherently bad and who needed to be controlled. He began to question them, challenge them and disobey them. They in turn saw this behaviour as confirmation of his 'type'. Yusuf decided he needed to avoid the conflict and always doing the wrong thing so he chose to 'hang around' the shopping precinct rather than school. He thought his teachers and the other children would be happy not to have him around.

(Continued)

(Continued)

Secondary school

Despite secondary school offering a new start, he continued to be faced with disadvantage; he was unprepared for the new routines and expectations in his new school, he had few friends and poor reading and writing skills. He began to avoid work so that no one knew that writing was difficult for him. He was picked on in the playground and got into fights. Eventually he teamed up with a few other like-minded boys. He felt that only they really knew him and cared about him. They understood what it was like to be 'picked on', mistrusted and disrespected. Together, these boys became increasingly disaffected by school and reacted with disobedience, truanting, fighting and challenging all around them. Eventually Yusuf was excluded from school.

Beyond ...

Yusuf didn't attend the pupil referral unit to which he was allocated. He left school with no real qualifications and little chance of employment. He drifted along with his friends, and with little direction 'fell into' drugs and crime. He became known to the police and was eventually convicted. He felt rejected by all of those around him (society) and rejected them in turn. He had become anti-police, anti-authority and anti-social.

(*Source*: adapted from Richardson and Wood (1999: 6), based on work in Lambeth schools and youth service, and developed from material in *This is Where I Live: Stories and Pressures in Brixton*, published by The Runnymede Trust, 1996.)

How would you analyse Yusuf's experience in terms of the themes of this chapter? What do you think the various practitioners Yusuf encountered could have done to steer him on to a different path?

Summary

Promoting equality and inclusion is about making a difference to children and young people's lives. It is about recognising and celebrating the rich differences and diversity of the communities and society in which we live. It is about the belief and commitment that our services and provision should extend to and benefit all children and young people, respecting and celebrating their individual identities, abilities and their set of individual circumstances and attributes. But it is also about recognising that equality and inclusion have not always existed and that much still needs to be done to remove barriers to achievement, health and well-being. As individual practitioners, we have a duty and responsibility to promote inclusion and equality in our own services and settings. We also share a collective responsibility to create an inclusive society.

Further reading 📖

Asare, Y. (2009) *Them and Us: Race Equality Interventions in Predominantly White Schools*. London: The Runnymede Trust. Available online at: http://www.runnymedetrust.org/uploads/publications/pdfs/ThemAndUs-2009.pdf (accessed 21.07.11). A very helpful and insightful resource that addresses some challenging issues.

Centre for Studies on Inclusive Education (2006, 2011) *Index for Inclusion* (schools and early years) Available online at: http://www.csie.org.uk/publications/current.shtml#early-years-insert (accessed 21.07.11). These files will give you a practical guide, including materials and ideas, to assessing and making improvements in inclusion within settings.

Knowles, G. and Lander, L. (2011) *Diversity, Equality and Achievement in Education*. London: Sage. This book supports us in understanding and building empathy for some of the diverse experiences and backgrounds of the children and young people with whom we work in educational contexts.

Price, M. (2007) *All of Us: Working Together to Create a Safe and Supportive Learning Community for Lesbian, Gay, Bisexual and Transgender Young People and Staff in Secondary Schools*. Brighton: Brighton & Hove City Council/East Sussex County Council. Available online at: http://www.spectrum-lgbt.org/downloads/safety/All_of_Us.pdf (accessed 21.07.11). This resource pack and the accompanying DVD, 'Fear and Loving', gives guidance on policy, curriculum and whole-school initiatives to address homophobia in secondary schools.

World of Inclusion: www.worldofinclusion.com (accessed 21.07.11). This is a really useful website which, amongst other things, provides free downloads of books, up-to-date information and teaching materials, including some really interesting and informative videos relating to disability.

Wilkinson, R. and Pickett, K. (2009) *The Spirit Level: Why Equality is Better for Everyone*. London: Allen Lane. A readable and insightful book which explores the link between lack of inclusion and wider social problems.

References

Ainscow, M., Booth, T. and Dyson, A. (2006) *Improving Schools, Developing Inclusion*. London: Routledge.

Booth, T. and Ainscow, M. (2002) *Index for Inclusion: Developing Learning and Participation in Schools*. Bristol: Centre for Studies on Inclusive Education.

Booth, T. and Ainscow, M. (2011) *Index for Inclusion: Developing Learning and Participation in Schools* (3rd edn). Bristol: Centre for Studies on Inclusive Education.

Booth, T., Ainscow, M. and Kingston, D. (2006) *Index for Inclusion: Developing Play, Learning and Participation in Early Years and Childcare*. Bristol: Centre for Studies on Inclusive Education.

Brown, B. (1998) *Learning the Anti-discriminatory Way in Unlearning: Discrimination in the Early Years*. Stoke-on-Trent: Trentham Books.

Council of Europe (1950) *The European Convention on Human Rights*. Rome: Council of Europe. Available online at: http://www.hri.org/docs/ECMRSO.html (accessed 20.10.11).

Department for Children, School and Families (DCSF) (2008) *Statutory Framework for the Early Years Foundation Stage*. Nottingham: DCSF.

Department for Education (DfE) (1994) *Code of Practice on the Identification and Assessment of Special Educational Needs*. London: DfE.

Department for Education and Employment (1997) *Excellence for All Children: Meeting Special Educational Needs*. London: DfEE.

Department for Education and Skills (DfES) (2001) *The Special Educational Needs Code of Practice*. London: DfES.

Department for Education and Skills (DfES) (2003) *Vulnerable Childrens' Grant: Guidance*. Available online at: http://www.education.gov.uk/standardsfund/VCG02rev3lmc7.htm (accessed 17.05.11).

Department for Education and Skills (DfES) (2004) *Removing Barriers to Achievement*. Nottingham: DfES. Available online at: https://www.education.gov.uk/publications/standard/publicationdetail/page1/DfES%200117%202004 (accessed 21.07.11).

Department for Education and Skills (DfES) (2005) *Youth Matters*. London: The Stationery Office. Available online at: http://www.education.gov.uk/publications/eOrderingDownload/Cm6629.pdf

Equality Act 2010. London: HMSO.

Evans, L. (2007) *Inclusion*. London: Routledge.

Nutbrown, C. and Clough, P. (2007) *Inclusion in the Early Years*. London: Sage.

Parker, W.M. and Fukuyama, M.A. (2006) *Consciousness Raising: A Primer for Multicultural Counseling* (3rd edn). Springfield, IL: Charles C. Thomas.

Richardson, R. and Wood, A. (1999) *Inclusive Schools, Inclusive Society: Race and Identity on the Agenda*. Stoke-on-Trent: Trentham Books.

The Runnymede Trust (1996) *This is where I Live: Stories and Pressures in Brixton*. London: The Runnymede Trust. Available online at: http://www.runnymedetrust.org/publications/36/32.html (accessed 18.05.11).

SkillsActive (2011) *Multicultural Counseling* (3rd edn). Springfield, IL: Charles C. Thomas. Available online at: http://www.skillsactive.com/playwork/principles (accessed 17.05.11).

Thompson, N. (2003) *Promoting Equality: Challenging Discrimination and Oppression* (2nd edn). Basingstoke: Macmillan.

United Nations Educational, Scientific and Cultural Organisation (UNESCO) (1994) *The Salamanca Statement and Framework for Action on Special Needs Education*. Paris: UNESCO. Available online at: http://www.unesco.org/education/pdf/SALAMA_E.PDF

Conclusion

Mark Price

Our narrative

In writing and editing this book, the authors and editors have been conscious of weaving together three interconnected themes we see as central to professional learning:

- **conceptual and theoretical frameworks** – which helps us understand and analyse children and young people's learning and development and the way society shapes and structures all our lives;

- **the policy context** – locally, nationally and globally, through which employers and government seek to influence, direct and legislate services and provision for children, young people and their families/carers and communities;

- **focus on practice** – the relationships, interactions, interventions and programmes practitioners undertake with children, young people and their families/carers and communities.

The challenge we set ourselves in writing this book has been to capture these themes and present them as separate strands but woven as a coherent fabric.

An additional challenge has been to capture the virtues, values and voices of the different professional identities, the range of student practitioners the book is aimed at, mirrored in a similar range of identities and experiences of the writing team. Between us, the authors of this text have worked in and hold qualification and membership of the following professions:

- early years;

- playwork;

- teaching;

- youth work;

- social work;

- educational psychology;

- psychotherapy.

And most of us can tick at least two of these. We don't think, though, that we're unusual, and the multi-faceted backgrounds and experiences of our students support this. Rather, we conclude that this is no accident: for to develop the flexible, adaptable approach to working with children and young people that the current service landscape requires, particularly in the newer, emerging professions, the ability to be a 'border crosser' (Giroux, 1992), a 'boundary spanner' (Daft, 1989) is demanded.

This range of experiences and identities has led to an interesting and at times challenging exploration of values and perspectives. In particular, for example, concepts such as 'quality', 'professional', 'self' and 'inclusion' are both slippery and sticky – dynamic terms which we interpret through our individual, professional lenses. But through examining these underpinning concepts, we reach new insights into issues and practices – a journeying towards meaning.

In examining New Labour discourses on social inclusion/exclusion policy, Levitas (2004) quotes Humpty Dumpty (Carroll, 1871): '"When *I* use a word," Humpty Dumpty said, in a rather a scornful tone, "it means just what I choose it to mean – neither more nor less"'. Hence, not only are the concepts themselves tricky, but governments, as well as their associated policy and underpinning discourse, change, which then provides a further challenge. Chapters 1, 2, 4, 10 and 12, particularly, attempt to both analyse and summarise policy developed in recent years, which at the time of writing still provides the foundations of our current practice, whilst acknowledging the changing landscape and language a new government brings.

academic and professional work-based learning programmes, such as those at as the University of Brighton, are life changing. The capacity and commitment to reflect on experience and loosen the hold on current understanding and values are central elements to professional development in higher education. But we know this process at times is not easy or comfortable. Atherton's (2005: 1) analysis of resistance to learning introduces the concept of 'supplanting learning which calls into question previous ways of acting or prior knowledge' and describes how the psychological cost of learning prevents 'shift' and the supplanting process 'leads to a temporary "trough" of diminished competence' (2005: 2).

Relating to the *conscious competence* model explored in Chapter 2, the challenge for all professionals is to remain consciously competent. Hence, through the process of critical reflection and analysis, the intention is that there develops a willingness to continue to look at things from a new perspective. Moon (1999: 14) echoes Freire's (1970) process of 'conscientization' and Mezirow's (1990) use of the term 'perspective transformation' in relation to the learner's potential for change:

> Emancipatory interests rely on the development of knowledge via critical or evaluative modes of thought and enquiry so as to understand the self, the human condition and the self in human context. The acquisition of such knowledge is aimed at producing a transformation in the self, or in the personal, social or world situation or any combination of these. (Moon, 1999: 14)

Predictably, our future working lives will be unpredictable. Children and young people's everyday lives, and that of their families and communities, will change and so will those services whose role it is to support them through learning and development processes. A commitment to informed, critical, compassionate practice, however, will always be central to working with children and young people.

References

Atherton, J.S. (2005) *Learning and Teaching: Resistance to Learning.* Available online at: http://www.learningandteaching.info/learning/resistan.htm (accessed 22.05.11).

Cameron, C., Moss, P., Owen, C., Petrie, P., Potts, P., Simon, A. and Wigfall, V. (2009) *Working Together in Extended Schools and Children's Centres: A Study of Inter-professional Activity in England and Sweden.* London: DCSF/Institute of Education.

Carroll, L. (1871) *Through the Looking-Glass.* London: Macmillan.

Daft, R.L. (1989) *Organization Theory and Design* (3rd edn). New York: West Publishing Co.

Freire, P. (1970) *The Pedagogy of the Oppressed.* Harmondsworth: Penguin.

Giroux, H. (1992) *Border Crossing.* London: Routledge.

Levitas, R. (2004) 'Let's hear it for Humpty: Social exclusion, the Third Way and cultural capital', *Cultural Trends,* 13(2): 41–56.

Mezirow, J. (1990) *Fostering Critical Reflection in Adulthood.* San Francisco, CA: Jossey-Bass.

Moon, J. (1999) *Reflection in Learning and Professional Development.* London: Kogan Page.

Index